D0088942

BLACK AND WHITE

BLACK AND WHITE

Dan Mahoney

ST. MARTIN'S PRESS ☙ NEW YORK

Library of Congress Cataloging-in-Publication Data

Mahoney, Dan.
    Black and white: a novel / Dan Mahoney. —1st ed.
        p.   cm.
    ISBN 0-312-20278-4
    I. Title.
    PS3563.A364B53   1999
    813'.54—dc21   99–21853

FIRST EDITION: JUNE 1999

10 9 8 7 6 5 4 3 2 1

FOR

DETECTIVE LEE FORD, STREET CRIME UNIT, NYPD,
KILLED IN THE LINE OF DUTY ON NOVEMBER 6, 1978.

GUNNED DOWN STOPPING A BANK ROBBERY,
HE KILLED THE ROBBER WHO KILLED HIM.

ACKNOWLEDGMENTS

For years cops and detectives in the NYPD have been asking me if Tommy McKenna was the real basis of my Brian McKenna. This book should put that question to rest. Tommy McKenna is a pal of mine, as well as a first grade detective assigned to the Manhattan North Homicide Squad. He was a famous guy in New York long before I used his name and personality in this book. I've tried to capture him as I know him, both professionally and personally, and made him one of my characters without his permission.

TIMMY REMBIJAS (TIMMY JFK) is a pal of mine, as well as an FBI agent assigned to the Airport Task Force. He's just the personality I described in this book, although I did so without permission.

RANDY BYNUM is a pal of mine, as well as a detective for the Santa Clara County (California) Sheriff's Office. He's just the competent, wild and crazy guy I described in this book, although I did so without permission.

JOE ARPAIO is the sheriff of Maricopa County, Arizona, and a famous lawman in his own right long before I put him in these pages. I like his style and appreciate the help members of his department provided me in researching this book, but I used his name without his permission and hope he doesn't mind the way I see him.

Additionally, I would like to thank Police Officer *Raul Camarena*, San Jose PD (retired), *Lieutenant Ad Reese* of the Maricopa County Sheriff's Office, and *Inspector Manuel Matamoros* of the Costa Rican National Police, for the assistance they provided me during the research of this book.

ONE

John Cocchi and Kathy Rynn had worked together for six years doing day tours in the 34th Precinct's Sector Eddie. Like most partners, they had developed a routine that made casual conversation unnecessary. Each usually knew what the other was thinking. They made their arrests, gave their summonses, and handled all the radio runs assigned to them with few words passing between them. They had a stoic attitude about their job, but that didn't slow them down. In a tough precinct they were known as good cops who weren't afraid to work.

And work they did, most of the time. The 34th Precinct covered Washington Heights, a poor neighborhood at the northern tip of Manhattan where the vast majority of the residents were immigrants from the Dominican Republic, many of them illegal aliens. It was a tough life for the new arrivals. Most had learned to live by their wits, but there were always those prepared to prey on their neighbors. Consequently, crime was a sad daily fact of life for the good people and a livelihood for the bad.

As usual, Rynn and Cocchi expected that they would spend the day "tied to the radio," going from one call to the next if they didn't run into an arrest. However, like most radio car teams throughout the city, they tried to reserve to themselves the first half hour of the tour. They bought their coffee and bagels and headed for their spot in Fort Tryon Park, under the Cloisters. Although it wasn't in their sector, they had used the spot for years and considered it their own secret preserve.

Rynn drove into the park, up the steep road leading to the Cloisters, the medieval castle perched overlooking the Hudson River. A quarter mile before the Cloisters, Rynn left the road and drove across a small meadow and into the woods on a narrow dirt track. Their spot was a hundred yards into the woods, where the road ended at a steeply pitched hill that ran straight down to the New York Central Rail Road tracks paralleling the Hudson. There was another car in their spot, a late-model two-door red BMW. The passenger door was open, but they didn't see anybody sitting in the car. What immediately caught their attention was the rear license plate, NYC-9. Cocchi and Rynn naturally assumed that the politically important occupants of the BMW were trespassing and otherwise engaged in the backseat, using their spot as a lovers lane. That wasn't allowed.

"Let's be nice to the big shot when we break up his session," Cocchi said as he got out of the radio car.

"Let's," Rynn said. She approached the car from the driver side and Cocchi headed for the passenger side. Then Rynn stopped and motioned for Cocchi to do the same.

"Problem?" he asked softly.

"Maybe," she answered, pointing to the driver's door. "Window's shattered and there's glass on the ground. Be careful."

Both cops unholstered their guns and reached their positions at the sides of the BMW, nerves on edge and ready for anything. They relaxed a bit when they saw the body. He had been behind the wheel, but the force of the bullet fired into his head through the closed window had knocked his upper torso across the front seat. He was white, about thirty years old, and dressed casually in tan slacks and a green shirt. Death had caught him in an embarrassing position. His pants were pulled down to his knees and his eyes were wide open in shock. Hours before, a small puddle of blood had flowed onto the seat from his head wound. The blood had congealed and hardened.

"He looks Irish. Unusual for this neighborhood," Cocchi observed.

"Probably grew up around here in the old days, when the Irish were still in charge in the Heights. That's how he knew about this place," Rynn surmised.

"Probably," Cocchi agreed. "Let's go find the other body, if there is another one."

"Okay. But remember crime scene protocol. No need to give ourselves more problems than we already have."

She didn't have to say more. Both had been around long enough to know that many crime scenes were damaged and evidence inadvertently destroyed by the first officers on the scene. They prided themselves on doing the job right. Their problem would be explaining how they had stumbled on the BMW, deep in the woods and out of their sector. Both knew that they were headed for some grief from their cranky old sergeant, but what bothered them more was that their wonderful spot would no longer be a secret.

It took them only a minute to find the woman's ripped and bloody clothes at the edge of the hill and another minute to sight her body. They couldn't get to her. The killer had thrown her down the almost-vertical incline and the body had tumbled down until hitting a large rock protruding from the hill.

Even from a distance, Cocchi and Rynn could see that she was dead. She had come to rest face up, she had deep slashes all over her torso, her face was battered, and they were sure that her neck was broken.

"That poor girl surely suffered before she died," Rynn observed.

"You got that right. There's a real sick bastard responsible for this mess," Cocchi answered. "You ready yet for our own dose of misery?"

"Not really, but let's get the ball rolling and get this over with. I feel a fit of depression coming on."

TWO

Detective First Grade Brian McKenna of the Major Case Squad was easily the NYPD's most famous detective and had been involved in many news-worthy cases over the years, so many that people he had never met before stopped him on the street to ask him how Angelita and the kids were doing. McKenna figured folks overrated his skill and intelligence, but he was still New York's darling and he loved it.

McKenna arrived for work at the squad office in Police Headquarters at 9:30 A.M., half an hour early. Inspector Dennis Sheeran, the Major Case Squad CO, was sitting on McKenna's desk, waiting for him.

"There's been a murder," Sheeran announced. "Two of them, in fact."

"So?" McKenna answered. Murders were handled by the Homicide Squads, not the Major Case Squad.

"One of the victims is Cindy Barrone."

"Cindy Barrone? Who's she?"

"The married daughter of Paul Barrone."

"Uh-oh. The speaker of the city council? That Paul Barrone?"

"The very same. Her body and the body of a man not her husband were found in a lovers lane by the Cloisters a couple of hours ago. He was executed straight out, one bullet to the head, but she got it much worse. Raped, tortured, and beaten to death. Some kind of sadistic bondage thing."

"Am I being assigned to this Magilla?" McKenna asked.

"I'd say so, but I don't think it was Ray's idea. He wants to see you."

McKenna understood at once. Paul Barrone wanted that famous Detective McKenna assigned to what was sure to become a very delicate and embarrassing case, aside from being a family tragedy. But Police Commissioner Ray Brunette didn't like political interference in his department and probably would have turned him down. No problem for Barrone; he'd gone straight to the mayor. By the time His Honor spoke to Brunette, McKenna's assignment to the case was no longer a request. It was an order.

Ray Brunette was on the phone, sitting back in his chair with his feet on Teddy Roosevelt's ornate desk when McKenna entered his large office on the fourteenth floor. Although he was ten years older than McKenna, the two appeared to be about the same age. It was Brunette's confident air, his outgoing personality, his straight black hair, and his dimples that made him look under fifty. People liked him minutes after meeting him, and nobody ever thought of him as one of the old guys.

Brunette closed the conversation with "Thanks a lot, Tommy. I owe you." Then he hung up, took his feet off the desk, and turned his attention to McKenna. "Whatcha been up to, buddy?"

"Been busy, but not killing myself," McKenna answered. "I found out where Freddie Buchanan buys his crack and I thought I'd be able to grab him today."

"Freddie Buchanan? Is he the note passer?"

"That's him. Eight banks in ten weeks for a total of more than eleven thousand dollars without ever showing a weapon. From what I hear, he doesn't even have a gun. He just gives them the note and they give him the money."

"Who's been working that one with you? Cisco?"

"Yeah, but it was my case."

"Sorry, but it looks like Cisco gets the collar and the glory. I hate to do this, but I'm under some pressure and I have to give you this Barrone case."

"I haven't worked in Homicide in years, but I don't mind taking it," McKenna said, lying to make Brunette feel better. Murders were always a sad business and he hated working them. "Are the bodies still there?"

"Waiting for you."

"Who's handling from Manhattan North Homicide?"

"Tommy McKenna."

So that's the Tommy who Ray was talking to, McKenna realized, shocked that Barrone would want Brian McKenna when he already had Tommy McKenna. Tommy was widely recognized as the best homicide detective in the NYPD. He had worked on all of the famous murder cases in Manhattan and had achieved a large degree of fame by solving most of them. His exploits had been featured in a book that was still in print and selling well.

Although McKenna had never worked with Tommy, he had no doubt that Tommy knew more about murder than he did. Barrone was making a mistake. "Doesn't Barrone know that he already has the best assigned?"

"When it comes to murder, that's what I told him. But he doesn't like it. Says he doesn't want his daughter's murder showing up in a book down the line with all the gory details."

"Tommy's still going to be working this with me, isn't he?" McKenna asked.

"Sure. I'd never think of taking him off a case. As far as we're concerned, you'll be helping him out. As far as the press is concerned, he'll be helping you out."

"What does the press know so far?"

"Probably quite a bit, but they don't know yet that one of the victims is Cindy Barrone. The pressure won't be on you until you tell them."

"Who was the other victim?"

"The guy? Don't know, yet. It's Cindy's car and the killer took his wallet, so he's not ID'd yet. I'm just hoping he's not the son of some other big-shot politico."

"Where's Paul Barrone now?"

"At Cindy's house with her husband, sweating it out and cooking up a statement through his tears. I imagine he'll give his to the press right after you identify her for them and give yours."

"Once I do, the press is gonna go crazy with that old McKenna-McKenna thing."

"You mean I'm giving them a chance to find out which one of you two is really the best?"

"Exactly. They're gonna read controversy and innuendo into everything we say to each other, and they won't be afraid to print whatever they think."

"I'm not worried about that. You get along with Tommy, don't you?"

"Love him, but that won't mean much to the press once they get their imaginations going. How's he taking this?"

"Not well, at first, but I eventually got him to see things my way. Now he tells me he's looking forward to teaching you a thing or two about murder."

"Wonderful, because he's the man to do it. Probably forgot more than I ever knew."

"We'll see," Brunette said, smiling. "I think I'm gonna enjoy reading about this one."

THREE

McKenna had a hard time finding the crime scene. He cruised slowly around Fort Tryon Park without seeing any signs of police activity until he got lucky. A radio car from the 34th Precinct passed him and he followed. McKenna saw the driver, a female cop, eye him in her rearview mirror and then her partner turned around to get a quick look. They turned off the road, across the meadow, and into the woods on the narrow dirt trail for fifty yards before stopping. The road was blocked by a Crime Scene Unit van. There were many cars in front of the van including radio cars, unmarked cars, and a morgue wagon. The uniformed cops got out of their car and waited.

McKenna guessed that both were in their early thirties and had been on the Job a while. The row of medals above their shields told him they hadn't spent their time idly. Sharp cops, was his first impression. He was the serious one in the team. Dark and handsome, he reminded McKenna of Valentino. Opposites sometimes do attract, and they did in this case. She was all smiles, and she exuded personality.

"Are you gonna be working on this case, Detective McKenna?" Rynn asked.

McKenna didn't know them, but wasn't surprised at being recognized. "Yes, I am."

"Then you're probably gonna want to talk to us. We discovered the bodies."

What a piece of luck for me! McKenna thought. I'm not gonna be going in dopey when I see Tommy. "I guess you've already talked to Tommy McKenna, haven't you?"

"Yeah, talked to him for quite a while."

"Okay, now talk to me."

While Rynn told him how they had found the bodies, McKenna noticed the cops had two cardboard trays of coffee containers on their backseat. Eighteen coffees told him a lot. He was headed into a crowded crime scene that was going to be in place for a while. Traditionally, the detective boss in charge at the scene of a long, drawn-out affair bought the coffee all around, and those folks usually didn't spring unless it was absolutely necessary.

"Who's there now?" McKenna asked.

"Our captain, our sergeant, and another team from the Three-four. There's a lieutenant from the Homicide Squad who came with Tommy, but I don't know his name," Rynn said, looking to her partner for help.

"Lieutenant Greve," Cocchi piped in.

"Yeah, Lieutenant Greve," Rynn continued, counting off the cops on her fingers as she listed them. "Then there's four from the Crime Scene Unit, but the only one of them I know is Joe Walsh. A crew from Emergency Service, but I don't know if they're still there. They went down the cliff and brought Cindy Barrone's body up." Rynn turned to Cocchi. "Who am I leaving out?"

"Dr. Andino," Cocchi said.

A real high-powered crime scene, McKenna thought. The precinct CO being here is unusual. They usually deal in statistics, not specifics. And the chief medical examiner himself? A man in John Andino's position doesn't usually make house calls. John Andino, Tommy McKenna, and Joe Walsh on the case means that Cindy Barrone's murder is already being handled by the best the city of New York had to offer. "How many reporters are there?" he asked.

"Two," Rynn answered.

That didn't make sense to McKenna with a victim like Cindy Barrone. This crime scene called for a gaggle of reporters, both print and TV. "Just two?"

Rynn and Cocchi exchanged a smile. "When we saw that NYC-9 license plate, we knew these were hot murders and a big splash," Rynn explained. "We figured that maybe whoever caught it would like some time to get a story together before the press caught on and started up the pressure, so we didn't put anything over the radio."

"Nothing?" McKenna asked, impressed with Rynn and Cocchi's logic and actions. They knew that the sharper reporters monitored the police radios, but nothing?

"Not a peep, used landlines for everything," Cocchi said. "Kathy stayed here to guard the crime scene and I went to the station house. Ran the plate from there on the computer and found out who the car was registered to. Then I went in to see the captain with the news. Got a big 'attaboy,' and the captain got on the horn to everybody else. Nothing on the air."

"Captain's a sharp guy, too," McKenna said.

"A sharp lady and a square shooter," Rynn corrected, but both she and Cocchi were obviously pleased with the implied compliment. "We were set for some misery with these murders, but she saved us some problems."

"This isn't your sector?" McKenna guessed.

"Unfortunately, no, and our sergeant has been in this precinct since before we were born. A real old-timer with old-time ways."

It had been years since McKenna had worked for one of those types, but he remembered. Run afoul of them by breaking one of the sacred old rules, and each eight-hour tour seemed to last forever. But if the captain thought they had done a good job, then that was it. Case closed.

McKenna searched his mind for more questions, something to give him more of an edge over Tommy. He came up with a few. "Do you know if your spot has been used as a lovers lane before?"

"Sometimes, but they're always gone by the time we get here in the morning," Rynn said. "We find empty beer cans, wine bottles, pizza boxes, things like that."

"We like to keep our spot tidy, so we always clean up after the slobs," Cocchi added. "It's pristine, and Tommy really liked that."

Another piece of luck for Tommy and me, McKenna thought. Anything found there was probably left by the killer. Now for the small question that could tell me quite a bit. "Are two of those coffees for the reporters?"

"Yeah," Rynn answered. "I think they're pals of Tommy's and he told us to count them in."

So it was Tommy who called them, McKenna thought. Called two old, trustworthy pals to watch him work his wonders. "Thanks for the briefing."

The two cops nodded an acknowledgment, then grabbed the trays from the backseat. McKenna followed them up the trail to the crime scene tape stretched across it. John Harney of the *Daily News* and Phil Messing of the *Post* were there, chatting and looking bored. They were both in their forties, but the stress of their jobs hadn't gotten to them. Each had a full head of wavy black hair with no gray, and they looked as if they didn't have a care in the world.

McKenna knew both and counted them as friends, two good men who had been around long enough to know that breaking a confidence meant burning a source forever. There was no need to assign a cop to the crime scene tape to keep them at bay. They would wait for their statement and permission to get close enough to take pictures.

Harney and Messing's casual and unexcited demeanor told McKenna that Tommy hadn't given them the victims' names. It looked like they still considered the crime a routine double murder, no big thing.

That all changed when they saw McKenna. McKenna on the scene meant they had missed something. It wasn't routine; something extraordinary had happened and they were in the right spot at the right time. "You gonna talk to us, Brian?" Harney asked.

"Don't know much yet, but we can chat for a moment."

Harney and Messing each grabbed a coffee container from Rynn's tray and the cops ducked under the tape to deliver the rest.

"You gonna be working this case?" Harney asked.

"Yep. Just got assigned to it by the PC."

"You been transferred to Homicide?"

"Nope. I'm still in Major Case."

"So this is a major case?" asked Messing.

"Yes, turns out that it is."

"Why's that? Something special about the victims?" Messing guessed.

"You got it, Phil. It's the victims."

"Who are they?"

"As I understand it, we've only got one of them identified so far, the woman. I'll leave it to Tommy to tell you who she is."

"Is he still on the case?" Harney asked.

"Yes."

"So who's case is it then? Yours or Tommy's?"

"It's been assigned to me, but Tommy's gonna still be on it with me."

"Let me make sure I've got this straight," Messing said. "Tommy's not in charge of the case. For some reason it's been given to you by Brunette, but Tommy's still going to be working it."

"That's right."

"So he'll be working for you?" Harney asked, choosing his words carefully. "Tommy McKenna will be working for Brian McKenna?"

"In a manner of speaking, but that's not the way I'll be looking at it. I regard it as a learning experience for me and I feel lucky to be able to work with him, no matter how it looks to you right now."

"These murders are going to be a big story, aren't they?" Harney asked.

"Yeah, John. It's gonna be a big one, so you and all your pals are gonna be putting a lot of heat on me before it's over. Now, if you don't mind, I'm gonna get to work."

McKenna left them. As he ducked under the tape, he looked back and saw that both men were on their cell phones calling their editors to suggest that real photographers be sent over in a hurry. The circus was warming up and about to begin.

Cindy Barrone's BMW was still at the end of the dirt road. Two Crime Scene Unit detectives were photographing the scene and another was scanning the ground around the car with a metal detector. Tommy was in the coffee clutch gathered around Cindy's body at the edge of the hill, about a hundred feet away. Detective First Grade Joe Walsh was busy dusting the passenger door handle of the BMW while the uniformed cops watched and sipped their coffees. Walsh kept up a running commentary as he worked, explaining his craft to all who cared to listen. The cops looked bored, which told McKenna they had been standing there too long.

McKenna had expected Walsh to be there for the big case because Walsh kept his ear to the ground and somehow always knew which cases were likely to put his name in print. Universally recognized as the Crime Scene Unit's leading expert on processing evidence and the NYPD's leading ham and glory hound, Walsh was a big, gregarious man in his late fifties.

McKenna didn't feel like talking to Walsh at the moment, so he just glanced into the car at the body still lying there. Unfortunately, Walsh saw him and stood up. "What are you doing here, Brian?" he asked. "Come to get your picture in the papers?"

"No, Joe. Unlike yourself, I'm here because I was sent here."

"The PC?"

"Yeah. He assigned this one to me."

"He assigned Tommy's case to you?" Walsh asked, incredulous. "Why would he do that?"

"Politics."

Walsh understood and he shook his head to indicate his disapproval. "Dopey meddling bastards."

"Yeah, it's a dopey move, but it's not Ray's fault."

"The mayor?"

"I guess so."

"Wanna hear what I've got so far?"

"Not now, Joe. I'll talk to you later," McKenna said.

"Just as well because I don't have much. This might be the cleanest crime scene I've ever seen. Guy was real careful."

That piece of news was a disappointment for McKenna, but he believed it. If Walsh couldn't find it, then it wasn't there. He walked toward the crowd gathered around the body, but the view was so beautiful that he had to stop for a moment to admire it. It was a great spot for a lovers lane, secluded with an expansive view of the Hudson, the Palisades on the Jersey side, and the George Washington Bridge. Unfortunately for Cindy Barrone and her late pal, those same characteristics made it a perfect spot for murder. Then he noticed that Tommy was staring at him, but he had a friendly smile on his face. By the time McKenna walked over and joined the group, everyone was staring at him and he felt self-conscious.

Tommy McKenna was the epitome of a detective. Always well dressed, he radiated authority and confidence. He had a reputation as a kind man, a great socializer, and was so well liked and respected that he had long ago been elected as the Manhattan trustee of the Detectives Endowment Association, the detectives' union. It was a position he would hold as long as it suited him.

McKenna had known Tommy for twenty years, and the man hadn't changed much. Tommy looked fifty-something then and he still did.

The first thing Tommy did was hand McKenna a container of coffee.

Then McKenna shook hands all around, trying not to look yet at the covered body lying at their feet. Although he had spent years in the Manhattan South Homicide Squad and had seen more than his share of murder victims, McKenna knew it would take him a while before he could again regard death as objectively as did Tommy and the rest of his Manhattan North crew. He felt uncomfortable making small talk with the victim on the ground in front of him, but the amenities had to be observed.

John Andino was an old friend and he greeted McKenna warmly. He was a friendly, unassuming, outgoing character in his late forties, usually so cheerful that it was hard to imagine him cutting up bodies for a living.

Lieutenant Greve was the opposite, a serious man in his fifties with a detached air and slicked-back graying blond hair. He wasn't tall, but his square jaw and weightlifter's build made him look like a tough guy. "Are you going to be officially working for me?" Greve asked as he shook McKenna's hand.

"I guess so, Lieutenant, but it hasn't officially been worked out yet."

Captain Uhlfelder was the surprise. She was an attractive woman in her thirties. McKenna would have thought her too young to be a captain, but there she was with the double gold bars and a row of medals besides. "My, my! First one famous Detective McKenna, then Dr. Andino himself, and now the other famous Detective McKenna? We're getting quite a few distinguished visitors around here today, aren't we?" she said with a smile as she shook McKenna's hand.

McKenna felt that a reply was called for. "Just going where I'm sent, Captain. I thought it was pretty sharp, the way you kept this whole thing under wraps."

"I'm not the sharp one," she said. "One of my cops suggested it and it sounded like a good idea to me. Just another case of good cops making the captain look good."

Why is Ray hiding this lady up here? McKenna wondered, very much taken with Uhlfelder's appearance, modesty, intelligence, and sense of fair play. He should be showing her off in midtown, commanding a precinct under the bright lights.

After Tommy finished introducing McKenna to the few detectives there he didn't know, it was time to look down and see what had been done to Cindy Barrone. McKenna reached down and grabbed a corner of the blanket.

"Let's have our coffee and talk first," Tommy suggested.

That was fine with McKenna. They left the group and walked a little further into the woods. For a few minutes, not another word was said. Both men drank from their containers as they surveyed the crime scene.

Tommy finished his first. "I just want you to know that I've got no hard feelings over this. I know it wasn't your idea, and I don't blame Ray either. That prick Barrone put him in check," he said.

"I still feel bad about it," McKenna said.

"Don't. You never were the grandstanding, piggy type, so we'll probably make a good team. Matter of fact, we're gonna have to be if we're gonna solve this one."

"Mind telling me one thing before we get into these murders?"

"Let me guess," Tommy said. "What's the real reason Barrone doesn't want me in charge of this one?"

"Exactly."

"What did Ray tell you?"

"That Barrone's worried about this case winding up in a book of yours someday. Even in the middle of this, Barrone's still thinking like a politician. I'm sure he's going to want this case forgotten as soon as it's over."

"Then that's a pretty good lie he fed the mayor," Tommy said, shaking his head. "The truth is that his daughter's murder means he'll always be reelected, if he plays it right. He can count on the sympathy vote and that's a big thing."

"Then why?"

"He doesn't want me working this because he hates me, and the feeling is mutual. Years ago, he welshed on a deal with me and I dragged his name through the mud for anyone who'd care to listen."

"Union business?"

"Brian, it pains me to think that you're one of the many who don't pay attention to what we're trying to do on your behalf," Tommy said, smiling.

"Sorry, I'm one of those people," McKenna admitted.

"Don't worry about it. Most of the time this union crap bores me to tears. Anyway, about fifteen years ago Barrone was the city councilman from my home district and he was running for reelection in a tough race. This was before we had tenure, but it was our main concern. You remember what it was like back then, don't you?"

McKenna did. The issue had finally been resolved, but in the old days even a first grade detective making lieutenant's money still served as a detective "at the pleasure of the police commissioner," or at the pleasure of any politician who could get to the PC. Many who had been detectives for years found themselves demoted and back in uniform after making errors on a case, disagreeing with the boss, or getting into some other kind of jam. But no longer. Tenure was now part of the DEA's contract with the city, meaning that any person who works three years as a detective stays a detective. "So what was the deal you had with Barrone? Support us on the tenure issue and you'd work to get him reelected?"

"That was it, basically, and work I did. Me and my whole family, plus anyone else I could get to come out with me. Ringing doorbells, handing out pamphlets, making speeches, raising money, the whole rigmarole. Even got the DEA to endorse him as 'the crime-fighting candidate' for all the good it did us. Soon as he's reelected, the slimeball doesn't know me anymore. He got in bed with the mayor and worked against us on the tenure clause. Made me look like a horse's ass, but I get him back every time I can. Hard as I worked for him, every time he's up for reelection I work even harder against him. He's won them all, but some were squeakers. Thanks to me, he's had to spend considerably more time and money to keep his job than he would've liked."

"I understand, but you've made yourself a powerful enemy," McKenna observed.

"So has he, Brian. So has he, but he must know that I'd never use his daughter's murder against him. I'll work just as hard to catch her killer as I do on every other case. Barrone having the mayor send you here is just a personal slap at me, nothing more."

"Are you gonna tell Harney and Messing that?"

"Yeah, but I'll ask them not to print it. I'm not sinking to Barrone's level just yet. He's got enough on his mind right now, so I'll let him think he's won."

Tommy's still a kind guy, McKenna thought. He's been officially embarrassed, but he's not lashing back at his grieving tormentor just yet. "Should we set up the ground rules on how we're gonna work this case?" McKenna asked.

"No need to. You just run it and I'll help you out as much as I can. Maybe we'll both learn some more about murder by the time this is over."

"If you say so. I guess you've got a pretty good idea by now of how these two were done."

"I know exactly how it was done. Let's walk through it."

McKenna followed Tommy a short distance deeper into the woods to a fallen tree. "This is where he waited for them to arrive. Sat here quite a while," Tommy said, then crouched down on his knees. McKenna followed his lead and Tommy pointed to some cigarette ashes intermingled with the dead leaves. "No way of telling how many smokes he had, but he was careful. Took his butts with him. Left not another thing anywhere after he finished."

"But it tells us something," McKenna said. "He didn't follow Cindy and her pal here. He was here waiting for them, targets of opportunity. He must've walked in and walked out of the park."

"That's the way it looks, unless Cindy or her boyfriend made a habit of coming here. The only clue the killer left us is that he has to be from this area to know about this spot. After the victims arrived, he waited a few minutes longer while they went at it in the car. Her boyfriend gets his pants down, but we don't know what state of dress or undress she was in. In any event, none of her clothes are in the car."

McKenna stared at the ground, searching for something the killer might have left behind, but Tommy was right. There was nothing but the ashes. No footprints he could see, no butts, nothing.

"Ready to go on?" Tommy asked.

"Let's go." He followed Tommy to the driver's side of the BMW.

"He walks over and fires one shot through the closed window, killing this poor slob," Tommy said.

"Any brass?"

"No, but I'm betting he used an automatic. Held the gun in a paper bag to catch the ejected cartridge when he fired. I'm also betting that when Andino pulls the slug out of his head, he's gonna find paper residue burned into it from the bag."

So we're dealing with a serial killer here, McKenna thought. Tommy's seen his work before. "What kind of gun is he using?"

"If I had to guess, I'd say a .380 Colt Commander."

McKenna waited for more facts from Tommy to justify his guess, but Tommy wasn't ready to show his cards yet. It could wait. "What happens next?"

"The boyfriend never saw it coming, but whatever she was doing, maybe Cindy did. After the shot, she was sharp enough to open her door and run. But she wasn't fast enough and didn't get far."

McKenna followed Tommy around the car and into the woods on the other side. "This is where he caught her," Tommy said, pointing to the ground. "Tackled her from behind and brought her down."

McKenna could see that the fallen leaves on the ground had been shoved aside, exposing the ground where Cindy had been pulled down.

"Found two things here," Tommy said. "There was some blood on one of the leaves here, presumably Cindy's, so he must have smacked her to bring her under control. I'm assuming he hit her on the side of the head with his gun because she's got a nasty lump there and I found this here." Tommy reached into his pocket, took out a handkerchief, and unfolded it to reveal a thin gold hoop earring with a small blood smear on it.

"Which side of her head is the lump on?" McKenna asked.

"The right side."

"Doesn't look like there was much of a struggle here, so I'd say he hit her from behind when she was on the ground. If so, he was holding the gun in his right hand."

"That's my thinking, too. We're looking for a right-handed killer, but that doesn't help us much. After he had her under control, he brought her over here."

McKenna followed Tommy to a large tree growing at the the edge of the precipice. "Be careful, but take a look at the other side of this tree," Tommy said.

McKenna held on to the tree and saw that the bark was recently scarred on the far side, two small marks. One was three feet up from the base of the tree and the other was about five feet up. "How tall is Cindy?"

"Pretty tall. I'd say about five foot six."

"Looks like he tied her to the tree at her neck and at her waist. Must have used some kind of chain to make those marks."

"I'd say he used a couple of chain dog leashes, but the way he tied her is unusual. He used two sets of handcuffs, put one on each of her hands. He has her back against the tree with the chain tied around it at her neck. Then he stretched her arms back, ran the chain through the cuffs, and pinned her to the tree. Gagged her, then he probably went back to the spot I showed you before. Had a few more smokes and waited. If anyone else would've shown up here last night, maybe he would have left. But Cindy wasn't that lucky."

"What was he waiting for?"

"Dawn. He wanted to be able to see in order to enjoy himself thoroughly. Andino puts the guy's time of death at about one this morning, but Cindy's only been dead about four hours."

McKenna checked his watch. Eleven-fifteen. "What time was dawn this morning?"

"Five-ten."

"So he tortured her for about an hour before he finally killed her."

"Right, but it gets even more bizarre. Take a look here," Tommy said, pointing to the base of the tree. The ground had been stamped down there and many of the leaves had been broken into small pieces. Thousands of small drops of blood speckled the ground to the left and right of the tree, but there was no blood at the base. "She lose a lot of blood when he tortured her?"

"Most of it."

"So he spread a tarp on the ground under her feet," McKenna said. "Real careful. Caught most of her blood and anything he might have left."

"You mean semen?"

"Yeah, semen. I'm assuming he raped her, but pulled out because he didn't want to leave his semen behind."

"Maybe you're right, but I don't think so. Andino says he shoved something in her orifices, but I don't think it was his dick. That's not the way this type gets off. He likes to watch the pain and degradation he's causing while he jerks off."

McKenna took Tommy's opinion as a fact only because it was Tommy who was saying it. But it was time for Tommy to justify his opinions. "I guess you've seen this type of thing before."

"Seen this very type of thing."

"When?"

"Eighteen years ago. August 10th, 1981."

"Where?"

"Right here. I knew just where to look for those marks on the tree because he chained his victim to the same tree last time. Also went right to the spot where he sat and waited. That fallen tree where he sat and had his smokes was still standing back then, but the ballsy prick had brought a lawn chair with him. Found the indentations in the ground where he had sat it down."

"And how about that victim? Same type of torture?"

"When the emergency service guys finally got Cindy's body up, I knew it was the same man. She suffered through the exact same kind of torture."

"I guess you didn't solve that case."

"Never even got close. It's not one of the ones I brag about. Matter of fact, hardly ever mention it to my fans."

"Does Ray know we've got a serial killing case?"

"Not yet. When I talked to him, Cindy's body was still down there," Tommy said, pointing down the precipice. "I wasn't certain until the ESU guys went down and brought her up, so you'll be the one to tell him."

Problems for everybody, but especially me. A big case just got bigger, McKenna thought. Probably much bigger. "Serial killers don't kill once every eighteen years. There's other cases," he said.

"That's what I thought, but not in this city there aren't. I take a look at every lovers lane case that comes up and I looked at all the older ones, but it was never the same killer."

"How about the rest of the country?"

"Thought I had another one in San Jose, California, about ten years ago. So many things were close. Gun used in that one was a .380 Colt Commander fired through a paper bag, but it wasn't the same gun. Victim was different, too. In that case the killer executed the woman right away, but it was the man he had his fun with. Tied him to a tree the same way and tortured him."

"Same kind of torture?"

"Different. Used the gun to kill the girl, but that guy was a slasher. This one's a whipper."

"He used a whip on Cindy?"

"Sure did. Really punished her, opened her up good."

"And splattered her blood everywhere but in front of her," McKenna observed, pointing to the blood on both sides of the tree. "He must have gotten quite a bit of it on himself when he whipped her."

"I'm assuming he did, but you've seen how careful he is. Maybe he was naked when he did it. If so, he just cleaned himself up before he left. If not, he brought a change of clothes with him."

"That's another reason for the tarp in front. He didn't want to leave us any of his bloody footprints."

"Like I said, real careful. You ready to take a look at Cindy?"

"I guess so, but just one more question. Is Walsh gonna find anything here?"

"Not a thing that'll help us. For once, the great Joe Walsh is gonna come up blank."

"Too bad. Might as well get the unpleasantness over with."

The two men walked to Cindy's body. Everyone was gone except Walsh and Andino. The blanket still covered her, but Walsh had pulled out her left hand and was busy taking her fingerprints.

McKenna could see that Tommy was right about the handcuffs. He had seen the same circular marks before on the wrists of prisoners who had struggled to free themselves from the cuffs, but never so severe as Cindy's injuries. Her wrist was tattered, damage she had inflicted on herself as she struggled against her restraints during her painful ordeal.

Since bodies are usually fingerprinted at the morgue, not the crime scene, McKenna assumed that Walsh had come up with some prints and wanted to compare them himself. "What'd you find, Joe?"

"Nothing except many, many latent prints in and on the car. Guy was very cagey, but maybe I'll get lucky for you. Already printed the boyfriend and I'll just be another few minutes here," Walsh answered without looking up.

While waiting for Walsh to finish, Tommy used the time to show Cindy's clothes to McKenna. She had worn a flowered pink blouse, a white skirt, panty hose, and a matching gray bra and panty set. The killer had used the whip to undress her. The clothes were ripped and in shreds, with bloodstains forming the boundaries of many of the tears in the fabric, but only the front of the clothing showed the damage wrought by the whip. The killer had whipped her to a pulp, then had torn off her clothes to check the damage and have some more fun.

Neither man spoke as McKenna inspected the clothes. The shape the clothes were in gave McKenna some idea of the shape Cindy was in, and he dreaded the prospect of seeing the damage done to her. "No purse?"

"No, the killer took it with him. Can't find her other earring, so he probably took that too."

Walsh was done. "I'm gonna do a quick comparison right now and I'll let you guys know if any of the prints I've lifted don't belong to the victims," he said, then walked off toward the Crime Scene Unit van.

"Ready?" Tommy asked. McKenna braced himself and nodded. Tommy reached down and pulled the blanket off the body.

McKenna had known what to expect, but the bloody sight caused him to gasp. Cindy Barrone hadn't just been murdered, she had been professionally savaged. A whip had been the killer's main instrument, and the torture had lasted long enough for welts to form while she was still alive. She was cut to pieces, with welts and long, ugly cuts all over the front of her body, but the killer had concentrated his fury on two places—her breasts and her face. Her nose, lips, ears, and breasts were gone, shredded by the whip.

McKenna could see that Tommy was right. Most of her blood was gone, but not all of it. Her skin looked white and waxen, contrasting starkly with the red muscle and white bone where her insides had been exposed by the whip. The bruise on the right side of her head where the killer had struck her with the gun was still discernible, but too much of her face was gone for McKenna to judge her age with any degree of confidence.

Cindy Barrone was to be a closed casket, McKenna was sure. He doubted that Paul Barrone would be able to recognize the face of his daughter.

After looking over the rest of her, McKenna decided that she had the body of a young woman in her twenties who took care of herself. "How old was she?" he asked.

"Twenty-six," Tommy answered.

Young, rich, and everything to live for, flashed through McKenna's mind. Then he noticed that the sides of her buttocks had also received the ministrations of the whip. He had missed it at first because he had focused on the obvious damage on the front of her body. There was no blood, welts, or bruises on the side of her buttocks, just shredded skin over white, fatty tissue. "What did he do to her behind?" he asked.

It was Andino who answered. "Another unusual twist. After she was dead, he unchained her and went to work on her buttocks with the whip. Pretty thorough job; man has a lot of rage in him. Fatty tissue exposed, but besides that there's anal penetration. I'm betting that was done with the whip as well. There's tearing and I'd say there's also internal damage."

"You think he shoved the whip handle into her?" McKenna asked.

"Yep, and she was already dead at the time. No rectal bleeding. Want to roll her over and take a look?"

"That won't be necessary."

"You'll also notice that her vagina is torn. I'd say he used the handle there as well, but the poor girl was alive for that."

McKenna had to agree. Cindy's groin area showed no evidence of having been lashed, but there was dried blood congealed on her thighs around her vagina, and a lot of it.

McKenna had seen enough. "You ready to venture a cause of death?"

"Right now, I'd say she simply bled to death," Andino stated.

"You ever seen anything like this before?"

"Never even heard of a case like this."

"How long you been the medical examiner, John?"

"Seven years as the chief, three as the assistant chief. Before that, I was the medical examiner in St. Louis for seven years. Why you asking?"

Tommy answered. "Because these aren't his first murders. He did another two in this same spot, same way, eighteen years ago. We figure he did other killings in between, but Brian just wanted to make sure he hasn't been doing them here."

"Sounds like you've a lot of work ahead of you."

"Sure do," McKenna agreed. "We'll be talking to every homicide detective in the country who's got an old unsolved torture case on his books."

"Not just whipping cases?" Andino asked.

"No. Not just whipping cases, only because there aren't any more. Tommy's had his ear to the ground for eighteen years and there hasn't been anything else like this one."

"Still, there must have been hundreds of other unsolved torture cases in this crazy country over the past eighteen years," Andino observed.

"Maybe thousands," Tommy said. "But thanks to the victim in this case, it looks like Brian's going to have the time and support to do it right."

"I've got a worse job ahead of me when I go to see Paul Barrone and Cindy's husband," McKenna said. "I'm probably gonna bring them right to the morgue, so can you hold up on her autopsy until I do?"

"Fine by me. I'll work on the guy first and get that bullet to your lab. Are you gentlemen done here?"

"Are we?" McKenna asked Tommy.

"Yeah, we're done."

"Then so am I. See you later," Andino said, and left for his car.

"What's next? Harney and Messing?" McKenna asked Tommy.

"Yeah. I guess the guy in charge should be the one talking to them. That's you now."

"Sorry, but you're right. Officially, it's me, so we can't have Barrone and the mayor reading interviews from you."

"It's gonna be quite a story, especially when you throw in the old murders. Unfortunately, it's also going to tarnish my rep a bit. Messing and Harney will know better, but it's going to look to the readers like I don't have the new case because I screwed up the old one."

"Nobody solves them all," McKenna offered.

"But I sure wish I had solved that one. Would have saved these two lives."

"This press thing brings us to our first problem," McKenna said. "This case is too big to give your two pals an exclusive. We're gonna have to have a full-blown press conference later on, probably sometime today."

"I know that, but I figure that Barrone will be in on that one and he'll have his share to say. I'm sure he's going to try to make me look like a bumbler, so I'd rather you give Harney and Messing the jump and start the coverage with friends having sympathetic ears. You mind?"

"Not at all. Let's go talk to them and then I have to get on to the next unpleasant task."

"Barrone?"

"Yeah, Barrone. I have to pay him a visit, but I don't think you should go with me."

"I'd like to go along," Tommy said.

Bad idea, McKenna thought. Why antagonize Barrone right now with Tommy's presence? He'll just run to the mayor and cause a problem for Ray.

Tommy read his mind. "Don't worry, I'm not gonna cause any problems. I'll make it clear to him that he's won this time, that you're the man in charge."

He'll make it clear that he's down, but not out, McKenna thought. What can I say to that? "Okay, suit yourself."

Joe Walsh was waiting for them outside his van. "You going to be seeing the Barrone family?" he asked.

"That's where we're headed," McKenna said.

"Then you should print Cindy's husband and anybody else who had access to that car. Just a quick look tells me that I've got lots of prints that don't belong to the victims."

"Good ones?"

Walsh looked hurt by the question. "You should know by now that they're always good when I lift them. Want me to loan you a fingerprint kit?"

"No, thanks. I've got a kit in my car," Tommy replied. "Besides, you should know by now that I'm in real trouble whenever I need something from you."

FOUR

Harney and Messing had been joined by two photographers. McKenna was content to let Tommy show them around the crime scene and explain what had happened. The photographers wanted to photograph the uncovered bodies, but Tommy wouldn't permit that. He gave them free rein to shoot whatever else they liked, but there wasn't much that interested them. They took pictures of the tree, the BMW, and shots of the covered bodies being loaded into the morgue wagon.

To save the Barrone family some dignity, Tommy asked Harney and Messing not to print that the male victim's pants were down. He also asked them not to characterize the murders as "lovers lane killings" when they filed their stories. They said they wouldn't.

Then came the official interview. McKenna gave the story for the record and they had very few questions for him. After he told them about the 1981 murders, Harney and Messing wanted to interview Tommy once again.

Fine by McKenna. These murders were his case and those were Tommy's. Even Barrone would have to understand that.

Because so much work had been done on those old murders, it took Tommy a while to tell them about it. McKenna listened with interest and learned a few things. By the end of Tommy's interview it was clear to him that Tommy had done everything that should be done, and then some.

"Off the record, Tommy. Is Barrone the reason Brian's in charge of this case, not you?" Messing asked.

"He's the reason. The PC doesn't know about that old case yet, and neither does Barrone. Barrone and I have got some bad blood between us."

"But you're still going out of your way to be nice to him, asking us not to print things in this story that would be embarrassing to him."

"Not nice. Just decent. No reason to make this any worse for him unless we have to."

Uhlfelder had given Tommy the DMV printout on Cindy's car. It listed her address and he knew just where it was. They decided to take two cars there. After talking to Barrone and Cindy's husband, McKenna would drive one or both of them to the morgue to ID her body. Tommy would make the rounds, picking up the crime scene photos and sketches at headquarters and delivering the fingerprints to Walsh at his office in the 20th Precinct.

It took them half an hour to drive to Cindy Barrone's residence in

Bayside, Queens. It was a large colonial, a nice house in a nice neighborhood. Paul Barrone's official car, a new Mercury, was parked at the curb outside. Its plate number was number NYC-2, second only to the mayor. Another new BMW, a black one with MD plates, was parked in the driveway.

"Looks like they were doing all right, before today," Tommy said. He took a black briefcase from the trunk of his car and the two men went to the door. A maid answered the bell and admitted them to the living room.

Paul Barrone was a tall, slim man in his sixties. His gray hair was thinning, but that didn't detract from his appearance. He had a patrician face with thin lips and a straight, aquiline nose and was dressed for the occasion in a black suit, white shirt, and black tie. As expected, he appeared distraught, and he had a drink in his hand.

Cindy's husband was nothing like Barrone. He was a short, paunchy man in his late thirties with a full head of brown curly hair. He wore jeans, a Polo pullover shirt, and brown loafers without socks. He sat on the sofa dressed for watching a ball game on TV, not to grieve over a dead wife. However, he had placed a framed 8x10 photo of Cindy on the coffee table next to the sofa, and McKenna could easily see that she had been a stunning beauty before that day.

A surprised look flashed across Barrone's face when he saw Tommy, but he was prepared to be the gracious host in trying circumstances. He stood up, offered his hand to McKenna, and said, "Thank you for coming, Detective McKenna."

McKenna shook his hand and then Barrone turned his attention to the other McKenna. "Tommy, I have to admit that I didn't expect to see you here," he said, offering his hand.

Tommy took it, a short perfunctory handshake. "I'm sure you didn't, Mr. Barrone, but here I am. I don't know if you'll believe me, but I'm truly sorry about your daughter."

"I always believe whatever you say. Despite our differences, I've never known you to lie."

Cindy's husband had sat up on the sofa, but he remained seated. "I'm sorry, sir, but I don't know your name," McKenna said.

He shook his head, amused. "You don't know my name? Then how did you find my house?"

"Cindy's car is still registered in her maiden name, but this is the address listed."

"I see. My name is one of the many things she decided she didn't like about me," he slurred, clearly drunk. "Always used her maiden name on everything—checkbook, credit cards, driver's license, you name it. I'm Dr. Roger Valenti."

I didn't ask your occupation, I just asked your name, McKenna thought, deciding he didn't much care for Dr. Roger Valenti's attitude. "I'm here to tell you how Cindy was killed, answer your questions, take your fingerprints, and then I'll take one or both of you to the morgue to identify her body."

"Why do you need my fingerprints?" Valenti asked, belligerently. "Are you considering me a suspect?"

In any other circumstances I would, McKenna thought. "No, you're not a suspect. Some fingerprints were found in Cindy's car that don't belong to her or the other victim. I need the prints of everybody who had access to the car, and I'm assuming you gentlemen were in it at one time or another."

"I've used it a few times, but not much," Valenti said.

"When was the last time?"

"I backed it out of the driveway yesterday. She had me blocked in, as usual."

"And you, Mr. Barrone?"

"We went shopping for some shirts and ties for me last week," Barrone replied.

"Who was the guy she was with?" Valenti asked.

"We don't have him identified yet. The killer stole his wallet. You'll be able to take a look at him at the morgue, maybe tell us who he is."

"I doubt if I know him. She wouldn't embarrass me by going out with anybody I know. She wasn't mean that way," Valenti explained without emotion, and then he had a question. "Were they going at it when they got shot?"

McKenna had worried about explaining that part of the story, but Valenti was making it easy for him. He obviously knew his wife had a lover or lovers and he obviously didn't care. "I take it you and Cindy haven't been getting along lately."

"Cindy and I agreed to dislike each other, but we got along in our own way and I certainly never wished her any harm. What she did whenever she went out no longer concerned me, but I would like you to satisfy my curiosity."

"His pants were down when he was killed, but she was apparently fully dressed at that time."

"Too bad for him. He missed a really great time. Cindy was good and really liked her sex, as long as it wasn't with me."

McKenna couldn't believe Valenti was talking like that in the presence of his murdered wife's father. He stole a glance at Barrone and saw that he was glaring at Valenti with undisguised hatred.

"Don't worry about me, Detective McKenna. Both Cindy and I realized a long time ago that she had married classless dirt. Educated, but crass and classless," Barrone said, and then he forced a polite smile back onto his face.

"Yeah, I'm dirt and you're great. A real classy man of the people, a loving father, and a great father-in-law. Right?" Valenti casually asked.

Barrone ignored him. "Detective McKenna, I hope it's not necessary that the lurid details be given to the press. The public will certainly draw their own conclusions about what my daughter and her friend were doing there, but I see no reason to spell it out for them."

"Nor do I," McKenna said. "A few reporters were at the scene and know about it, but it happens that they're friends of Tommy's. They've promised him that it won't appear in their stories."

"Thank you, Tommy," Barrone said. "Quite decent of you, considering. Now, which of you is going to tell us what the killer did to my daughter and how she died?"

McKenna had expected that Tommy would tell them how Cindy had died, but Tommy wasn't there to rankle Barrone. "The detective in charge will tell you," Tommy said, then turned to McKenna.

"Fine, but I have a question before we begin," Barrone said to Tommy. "What will be your role in this case, exactly?"

"The loyal assistant."

"Murder expert and trusted advisor," McKenna said.

Barrone eyed McKenna shrewdly, but he didn't challenge the statement. "I'm ready to hear about Cindy."

"No you're not," Tommy said. "Finish your drink first and pour yourself another."

"That bad?" Barrone asked, terror in his eyes.

"Horrible. You should pour yourself another one, too, Roger. Love her or hate her, what happened to Cindy shouldn't happen to anyone."

There were no questions as McKenna told the tale of Cindy's death. There was no need; since they would be seeing the body shortly, he told them everything to prepare them for the shock.

The problems began when McKenna told them about the 1981 murders.

"Do you mean to tell me you've had eighteen years to catch this man, and you haven't?" Barrone asked, pointedly directing his question to Tommy. "I didn't read about that one in your book."

"Haven't even gotten close. No idea who he is," Tommy admitted.

"So that case is gone and forgotten until now. Two people murdered with impunity."

"It's not forgotten by me. Isn't a week goes by that I don't do some-thing on it, but it's been a waste of time."

"What, exactly, have you been doing all these years to waste this time?"

"Checking to see if he's killed again."

"That shouldn't take you long."

"Not only here. I check all around the country, mostly by phone, but I also spend a lot of time at seminars on serial killers with homicide in-vestigators from all over. I always make a point of asking them if they've ever had a case like mine and got nowhere."

"Then it would seem to me that he only became a serial killer this morning," Valenti said, taking a gulp of his drink. "Before that, he was just a murderer."

"That's the way it looks, but it just doesn't seem possible. According to everything I've seen, read, and heard, they never stop after one. If he's got it in him to be that kind of animal, once he got his first taste of blood he didn't just quit for eighteen years. He's been killing all along, and prob-ably for a lot longer than eighteen years."

"Because even back then, he was so good that you couldn't find him?" Barrone suggested.

"Basically, yes. He didn't make any mistakes."

"Did you?"

"None I'm aware of."

"Did he make any when he murdered my daughter?"

"I'm hoping he did."

"But probably not?"

"Probably not," Tommy conceded.

"If he's been killing as many people as you think, where are the bod-ies?" Valenti asked.

"I don't know. Maybe he buries them."

"I don't mean to disparage you personally, but I'm sure we all realize the harm your failure has done to me," Barrone said, glaring at Tommy. "Maybe it's good that there's some new blood working this case."

McKenna was braced for the explosion, but Tommy was true to his word. "Maybe."

FIVE

Valenti was too drunk to go to the morgue, Barrone told him. An embarrassment, and Valenti agreed. He was a man who recognized his own weaknesses and limitations and he hadn't been looking forward to the morgue trip anyway. He had seen his wife for the last time and preferred to remember her the way she was.

McKenna and Barrone rode in silence, each lost in his own thoughts until the skyline of Manhattan came into view. "Did Tommy tell you the cause of our dispute?" Barrone asked.

"Yeah, said you welshed on a deal with him."

"He's right, but he didn't understand the nature of politics. At the time, neither did I. We've both learned a lot since then, painfully at times."

Barrone wasn't inclined to say more and they drove on in silence for another few minutes, but McKenna's curiosity was whetted. "Why did you do it?"

"I was a first-term city councilman running for reelection in a tough race. My opponent had all the unions behind him and my district was working class. I thought I was going to lose, then Tommy came to me with his tenure deal. I was desperate and I took it, and nobody was more surprised than me when Tommy pulled it off. Won me the election, I'll be the first to admit. However, at the time I wasn't able to keep my part of the bargain and he never forgave me."

"Why couldn't you?"

"A few reasons. As a two-term city councilman, I didn't have the weight. Besides, the mayor wouldn't hear of it. There was a scandal going on in the police department at the time and he knew that heads would have to roll if he was to get reelected himself. Tenure would have tied his hands when it came to the detectives and he couldn't be seen making concessions to the police when your popularity was down in this town."

"Which scandal was that?" McKenna asked, trying to get a handle on the time frame. It seemed there was one every five years to be suffered through by bosses, cops, and detectives who had nothing to do with the incident that had provoked the public outrage.

"The stun gun."

The early eighties scandal, McKenna knew. The 106th Precinct in Queens. Questioning a drug dealer while using a stun gun to refresh his memory. Heads rolled from the top on down and every cop on the Job was given a black eye. "Bad timing for a tenure deal," he said, understanding Barrone's position.

"I tried to explain that to Tommy, but you know how he took that."

"Sure. A deal's a deal. He delivered on his end and it was your turn to deliver. That's the way he would see it, no matter what."

"Exactly, but tenure just wasn't possible at the time and I told him that we'd have to wait. Tommy wasn't prepared to listen and didn't understand that I had to ally myself with the mayor if I was ever going to have any real power in the city council. Eventually, I was able to keep my end of the deal and get tenure for the detectives, but by that time Tommy was the enemy. Caused me a lot of problems over the years, but I never retaliated."

"Until now," McKenna observed.

"Yes, until now. But you can understand my position, can't you?"

"I understand how you're thinking, but you're wrong. Tommy would never use your daughter's death to hurt you."

"I see that now. Seems he even went out of his way a bit to help me with the press."

"He did."

"Would you have done that?" Barrone asked.

"I guess so. The dead person isn't the only victim when there's a murder. The family suffers as well and I try never to cause unnecessary damage or pain to them."

"Then I made the right decision," Barrone said. "Got all of the benefits and maybe a better detective to catch my daughter's murderer."

"You made the wrong decision. When it comes to homicides, Tommy's better than me. He's the expert."

"I'm told by some cops that you're better. In light of Tommy's failure to find the killer eighteen years ago, I'm inclined to agree. I've also heard that you're more discreet, and I might need some of that discretion."

"Why's that?"

"It's possible that I know the person lying next to her in the morgue. If so, I'm not asking you to cover it up. All I ask is that you throw the best possible light on an unfortunate situation."

"Who do you think this poor guy might be?"

"I don't want to step out on a limb unnecessarily. Let's wait and see if it's him before we start talking about Cindy's love life."

"Fair enough. We'll wait and see. If it's who you think, I'll try to help— but I don't do cover-ups."

"Fair enough."

McKenna reflected for a moment on the tacit deal he had just made and found nothing wrong with it because he got nothing out of it. "While we're being somewhat candid with each other, mind telling me what's going on between Valenti and you?"

"Since we're being somewhat candid and discreet, not at all. He hates me because I backed out of a deal with him and I loathe him because he's weak and lazy. He used all the ambition he had in him just to get out of medical school and marry my daughter."

"What was the deal you had with him?"

"A promise, really. When they got married, I told him that after he got some more experience, I would get him on the board of the Health and Hospitals Corporation."

"A nice, cushy job?"

"I suppose so, and right up his alley. It soon became apparent that he'd rather drink than work, so I couldn't afford to have my name linked with his by recommending him for a public position. He would've turned out to be an embarrassing political liability, one that Tommy would be sure to point out the next time I came up for reelection."

"Did the drinking bother Cindy?"

"No, the lack of ambition was what did it. She no longer loved him, so I urged her to get a divorce and start over. She didn't, hung on because it was convenient. He basically gave her her freedom to do whatever she liked."

"Does he know that you wanted her to divorce him?"

"I guess it came up. Gave him another reason to hate me, which I think makes him happy. He likes to think of himself as the aggrieved party."

Who is to blame in this family mess? McKenna wondered. Oh well, doesn't make much difference now.

The New York City morgue is a modern four-story building located on the corner of First Avenue and East 30th Street in Manhattan. In a city with more than its share of unpleasant places, it was the one McKenna hated most, the place where death was treated casually in an analytical fashion. Aside from being used as a temporary storehouse for unclaimed bodies and those who died in police cases, the main activity of the professionals working there day in and day out was to determine how the piece of meat on the table in front of them wound up there in the first place.

Years spent in the Manhattan South Homicide Squad had done nothing to assuage McKenna's distaste for the building. Although he had long ago gotten used to the sights of bloody, mangled bodies at crime scenes, the sight of those same bodies at the morgue, cleaned up, professionally dissected and probed, sickened him and filled him with sadness. The passing of a human being, he felt, should never be treated so impersonally.

McKenna took Barrone to Andino's second-story office, but his secretary told them that he was "working on the floor." She would call him and he would meet them downstairs. McKenna took Barrone down and they waited in the large room dominated by a large refrigerator with banks of stainless steel doors. Two autopsy rooms were on their left and each door had a porthole, but neither man thought about looking in to locate Dr. Andino. They were content to wait for him, both men uncomfortable with the strong smell of antiseptic assaulting their nostrils.

Five minutes later Andino emerged from one of the autopsy rooms, buttoning a fresh white smock. "Sorry to keep you waiting, Paul, and I can't tell you how sorry I am about your daughter." Andino offered his hand and Barrone shook it warmly.

"Thank you, John. I appreciate your feelings."

McKenna wasn't surprised that the chief medical examiner knew the speaker of the city council. Andino would have been before the council many times to justify his budget. What surprised him was that the two men appeared to be friends.

"I wish it could be avoided, but this is going to be an unsettling experience for you," Andino said. "You should prepare yourself for a shock."

"I was a medic in Korea. I can handle it, so let's get it over with."

Andino opened the refrigerator door number 103 and slid out the stainless steel tray containing the body. It was covered with a sheet and Andino pulled it back just far enough to reveal the battered, tortured, savagely damaged face that, until that morning, had been so beautiful.

Barrone was visibly shaken at the sight of his daughter. "My god!" he wailed, losing all reserve.

McKenna thought Barrone was going to faint and was prepared to catch him, but he recovered sufficiently to support himself by holding on to the sides of the tray. He stared at her face for an uncomfortably long time. Neither Andino or McKenna said a word. "That's my daughter, Cindy Barrone Valenti," he said finally, making it official.

Andino started to cover up Cindy's face with the sheet, but Barrone stopped him by grabbing his hand. "John, show me what else he did to her."

Andino looked to McKenna for guidance and McKenna nodded. He pulled off the sheet, revealing the full horror, but Barrone was prepared this time. He inspected the damage with an almost-clinical, detached manner. Then he bent over and kissed her forehead. "Good-bye, baby. I'm going to miss you," he said softly.

Although Barrone was dry-eyed, McKenna was so touched that he felt his own eyes filling with tears. He wiped them with his coat sleeve, hoping Andino and Barrone wouldn't notice, but of course they had.

"Thank you, Detective McKenna," Barrone said, placing his hand on

McKenna's arm. "Just another reason why you're the man for the job. I have every confidence that you'll catch this monster and prevent him from doing this again to someone else."

"I'll do my best," McKenna said, but it sounded weak to him as he said it.

"That's all I can ask, isn't it?" Barrone said, but it came across to McKenna as, "Your best better be good enough to do the job."

Andino replaced the sheet on the body and slid the tray back into the refrigerator.

"Where's the other body?" McKenna asked.

"I just finished autopsying him. Pretty straightforward, death instantaneous caused by one bullet to the head. He's being stitched up now, should be out in a moment."

"I'd like to show that body to Mr. Barrone as well. It's possible he knows who it is."

Andino weighed the implications of that statement, but said nothing.

"What kind of shape is the bullet in?" McKenna asked.

"Slightly deformed, but usable. Looks to me like a .380 or a .38 caliber. You want to take it with you and deliver it to Ballistics yourself?"

"Please."

A few minutes later two morgue attendants emerged from the autopsy room pushing a stretcher with a covered body on it. Andino stopped them and pulled back the sheet to expose the face.

"Well?" McKenna asked.

"That's Arthur McMahon, one of my aides. A very nice young man."

McKenna had been prepared to learn that Barrone knew who his married daughter was spending time with, but one of his aides? Did Barrone introduce them and encourage the relationship? he wondered. If Roger Valenti already knew about Arthur McMahon, it was another reason he hated his father-in-law. If he didn't know, he soon would. No way to keep this under wraps. A scandal's brewing here, McKenna concluded. Nothing criminal, but unsavory all the same. "How old is he?"

"He was thirty-two yesterday."

So Cindy and her lover were having a little birthday celebration, McKenna thought. "How long has he been working for you?"

"About two years. Very ambitious young man and extremely bright. He was a cop in Arlington, Virginia, and he put himself through law school at night. I had gone to law school with his father and we persuaded Arthur to join my staff right after he graduated."

"Where does he live?" McKenna asked.

"Inwood, near the Cloisters. He was saving to buy a co-op downtown in a much better neighborhood and closer to my office in city hall."

"Any relatives in New York?"

"No. Would you like me to notify his family?"

"Please. That would be a burden off my mind."

"I intend to make myself unavailable to the press until after the funeral. I would appreciate it if there were no major news conferences on this matter until then."

"That's going to be difficult. They're going to be clamoring for information."

"I'm confident you can handle them," Barrone stated.

"I'll try, but before I do I'll run your request by Commissioner Brunette. If it's okay with him, it's fine by me. No news conference, but I'm still going to have to handle questions from individual reporters and there's no way I can withhold this man's identity and occupation."

"I realize that and wouldn't ask you to withhold that information. Just no news conferences, if you can."

McKenna understood Barrone's motives. He wasn't as worried about the print reporters as he was about the TV people. News conferences meant TV cameras and embarrassing questions asked over the air and re-played on the nightly news. Visual images were more easily recalled by voters than something they might read in the papers. Barrone wanted to do the news conference right after the funeral, probably so it would be carried at the same time on the nightly news.

Folks seeing him screaming for justice after watching him follow his daughter's casket out of the church would remember that in the voting booth. The sympathy factor would cause a great many of them to disregard the fact that his daughter, a married woman, had died in a lovers lane with her boyfriend and her father's aide, the same man. If politics is played right, every kick's a boost.

SIX

After dropping Barrone off at a side entrance to city hall, McKenna called Brunette to seek his approval on the press deal he had made. Brunette wasn't in—he was at city hall with the mayor—so McKenna wound up talking to Camilia Wright instead. Brunette's trusted secretary was loaded with common sense and was possibly the most efficient woman in the department. Camilia saw no problem with the Barrone arrangement, which made McKenna feel a little surer of himself. She would tell Brunette about it when he returned.

Next stop was the 13th Precinct on East 21st Street, where McKenna officially vouchered the bullet as evidence, but he kept it with him. Then he walked through the building to the Police Academy on East 20th Street and took the elevator to the Ballistics Section lab on the eighth floor. After filling out the required forms requesting the ballistics examination, he was admitted to the inner sanctum, Detective Brady Wilson's workshop. Wilson had been in the Ballistics Section as long as McKenna could remember and was considered one of the nation's experts in the science of guns and bullets.

Since the bullet from the 1981 homicides should have been kept someplace in the Property Clerk's Office in the bowels of headquarters, McKenna had expected to spend just a few minutes in Ballistics, finding out at most what kind of gun had been used in the present murders. But he hit it lucky, thanks to Tommy and his persistence in that old case. Eighteen years before, Tommy had given the bullet to Wilson and insisted that he make a comparison to every .380 round that came to Ballistics. Consequently, Wilson kept the bullet in his top desk drawer and had been doing just that over the years. He had taken that bullet out of his desk at least once during every working day for the past eighteen years and knew its characteristics by heart. There hadn't been a single match.

After half an hour with Wilson, McKenna knew that Tommy had been right in all things so far. The bullet came from a .380 Colt Commander and it was the same gun used in the old homicides, eighteen years before. And, as Tommy had predicted, burnt paper residue was still imbedded in the slug; the killer had held the gun in a paper bag when he had shot Arthur McMahon so that he wouldn't leave the ejected cartridge at the scene as evidence.

By three o'clock McKenna was in Joe Walsh's office in the 20th Precinct. Tommy and Walsh were both there waiting for him. Tommy had the crime scene photos and the sketches made with all the dimensions and distances indicated. McKenna took a moment to look them over while Walsh waited to report and show off a bit.

Although, officially, fingerprints are classified and compared at the Identification Section in headquarters, Walsh considered himself the department's fingerprint expert and nobody in the Identification Section cared to argue that point with him. When it came to fingerprints, for twenty years Walsh had been free to roam through any case he liked. He had finished comparing the sixty-one latent fingerprints he had taken from Cindy's car against hers, her father's, her husband's, and her boyfriend's.

"Got five prints that don't belong to the known players," Walsh proclaimed. "I think I might have the killer in one of those five, but Tommy said I'm nuts."

"Bad news for you, Joe," McKenna said. "Tommy's been right in everything about this case so far, so I'd have to agree with him. You're nuts."

"Maybe I am," Walsh conceded.

"But let's forget everything we know about you and assume for the moment you aren't," McKenna said. "Where in the car did these unidentified latents come from?"

"Good idea and good question," Walsh said. "Got one on the back of the rearview mirror, so that has to belong to someone else who drove the car. Probably adjusted the mirror as soon as he got in. No indication that the killer drove the car, so I'm discounting that one. Got two on the inside of the glove-box door and two on the inside door frame of the driver's door. Any one of those and maybe all of them could belong to the killer. He was in the car to steal McMahon's wallet. Probably opened the driver's door to get at it, and he might've gone through the glove box as well."

"Good points, Joe," McKenna conceded.

"All he's done is given us more meaningless labor," Tommy countered. "I'm telling you, this killer didn't leave a print for us to find. But now, thanks to Joe, we have to waste time fingerprinting any friend of Cindy's who might've been in the car, we have to find out if she had any other lovers and then fingerprint them, and we have to find out where she had her car serviced and fingerprint every mechanic in the place. A lot of time and trouble for nothing."

McKenna accepted Tommy's opinion at face value; all those people would have to be found and their fingerprints would have to be compared to the latents. There was no way around it. Since Joe Walsh, in his quest for ink, spent more time talking to reporters than he did talking to his wife, McKenna didn't want to tell Tommy everything he had learned that day from Barrone and Brady Wilson. He indicated with a head movement that it was time to go and Tommy caught on.

"Thanks a lot, Joe," Tommy said. "Go home and read your scrapbooks."

"You think that's all I do at home?"

"That's exactly right."

"How'd you know?"

Moonlighting is a restaurant and club on Broadway and West 75th Street that features good food served in an upscale atmosphere at reasonable prices. Since it was on the way to Tommy's office uptown, he suggested that they stop there for dinner. McKenna wasn't surprised. The place

ranked high on Tommy's extensive list of hangouts in Manhattan and Mc-
Kenna had met him there before socially. Tommy was greeted as visiting
royalty, and they were given his usual table in the rear.

While enjoying their late lunch, McKenna told Tommy about Arthur
McMahon and everything else he had learned from Barrone. Tommy un-
derstood Barrone's desire to avoid a press conference, but surprised Mc-
Kenna by agreeing with his inclination to comply with Barrone's wishes.
"Helps the prick keep his job, but it's the decent thing to do under the
circumstances."

"You getting mellow in your old age?" McKenna asked.

"Not at all. He won the last battle, but in every war there should be a
truce to bury the dead. He's got his."

McKenna next told him what he had learned from Brady Wilson. It
didn't surprise Tommy, but it seemed to make him happy. "After eighteen
years, he's still using the same gun? Good!" he said.

"How does that help us if we have no other known cases in those
eighteen years?"

"I don't know if it does, but I've had a lot of time to think about it.
One of the questions I ask myself is: Why does he go to the trouble of
firing through the paper bag if he's going to leave the slug in his victim
anyway? The slug is enough to tie him to the killing if we ever get him
and the gun together in the same place, so why does he do it?"

McKenna thought that over and could come up with only one possible
explanation. "He's got more barrels for that gun."

"That's what I've been thinking for years. If you know what you're
doing, you can break an automatic down, change the barrel, and reassemble
it in under a minute. New barrel, new ballistic markings on the slug. But
changing the barrel doesn't change the ballistic markings on the ejected
cartridge. He knows that the chamber, the firing pin, and the ejector all
leave identifiable marks on the ejected shell, so he uses the bag to recover
it."

"Meaning he could be using the same gun with different barrels to kill
other people, and we'd have no way of knowing."

"Right. No way of knowing, as long as he varied his technique a bit.
Any whippings we'd catch, but he must have other ways of torture that get
him off. Maybe there's something about that Fort Tryon location that
makes him think that the whip is the way to go. Whip her to death while
admiring the scenery. He can see a thousand people from there and nobody
can see him and the horrible things he's doing. Might be a real power trip
for him."

"Solve one problem and create many more," McKenna said. "As it stands right now with this theory, things are probably a lot worse than we know."

Unlike most detective units spread throughout the city, the office of the Manhattan North Homicide Squad is not located in a station house. Home for them is a nondescript city-owned office building at Broadway and West 133rd Street in Harlem that also houses Manhattan North's detective borough headquarters, its Sex Crimes Unit, and the Internal Affairs Bureau unit for the borough.

The office was empty when the McKennas arrived. Everyone was still in the Fort Tryon Park area doing the mundane things always done after a homicide—searches and canvasses. The fact that this was a double homicide and a newsworthy case bound to generate pressure meant that those mundane procedures were being diligently performed with a sense of urgency. All the *t*'s were being crossed and all the *i*'s dotted. Detectives had been called in from home, manpower had been requisitioned from other commands, and Emergency Service people were out getting dirty. Evidence and witnesses were the focus of activity.

Evidence in this case consisted of the gun, McMahon's wallet, Cindy's purse, the whip, the chains, the handcuffs, and the bloody tarp—all things at the crime scene during the murders that weren't there when the cops arrived. On the chance that the killer had discarded any of these items soon after the crime, the park and the surrounding area was being combed foot by foot, garbage in every receptacle was being sifted, manholes were being opened, and sewers were being searched. There was also the possibility that the killer had driven into the park and had left his car in another secluded area while he waited, tortured, and killed. If so, that spot had to be found.

Anyone in the vicinity of the park during the night and early morning could be a witness, not necessarily to the crime, but to something connected to it. The killer had entered the park the night before, stayed all night, and left after 6:00 A.M. He had gear with him and was probably carrying a suitcase containing the tarp, his whip and chains, and possibly coveralls. Somebody had seen something and that somebody had to be found and questioned. That meant questioning every parks department employee in Fort Tryon Park, every cop who had worked the late tour in the 34th Precinct, and going door-to-door in every apartment building near the park.

Lieutenant Greve knew what had to be done and Tommy didn't give it a second thought. All the bases would be covered. Any evidence still there would be recovered and brought in and anyone who had seen anything even remotely connected to the crime would be found and interviewed.

As detectives started arriving to work for the evening tour, the Mc-Kennas got busy on their paperwork. Knowing that Greve would be getting a steady stream of questions from the chiefs, everything they had done during the day had to be documented on a COMPLAINT FOLLOW-UP form, the DD5, so that he would have the information at his fingertips. McKenna used separate reports to document his assignment to the case and presence at the crime scene, his visit to Barrone and Valenti, the identification of Cindy's and McMahon's bodies at the morgue, and his visit to the Ballistics Section and what he had learned there. Absent from his reports was the relationship between Cindy and McMahon, but he did note that McMahon had been employed by Barrone and that Barrone would make the death notification to McMahon's family.

McKenna was still typing when Tommy handed him his completed reports, three short ones. He had documented his presence at the crime scene, his visit to the Photo Unit in headquarters, and the results of his meeting with Walsh. Tommy had also filled out a form that McKenna had never seen before. It was an FBI form titled "VICAP," and it listed the particulars of the 1981 homicides as well as the present ones. In the Details section Tommy had also requested information on any unsolved homicide nationwide in which a .380 Colt Commander had been identified as the murder weapon.

"What does VICAP stand for?" McKenna asked.

"Violent Criminal Apprehension Program, something the feds have come up with. Makes things easier now that they're involved. Think you got a serial killer case, fill it out and fax it in. Feds run it through their computer looking for similar cases that have been submitted to VICAP. If they come up with one, they send you the particulars and it's up to you to contact the detective in whatever department submitted it."

"That's the limit of their involvement?"

"Not necessarily. They'll help with the coordinating, if requested, and they just about insist on helping if there's more than one case around the country that's connected to yours."

The VICAP form had not been around when McKenna was last in Homicide, but he liked it. In the past, he'd had to go to the thick directory of police agencies in the U.S. and fax the information and request to each one of them, a very time-consuming and expensive process. "How long has this form been around?"

"About five years, give or take. Ever since serial killers became the public rage."

"Did you ever submit the old case to them before?"

"Tried, but they wouldn't take it. Too old and I only had one double murder. It didn't fit their guidelines for a serial killer case, but that's all changed now."

"We're going to be getting a lot of calls on the .380 cases," McKenna said.

"And we'll look at each one of them. Who's to say that besides being a low-life, murdering pervert, our guy isn't doing robberies as well. After all, he did take Cindy's purse and McMahon's wallet."

"Which brings us to another point," McKenna said.

"The credit cards?"

"Yeah. We've got to know."

"Of course we do. Who do you want to use?" Tommy asked.

"Bob Hurley. You know him?"

"Hurley? Who doesn't? We go back a long ways and he owes me for all the jams I got him out of over the years. Thank God he finally retired. Always had a problem, but he always had a great story with his version of events to entertain the chiefs."

"Good. Could you call him, then?" McKenna asked. "In my case, it's me who owes him."

Tommy called Hurley, gave him Cindy Barrone's and Arthur McMahon's names and dates of birth, and requested the numbers of all their credit cards and whether they had been used that day. Then they gossiped for five minutes about who had retired, who was doing what, who was up and still rising in the detective bureau, and who was down and on their way out. "He'll fax it to me in fifteen minutes," Tommy told McKenna after hanging up.

It wasn't the only way to get the information, but the McKennas knew it was the best and certainly the fastest. They had to know if the killer was using the victims' credit cards and, if so, where. But due to the many laws passed and court decisions rendered over the past years regarding privacy and confidentiality of financial information, that information would be legally denied to them unless they went to extraordinary lengths to get it. The only persons who could authorize the disclosure of the information was a judge, an ADA willing to use his subpoena power, or the executors of Cindy's and McMahon's estates, and only after their wills were probated. A long wait, and if they had died without a will, even that option was out.

Asking an ADA in the homicide bureau for the subpoenas directing the credit reporting agencies and banks to provide the information needed would be faster than going to a judge, but it was an option neither McKenna nor Tommy would ever seriously entertain. Involving the DA's office that early in the investigation would mean that the DA assigned would have a hand in supervising it from then on, a prospect any detective would find unappealing.

Going to a judge for court orders directing the credit reporting agencies to release the information would be preferable, if worse came to worse. Establishing to the judge's satisfaction why they needed the information would be the easy part and serving a court order on TRW or some other credit reporting agency wouldn't be hard, either. Then they would legally possess a list of the victims' cards, but not what they needed. They would have to return to the judge and get court orders addressed to each of the credit card companies, directing them to reveal when and where the cards were used. Of course, each would comply, but they weren't dopes. Because of the police inquiry, they would figure that something was up and they would do one of two things: either try to call the victims—bad news for the McKennas—or simply cancel their cards, just as bad.

The reality of the situation was that the McKennas weren't overly concerned with the financial health of the credit card companies; they wanted those cards active as long as possible and fervently hoped that the killer used them or sold them to someone who could lead them back to him after they applied the appropriate amount of pressure.

Although it violated all the rules, and probably just as many laws, Bob Hurley was the intelligent choice. During his time in the department, Hurley always had some scam going to make money somehow. The chiefs wisely considered him a detective of questionable integrity, but they never really got him good enough to lock him up or fire him—close, but not quite. Hurley was just too sharp for them and they all breathed a sigh of relief when he retired, freeing up the four detectives from Internal Affairs who usually worked on him full-time.

After retiring, Hurley went into the PI business, a trade loaded with hacks who still managed to make a pretty good living. Hurley had correctly figured that a sharp, experienced, and possibly unscrupulous character like himself, fully armed with money, connections, sources, and friends in places high and low, could quickly obtain more information on anybody or anything than all the PIs in town, and he was right. Reliable information was the lifeblood of the PI business and Hurley's ability to gain it quickly soon made him one of the major players in the city. He had found his place in life, president of the Holmes Detective Bureau, hiring his old cronies from the NYPD as soon as they retired, living the high life, and enjoying himself day in and day out.

Although Hurley found it laughable that the NYPD had to go to such lengths to get the information he obtained in minutes with a computer terminal, the appropriate passwords, a chat with some old friends in the credit bureaus, and a few favors spread around, Hurley never forgot where he came from. He always assumed that if an old friend still in the Job called him, it must be important and he always got the information requested.

The nominal price for Hurley's information was a dinner at Kennedy's, his primary hangout, but it went deeper than that. Although the chiefs never wanted to officially know if Hurley was their detectives' source of information on a big case, they were also under as much pressure as their detectives to get those cases solved. But they knew, and one hand always washes the other. Consequently, Hurley always seemed to know when he was hot and under investigation by this regulatory agency or that police agency. An inconvenience, but at those times he would become the model PI, following the rules and laws to the letter for a while.

True to his word, Hurley faxed Cindy's and McMahon's credit reports. McMahon had four cards and Cindy had five. Each also had a debit card for their checking accounts. Next the machine spewed a note from Hurley:

> Tommy:
> Nothing on McMahon, but you've got a hit on Barrone. Heavy activity. I'm still investigating and on the phone; call you when I get all the details. You and I are square, but tell Brian he owes me big time once again.

"The killer's got her PIN numbers. Bet it's all gonna be cash advances," McKenna guessed.

"Of course he's got them," Tommy replied. "Poor girl, I'm sure she told him anything he wanted to know before he was through with her."

While waiting for Hurley's call, McKenna noticed that in violation of law and all ethical business practices, the header on the faxes listing the name and phone number of the sender stated that they came from O'Shaughnessy Investigations, Inc. Jerimiah O'Shaughnessy was a recently retired chief who had started his own company and foolishly placed himself in competition with Hurley. He had been hated by most in the NYPD, but none despised him as much as Hurley. If the illegally obtained credit reports were ever shown to the wrong person, Hurley couldn't care less. McKenna was sure that the phone number at the top of the faxes must be the unlisted personal line sitting on O'Shaughnessy's desk.

By the time Hurley called, all the detectives working the night shift were standing by, waiting to learn where Hurley was sending them. When the phone rang, both McKennas reached for an extension at the same time.

"Detective Forever-in-my-debt McKenna, please," Hurley said.

"You got me," Tommy said.

"Me too," McKenna added.

"I sure do. Don't worry about the addresses, I'll fax them to you. First use, nine-ten this morning, Mobil gas station on Kissena Boulevard and the Long Island Expressway in Queens. Put twenty-nine dollars on her Chase Manhattan Visa. Does a little traveling and at nine-fifty he's at an ATM in a 7-Eleven in Wantagh in Nassau County. Took two cash advances, three hundred dollars each on her Citibank Visa and her First USA Visa. Ten minutes later, another 7-Eleven in Wantagh. Same thing, three hundred dollars on her Planet MasterCard and five hundred on her American Express. On to a K-Mart in Levittown, another ATM, ten-twenty this morning. Took five hundred from her checking account on her Citibank debit card and three hundred on her Chase Visa. Then he tried the First USA Visa again, no good. He'd already exceeded her daily cash advance limit, got rejected on that one."

"Is that it?" Tommy asked. "No purchases?"

"Why should he take a chance on some sales clerk remembering him? He made twenty-two hundred in less than an hour with very little risk. Faceless machines and I'll bet there's no security cameras at any of those ATMs."

"I'm not taking that bet," Tommy said. "Another favor?"

"Already done. If he uses them again tomorrow, I'll let you know two minutes after he punches in her PIN. It cost me, but I've got all her accounts flagged."

"They're keeping her cards active?"

"Like I said, it cost me. She's got eleven hundred left in her checking account, so that's still good. She's close to her limit on the Planet card, but all the rest are good for at least another three hundred tomorrow."

"You got my beeper number?" Tommy asked.

"You kidding? With all the problems the Job gave me, I used to write it on my hand every morning before going to work. Talk to you later if we get lucky and he stays greedy. Take care, brothers."

"One more thing, Bobby," McKenna said. "Can you get us a list of anyone who used any of those machines at about the same time?"

"Tough one and a little risky for me. If there are any and you question them, they might start wondering how you knew who they were."

"It'll never get back to you. Trust us to bamboozle them and leave them smiling."

"I do. You going to be there for a while?"

"Always at your service."

"Nice thinking, kid," Tommy told McKenna after they had hung up. "We get a witness out of this and you're my hero forever."

McKenna could hardly believe it, but he felt himself blushing at the compliment from the great Tommy McKenna. "Think he'll try to get some more cash tomorrow?" he asked, looking to change the subject.

"Don't know, but we've got to be ready to waste the time. One thing I'm sure of is that he won't use the same machines again and he's not from either Levittown or Wantagh. If I had to guess, I'd say he lives in the opposite direction. Upstate, Staten Island, or Jersey."

"But he sure knows the area. Knew just where to go, three ATMs in twenty-two minutes."

"Knew Fort Tryon Park, too, but I know he's not living there. If he was, I'd have found him a long time ago," Tommy stated, sounding very sure of himself.

"So all we know for sure from this is that he's a thief as well as a murderer and he's got a car with a tank that'll hold twenty-nine dollars' worth. That's a big car or an old gas guzzler."

"That's more than I knew before," Tommy said.

"What do we do after we hear from Bobby again? On to Nassau County?"

"Only if somebody was at those machines with him. Then we'll do them ourselves to keep straight with Bobby."

"If not? Somebody's got to talk to the clerks at those stores and question them hard."

"Somebody will, but I don't know if it should be us," Tommy said. "Don't forget, pardner, we're the top hands on this spread. We've got nothing but good people here, so let's decide after we find out how Greve did today. I imagine we'll just go out and poke around a bit before we go home."

"Fine by me. I wouldn't mind an early night. Haven't been home much lately."

"Been working a lot?" Tommy asked.

"Yeah, been putting in a few hours."

"On what?"

"Nothing you'd find interesting," McKenna answered, reluctant to tell him that he spent most of his time chasing note passers. Most homicide detectives regarded their lesser brethren simply as okay folks who had found a way to get a pension by performing meaningless little make-work projects.

Tommy was one of them. "You're probably right," he said, giving McKenna a sympathetic smile. "Not everybody gets to do the real stuff."

Greve came in with his day tour crew. They looked beat and none of them looked like they had enjoyed a particularly successful day.

"Looks like a big zero shaping up," Tommy said, then followed Greve into his office.

McKenna felt he needed a boost, so he called home to tell Angelita he would be on time for a change.

"Good," she said, sounding upbeat. "Ray called. He wants to take us out to dinner tonight. Sotto Cinque at eight, if that's okay with you."

"Fine, but is it his turn?" McKenna asked.

"I can never keep track, but he says it is."

"He's the boss. See you soon."

McKenna wasn't surprised at the invitation. He figured that the meeting with the mayor today had something to do with the Barrone case and Brunette would be under pressure to get it solved quickly. Dinner was the best way for him to find out how the investigation was going without spreading the pressure around. Fine by McKenna, but he wished he had some good news to give his friend.

SEVEN

As it turned out, events mandated a late night. The top hands had to stay after all, traveling up to Washington Heights and out to Nassau County before calling it a day. By the time McKenna got home to his Greenwich Village apartment at nine-thirty, Angelita had been dressed and ready for hours, the kids were finally asleep, and the baby-sitter was doing her homework, grateful for a night of easy money watching Mommy play with her charges before putting them to bed. Dinner with Brunette had been delayed, but they were still on.

Brunette, of course, took it in stride. The delay meant that progress was being made in an important case and work always came before food with him. He was content to wait for them in the restaurant while McKenna finished whatever he was doing.

Angelita understood as well, but was unable to accept this particular delay as part of any routine. Although she had been a rookie cop when she had first met McKenna and Brunette, one of the reasons the Job had not been for her was that she always expected to have what she really wanted when she wanted it, and what she really wanted by nine o'clock that night was to be having dinner in a nice restaurant with her husband and their friend while looking great in her favorite red dress.

It wasn't that Angelita was a spoiled, something-for-nothing type of person; she worked hard at cooking, keeping the apartment immaculate, and raising the kids. She kept herself in great shape and gave McKenna every chance he liked to show her off. She was a good trooper, accompanying him with a smile and without complaint to all those boring promotion and retirement galas he seemed to enjoy so much. Aside from the some-times-irrational jealous streak she found hard to control, she was almost the perfect wife as far as McKenna was concerned.

Almost perfect, but long before he finally walked in the door, McKenna knew he had a problem. He loved Angelita deeply and appreciated her, but he also understood her. He knew that Angelita liked Brunette, enjoyed his company and the fuss he always made over her, and considered his boss to be her friend as much as his. She looked forward to their informal once-a-week-or-so dinners with Brunette so much that she was always ready on time, a rare event in all other circumstances. Being late meant cutting one of her favorite evenings short, and McKenna knew that Angelita didn't like that. Two hours late made even the best excuses inoperable; she would have to be pampered and he was ready to do just that as he made his entrance.

Angelita was sitting in the living room helping the baby-sitter with her Spanish homework. Open on the coffee table were a Victoria's Secret catalog and a Macy's catalog, giving McKenna his first indication of how bad things really were. Repentance was going to be an expensive affair, but he felt it was worth an attempt to minimize the damage. "Sorry I'm late, baby, but I have to tell you something before I say another word. That dress looks just great, especially on you."

"You still like this old thing?" she asked, giving her dress the once-over before shooting him the barest deprecating glance.

"Old? Only seen it once or twice at the most. How old is it?"

Angelita made a small show of looking at her watch. "About two hours older than it should be. I've been sitting here waiting so long that it went out of fashion."

Uh-oh! McKenna thought. What approach do I take now? Contrite and humble or indignant and stupid? "A lady with looks like yours doesn't have to worry about fashion. The older it gets, the better it looks on you."

"If you say so, but I feel a little shopping spree coming on."

"Whatever makes you happy, baby. Lord knows you deserve it."

"It would be nice if you came with me," Angelita said, blatantly pushing the envelope.

Whether it was for herself or him, Angelita loved a slow, thoughtful day of shopping that allowed her plenty of time to ponder each selection. But not McKenna. He hated shopping so much that he could buy himself two suits, five shirts, and ten ties in fifteen minutes while Angelita would still be searching for a new belt for him, but he kept the contrite smile on his face. "Shopping? Love to. Why don't we make a day of it?"

She knew she had him. "Really?" she asked, excited and suddenly all smiles.

"Of course, on one condition. Nothing for me. I've already got enough clothes, but I'm sure you could use a few things."

"I do keep you extraordinarily well dressed, don't I?" she said as she got up and walked toward him, looking him up and down with a hint of pride and satisfaction.

"Sure do. I should be on the cover of *GQ* every other month, thanks to you."

She hugged him and pecked his cheek, but then wrinkled her nose in distaste as she sniffed his suit. "You been to the morgue today?" she asked, pushing herself back.

"Unfortunately, yes. You can still smell that antiseptic?" McKenna asked, amazed.

"It's overpowering. We're late enough as it is, so another few minutes won't matter. You have to change or they won't let us in."

Angelita took her seat on the couch, leaving McKenna sniffing his sleeve. He couldn't smell a thing, but he took her word on it. As he passed her on his way to the bedroom, she gave him a compassionate smile. "Was it bad?" she asked.

"A horror," he answered. "Really sad."

She deliberately closed both catalogs as she continued smiling at him. "You know, I'm trying, but I can't think of a single thing I need. This old dress will do just fine for a while."

With his job and his personality, Brunette never found himself alone for long. When McKenna and Angelita finally entered the restaurant, he was munching a zucchini stick while happily engaged in conversation at the bar with Mike Brennan, an old friend and the *New York Post*'s premier columnist. While Brennan wasn't a reporter, with an inquiring paragraph or two he could put his colleagues in a feeding frenzy, mandating a P.M. press conference the next day.

As usual, Brunette knew what McKenna was thinking. "Mike and I were just having a little off-the-record discussion about how this tragedy you're working on could affect local politics here," he said.

McKenna felt a tinge of relief. "Off the record" with Brennan meant just that. But it would be nice to know Brennan's take on the matter. McKenna didn't say anything, but he gave Brunette an inquiring look.

"I told him everything I know, which isn't too much at this point," Brunette said in response.

"And?" McKenna said to Brennan. "What do you think of the deal with Barrone?"

"Understandable. It's politics, but it doesn't hurt anybody. As long as there's no cover-up of anything the public has a right to know, there's nothing wrong with helping Barrone along through his time of grief." Brennan took an emergency sip from his martini before he continued. "Besides, Barrone's done some good things for the city. He's a fiscal realist."

"So you like him?"

"Can't stand him personally, but he's good for the city," Brennan said, then turned to Brunette. "Matter of fact, it's a smart deal. Can't hurt you when it's time to present your budget to the city council."

"That never crossed my mind," Brunette said with a smile. "See you later." He nodded to a waiter and they were led to their usual table in the rear, leaving Brennan at his usual spot at the bar.

Angelita gave no indication that she wanted to talk about anything but the food, so Brunette and McKenna made small talk with her until they finished ordering. Angelita knew nothing about the case, but she had been through it before and knew that both men wanted to talk about the reason they were eating so late. "You've both been so gracious to me," she said. "I realize my allotted time must be up by now, so why don't you boys talk cops and robbers and pretend I'm not here?"

"Angelita, you're impossible to ignore," Brunette said. "However, I do have some questions for Brian."

"Fire away," McKenna said. "What do you know so far?"

"The press has been bothering me, but I've made no inquiries," Brunette said. "I'm in the dark."

McKenna felt a pang of guilt. When he had called Brunette to tell him he would be late for dinner, Brunette hadn't asked a single question. At the time, McKenna had figured that Greve was keeping him informed of the progress they were making. Apparently, that wasn't the case. "Sorry, I thought someone else was talking to you."

"You mean Greve?"

McKenna didn't want to give up the man for whom he might be working, so he said nothing.

Brunette knew. "Don't worry about it. After Camilia told me about the deal, I made a point of not asking for information. Figured the less I know, the fewer lies I have to tell them. Greve was sharp enough to keep his mouth shut and not send anything to DCPI. Besides, you know how things sometimes slow down when the PC starts asking questions. I didn't want that."

McKenna realized that both Brunette and Greve had been right on the money. Brunette knew that official high-ranking interest in a case frequently slowed it down because the detectives and bosses became too careful, sometimes making them unwilling to climb out onto that important limb. Official pressure on Greve might have worried him to the point that he wouldn't have let his men profit from the information illegally obtained from Hurley. According to the Supreme Court, detectives were not allowed to enjoy fruit that fell from the poisonous tree.

Greve had been sharp enough to realize that the apparent lack of official interest in what he knew was a very important case meant that he was being told, indirectly, to pull out the stops. And, since nobody was asking, he wasn't answering by sending routine progress reports to the office where the press gets most of their information from the NYPD, the deputy commissioner of public information. Sharp.

Greve was a man to be trusted, McKenna concluded, and he tucked that information away in the back of his mind. "How are we gonna handle the press until the funeral?" he asked.

"I'll direct all inquiries to you and you handle the reporters on an individual basis. Be nice to them, give them a little, but generally stonewall them."

"Got it," McKenna said. "Down to business?"

"I'm listening."

McKenna told him about the bullet match with the .380 Colt Commander used in the old homicides and his and Tommy's theory that the killer had been using the same gun with different barrels over the years to commit other crimes, either robberies or murders. He expected a comment on it, but Brunette remained noncommittal.

Walsh's unidentified latent prints were another story. "Where in the car were these prints found?"

McKenna told him, then added, "Tommy thinks it's a waste of time. He's sure the killer left no prints."

Brunette smiled. "I've found over the years that I'm usually right whenever I agree with Tommy. However, I've got some bad news for you. When you catch this guy, even if you do it tomorrow and get him good, you still have to find out who those prints belong to."

"Why? Accomplice?" McKenna asked.

"Sure. If you get him good enough, he'll say he was there with somebody else and the other guy did all the mean stuff while he just watched."

McKenna knew Brunette was right, but he still got some simple satisfaction from Brunette's reasoning. He had said "*When* you catch this guy," not "*If* you catch this guy."

Angelita had been making a show of not listening, but she had also noticed. "Is it going to take you long to catch him, Brian?" she asked.

It was a question McKenna hadn't wanted to hear, and it forced a commitment from him. "Maybe not. If we stay lucky, it could be soon."

That was what Angelita had expected to hear, but not Brunette. "I take it you and Tommy have forced some breaks in this case," he said.

"Forced is the right word. We went to Bob Hurley."

"Hurley?" Brunette asked, concern etched on his face. "Who else knows about that?"

"We kept it a secret on a need-to-know basis. Right now, it's just the Homicide people."

"Whew! I should know better, but you had me worried for a minute. There had to be a lot of people assigned to this case today from other squads, and I'd hate to have to vouch for all of them."

"Anybody in the Homicide Squad that worries you?"

"Not a one. I'd go to the wall with any of them, and that's why they're there doing God's work. I'm very careful when I select his disciples."

Brunette didn't have to explain his feelings any further to McKenna since they shared the same creed, but Angelita didn't get it. "You're choosing God's disciples? Sounds a little sacrilegious, don't you think?" she asked.

Brunette just shrugged, so it was McKenna who decided to answer. "Killers *have* to be caught, and it isn't just a matter of vengeance or soothing the feelings of the victim's family. A killer who gets away with it is likely to kill again for whatever reason. We usually can't stop him from killing the first time, but any victims after that are our fault—a failure of government to protect its citizens. You agree?"

"Sure, but what's the point?" Angelita asked.

"Sometimes the Constitution and the Supreme Court discourage the mission, but that doesn't bother a good homicide detective. Their motto is 'We work for God,' so they're not overly concerned with the risks they take to save lives and get their man behind bars."

"And you're taking those risks?" Angelita asked.

"Yes, and everyone in the Homicide Squad who knows that Bob Hurley is feeding us information is taking the same risk. We could all lose our jobs over this if it got out, Ray included. In all likelihood, we'd be treated as criminals and we'd lose our pensions as well."

"And you're sure it's worth it to get this one man?"

"Absolutely certain. If I showed you pictures of what this guy does to people, you'd have to agree."

"Not necessary, Brian. I like the way you think," Angelita said as she smiled at him and patted his hand. "Besides, it makes me proud to know that you are a good homicide detective and you both know what you're doing. It's one of the reasons I like hanging out with you guys."

The appetizers arrived at that moment, a case of perfect timing as far as McKenna was concerned. He found himself wondering if he was taking unnecessary chances early in the game. They trusted his judgment, but a point had been made by both Angelita and Brunette and it hadn't been lost on him. He was playing with futures when he took chances—Ray's, his, and even Angelita's and the kids'. He resolved to keep that in mind as he went along.

"How did the rest of Greve's people do this morning?" Brunette asked.

"Did all the standard things and spent a lot of time at it, but they didn't get too far this morning. Talked to the cops who worked the late tour in the Three-four last night and checked the parking summonses. Nothing there. Then they got the park workers and did a sweep of the park with them, looking for fresh tire tracks. Nothing."

"So the killer walked into the park," Brunette surmised.

"Or took the subway in. There's an A train stop right in the middle of it, the Cloisters station. Figuring that the killer knew the area and since the park neighborhood was mostly white when he first hit in eighty-one, Greve's men went on the assumption that they were looking for a white male in his forties, at least, carrying his killing gear in some kind of bag or suitcase. He left the park sometime after six, when Cindy died, and before seven-thirty, when the bodies were discovered. They started with the token booth clerk, but she doesn't remember seeing such a character. Understandable—it's a pretty busy station in the morning."

"He didn't stop at the token booth," Brunette said. "He's careful, right?"

"Very careful. Tommy and I are convinced that he's been at this for a long time, and Tommy hasn't heard so much as a whisper about him and his fun for the past eighteen years."

"Then if he took the subway, he already had a token or a Metrocard with him. He wouldn't take a chance on buying a token and being remembered by the clerk."

"As it turns out, that's probably what he did," McKenna said. "Unfortunately, it took a long time and a lot of interviews to find that out. Six hundred and eighty of them by the day crew and more than a hundred by the night crew."

"All the people living around the park?"

"Everybody in every apartment facing the park and every store owner and clerk. Nothing, nobody remembered seeing a white man leaving the park with a package this morning. Not a black man either, for that matter."

"If he left on foot, someone had to see him," Brunette said. "So if he isn't one of the parkies, he had to take the subway out."

"He's not and he did. Every parkie remotely fitting the profile was checked out. Turned out there were two of them, but they had no criminal records of any consequence and each could account for their whereabouts last night. Family men both, and they were home sleeping next to their wives. It had to be the subway, so Tommy and I kept ourselves on the clock. Figured we'd only be getting a couple of hours overtime, but then we got lucky."

"You found someone who saw him in the subway?"

"Two people, in fact, but we didn't think much of it at the time. They don't know each other, but both saw him on the subway platform about six-thirty this morning. He's about fifty and he was carrying a military duffel bag."

"Any blood on his clothes?"

"None that they saw. One of our witnesses, the woman, was even in the same subway car with him riding downtown. Says he got off at the Hundred and Eighty-first Street station, three stops."

"You get a good description?"

"They really had no reason to take a good look at him, so you know how these things go when you have two witnesses who don't know each other."

"Two different descriptions," Brunette guessed.

"You got it. Different heights, different weights, even some small differences in his clothes. Had them down to the Artists Unit for a sketch, drawings look like two different people. Both have him either bald or with a shaved head, one says he has a mustache and the other says he doesn't, but they're both describing the same man—five-eight to five-ten, one sixty to one hundred and eighty pounds, but he's the well-dressed, well-built guy with the duffel bag."

"Well dressed and well built?"

"Dressed in a casual way, might even call him a yuppie. Blue sports coat, tan slacks, white or beige pullover shirt open at the neck, loafers in some shade of brown, and both say he looks like a weight lifter."

"So why didn't you think much of it at the time?"

"Because he didn't fit one big item on our profile. Our man in the subway is black, and the overwhelming majority of identified serial killers are white males."

"Up until now," Brunette said.

"Yeah, up until now," McKenna conceded. "Tommy and I put our heads together and the only black, sex-oriented, long-term serial killer we could come up with was Wayne Williams."

"Wayne Williams? Who's he?" Angelita asked.

"A black guy who killed a bunch of young boys in Atlanta in the eighties. Except for him, this sick type of carnage has always been one of our sins."

"If this is the guy, it shoots down Tommy's whole local-resident-knows-the-neighborhood theory," Brunette observed. "The area around the park was mostly white when our killer first hit in New York."

"I know, and it's killing Tommy. Based on everything commonly known about serial killers, he'd spent eighteen years searching for a white guy. That was the whole focus of his investigation when he was looking for suspects."

"Will these two witnesses of yours stand up to inspection?"

"You mean, Did Hurley have anything to do with us finding them?" McKenna asked.

"That's what I'm asking."

"They'll do. We found them the hard way—old-fashioned door-to-door police work."

"I see. They're two that Greve's people missed this morning when they did their canvas of the neighborhood," Brunette surmised. "They missed them because your witnesses weren't home."

"That's right. They were at work then, but on their way into work was when they saw our man on the subway."

"What finally made you two so sure that he's the guy?"

"That's where Hurley comes in," McKenna said, then briefly told Brunette about the information he had gotten from the PI on Cindy's credit cards.

"Did you ask him for the names of the people who used those ATMs around the same time as the killer?"

"Hold on, Ray. I'm supposed to be the sharp guy," McKenna said, impressed with how quickly Brunette had come up with the same idea Tommy had thought so brilliant.

"Okay, you're still the sharp guy. But did you?"

"Yeah, and that was the clincher. One of the night teams went out to Nassau County. They stopped at the gas station off the expressway where the killer used Cindy's card to buy gas. Got nowhere there."

"He just swiped her card at the pump and filled up?" Brunette guessed.

"Exactly, spoke to no one. Next they went to Wantagh and interviewed the clerk at the 7-Eleven. Got lucky there. He remembered a well-dressed black man using the ATM this morning at around nine o'clock. Stood out in his mind because that neighborhood is lily white, but he couldn't give them much in the way of a description because nine is one of their really busy times there."

"So how about the other places he used the card. Anybody remember him there?"

"I hope so, but we won't know for a while. Soon as Tommy and I heard about the black man using the card in the first 7-Eleven, we knew the subway guy was the one we should be looking for. We went to Greve and had him bring back that team from Nassau County."

"Because you're gonna take the time to make the rest of those interviews legal?"

"Exactly, with one exception. We know who we have to talk to, but we can't legally know that yet without risking getting indicted. So we decided to do it legal, put a rush on those court orders, and hope our potential witnesses out there won't forget seeing our guy, if they saw him at all."

"Who's the one exception?"

"His name's Teddy Wozniak, saw our man at that Wantagh 7-Eleven this morning. Gave us a pretty good description, the best so far."

"What made him the exception?"

"He's safe because he's one of us, or at least we're hoping he is. He's a cop, works in the Tenth Precinct, lives out there. Today's his day off, but his wife's away and he was running short on funds. So he went to the 7-Eleven to get a cup of coffee, a pack of smokes, a quart of milk, and some cash from the ATM."

"How did you know he was a cop?"

"Because Hurley threw in a bonus, sent us the credit reports on all our potential ATM witnesses. Employment listed as NYPD, but I still checked him out a bit before we went out to see him. Called the squad commander in the Tenth and he told us that Wozniak is a pretty active cop. Considers him reliable and, most important, stand-up."

"Wasn't Wozniak wondering how you found him?"

"I'm sure he was, but he didn't ask and we didn't tell him. We just asked questions and he gave answers."

"What was his story?"

"Went to the 7-Eleven and parked in front. From his car he could see our man at the ATM through the store's window. Since Wozniak didn't have enough money to make his purchases, he decided to sit in his car and wait for the guy to finish getting his money from the machine. Saw him get cash on two of Cindy's cards. After he gets his money, the guy leaves the store and Wozniak starts in. Passes the killer, gets to the door, then he hears a noise and turns around. The killer had been parked next to him and had accidentally banged Wozniak's car door with his own when he got in. The guy sees Wozniak looking and says 'Sorry' real politely. Wozniak's driving a shitbox and he's not concerned about any dings, so he yells back,

'Don't worry about it.' Then he goes into the store without another thought."

"Does he remember what kind of car the killer was driving?"

"Not very well. Big car, not too new, maroon or red, possibly an Olds or a Buick was his impression."

"How about a paint chip on Wozniak's car? The killer might have left one there when he banged Wozniak's door."

"Thought about that. Tommy and I checked his car over real good, saw nothing. Just to be sure, we called Walsh at home. He was happy to come out to Wantagh for some easy overtime, and he gave the car a good going-over with his magnifying glass. Came up with some paint from a few other cars, but nothing recent and nothing red or maroon."

"If Walsh couldn't find it, it wasn't there," Brunette said. "Too bad you couldn't bring Wozniak to the Artists Unit and get his version of what this guy looks like."

McKenna smiled, reached into his pocket, and took out three folded pieces of paper. "Couldn't risk taking him to the Artists Unit yet, but we did just as good," he said as he passed them to Brunette.

Brunette unfolded the papers and spread them out on the table. Two were standard Artists Unit wanted-for-questioning sketches, but the third was a sketch done in pencil on a plain piece of paper. Brunette studied them all, then pointed to the plain paper sketch. "This one was made with Wozniak's help?" he asked.

"Yep. Can't show the muscles, but that's his face."

"Who's the artist?"

"Believe it or not, Tommy McKenna. Took him about ten minutes and Wozniak says that's the guy. Also pinned his height and weight down a little better. Says he's five-nine, about a hundred and seventy pounds, right in the middle of what our two subway witnesses say."

"That Tommy never ceases to amaze me, and I'm inclined to agree with Wozniak," Brunette said, staring at the sketches. "These other two look like sketches of two different people, but Tommy's looks like a composite of both of them."

"That's why we can use it tomorrow. We'll put it on the circular form, give it a number, and show it around One Hundred Eighty-first Street. We figure that's where he had his car parked, so somebody must have seen him there."

"If you stay lucky, somebody might even know him," Angelita said. "Easy job, case closed."

Brunette and McKenna exchanged a smile. It was never that easy, they knew. Sketches are routinely made and circulated in major cases, but seldom turn out to be any help at all in catching the suspect. Detectives considered them the outside shot, something they could pin their hopes on when they had nothing else and everything was going wrong. But there was a big down side; sketches generate meaningless investigative hours checking out calls from people who say the sketch looks like their old boyfriend, their boss, their neighbor, their mailman, or whoever else strikes them as a little strange.

Angelita caught the smile and felt miffed. "It could happen," she said defensively.

Her point had to be addressed. "Probably will. We should have this guy in irons tomorrow," McKenna answered, trying not to sound condescending.

He didn't pull it off and Angelita pouted a moment before she won her argument with her standard retort. "You never know," she said emphatically, challenging them to dispute that statement.

Brunette and McKenna just shrugged. They were the losers because, after all, you never did *really* know.

EIGHT

Dawn found McKenna alone in Fort Tryon Park, sitting on the same fallen tree the killer had used twenty-four hours before. He was trying to reconstruct the crime from his quarry's point of view, trying to get into his head. It was an uncomfortable place to be.

By that time the day before, the man had already killed Arthur McMahon and he had Cindy Barrone, bruised and terrified, securely fastened to the tree at the edge of the precipice. From where he sat, by dawn's light McKenna could just make out that tree through the woods. He wondered if the man enjoyed watching Cindy struggle as he waited, wondered if that was part of the fun attached to his perversion. Did he taunt her as he sat here, increasing his pleasure as he yelled to tell her all the horrible things he was going to do to her? Or was he quiet and composed, waiting and watching, biding his time?

He was quiet, quiet and wary, McKenna decided. This man was a patient and meticulous planner, not given to outbursts of pain or pleasure. As Tommy had said, he was just being careful, smoking and relaxing, making sure he and Cindy were alone while waiting for the light of day. For whatever pleasure it gave him, he had come here to torture and kill, and this man knew just how he would do it. Nothing was left to chance with him. Since the spot wasn't frequently used as a lovers lane, he had probably come here many times before, prepared and eager, like a spider on its web waiting for an unlucky victim.

At five-twenty McKenna got up and walked slowly to Cindy's tree, trying to imagine her pinned there, gagged and already in pain as she watched her tormentor approach. Then came the methodical preparations, spreading the tarp on the ground in front of her, showing her the whip and maybe snapping it a few times to heighten her terror. This perverted killer would relish that, McKenna thought, but what would be going through his mind next? Would he tell her where the first blow would rip her flesh, then enjoy watching her panic as she strained at her bonds?

No, he didn't do that, McKenna concluded for reasons he couldn't entirely fathom. Not this guy, not a man who could whip her to death, then throw on a sport coat and climb on the subway looking like an ordinary human being. No, this guy just went to work without saying a word, lashing her and gauging with satisfaction the effects of each blow. He had probably stopped to question her every once in a while about her PIN numbers, but that wasn't why he was there. What was important to this man was Cindy's pain, terror, mutilation, and degradation, not her money. He tortured her in a controlled frenzy, seeking to satisfying whatever inner demons sent him there in the first place. The sex in whatever form it took was almost incidental, McKenna thought.

Cindy Barrone had to suffer and die, but even her death didn't assuage the demons. One particular action among all the other horrible things he did to Cindy led to a question McKenna hoped to ask him soon—Why did you take her down and whip her buttocks to a pulp after she died, after she was past feeling or caring? McKenna was certain that the answer to that question would go a long way toward solving the riddle of what made him tick, what made him so different from everyone else while appearing the same.

As the sun came up behind him, illuminating the Palisades across the Hudson in a spectrum of colors, McKenna tried to stay objectively focused on the killer. He couldn't do it. He had a good description of that man and a picture of him in his mind's eye, but he had seen Cindy Barrone and what he had done to her. He found himself in her mind as she struggled against her bonds, even before the real pain began. She had spent hours in the dark fastened to that tree, looking at the car containing the body of her murdered boyfriend and maybe catching a moonlit glimpse of her tormentor watching her. By the time he approached her at dawn, she knew she was going to die. As she watched him unfold his whip, she hoped

it would be soon. After she felt the searing pain of the first lash, she wanted to die in that instant. But she didn't, couldn't. Merciful death wasn't part of his procedure. She first had to suffer pain McKenna knew he couldn't begin to imagine.

"I'm going to get this cruel bastard," McKenna was surprised to hear himself say. What surprised him more was the intense hatred in his voice. He suddenly knew how Tommy felt and wondered if this man was the reason Tommy hadn't retired. Maybe, so McKenna made himself a promise. He wasn't leaving either until they got him.

McKenna decided he had been at the spot long enough. As he turned to go, a glint in the trees caught his eye. He almost ignored it, but his curiosity got the better of him. He had to search the trees before he saw it again, a shiny object stuck on a twig midway up a tall, slender sapling. He knew what it was and he knew how it had gotten there, ripped loose and propelled by the lash of the whip across the side of Cindy's head. He shook the sapling until her missing earring fell to the ground. He picked it up reverently and examined it. The gold hoop was bent almost in half and speckled with dried blood.

McKenna considered it an omen and he reached a decision. To help him stay focused, he would keep the earring until they caught the man who had damaged and soiled it. He wiped off the blood with spit and his handkerchief and attached it to his key ring so that every time he unlocked a door, he would remember Cindy Barrone and the way she had suffered at the hands of the monster.

McKenna picked up the *News* and the *Post* and read them while having breakfast in a Dominican luncheonette on Broadway. The murders were banner headlines in both papers, and each had a picture of the crime scene on the front page. The articles on the inside pages of both newspapers reported without additional comment that, due to the heinous nature of the crime, Detective First Grade Brian McKenna of the Major Case Squad had been assigned the case with Detective First Grade Thomas McKenna of the Manhattan North Homicide Squad assisting.

In their stories both Harney and Messing attributed a statement to McKenna that he didn't remember making, but he didn't mind. The two reporters had gotten together to give him the proper quote: "After consulting with Detective McKenna of the Homicide Squad, I'm convinced that this is the second set of murders committed by this cruel, demented killer in the very same place." That sounded eloquent enough to McKenna and he was sure that Tommy wouldn't be offended by it. Harney went even one quote better, but McKenna thought he might have said that one in so many words: "Detective Brian McKenna stated that he 'feels honored to have the opportunity to work with Detective Tom McKenna on this very important case.'"

The *News* had a file photo of the 1981 crime showing two covered bodies being loaded into an ambulance with an inset of an old Tommy photo. McKenna couldn't help thinking that Tommy looked like an old young guy then and a young old guy now.

Messing wrote that the 1981 murders were "the perfect crime" since the killer hadn't left a single clue at the scene and, despite years of intensive investigation by Thomas McKenna, described by Messing as "one of the best detectives in the NYPD," the killer hadn't been identified or even described.

After finishing the articles, McKenna thought both Harney and Messing had done a good job without stepping on Tommy's toes. They had reported the crime in more lurid detail than Paul Barrone would have liked and had even gone to the Valenti residence, presumably to inquire about what his wife had been doing with another man, but there had been no answer at the door. Paul Barrone was unavailable for comment, but a spokesman at his office said that "Mr. Barrone has every confidence that the New York City Police Department will bring the killer to justice," and that Barrone would make a statement "at the appropriate time."

McKenna was especially pleased that there was no speculation or progress report on the investigation from that usual "high-ranking police official who spoke on condition of anonymity," which meant to him that Brunette had put a very tight lid on the case. Then he turned the page and all good feeling vanished. It had already begun. Messing and Harney had come through for Tommy on their end, but they didn't run their papers, their editors did—and editors are charged with stimulating public interest in a story in order to sell papers, and that is best done by creating controversy. According to the byline, they used staff reporters to do that, not Phil Messing.

Beginning on page four of the *Post* was a two page spread titled MC-KENNA VS. MCKENNA. Page four was Brian's and page five was Tommy's. The top of each page carried a head shot file photo, that gave the appearance that they were staring hard at each other across the pages. The articles gave career summaries and went on to list their most famous cases. At the bottom of each article was printed "More on Page 26."

McKenna skipped what he already knew and went right to page 26, where the articles came together in a single column designed to create the controversy the editor desired. Sergeant Winterbottom was the usual police spokesman at DCPI, the man charged with doling out to reporters the NYPD's official party line on anything newsworthy, and he had apparently been caught unaware and professionally ambushed. When questioned, he naturally denied that Det. Brian McKenna's assignment to the case had anything to do with the identity of the victims. According to him, political influence was never a deciding factor in the NYPD's personnel decisions.

When asked why Det. Brian McKenna had been placed in charge of a case that normally would have been Det. Thomas McKenna's, Winterbottom stated, "It was a command decision intended to put the best investigators in the department on an important case that will certainly receive national attention."

So far, so good, McKenna thought, and then read on as Winterbottom failed his final exam in advanced doublespeak. "Who makes the command decisions in cases of this nature?" was the question. Poor Winterbottom must have been stuttering by that time and didn't know if he was authorized to give up the PC. "Commanders" was his answer for the record, an answer that immediately evoked in McKenna's mind an image of Winterbottom in uniform, sitting in a radio car and patrolling one of the city's most unfashionable neighborhoods, a neighborhood located as far as possible from where Winterbottom lived.

The final question, the merciless coup de gras for Winterbottom, was "Is it possible that the reason Det. Brian McKenna was placed in charge of this case is that Det. Thomas McKenna hasn't been able to catch this killer since 1981?"

Winterbottom failed to exercise either of his two sensible options under the circumstances—he didn't fake a heart attack and fall to the ground, clutching his chest and writhing in pain, and he didn't give them a simple "No, that's not possible." Instead he answered, "I can't say for sure, but I don't think that's the case."

That failure to deny unequivocally was all the editors needed to exploit the story and speculate in print for the final two paragraphs of the article. One McKenna was in and the other was out. Dismissing the possibility that the McKennas were friends who were working as a team to catch a fiendish murderer, the contest was on. Which McKenna will prove to be the better? Can Tommy McKenna resuscitate his soiled reputation by finally catching the killer? Or will Brian McKenna catch him first and deny the old-timer the chance to make good? These questions weren't printed in black and white, but they were certainly planted and growing.

NINE

Although McKenna wasn't scheduled to start work until ten, he was at the Homicide Squad office at seven-thirty. The place was empty and he expected to be alone for a while, but Tommy came in ten minutes later carrying two cardboard file boxes.

"Whatcha got?" McKenna asked.

"My files on the Lenore-Crudo killings. Figured it was time to bring in all the paperwork."

"Your 1981 case?"

"Yeah. Sharon Lenore and Patrick Crudo. The files were taking up too much space around here, so I'd brought them home."

Very unusual, McKenna thought, and another indication that Tommy's obsessed with those old killings. "Light reading?"

"Better than watching TV. You see the papers yet?"

"Yeah, I read them. Have you?"

"I browsed through them just long enough to realize that I'm not saving today's copies."

"Don't you think we should talk about it?"

"Nothing we can do about it, so don't go feeling sorry for me. This will all pass and my ego can handle it."

"I'm gonna say it, anyway. I'm sorry about the trouble this must be causing you."

"Brian, if you insist on feeling sorry for somebody, then why don't you make it Winterbottom? That poor slob's a goner and he could probably use the sympathy."

"Okay, you win. Winterbottom's the only one I feel sorry for."

"That's the spirit. C'mon downstairs with me. You can give me a hand bringing up the rest of the files."

"There's more?"

"Lots more. Eighteen years' worth of no results."

McKenna followed Tommy down to his car. In his trunk there were four more cardboard file cartons of reports. "I don't think the Warren Commission generated this much paper," McKenna commented as he hefted two of the cartons.

"Course not, and it was all bullshit because those amateurs didn't know what they were doing. This squad could've done a better job with half as much paper."

McKenna didn't know whether or not Tommy was kidding, but he decided to leave it alone. Once they were back in the office, Tommy began unpacking his files. "You going to be reading these?" he asked.

"If it's all right with you."

"Fine by me. Let me know if you come up with anything I missed. Which desk is gonna be yours?"

"Don't know. Greve didn't officially give me one yet."

"Then you better wait until he does."

"Why's that? Is he a stickler?" McKenna asked.

"Typical old-time boss, doesn't say much unless something is bothering him. In the office he's king and he's got his ways."

"How about in the street?"

"Leaves us alone and lets us get our work done. He's there if you need him to get some other boss out of your hair, but otherwise your case is your show."

Considering the talent Greve had working for him, McKenna decided he had a good policy. Most of the detectives in Homicide were first graders with thirty years on the Job, so Greve didn't have much to worry about. However, McKenna did. He had much to do that day, he had come in early, and he wanted to get to work. Not having a desk bothered him. "What time does Greve get in?"

"Soon. Usually he's the first one here. Makes the first pot of coffee, goes into his office, closes the door, and spends his day signing our reports. Never see him unless we all go out on a fresh kill."

"Then I'll save him a big part of his job today," McKenna said. "The new kid on the block makes the first pot."

"Long as you know how to make it strong, fine by me."

No matter where in the city they were located, the interior of most detective squad offices looked the same. Although this one was not in a station house, it could have been. There was a small reception area just inside the front door and two rows of desks in the squad room where the detectives handled their calls and typed their reports. The squad commander's office was at the end of the squad room, next to a door that led to a combination lounge/bunk room. That was where the refrigerator and coffee pot were kept, and McKenna had no trouble finding everything he needed.

McKenna also liked his coffee strong and he brewed it to his taste. By the time he had it ready, Greve was in. The boss looked disappointed to see the pot full, but he poured himself a cup and savored the first sip.

"Well?" McKenna asked.

"Sissy headquarters coffee. We drink a manly brew up here, but it'll do for now," Greve said, then turned and walked to his office. McKenna thought the orientation interview was over, but Greve stopped at his door. "Give me fifteen minutes to go through my mail, then come on in," he yelled to McKenna.

McKenna made Tommy and himself a cup and brought it over. Tommy made a face after his first sip.

"I know. Sissy headquarters coffee," McKenna said.

"You'll improve. Up here we drink it stronger than the Cubans do."

"Is Greve gonna want the plan for the day?"

"Probably not. He knows your rep and he knows who sent you here, so you'll get plenty of latitude from him. What he'll tell you is that he doesn't want to find out what's going on by reading about it in the papers. Talk to him before talking to the press."

"Understandable," McKenna said. "Standard procedure. Anything else he'll want to talk about?"

"In your case, not a thing."

"Nothing about talking to him before talking to Ray?"

"No, he doesn't have to worry about that."

McKenna felt satisfied thinking that Greve had enough faith in him to know that, friendship aside, he wouldn't tell the PC anything about the case without telling his immediate boss first. Brunette wouldn't have it any other way.

Just in case Greve did ask, McKenna and Tommy spent a few minutes going over their plan for that day. Brunette had a friendly judge standing by, so McKenna would go downtown to court to get the court orders he needed to make Hurley's information legal. Then he would run around town to credit agencies and banks to get the information he already had. Sometime during the day, he would stop at the morgue to pick up the autopsy reports on Arthur McMahon and Cindy Barrone.

Tommy would take a team to West 181st Street, the place the killer had gotten off the subway. It would be a repeat of the tedious door-to-door questioning done the day before, except this time they had a better description. They would want to know if anyone had seen that well-dressed black man get into a car. If so, what kind of car was it? They would also check all the parking lots and garages in the area and, on the off chance the killer had parked illegally and gotten a parking ticket, they would check the summons box at the 34th Precinct. Anybody who had gotten a parking ticket near West 181st Street on their big, old red or maroon car the night before was up for a look.

"This is the stuff you don't see on TV," Tommy commented. "Good old-fashioned, boring police work done with a smile."

"Think we'll get anywhere with it?" McKenna asked.

"Maybe. We've already gotten further than I did the last time."

"Did he take their wallet and purse on that one?"

"Sure did. They had credit cards, too, but he was only in for the cash."

"He didn't want to take a chance on being recognized if he tried using the cards," McKenna surmised.

"No way, not our scumbag. We weren't in the computer age back then. No ATMs where he just swipes the card, enters the PIN number, and gets money without talking to anybody."

Tommy looked so down when he said it that McKenna felt compelled to add something. "Too bad. Even a Bob Hurley wouldn't have done you much good back then."

"Yeah, too bad."

Four more homicide detectives reported in for work, more than an hour early. They all greeted McKenna cordially enough, but he got the feeling that they weren't overjoyed to see him.

"You'd better go see the boss," Tommy suggested.

McKenna went to Greve's door, checked the shine on his shoes, and snugged up his tie. He was a traditionalist and believed a detective should always look his best when reporting to his squad commander. He knocked and went in.

A quick look around told McKenna that Greve was a conscientious, practicing neatnik, and a little unorthodox to boot. The office was spotless, the rule books and law books in his bookcase were all perfectly aligned, the place was freshly painted, and even the floor was waxed. Then there was Greve's desk. It wasn't the city-issued gray metal type. Greve had bought his own walnut desk and it glistened with polish. On top, his in basket was empty and his out basket was already full of neatly stacked reports. Unusual, but McKenna had known another neat squad commander who had bought his own desk. What made Greve unorthodox were the curtains on his windows, a rarity in any city office; the crucifix hanging on the wall over the bookcase; and the calico cat stretched out on his desk.

Even the cat was neat; on the floor under the window were two shiny silver bowls resting on a shiny silver tray. There was water in one bowl and dry cat food in the other, but not a speck of cat food or a drop of water on the tray. Next to the row of file cabinets was a covered litter box, but there wasn't a hint of odor or a bit of cat litter on the floor.

Greve was seated behind his desk, reading a report while stroking his cat's head. Both looked up when McKenna entered, but only for a moment. "Be with you in a minute, Brian. Pull up a chair," Greve said, then continued reading while his cat watched him. Both ignored McKenna.

McKenna sat down and was immediately taken by the polished brass nameplate on the desk that announced he was in the office of Lt. Stephen Greve. Steve Greve? was all he could think. Even his name sounds tough.

Greve finished reading the report, signed it at the bottom, and placed it in his out basket. He took a moment to align it properly on top of the other reports there, then he focused on McKenna. "Sorry to keep you waiting, but you really have to read between the lines of the stuff those guys crank out. If I didn't know better, after reading their reports I'd think that they were following the rules to the letter." Greve allowed himself a small chuckle. "Every murdering bastard's got countless constitutional rights, with the courts adding new ones every day. Makes no difference. Those guys out there are way up on any money-grubbing, cocksucking, double-talking scumbag lawyer who winds up defending those filthy bastards."

The sentiments were fine, as far as McKenna was concerned, but those weren't exactly the words he had expected to hear from Greve. He took a quick look up, halfway expecting to see the crucifix fall off the wall. It didn't, so he figured everything was fine. "Isn't that the way it's supposed to be?" he asked, just to get Greve's reaction.

Greve looked confused by the question. "Following the rules? Of course not. They'd get nothing done and we'd have those murdering bastards wandering all over the city."

"That's not what I meant."

"You mean the lawyers and all that rights crap?"

"No. What I meant was, Shouldn't their reports somehow tell you the whole story and, at the same time, shouldn't they tell the defense attorney who's going to wind up reading them only what he's supposed to know?"

"Of course they should. They're New York City homicide detectives I've got out there writing them," Greve said, dismissing the question with a wave of his hand. "Let's get down to business. Orders came down this morning transferring you to this squad on temporary assignment. It's official now, you're working for me. It wasn't yesterday, but it is now."

"So it's official. Does that make any difference?"

"To me it does. If you're going to wander way off base with a bright idea, let me know first. If worse comes to worst, we'll deny everything together, but I'd like a little lead time."

"You mean like calling Bob Hurley?"

"Yeah, Bob Hurley. Bright idea, but next time whisper something in my ear first."

Okay, so Greve's not one of those common don't-tell-me-anything, just-give-me-results type bosses, McKenna realized. But why didn't Tommy tell me that before we made the call? "Sorry. I wasn't sure you'd want the details."

"Don't worry about it. Aren't you wondering why Tommy didn't come to me before you guys made the call?"

This guy's uncanny, McKenna thought. "I guess I am."

"Because I go ask Tommy whenever I'm not sure of something. He's the best I've seen, the exception to the rule. I guess he figured you were, too."

"But I guess I'm not?"

"Not yet. From what I hear about you, you probably will be soon. But not yet. I'd like to see some of your stuff first."

"Fair enough. I hope I measure up."

The cat got up and stretched, arching its back, and Greve turned his attention to the animal, stroking its ear and uttering a few ridiculous sounds that only the cat understood. It licked his hand, then stretched out once again on the desk. Only then did Greve turn his attention back to McKenna. "You ready for a few questions?"

"Shoot."

"How long has it been since you've worked homicide?"

"About ten years."

"Why'd you get out?"

"Because murder depresses me. Saddest crime of all."

"That's for sure. Depresses me too. That's why I hate killers, but I have to tell you something. I try to keep my emotions in check, but that Cindy Barrone kill was the worst I've ever seen. That killer I really despise, so I hope you can get him."

McKenna didn't think Greve sounded very confident and he knew the reason why. If Tommy McKenna couldn't get him, then who could? Nobody, Greve believed. "I'm here until we do," McKenna said confidently.

"Glad to hear it. If you can manage it, try to get him before I retire."

"When will that be?"

"In about six years, I figure."

What a vote of confidence that is, McKenna thought. He searched his mind for a clever rejoinder, but couldn't come up with one. "Okay, I'll try."

"Thanks. Now for a few more ground rules. I'm sure you've got more than a few reporters in your pocket and I don't mind you talking to them. I just want to know what's in the paper before I buy it."

"You will. There shouldn't be much coming from me for a few days."

"So I hear, and I'll do my best to keep them off your back. When they call, you're in the field. Already told a few lies to them on your behalf."

Thanks, but who told him to do that? McKenna wondered. Was it Ray, Tommy, or did he just figure it out himself?

Greve gave no indication, but the interview was over except for one more thing. "There's an empty desk next to Tommy's and it's in pretty good shape. Even the locks on it work. Use them, because we don't want the cleaners finding out what you're doing on this case and then selling the story to the *Enquirer*," Greve said. He reached into his pocket, took out a key, and looked at it fondly for a moment before he passed it to McKenna. "It used to be my desk before I bought this one. There's a bottle of polish in the bottom drawer, right side."

Greve's a strange one, McKenna thought, certain of one thing. Brunette had the right man for the job.

TEN

McKenna spent the morning and most of the afternoon making Hurley's information legal the hard way: visiting Brunette's judge three separate times for court orders. Each time he had to prepare and swear to an affidavit listing the information he needed and why. Before it was over, he had legally obtained it all from the Eastern District Credit Agency and the midtown offices of four separate banks. He was sure that Cindy's credit cards were cancelled within minutes of his departure from those banks, but he still had an ace up his sleeve. He had enough to legally interview the people on Long Island who might have seen the killer use Cindy's cards and he wanted the killer to keep using the cards, so he didn't serve his court orders on American Express and Citibank. He hoped his killer would get another day or two of good plastic from Amex and Citibank before they caught on and cancelled those cards.

McKenna's last stop in midtown was the morgue. He was happy to find Andino in his office, munching on a sandwich.

"I was right in all things," Andino said as he passed McKenna copies of the autopsy reports. "Cindy Barrone bled to death. No injury to any of her vital organs. When her blood pressure dropped, her brain just shut down due to lack of oxygen. Her heart followed moments later and it was finally over for her."

"It looked to me at the scene like her neck might've been broken."

"It was, along with four ribs, but those injuries were sustained when she was thrown down the cliff. All postmortem, no internal bleeding at the fracture sites."

"Was she raped?" McKenna asked.

"Couldn't determine that with absolute certainty, but I'd say no. Found no semen or foreign pubic hairs anywhere on or in her. He could have used a rubber, but I consider that unlikely. They always leave a pubic hair or two behind and he didn't."

"And the tearing? Were you right about that, too?"

"Like I said, he stuck the whip handle in her. Hard and frequently, both in her rectum and her vagina. Caused some internal damage, but not as much as I'd originally thought. The interesting thing for you to consider is that I was also right about the rectal damage. All postmortem, something I've never seen before. Means that you're looking for a really sick and twisted individual, a genuine classic."

"How do you know it was the whip he used?"

"Another assumption, but it was something leather. There's tannic acid residue on the inside wall of both her vagina and rectum. That's the chemical used to cure leather."

"Anything under her fingernails?" McKenna asked.

"Sorry, nothing on the fingernail scrapings. She never laid a glove on him."

"How about her blood?"

"Extremely high levels of adrenaline, but we expected that. She was petrified. Alcohol level of point oh eight. Not drunk, but she'd had a few drinks."

"Are you releasing the body?"

"Yeah, I already called Barrone. He's sending a funeral director around to pick up the body after six."

"Did he happen to mention where she'll be laid out?"

"Walter B. Cook's in Bayside. Wake begins tomorrow. The funeral's on Friday at Our Lady of Sorrows, also in Bayside."

"Are you going?" McKenna asked.

"I'll be there. Probably go to the wake as well. Yourself?"

"I'll go to both. If I don't see you at the funeral home, I'll catch you at the funeral. How about Arthur McMahon? Anybody from his family come up?"

"His father, Arthur McMahon, Sr. He was here a couple of hours ago. He didn't call you?"

"Not yet."

"He will. I gave him the Homicide Squad number. From the looks of him, he's another heavyweight. He's staying at the Pierre."

"How'd he take it?"

"Same as Barrone. He's a dignified gent. Very reserved, but I've got the feeling he's taking it hard. He did mention that Arthur was his only child."

"You know, I never thought to ask Barrone. Do you know if he has any other children?"

"No, he doesn't. Makes this whole affair even sadder. The last of both lines ended in Fort Tryon Park. The hopes and dreams of two families gone in one horrible crime."

It was sad, but it was one of the things McKenna didn't want to think about at the moment. Emotion fogs objectivity. Since he was in midtown he would go see McMahon before McMahon called the office, and he wanted to remain clear-headed for the meeting. "Anything else you can tell me, John?"

"Nothing you'd consider significant. The contents of their stomachs were almost identical, so they probably had dinner together. They were celebrating his birthday with Italian food, sometime around nine o'clock Sunday night."

"You're right. That doesn't help," McKenna said. The autopsies had disclosed nothing positive of any consequence that he hadn't already known.

McKenna called the office as soon as he left the morgue. He was told that Tommy still hadn't returned from Washington Heights, so he didn't feel he was upsetting their schedule much by stopping to see Arthur McMahon. He called the Pierre Hotel, asked for McMahon's room, and was surprised when Paul Barrone answered the phone.

"We were just about to call you," Barrone said. "Have you been making any progress?"

"Some, but we've got a long way to go. Is Mr. McMahon there?"

"He went downstairs to get some cigars, but he'll be back in a moment."

"I'd like to stop by, if it's convenient."

"Very convenient. Please do. Room six-fourteen."

It was rush hour, so it took McKenna thirty minutes to get to the Pierre Hotel at Fifth Avenue and East 61st Street. Arthur McMahon, Sr., opened the door to Room 614 and McKenna saw at once that Andino was right on both counts. McMahon *was* a dignified gent, in his sixties with a full head of white hair and a face that reminded McKenna of Thomas Jefferson. His expensive dark blue suit and the fact that he was in one of the better suites at the Pierre was enough for McKenna to consider McMahon Sr. a wealthy man. The big Churchill in his hand only added to the effect.

"So good of you to come, Detective McKenna. I'm very pleased to make your acquaintance," McMahon said with a slight Southern drawl. "Do come in."

Paul Barrone was seated on the sofa with a drink in front of him on the coffee table and an open newspaper on his lap. He closed the newspaper, placed it on the coffee table, and got up briefly to shake McKenna's hand.

The newspaper headline gave McKenna yet another sign that McMahon was a heavyweight. ARTHUR McMAHON'S SON MURDERED IN NEW YORK told McKenna that McMahon's local paper considered his son's death more important than the murder of the daughter of the speaker of the New York City Council.

"Can I get you anything, Detective McKenna? A drink, perhaps?" McMahon asked.

"No. Nothing, thank you."

"Then please make yourself comfortable while I make one for myself."

McKenna settled onto the sofa opposite Barrone and saw that the newspaper was the *Richmond Ledger*. McMahon took a sip from his drink, then sat next to Barrone. "Detective McKenna, I'm looking forward to sitting front row at the trial of the man who murdered my son, and I think we can stand some good news," McMahon said, getting right down to business.

"Then you may be disappointed. I've got some news, but it's just a start. Tommy McKenna and I have developed a description of the killer, but not much else yet."

"I see," McMahon said. "Will you and this Tommy McKenna be working full time on this case until you catch this man?"

"I will be, exclusively. Tommy will be working with me for a while, but if it drags on he'll probably be reassigned to other cases."

"Do you think it will drag on?"

"Unfortunately, I do. Tommy's been searching for this man for eighteen years and he's the best in the business."

"Yes, I've heard that he's quite good," McMahon said, nodding to Barrone and surprising McKenna. "As a matter of fact, I've started reading his book and you can tell him for me that I'm quite impressed. I had hoped to meet him before I left town, but he'll understand that I've got to take my son home."

"I'll tell him and I'm sure he'll appreciate it."

"For my own information, which of you was it that developed this description?"

"It was a team effort."

"According to the newspapers, your friend Tommy didn't get a description of the killer in 1981. Is that correct?" McMahon asked.

"Things were different then," McKenna said, not liking where the conversation was leading.

"I see. Then let's just say that I'm glad you've joined the team and leave it at that. Now, tell us, please, everything you know about this killer and how you now have his description after eighteen years."

Can I put our cards on the table? McKenna wondered. Can I tell the speaker of the city council that members of his police department have been committing a few improprieties on his behalf? He looked from McMahon to Barrone and back again. Each was watching him, waiting expectantly. "I will, but first I want you to understand that this is privileged information that can never be repeated to anyone because we went out on a limb to get it."

"Agreed. I never heard it," McMahon said.

McKenna looked to Barrone.

"Of course I agree," Barrone said. "I don't want you to catch the man who murdered our children, I want you to kill him. If I could do it myself, I wouldn't mind spending the rest of my life in jail."

I can go with this team, McKenna decided. For the next ten minutes he brought them up to date on the investigation, omitting nothing.

"I see you *have* gone out on a limb for us, and we thank you for that," McMahon said.

"To tell you the truth, we wouldn't have climbed out on that limb if this was a case of one drug dealer shooting another," McKenna stated. "But we would have done it in any case where innocent victims were murdered this way, and it has nothing to do with you two being heavyweights."

"Heavyweights?" McMahon asked.

"Yeah, heavyweights. Mucky-mucks. Shakers and movers like yourselves."

"I'll admit that I'm sometimes thought of as a shaker and mover in Virginia politics, but exactly what is it you think I do?"

"Nobody told me, but I'll admit I'm curious."

"Briefly, I'm now with a large Richmond law firm doing corporate law, mostly. I'm interested in politics and years ago I served in Congress briefly, but that wasn't for me. I prefer not being directly involved in the political process, although our law firm does quite a bit of political lobbying in Washington for various clients."

"So you're a party boss?"

"I hold no official position, but I guess you could say I am," McMahon said with a smile. "Back home, people tend to listen to what I have to say."

Just what I needed, McKenna thought. First the city council speaker and now an ex-congressman. But something doesn't make sense. "I take it you're not hurting for money?"

"No, I'm not. You're wondering why Arthur put himself through law school and then came to New York instead of working for me?"

"It crossed my mind," McKenna said.

"We always got along and I loved him dearly, so let's just say that he wanted less out of life. He always had an independent streak, wanted to do everything on his own. I respected him for that," McMahon said, but all of a sudden his reserve was crumbling. He trembled a bit and slouched slightly, seeming to McKenna to shrink right in front of his eyes. He picked up his drink and took a sip while he tried to compose himself. He couldn't do it, so he puffed on his cigar, blowing smoke to hide his tears.

Next, to McKenna's complete surprise, Barrone started falling apart as well. Tears formed in his eyes and he looked embarrassed as he dried them with his handkerchief. He picked up his glass and drained his drink. It was all he needed. "You would have liked Arthur, Brian. Lord knows I did. A fine young man," Barrone said evenly.

"I'm sure I would have," McKenna said.

Barrone placed his hand on his old friend's arm and McMahon put his hand on top of it.

McKenna was touched and felt like crying himself. Neither man was paying any attention to him and he thought they needed some time. "Mind if I use the bathroom?"

"Go ahead," Barrone said, indicating with a nod of his head the direction of the bathroom.

When McKenna returned, McMahon and Barrone were talking to each other in hushed tones, all business again. He sat down and was surprised to see that they were smiling.

"Detective McKenna, what are the chances you'll get anything substantial from the witnesses tonight?" McMahon asked.

"Not great. It's been more than a day since they've seen him and they really didn't have much reason to take any notice of him in the first place. They might not even remember having seen him."

"So this delay has really hurt our case, hasn't it? If you could have spoken to them this morning, it's probable that they'd remember more."

"Yes, but the delay was unavoidable. Can't legally be done any other way."

"Not by you it can't. You're an agent of the state. What was the name of that friend of yours, the private detective?"

"Bob Hurley."

"And his firm?"

"The Holmes Detective Bureau."

"I'm assuming he's good?"

"The best. Plays the edges, but maybe that's what makes him the best."

"So much the better. I intend to hire him. Please have him call me and, while you're at it, give him your impression of me. Tell him he will receive any advance he requires and that I pay my bills on time. You might also tell him that, if this works out, my firm represents many influential clients who would have need of a man of his abilities."

"If what works out?"

"The type of information he gave to you he will now be giving to me, a private citizen. I will immediately forward it to you for your use."

It was a twist McKenna hadn't heard before. "And that will make the information legal? I can use it and get away with it?"

"Absolutely. Evidence and information that falls into your hands will stand up in any court as long as you, a police officer acting under color of governmental authority, didn't break any laws or conspire with me to get it. You didn't and you won't. It's all my idea. As a matter of fact, you'd be remiss in your duty if you didn't use it."

"But there are laws being broken here."

"Like privacy laws, computer theft of information, and possibly bribery of banking officials if Hurley's really good?" McMahon asked, not appearing at all disturbed.

"That's a start."

"But the only one breaking those laws is Bob Hurley. I imagine he breaks them every day without giving it a second thought and he must be quite good at covering his tracks by now," McMahon said. "That doesn't affect you, as long as you're not aware of the source of my information."

"Of course I'm not, but are you sure about all this?"

"Believe me, I'm well versed in constitutional law and I had a hand in writing some of the laws relating to privacy."

"Okay, but there's a down side. I'll have to say that this information is coming from you."

"Of course you will. It's coming from the grieving father of a murder victim, a sympathetic character with money to spend. You can tell Bob Hurley that I'll pay him in cash, if he likes, and that I'll never reveal the source of my information. Tell him that I'll go to jail first, although I hardly think it will ever come to that."

"But you'll be under some pressure if this thing blows up in our faces, won't you?"

"There will only be pressure if one of the people you interview squawks, but I consider that unlikely. After all, you're investigating a particularly heinous crime that's in the news. But even if they do squawk, what's the most that can happen? A grand jury investigation? Fine, but unlikely. I'd simply refuse to divulge my source, and then what?"

"I don't know," McKenna said. "What?"

"If I was a police officer, they'd throw the book at me. But I'm not. I'm a victim, an object of public sympathy."

"They could throw you in the can for contempt of the grand jury."

"Fine, but we're forgetting that these are federal laws that are being violated, and I'm going to be in Virginia when they are. Presumably, that's where the laws are being broken. So, in the unlikely event there is a grand jury investigation, I think that, in my case, it will be in Richmond. As a matter of fact, I can assure you that it will be in Richmond Federal Court."

"You can do that?" McKenna asked.

McMahon and Barrone exchanged a smile before he answered. "Yes, I can. I've been around a long time and I'm owed my share of favors."

"Okay, let's say it's in Richmond. Then what?"

"And then, nothing. Closed proceedings, no true bill. In Virginia people ask themselves what's right, not what's the law."

"I think the same thing would happen here. Our folks aren't blind to justice, either," McKenna said. "But aren't you going to a lot of trouble for another unlikely event? Hurley comes in handy only when the killer uses Cindy's credit cards. I'm sure that the banks I visited today already have cancelled her cards and it'll only be another day or two before American Express and Citibank catch on. After they're cancelled, we won't be able to get a fix on the killer."

"Paul and I have already discussed that. We'll arrange to keep her cards active, funded by us. Any cards that were cancelled will be reopened this evening. I need the names of the people you spoke to at those banks today. I presume they were all persons in positions of authority?"

"They were, but the banks are already closed."

"Then Hurley's first mission will be to get their home numbers. They're all going to be getting a call from the speaker of the city council and I think they'll soon be on board."

Will this work? McKenna wondered. Assuming the killer's pulled this type of crime before, he must know that he's only got a day or two to work the cards before they're cancelled. What will he think if those cards stay good? That something's up, or will he just think that the banks screwed up and he got lucky? In any event, we've got nothing to lose. "Okay, we'll go with your plan. There's a good chance that he won't try those cards again, but we'll go on the chance he will."

"And if he does, you'll get him?" Barrone asked.

"Maybe, as long as he stays in the same area going from machine to machine. If we don't get him, we'll get close and firm up his description."

"I'm willing to take that chance," McMahon said.

"Me too, although it pains me to think we'll be funding the man who killed our kids," Barrone said.

"There's no better use for money if it helps to get him," McMahon said.

"Right. We'll do our end," Barrone said to McKenna. What he didn't say was, "Now you do yours," but McKenna got the message.

"I've got one other request, Mr. Barrone, and I'm afraid it will cause you some inconvenience and maybe some embarrassment," McKenna said.

"Anything. What is it?"

"I'm assuming that everyone Cindy knew will show up at the wake at some time or other. I want you to ask each of them if they've ever been in her car. If so and if you agree to this, you can save us some time. I'd like to have a detective there to fingerprint them at the funeral home. We have to account for every set of latent prints that were lifted from her car."

"Why go to the trouble? Didn't you say that there's almost no chance they belong to the killer?"

McMahon answered before McKenna could. "It has to be done, Paul. Otherwise, after Detective McKenna gets the killer, his lawyer will tell the jury that the owner of those prints was the man mainly responsible for the murders. If he's good, he might be able to implant that thread of reasonable doubt in the mind of at least one dopey juror, and that's all he needs."

"All right. If it makes things easier for you, all right," Barrone said.

"It does. Thank you," but the speed with which McMahon had given the answer made McKenna curious. "What kind of law did you say you practiced, Mr. McMahon?"

"I probably shouldn't tell you this, but I started out as a criminal defense attorney. Still take a case now and then when a friend's kid gets in trouble."

"That's all right. A few of my friends are defense attorneys," McKenna said, not thinking it necessary to mention that those friends weren't exactly top shelf and that they all suffered from a streak of incompetence that McKenna found endearing in defense attorneys. But McMahon impressed him so much that he made himself a promise. If he ever walked into a courtroom to testify and saw Arthur McMahon, Esq., seated at the defense table, then he would tell the truth, the whole truth, and nothing but the truth.

ELEVEN

McKenna called the office and asked for Tommy. "Just got in," Tommy said. "It's been a long day, so far."

"How'd we do?"

"Not great, but not bad, either. Nobody saw him get into his car, but we found a bodega owner who remembers him. Walked in yesterday morning, got two packs of Marlboro Lights and ten dollars' worth of lotto tickets, Quik Pick. But our killer's lucky, so we got lucky. Probably the only reason the bodega owner remembers him is that he cashed in an old winner for him. Had to shell out sixty-four bucks."

"You get the ticket?"

"I'm way ahead of you, Brian. Got the ticket and fingerprinted the owner, but I'm not optimistic. He ran it through his lotto computer to check the numbers, so any of the scumbag's prints on it are probably smudged."

"You said it's an old ticket?"

"Three weeks old. Bought it May eighteenth."

"Can we find out where he bought it?"

"Sure can. Already got the Lotto people working on that, gave them the serial number on the bottom of the ticket. Said they'd check and get back to me sometime tonight."

"Sounds to me like you did real good," McKenna said. "Where's this bodega?"

"Fort Washington Avenue and One Hundred Eighty-first Street, right by the subway station. Must have stashed his car right near there because he didn't have the duffel bag with him in the bodega. Greve's sending another team out tonight to talk to anybody we missed, but I've got a bonus for you. The scumbag speaks Spanish."

"He's Hispanic?" McKenna asked.

"No. All I said was that he speaks Spanish, but that's part of the bonus. According to the bodega owner, the guy spoke to him in textbook Castilian Spanish, but he's a gringo with his English accent coming through."

"A well-educated gringo," McKenna surmised.

"Can't be certain, but probably. Lots of people learn Spanish, but the bodega owner said he spoke it like a high school Spanish teacher."

"How'd you make out at the Three-four?"

"A bust, no summons we could connect to him. Most of the parking around One Hundred Eighty-first Street is legal at night. Getting a space is difficult, but we already know that he's lucky."

"And so are we," McKenna said.

"I'll agree once we get him in irons. When are you getting back?"

"In about an hour. I've got to go see Bob Hurley."

"What for?"

"I'm on a cell phone."

Enough said. Tommy knew that anything connected to Bob Hurley shouldn't be on the air waves. "Okay, tell me when you get back. I'm gonna go out for a bite, so take your time."

Hurley's office over the Hard Rock Cafe on West 57th Street wasn't far from the Pierre, so McKenna decided to give him the case in person. He called the Holmes office, but was told by his secretary that Hurley was "in the field."

"Would that be his usual field?" McKenna asked.

"Yes, Brian, I believe it is," she answered.

Ten minutes later McKenna entered Kennedy's Bar and Restaurant on West 57th Street, one of the city's larger and more fashionable Irish establishments. The place was crowded, but McKenna didn't see anyone he knew and didn't bother looking for Hurley until he walked through to the second dining room and bar in the back room. That room was crowded as well, but McKenna knew most of the people there. The back room of Kennedy's was one of New York's upscale law enforcement hangouts. Crowded at the bar were well-dressed active and retired detectives, bosses, and federal people, along with a few reporters. It was a festive place, fancy and well lit, with an Irish band in the dining room singing a melodious little tune about killing Brits somewhere.

Bob Hurley was holding court at his usual spot at the far corner of the bar. With him were two people McKenna knew well. One of them was George Hill, a retired captain from IAD who used to spend most of his time on the Job chasing Hurley, without much success. However, Hill had so impressed Hurley with his efforts that Hill now worked for him. The other man was Richie White, a former partner of McKenna's. After he retired, White had taken a job as an investigator at the Eastern District Credit Bureau, so it was the second time that day McKenna was seeing him.

McKenna began working his way down the bar to Hurley, stopping to shake hands and say hello to many old friends, and then he hit an obstacle. John Harney was seated midway down the bar waiting for him, and a simple hello wouldn't do. "Can you give me a few minutes of your time?" Harney asked.

McKenna didn't want to talk to any reporters just then, but he had placed himself in a social setting and Harney was a friend, so there was no way out. "Sure, John. I'll get back to you in a few minutes."

"You here to see Hurley?"

Harney knew that a visit to Bob Hurley meant that some unorthodox means were being used in the case, but that didn't bother McKenna. Kennedy's was one of those off-the-record places, an unofficial sanctuary where cops could talk candidly to reporters without worrying about their conversations appearing in print. "Yeah, I have to see him," McKenna admitted.

"Then I assume you're making some progress."

"Nothing I'd want the world to know."

"Understood. See you later."

By the time McKenna finally got down to Hurley, an O'Doul's nonalcoholic beer was waiting for him at the bar. He greeted Hurley and his entourage and then took a long gulp from his beer while Hurley watched him, waiting.

The years had been kind to Bob Hurley, but not as kind as he had been to himself. McKenna figured he had to be sixty, but he looked fifty with his sun-parlor tan. Although he could stand to lose twenty pounds, he was broad-chested and the extra weight made him look successful rather than fat. Except for Morris, the bartender, Hurley was the only one in the room not wearing a suit. He rarely did, figuring the boss could dress any way he liked and knowing that what he was wearing cost more than any suit in the place. He favored the European look, wearing a tailored, monogrammed silk shirt, and hand-made Italian loafers with a belt that matched the leather weave of his shoes. No matter how well he dressed, Hurley was a gaudy type of guy who could easily be mistaken for a successful gangster. There was the obligatory gold chain around his neck and on his left pinky was the gold detective ring many detectives wore, its face fashioned into a miniature version of his old shield. However, unlike most such rings, Hurley's shield number was in diamonds. On his left ring finger was a ruby-studded horseshoe ring.

"I assume this is a business visit," Hurley said.

"Yeah, we have a few things to talk about. I've got a nice case for you, if you want it."

"When you say nice case, do you mean an interesting case, or do you mean . . . ?"

"An expensive case."

It was just what Hurley wanted to hear. He nodded to Hill and White and they took their cue, leaving Hurley and McKenna alone to talk business. "You have my undivided attention."

McKenna gave him the deal, explaining who McMahon was and exactly what he wanted.

"Oh, boy!" was Hurley's only comment, but then he thought it over for a moment. "Do you vouch for this guy?"

"Yes."

"Does he know my services aren't cheap?"

"He knows you're the best and the best never come cheap."

"Let me get this straight. I'm finally going to get paid for what I do for you guys for nothing?"

"Yes."

"Oh, boy!" Hurley said again, smiling broadly. "Morris!" he shouted. "Buy all my friends a drink."

"Your friends? Who might they be, Bob?" Morris asked.

"Right now, everybody," Hurley answered, then turned his attention back to McKenna. "Did my wonderful new client happen to mention any payment arrangements?"

"In cash, if you like. He also mentioned something about an advance."

"Oh, boy!"

"There is a small hitch," McKenna said. He reached into his pocket and passed Hurley a piece of paper. Listed on it were the names of the people he had spoken to at the banks, their titles, and the places where they worked. "Mr. McMahon needs the home phone numbers of those people before he'll hire you, and he needs them tonight. Consider it a test to see how good you are."

"That's it? That's the hitch?" Hurley said contemptuously after barely glancing at the paper. "I'll get their numbers, their mothers' numbers, their kids' numbers, any number he likes, listed or unlisted. Hell! He's paying in cash, so I'll even get the phone numbers of their kindergarten teachers if the old biddies are still alive."

"I don't think that will be necessary. Just those numbers will do."

Hurley called Hill over and gave him the paper. "George, you're back on the clock. Priority job. I need the home numbers of those people."

Hill gave the paper the same cursory, contemptuous glance Hurley had, but Hill hadn't changed much. "Priority pay?" he asked.

It was the first time the smile left Hurley's face since McKenna had sat down, but it was back in a second. "What the hell, we all gotta eat. Priority pay. Now run along and come back with those numbers."

"Sure thing, boss."

"Sometimes I treat these pricks too good," Hurley said as soon as Hill had left. "Guy spent fifteen years trying to put me in jail and now I've got him driving a Cadillac."

"You always were a kind-hearted soul."

"Yeah, I know. It's my only fault. I'm just too nice a guy."

McKenna left Hurley happy, but completely out of touch with reality. He walked down the bar and joined Harney.

"You hungry?" Harney asked.

McKenna had been too busy to think of food, but realized he was starving as soon as Harney asked. "I'd love to chow down, but I don't have much time. Tommy's waiting for me at the office."

"Then we'll make it quick. No appetizers, no dessert, no espresso. How about it?"

Why not? McKenna asked himself. Tommy's filling his face right now and Lord knows when I'll get another chance to eat tonight. "Flip for the check?"

"Deal. Let's eat."

They sat down and ordered, each of them feeling lucky enough to believe that the other was going to wind up paying. McKenna ordered the lobster, but Harney went one better, ordering the surf and turf along with another Guinness.

"How'd you guys like my piece this morning?" Harney asked.

"I thought it was pretty good."

"And Tommy?"

"He didn't say, but I couldn't see anything in it that would have pissed him off."

"I treated that whole thing about you being assigned with kid gloves. My editor didn't like it, but he let me get away with it. Then he saw that McKenna vs. McKenna thing in the *Post* this morning and now he's pulling out the stops. We're running something pretty close to it tomorrow, making it into some kind of competition like the *Post* is doing."

McKenna had expected that. "It's not, you know. There's no personal competition going between me and Tommy."

"I know that, but two famous friends working together doesn't sell papers. It's got to be a race."

"Are you going to be working that angle?"

"No, I'm just covering the killings. The feature guys are gonna be the ones fanning the flames and keeping the race tally."

"Then it's a race I'm gonna lose," McKenna said. "Once we can go public with information, I'm going to feed you and Phil Messing everything positive that Tommy does on this case. If we get anywhere, he's got to be the hero. Probably will be, anyway."

"Fine by me. I'll take anything you give me, but are you sure you want to play it like that?"

"I'm not worried. Tommy's the type of guy who always shares the credit with those who deserve it, so I don't mind playing his competent second fiddle. What I really want is the public wondering why I was given this case in the first place. That's how good Tommy's going to look."

"I like it," Harney said. "It'll keep me one step ahead of the feature guys. Try and feed me late, after they get the type set on their story. Then I'll come in with some new information changing the score and keep those glory pricks there all night."

"Whatever you say."

"When are you going to start feeding me stuff I can use?" Harney asked.

"After the funeral."

"After the funeral? Too long, Brian. Give me a break, at least a little something now."

"I bet you were able to get a little something on your own," McKenna said cagily.

"Not enough. I have a friend at the morgue, so I found out who the other poor dead slob was. Then I dug a little deeper and found out that he worked for Barrone. Good story, Barrone's married daughter was killed with one of her father's chief aides. From what I hear, he introduced them. Add in that they were murdered sort of in flagrante delicto late at night in a lovers lane, and how does that look for Barrone?"

John's good, McKenna thought. He got to somebody at the morgue, he got to somebody in Barrone's office, and he got to one of the cops at the crime scene.

McKenna's curiosity got the better of him on one point. "Just between us, who told you about the in flagrante delicto business?"

"It's not my place to tell you and I don't know if I would. I never give up a source to anyone, but he's not one of mine."

"One of Messing's?"

"Yeah, Phil knows the guy for years."

Knows the *guy* for years? Harney saw him thinking and felt magnanimous. "Don't rack your brain, Brian. You never met the old crank and I can't even remember if he was there when you were."

Old crank? Now who can that be? McKenna wondered, and then remembered his conversation with Rynn and Cocchi. The patrol sergeant was the one. That's all right, a one-shot deal. He won't know anything about the investigation, so nothing else to worry about when it comes to leaks. "Thanks. I figured it had to be Walsh, but I'm glad it's not."

"Not that we didn't try. He worked us for a big breakfast, then stiffed us good. Told us anybody else's case, he'd give us what we need."

"Okay, let's forget that. How in flagrante delicto did you hear Cindy Barrone and Arthur McMahon were?" McKenna asked.

"Very. She was naked and he had his pants down."

"When are you gonna start running the steamy stuff?"

"I filed the story, but that's up to my editor. I think he's inclined to run it after we can get some kind of comment from Cindy's husband, but he's locked up in his house and won't talk to us. He's got to come out for the wake, so we'll get him then."

"So if you don't get a statement from Valenti tonight, you start with the dirt for tomorrow's edition?"

"I don't think my editor will have any choice, unless you give me something we can use."

"You've got people at Valenti's house?"

"Like he's Madonna on tour with Michael Jackson. Plenty of TV people there, too."

"Suppose he just gives you a 'No comment'?"

"Just as good. Think about it. He's going to be asked about his wife apparently running around on him with his father-in-law's aide and what he thinks about it. He might deny it and tell us we've got it wrong, but a 'No comment' is as good as 'I know. Isn't it terrible?' "

McKenna didn't particularly care for Roger Valenti, but suddenly his heart went out to the man whose wife had involuntarily given him unwanted fame, at least for a day or two. "I'm doing you a favor, but I wouldn't go with the in flagrante delicto story tomorrow if I were you."

"Why not?"

"Because it's not entirely true and could be completely false. If so, Paul Barrone might wind up owning both you and the *News*."

"Bad source?" Harney asked.

"No, the source is good, the conclusions are wrong. We off the record?"

"Sure."

"Cindy Barrone was fully clothed in that car. It was the killer who undressed her with the whip."

"And the guy? What about Arthur McMahon? Were his pants down?"

"Yeah, but who's to say the killer didn't take them down? He did take McMahon's wallet from his pants."

"What are you saying? McMahon was dead first thing, right?"

"Yeah, he was."

"So are you telling me that maybe this killer pulled down the pants of a dead man for some kind of thrill?" Harney asked skeptically. "After he tortures a girl to death, maybe then he finishes up his fun by playing with a dead man's dick? Is that what you're telling me?"

"All I'm saying is that it's a possibility. Let me tell you what kind of sick bastard this guy is, and then you tell me if you want to take a chance in court with Barrone. Okay?"

"Go ahead."

"After Cindy Barrone finally died, he took her down from the tree he had her chained to and then he whipped her behind into mush. Sometime during or after that process, he really went over the edge and sodomized her with his whip handle."

"Sodomized her?"

"He stuck the handle up her vagina while she was still alive, but that wasn't enough for him. He stuck it up the poor girl's ass after she died, hard and more than once. It's all in the autopsy report."

"Sick bastard!" Harney said, shaking his head.

"Sure is. Now, who's to say a guy that sick isn't also a switch-hitter when it comes to sexually abusing the dead? Who's to say that he didn't pull down McMahon's pants to take a look at his dick, but then maybe he didn't like what he saw and called it a day?"

"Something wrong with McMahon's dick?"

"Yeah, he's Irish. He never pulled it out and won any bets with it."

"The Irish curse?"

"Extreme case, poor guy."

"I see," Harney said, shaking his head and maybe really feeling sorry for McMahon for the first time. "Thanks for saving me some problems, but I've still got a big one. You just killed my story for tomorrow, but we've got pages to fill. Brian, now you *really* have to give me a taste of something I can use for the morning edition."

What can I give him that doesn't violate the deal or hurt the investigation? McKenna asked himself. While he was searching for an answer with Harney watching him and waiting for something, the waitress brought their dinners. It looked and smelled so good that both men forgot anything but food for a few minutes. Then the answer hit McKenna. "John, do you know who Arthur McMahon, Senior, is?"

"Let me guess. Could he be the father of Arthur McMahon, Junior?"

"Very good. But did you know that he used to be a congressman, and now he's just a rich and very powerful shaker and mover in Virginia politics?"

McKenna had the reporter's total interest. Harney put his fork down, took a long swig from his beer, then wiped his mouth with his napkin and stared at McKenna. "No, I didn't know that."

"Too bad, because everybody in Virginia does. The headline in this morning's *Richmond Ledger* was ARTHUR McMAHON'S SON MURDERED IN NEW YORK. Not a mention of Barrone's daughter in the headline. Probably wrote something about her in the story, but in Virginia she's not important and neither is Paul Barrone. Arthur McMahon is, and I just came from his hotel room."

"He's in town?"

"Uh-huh. Maybe I can get you an interview tonight."

"If you can, what's he gonna tell me?"

"Just what you'd expect to hear. He'll tell you what a wonderful man his son was, except in this case it's probably true. Got along with his father, but wouldn't take his money. Instead, he became a cop in Virginia and worked his way through law school. Barrone's one of Arthur Senior's old buddies, so the kid takes a job with him when he gets out of law school. Probably working hard for peanuts. Although it's there for him whenever he wants it, he's still not taking Daddy's money—even though he could really use it."

"Yeah, I heard from one of my sources that he was a nice kid. But what's the story?"

"I just told you. Rich powerful father, but the kid wants to make it on his own. He's smart, hardworking, and a nice guy to boot. Then he's murdered and a bright, promising future is over for no good reason. Explain who his father is, get a few quotes from him, then write good things about the kid and work the human interest angle."

"You want me to spoil a great, dirty story by writing something nice about the kid?" Harney asked, obviously not liking the idea.

"You said you needed something for tomorrow."

"I don't know, Brian. I'm a newspaperman. When folks want to read something nice about somebody, they buy magazines like *People*. When they open up the *News*, they're in it for the dirt on big shots. That's what they expect and that's what we give them. Good news doesn't sell."

"What would sell in this case?"

"Big-shot rich father and the kid turns out to be a no-good, low-life douchebag. That would sell nicely."

"But that's not true. The kid was okay."

"I know. I'm just wishing."

"Do it my way and I'll get you the interview," McKenna said. "Otherwise, there's nothing else I can give you today."

"Okay. See if you can arrange it."

"Right away," McKenna said. He took out his phone, called McMahon at the Pierre, made his request, and outlined the prospective story.

"Can you trust this man to write good things about Arthur?" McMahon asked, concerned.

"I'm sure I can. He's a pal."

"Then send him up. I'll be happy to talk to him."

It was getting late, so McKenna wolfed down the rest of his food. When it came to the toss, McKenna's luck held out. He called tails, and tails it was. Harney paid the bill and McKenna left the tip.

McKenna was ready to leave, but there was still something bothering Harney. "You ever gonna tell me what you and Hurley were just talking about?"

"Maybe someday."

"Someday? When's that, exactly?"

"In about seven years."

"Seven years?"

"Yeah, I'll tell you after I'm retired and after the statute of limitations on Hurley and me expires. That's seven years from today."

TWELVE

Back in the office, McKenna had started documenting his day's work when Tommy returned, all smiles. With him was a middle-aged Hispanic man in his forties who would stand out anyplace but uptown. There, his bright red-and-green flowered shirt and his chartreuse pants would pass unnoticed, but McKenna found himself wondering what color his socks were. Something in a dark pink would be appropriate, he decided.

"Permit me to introduce you to Jorge Espinosa, our man of the hour," Tommy said. "He doesn't speak much English, but from what I can gather with my miserable Spanish, Señor Espinosa saw our man in his car and even talked to him on the phone."

"About what?"

"That's what I want you to find out. It's my understanding that you're one of our language whizzes, so let's see how you do."

"Wait a minute. I thought you went out to eat."

"I was going to, but then a fresh kill came up in the Two-five and everybody else went out on it. Greve didn't have a spare team to send up to One Hundred Eighty-First Street to question any people the day teams might've missed this morning, so I went out and found Señor Espinosa myself."

"You haven't had anything to eat yet?"

"Not a thing all day, but I couldn't take a chance on anybody up there forgetting about seeing the scumbag."

"Where did you find Mr. Espinosa?"

"In his crib. Lives on One Hundred Eightieth Street between Wadsworth and Fort Washington Avenue, right around the corner from the bodega."

"Wonderful. You did the hard part, so now your humble servant will find out just how well you did."

In Spanish, McKenna formally introduced himself to Espinosa and then made him a cup of coffee. It was a short interview, with McKenna taking notes and enjoying the amazed look on Tommy's face as he questioned Espinosa in colloquial Spanish.

Tommy's amazement turned to total incomprehension when, midway through the process, Espinosa looked around the room, searching for something. He found it somewhere in Tommy's multicolored tie, then got up for a moment and pointed to a spot on it. McKenna nodded and Espinosa sat back down as the interview resumed.

"What was that all about?" Tommy asked.

"He likes your tie, but says it's a little gaudy for his taste."

"Gaudy for *his* taste?" Tommy asked, offended. "Doesn't this guy have any mirrors in his house? Take a look at the costume he's wearing."

"Please, Tommy. I'm trying to get some work done here. You think it's easy fathoming the intricacies of this very difficult tongue?"

"I'm sorry. It won't happen again," Tommy said, somehow managing to sound contrite. "Go ahead."

Actually, it was easy for McKenna. While he didn't consider himself a whiz, languages and traveling were his two hobbies and they went hand in hand. While other people might come home and relax in front of the tube after work, that wasn't his way. He enjoyed studying his languages or listening to his Spanish, French, or Italian instruction tapes, and got his satisfaction when the McKenna family went on vacation, usually to a place where he could fine-tune his skills.

Spanish was the least of McKenna's language problems. Although he usually didn't speak it at home because he didn't relish it when his daughter made fun of his English accent, Spanish was the language Angelita and the kids spoke whenever he wasn't around. For McKenna, Spanish was a survival skill that prevented his family from talking bad about him while he was sitting right there.

When McKenna was satisfied he had gotten everything Espinosa knew, he showed him the sketch Tommy had made with Wozniak.

"That's him. Maybe his face is a little wider, but that's him," Espinosa said in Spanish.

McKenna was satisfied with that as well. Wozniak's sketch would be good enough. He asked Espinosa if he needed a ride home. Espinosa declined the offer, saying he had an old girlfriend on 136th Street whom he had been meaning to see for some time. McKenna thanked him and Espinosa was at the door when he remembered something else. He came back, pointing to his left forearm as he spoke.

McKenna had a few more questions for him, and then Espinosa was off on his romantic adventure.

"You did *really* good, Tommy," McKenna said as the door closed behind Espinosa.

"Looks to me like you did pretty good yourself."

"What, the Spanish? How hard can it be if my two-year-old kids speak it?"

"They speak English?" Tommy asked sarcastically.

"Like you and me."

"I take it Espinosa said the sketch is good?"

"Good enough for our purposes. Says that's him. Maybe a little fatter in the face, but it's him."

"What else did he have to say?"

"Señor Espinosa is a marvelous man. He works nights and takes his car to work. Got home from work yesterday morning a little after seven and then had his usual problem with his car. There's alternate side parking on his block, eight A.M. to eleven A.M., so one side of the street is almost empty. Espinosa needs a spot for the day and can't park there yet without getting a ticket, so he does what everybody else uptown does."

Tommy knew. "He double-parks across the street until the street sweeper comes through, then grabs one of the empty spots and sits in his car until eleven."

"Right. Knows everybody and everybody's car, and they all know him. If he's blocking in someone from the neighborhood, they just come and get him to move his car and let them out. But yesterday morning the only double-parking spot he could get was next to a strange car, one he didn't recognize. He says that was very unusual."

"I imagine it would be. It's not exactly a tourist area, unless you've got an unhealthy adventurous streak running through you," Tommy said. "Or unless you really need a parking spot for the night while you go off to have some fun torturing and killing."

"Which is exactly what happened. Our killer is probably from some-place up there, he's armed, and we know he's dangerous, so the neighbor-hood doesn't worry him. Espinosa blocked him in, but he's a considerate guy. He wrote his phone number on a piece of paper and left it on his dash. Then he went upstairs to make himself breakfast, same as always. You know the rest."

"The scumbag gets back to his car after his night of mayhem and sees that he's blocked in," Tommy surmised. "He finds a pay phone, calls Señor Espinosa, talks to him in Spanish, and Espinosa tells him what . . . ?"

"That he just put his eggs on, but he'll be down in five minutes."

"What's the scumbag's reaction to that?"

"He tells Espinosa, 'That's all right. Take your time,' in his perfect Castilian Spanish."

"Sure it's all right," Tommy said. "He doesn't want to make any fuss in the neighborhood, and besides, he's running low on smokes and he's feeling lucky. He just committed the perfect crime, not a hitch, just like last time. There's a bodega right in front of him, so he goes in, buys his smokes and his Lotto tickets, and then he remembers that old ticket he's got in his wallet. He gives it to the bodega guy to check for him, and Voila! Just like he thought, he's the luckiest murdering scumbag for blocks around. Perfect crime, lots of fun, a pocketful of good plastic, and now, of top of everything, another sixty-four extra bucks to spend on whips and chains. He's laughing to himself as he shuffles back to his car, and then . . . ?"

"He gets in, starts it up, lights up a smoke, and waits. Espinosa comes down, knocks on his window, and tells him how sorry he is. 'Don't worry about it, amigo. I understand. I was lucky to get this spot myself,' he tells Espinosa in Spanish, all smiling and friendly. 'Not as lucky as me, because that's now my spot and I can go up and go to bed,' Espinosa says, then throws in something nice for us. It's important, so let me make sure I've got it word for word."

McKenna picked up his notebook and Tommy tried reading over his shoulder, without success. McKenna had been speaking to Espinosa in Spanish, so he had taken his interview notes in Spanish.

McKenna gave Tommy his best know-it-all smile before he continued. " 'Your Spanish is very good, señor. Where did you learn it?' Espinosa asks. Now our man's really happy because that's a very nice compliment coming from Espinosa. You see, he's Colombian and speaks the refined brand of Spanish himself. 'Here and there, but mostly in Spain,' he says. Espinosa's feeling chatty, so he says, 'I've never been to Spain, but I've always wanted to go there. Have you been to Colombia?' Our man tells him, 'Not yet, but I've heard it's beautiful. I'll probably get there someday.' Then he throws his car into drive and Espinosa sees that he's getting impatient, so he gets into his own car, pulls out past all the other double-parked cars, and lets him out. He stops to wave at Espinosa, and then he's on his way. Espinosa backs into his spot, happy as can be, end of interview."

"Or so you thought," Tommy said. "What was it that Espinosa remembered as he was leaving?"

"That the killer has a nice scar on his left forearm, right here," Mc-Kenna answered, pointing to a spot on his own left forearm halfway between his wrist and elbow.

"The scumbag wasn't wearing his sports coat?"

"Nope. Must've taken it off while he was in his car waiting for Espinosa to come down. He was wearing a short-sleeve shirt, had his left arm propped on his open window."

"What kind of scar?"

"Espinosa said it's from a knife cut. Clean, about three inches long."

"Then a knife scar is what it is. Espinosa's been living uptown long enough to know what one of those looks like," Tommy said. "What did he say about the car?"

"One of the bigger GM cars, either a Buick or an Oldsmobile, early nineties, four door, not too clean, no dents he saw, New York plates, a deep, dark red in color," McKenna answered, once again reading from his notes.

"Not maroon?"

"Definitely not. Deep, dark red."

"What's the difference?"

"What's the difference?" McKenna asked, then pointed to the spot on Tommy's tie. "What color is that?"

Tommy lifted his tie up and gave it a long, hard look before answering. "I don't know. Could go either way. Could be dark red, and then again, it could be maroon."

"Only to the untrained eye which, incidentally, is never the Hispanic eye. As you might've noticed from Señor Espinosa's decisions when he selected his apparel for this evening, he's really got an eye for color."

"I didn't notice, but only because the glare hurt my eyes whenever I stared directly at him."

"Just the untrained eye I was talking about. For instance, did you see how good he was when he picked out his socks?"

"You mean his pink socks?"

"*Dark* pink, Tommy, but I'm relieved. There might yet be some hope for your sense of uptown fashion."

THIRTEEN

Wozniak was the first one interviewed, and the easiest. He was at work in the 10th Precinct, and a phone call brought him to the Homicide Squad office to officially tell his tale and provide his description. After the quick interview, he left for the Artists Unit with a copy of Tommy's sketch in his pocket to help the artist along. Wozniak would have the official WANTED sketch faxed to the office as soon as it was completed.

Then the McKennas were off for the one-hour trip to Levittown and Wantagh in Nassau County. Tommy drove and soon had them eastbound on the Long Island Expressway. They talked over the case for the first half of the trip, but McKenna fell silent as soon as they crossed the city line. "What's on your mind?" Tommy asked after enduring five minutes of silence.

"Time."

"Scumbag time?"

"Yeah. How'd you know?" McKenna asked, surprised.

"Because it's also been on my mind ever since we passed that Exxon station where the scumbag gassed up on Cindy's card. However, unlike yourself, I can talk and think at the same time."

McKenna was sure that Tommy could and he let it pass. "How long did it take us to pass the gas station after we left the office?"

"Twenty-two minutes."

"You've been timing this trip?"

"Sure I am. We're probably taking the same route he took to get to those ATMs, so why not see how long it took him?"

"It took him too long," McKenna stated.

"That's what I'm thinking. Cashed in his Lotto ticket at seven twenty-one yesterday morning, then figure another ten minutes in his car waiting for Espinosa to come down. They chat for a few minutes and then he takes off. Had to be seven forty-five at the latest, and yet . . ."

"He doesn't gas up until nine-twenty. It took him more than an hour and a half to make a trip that took us twenty-two minutes. Even with morning rush-hour traffic, that doesn't make sense."

"Wouldn't have been too much traffic for him," Tommy added. "He was leaving the city when everyone else was coming in."

"So what did he do? Stop for breakfast before he gassed up?"

"That's one possibility. He'd already put in a long, strenuous night whipping Cindy to a pulp, and he probably lost quite a few calories jerking off while he had his fun. That kind of night could give a real happy scumbag quite the hearty appetite."

"That makes sense, but I don't think that's it," McKenna said. "He might've been hungry, but I don't think he stopped to eat."

"Why not?"

"Because he's greedy, and his greed would've made him too anxious to eat. First he'd have to know if he had tortured the correct PIN numbers out of Cindy. He got to those ATMs as quick as he could."

"So how do you think he spent that lost hour?"

"I don't know yet, but it tells me one thing."

"That we're not seeing this right? That we're missing something, somewhere?" Tommy guessed.

"Exactly."

Since both men were unfamiliar with the Levittown and Wantagh neighborhoods, they stopped at the Nassau County Eighth Precinct and enlisted the aid of two local detectives. To save time, McKenna and Tommy split up, each going out with a Nassau County detective. According to their plan, McKenna would locate and interview the 7-Eleven and Kmart personnel who had been working the morning before and Tommy would talk to the six people who had used the ATMs around the same time as the killer.

It took four hours for McKenna to come up with nothing new. When he returned to the Eighth Precinct, he found Tommy already back and typing away. One look at Tommy's face told McKenna that Tommy had fared no better.

"Bad?" McKenna asked.

"Wasted three hours talking to the dopiest people I've met in a long time," Tommy said. "Poor memories and very short on powers of observation."

"Nobody remembered seeing him?"

"Found two with a vague recollection of a black man at the ATMs, nothing else," Tommy said. "You do any better?"

"Just as bad, but it took me longer to do it. Except for Wozniak, it's a bust."

"Any ideas on what our next brilliant move should be?"

"You tell me," McKenna said, and then his cell phone rang.

"Cindy's cards are in play again," Hurley said.

McKenna felt a surge of adrenaline. "When and where?"

"Good news is less than five minutes ago. Bad news is San Jose, California. He was at an ATM in a 7-Eleven at the Almaden Expressway and Ironwood Avenue. Got nine hundred using three cards."

"Thanks, Bob. Keep us posted on anything new," McKenna said.

"Will do. Keep this line free."

Tommy saw that the call had excited McKenna, but there wasn't time for explanations. Two minutes later McKenna was talking to Sergeant Gary Newell of the San Jose Police Department's detective division. "Sarge, you've got one of our killers on the loose out there and I need a lot of help in a hurry. Unfortunately, there's no time to give you the whole story right now, so you're gonna have to trust me."

"Okay, you've got my trust," Newell said. "What do you need?"

"First of all, your fax number."

Newell gave it. McKenna wrote the number across the top of Wozniak's sketch and Tommy took it to the Nassau detectives' fax machine.

"There's a sketch of the man we're looking for being faxed to you right now," McKenna told Newell. "Seven minutes ago he was using some stolen credit cards at an ATM in a 7-Eleven at the Almaden Expressway and Ironwood Avenue. Do you know where that is?"

"Sure. Do the cards belong to the murder victim?"

"Yeah, to one of his victims. I think he's going to be using those stolen cards in ATMs all over your town in the next hour, most likely in convenience stores. I need as many of them staked out as you can, and it has to be done very quickly."

"Can get that done, but not by plainclothes people on this short a notice. It's going to have to be done by uniform, mostly," Newell said.

Using uniformed cops on stakeouts? Waste of time, our man's too sharp and won't go near the place! McKenna wanted to scream, but then his cell phone rang again. "Excuse me, I have to take another call. Please stay on the line."

"Another 7-Eleven in San Jose," Hurley said. "Curtner Avenue and Lee Avenue. Got six hundred from that one four minutes ago."

"Thanks again, Bob. I'm talking to the San Jose cops now. Got to go, but get back to me if there's another hit," McKenna said, then ended the call and turned his attention back to Newell. "Our killer just pulled the same deal in another 7-Eleven. Curtner Avenue and Lee Avenue. That close to the last one?"

"About four miles," Newell answered. "I just got your sketch, so in a couple of minutes every one of our units will have it on their screens. That's nineteen, and every free car is now heading for an ATM on their beats. That's the best I can do for you on short notice."

McKenna thought it was quite a bit. "All your cars are computer-equipped?"

"Have been for years. We're pretty high-tech here in the Silicon Valley. I also have investigators on the way to stake out the ATMs downtown, but there's only six of us working now, not counting the lieutenant. There have to be a few hundred ATMs in this city, so I wouldn't get my expectations up if I were you."

"I'm not overly optimistic, but I'm hoping to get lucky," McKenna said.

"You got anything on a vehicle your subject may be driving?"

"If I had to guess, I'd say a rental. He was here yesterday in his own car, so he must have flown there for some reason and might've rented a car at the airport."

"I'll give that information to our units," Newell said.

Then a thought struck McKenna. "If we don't get lucky in the next hour, I need another big favor from you."

"Let's have it."

"Rental agencies always make a photocopy of a customer's license. Compare the sketch against the photos on the licenses and we might be able to attach a name to our killer. I'd appreciate it if you could have someone check with your airport rental people."

"I'll handle it myself," Newell said. "I guess you'll also want those store clerks interviewed?"

"Please. Can you get right back to me with anything you or your people come up with?"

"Sure thing. Give me your number."

McKenna gave Newell his cell phone number and the Homicide Squad number.

"I think it's time to give that old San Jose case another good look," Tommy said as soon as McKenna hung up.

"You don't believe in coincidence?"

"Never did."

"Me neither," McKenna agreed.

McKenna whiled away the time by typing his interview reports, but his mind was elsewhere. Why had the killer gone to only two ATMs, settling for just fifteen hundred dollars? he asked himself. Had he seen one of the San Jose uniformed units staked out on another ATM and smelled a rat? And what was he doing three thousand miles away in San Jose anyway?

McKenna didn't have the answers. He continued typing his reports and had just finished when Newell called back. "According to our 7-Eleven clerks, it was the guy in your sketch who got the cash from the ATMs," Newell said.

"How was he dressed?" McKenna asked.

"Casual, but neat. Tan pants, a blue sports shirt, and brown loafers. Sounds like one of our yuppies."

"Did he make any purchases?"

"None. Just went in to use the machines. In and out in a minute or two without a word to anyone."

"Anybody see what kind of car he was driving?"

"Sorry, no clue. He didn't park right in front, so neither clerk noticed. I'm going to head out to the airport now, but first I'm going to need all the details on the man you've got us all looking for."

Fair enough, McKenna thought. Newell had already put his department through its paces on the basis of nothing more than a simple telephone request. He outlined the known activities of the killer and promised to fax Newell the paperwork to back up his account as soon as he returned to the Homicide Squad office. Newell was enthused by the time McKenna hung up, which was exactly the state of mind McKenna wanted him in.

There was another big issue on McKenna's mind, one that required some delicacy in handling. Whenever a detective traveled officially, that happy soul normally earned eight hours overtime a day. For that reason, detective bosses were reluctant to let their people follow their cases to the far corners of the globe. So far, the San Jose Police Department had shown itself to be competent in handling its end of the present case. In any ordinary fugitive pursuit, the ball would be left in their court. But nothing about this case was ordinary. It was a big one, a political bombshell. The fugitive was in or around San Jose and someone from the NYPD should go there. It was officially McKenna's case, so that someone to be paid would be him. However, Tommy's role had to be considered. He had chased this fugitive far longer than McKenna had, and besides, he knew intimately the details on those old San Jose murders. As far as McKenna was concerned, Tommy should be the one going.

The same subject was apparently on Tommy's mind, but he had reached a different conclusion. "I'll talk to Greve and tell him that he'll have to do without you for a day or two."

"Are you sure?" McKenna asked.

"Certain. It's your case, so you're the one to go," Tommy said with conviction, apparently considering the matter resolved.

That was good enough for McKenna. "Tell me more about that old San Jose case."

"The killings took place on July third, 1989. Same as our cases in a lot of ways, two lovers lane murders, but I didn't find out about it until 1991."

"How'd you find out?"

"I was on vacation in Omaha and I happened to attend a conference on serial murders."

"Wait a minute! You just *happened* to be on vacation in Omaha, of all places, and you just *happened* to attend this conference? Isn't there a little more to it than that?" McKenna asked, already knowing the answer. It was another case of Tommy's dedication to his job in those days when the NYPD wasn't spending money sending its detectives to conferences and seminars.

"Yeah, that's right," Tommy said. "I happen to like Omaha. Nice, quiet place to spend a week with the family."

So Tommy dragged his family there so he could attend this conference and then he further insulted them by telling them that they were on vacation, McKenna thought. "I'm sure it's a wonderful place. Go on."

"I was looking for a connection to my 1981 case and I met the guy who had the San Jose case, Detective Randy Bynum. Good guy, dedicated and competent. We compared notes, found quite a few things the same, but there were also some big differences. Still, his case had my interest and I went to San Jose to take a closer look at it."

"On vacation again?"

The sarcasm was lost on Tommy. "Yeah, in 1992. Nice city in the sun, weather's always good. Bynum took me to his crime scene and it was another version of Fort Tryon Park, a secluded lovers lane with a spectacular view. One victim had been shot with a .380 Colt Commander fired through a paper bag and the other one had been tied to a tree in the same way, two sets of cuffs with the chain running through the loops. The poor soul had been professionally tortured to death, but that was where the similarities in our cases ended. Like I told you, in San Jose it was the girl that got killed right away and it was the guy who got the torture routine."

"And with a knife, not the whip. Do you have the crime scene photos at the office?"

"Yeah, along with every report Bynum ever did on the case. Interesting reading."

They got back to the office at midnight. Everyone was still out working the murder in the 25th Precinct, so they had the office to themselves. McKenna called the San Jose PD and Newell answered. "Checked the airport car rental agency. Sorry, it was a bust," Newell said. "Nobody close to your sketch rented a car there yesterday or today."

"Too bad, but thanks anyway. Are you working tomorrow?" McKenna asked.

"For the next three nights. Why?"

"I should be there tomorrow. Do you remember a lovers lane double homicide you had in 1989?"

"Randy Bynum's case?"

"That's the one. We're thinking that it's possible the man we're looking for did that one."

"Really? Then I'll have to give old Randy a call. That case was a real obsession with him and he always swore he would never retire until he got that guy."

"Then why did he?"

"Age. Mandatory retirement, age sixty-three, but he went out kicking and screaming."

"What's he doing now?"

"Still hanging around and still driving everybody crazy with that case. He's always doing something on it."

"For free?"

"Like I said, it's an obsession with him. You've never seen anything like it."

"Yes I have," McKenna said, stealing a glance at that other obsessive detective standing next to him. As McKenna hung up, Greve returned with six detectives.

"How'd you do, Lieutenant?" Tommy asked him.

"We've got the shooter ID'd, but he split for Puerto Rico. Got to send a team down there to get him and bring him back."

"Then there's going to be a lot of traveling going on. Brian's got to go to San Jose, California."

"Is that so? Why don't you two come in and tell me about it?" Greve said, heading for his office.

The McKennas gathered up their papers and were on their way in when the phone on Tommy's desk rang. He picked it up, then said, "One moment please. I'll give you the appropriate Detective McKenna." He then offered the phone to McKenna. "It's the lottery people. Get the information and I'll handle Greve."

McKenna didn't want Tommy fighting his battles for him and making his requests, but Tommy knew Greve better and was more likely to prevail. He took the phone and Tommy went into Greve's office, closing the door behind him.

"Detective McKenna."

"This is Mrs. Palmero from the New York State Lottery. I've got the information you requested on that ticket."

"Go ahead."

"It was purchased at the Hudson News concession stand in the Port Authority Bus Terminal on May eighteenth at seven forty-one in the evening."

"I take it they sell a lot of tickets there?"

"More than anybody else. It's the number-one location in the state in sales."

"Thank you very much," McKenna said, then hung up, perplexed and a little depressed by the information. He had been hoping that the killer had bought the ticket at his local candy store, a place where the people who worked there might know him and recognize him from the sketch. That wasn't going to happen in the number one sales location, a place where tickets were sold to travelers.

So what does this tell us? McKenna wondered. He bought the ticket on May 18, but didn't check the numbers until June 8. He's in San Jose now and we already know from Espinosa that he does a lot of traveling. Add in that he bought the ticket in the bus terminal, and what have we got? Maybe he was out of town from May 18 until June 6, but where and doing what?

They were questions without answers for the moment. McKenna decided to join the Tommy-Greve discussion, but it had already been worked out during the few minutes he had been on the phone.

"Go home and get some rest," Greve ordered. "You're going to San Jose in the morning."

FOURTEEN

WEDNESDAY, JUNE 9, SAN JOSE, CALIFORNIA

It was a seven hour total flight to San Jose with a plane change in Chicago, but McKenna didn't mind. He had plenty to read to occupy his time, since Tommy's San Jose file filled his entire carry-on bag. He had decided to start with the crime scene photos, but just one glance told him that he couldn't examine them without horrifying the passenger sitting next to him. Instead, he began with the initial crime report.

According to the original patrol officer's brief report, the bodies had been discovered on the morning of July 3, 1989, in the lovers lane off White Road by a man hiking with his two young sons. It was such a grisly sight that the children had to be hospitalized for trauma.

The victims were a female white and a male white, both apparently in their twenties. The female's body was found in the backseat of a red 1979 Camaro. Her pants and underpants were off, her blouse was open, and her bra was unfastened. Death had been caused by a single gunshot to the head through the closed driver's side window of the Camaro.

The male's naked body was found at the bottom of a gully thirty yards from the Camaro and his clothes. His clothing was in shreds and apparently had been cut from his body while he had been bound to a tree. The patrol officer noted that very little of the male's blood was found in front of the tree and that the grass there was matted down, leading him to state that the killer had apparently spread a tarpaulin in front of the tree while he had tortured his victim.

The male's apparent cause of death was listed simply as "multiple knife wounds." It was also noted that he had suffered a gunshot wound to his upper right arm, but the bullet had passed through his flesh and had not been recovered. The crimes were classified as depraved sexual assault, murder, and, since no wallet or purse was found at the scene, robbery.

After reading Bynum's first three reports, McKenna had a clearer idea on how the crimes had occurred. He had identified the female as Sara Reinhart, age 23, of Ellen Avenue in San Jose, and the male as Robert Harrison, age 29. Harrison was the registered owner of the Camaro.

Bynum had been present at the autopsies of both victims and had also been at the morgue when the bodies were identified by their families. Reinhart and Harrison worked in the same Chevy dealership in San Jose and had been dating each other for two years. The lovers lane was located at the end of a dirt road and the only tire marks evident were those made by the Camaro, so Bynum assumed that the killer had hiked to the location and had waited in ambush.

The time of death for Sara Reinhart was estimated to be 3:00 A.M. on July 3. According to ballistics, the bullet that had been fired into her head came from a .380 Colt Commander. Since there was burned paper residue still imbedded in the bullet and no spent cartridge had been found at the scene, it was assumed that the gun had been fired while the killer held it in a paper bag. Reinhart's autopsy disclosed that she had had recent sexual intercourse, but the only semen found in her body was Harrison's.

Robert Harrison died at approximately 6:30 A.M., and the gunshot wound to his arm had very little to do with his death. Before torturing Harrison, the killer had administered first aid by applying a tourniquet to his arm to stop the bleeding. There were 109 separate slash wounds on his body, but the one that killed him was the one that hurt the most—he had bled to death after being castrated. Harrison had been tortured while secured to a tree, probably with handcuffs and a chain. There was very little blood at the torture site, leading Bynum to agree with the patrol officer's assessment; the killer had spread a tarp in front of the tree while he had tortured his victim.

Harrison's left arm and three of his ribs had also been broken. According to the autopsy report, the coroner concluded that those bones had been fractured postmortem and those further injuries had probably been sustained when Harrison had been flung into the gully by the killer.

Twenty-three latent prints had been lifted from the car and, by the third day of the investigation, nine remained unidentified.

McKenna looked up from the reports when the pilot shut the seat belt light off. Through the window, he saw that they were high over the farmland of New Jersey. To avoid shocking the woman sitting next to him, he took the envelope containing the crime scene photos into the bathroom.

The photo on the top of the thick stack showed Robert Harrison lying face up in the gully, white and bloodless, with his eyes closed. McKenna was immediately reminded of an ancient Chinese form of execution, the "Death of a Thousand Cuts," and he guessed that Harrison had been twenty pounds overweight before the killer had started on him. Besides most of the blood in his body, Harrison was also missing his nose, his ears, and his penis, but that was only part of the damage that had been inflicted on him. Four-inch cuts covered his face, his chest, and his inner thigh, but most of the blood had been wiped from the wounds, presumably by the killer so he could admire his work after he had finished. McKenna saw that the fiend had prolonged his pleasure by not cutting any arteries as he had tortured his victim. Harrison had suffered for a long time before finally dying after the final painful indignity of castration.

The next six shots in the stack were close-ups of the damage inflicted to the different parts of Harrison's body, including the cuts and bruises on his wrists as he had struggled against the handcuffs. McKenna examined the close-up taken of the gunshot wound and concluded that the medical examiner had been right. He could see the bruise on Harrison's arm where the killer had applied the tourniquet to keep his victim alive long enough to really suffer.

Another series of shots showed a panorama of the crime scene. Aside from the dirt road and the Camaro parked at the end of the road on top of a hill, there wasn't another hint of civilization. The countryside was beautiful and the view spectacular, surrounded by golden hills covered with high brown grass and occasional stands of trees and scrub bushes. McKenna found it strange that such a rural setting could be contained in any place that was called a city.

The next series of shots showed the exterior of the Camaro, the tree Harrison had been fastened to, and the area around it, with close-ups of the marks made on the bark by the chains. Like Cindy Barrone, Harrison had been secured to the tree with two chains, one running through the handcuffs and the other around his neck. There was no blood visible in any of the photos.

The final three photos documented the end of Sara Reinhart, slumped across the backseat of the Camaro with a bullet in her brain. Like Harrison, she had also been on the plump side and death had caught her half-undressed in embarrassing circumstances. She had a pleasant face and looked much too young to be so obviously dead.

McKenna put the photos back into the envelope and returned to his seat to learn what Bynum had done in his unsuccessful attempt to capture the monster who had inflicted the sorrow and suffering he had just seen. From the amount of paperwork Bynum had generated during his hunt, McKenna felt safe in assuming that the San Jose investigator had left no stone unturned.

By the time the plane was over California, McKenna had finished going through Bynum's investigation and was looking forward to meeting the man. He approved of the way Bynum had handled the case and appreciated the amount of time and labor he had put into it. It seemed that Bynum had questioned every known sex offender in California and he had met with cops all over the country who were cursed with sex-killing cases even remotely similar to his own. A special telephone number had been set up in San Jose after the murders, and there had been plenty of callers who thought they knew who might have done the killings. Bynum had acted on every reasonable call and had followed each wild goose chase to its meaningless conclusion.

One year after the murders, McKenna could tell by reading the reports that Bynum realized he wasn't getting anywhere with his investigation, but he had continued plodding along. There was at least one report every month detailing something he had done. He had run the gamut searching for help, enlisting the services of the FBI as well as more than one local psychic, all to no avail.

Bynum's last report was dated September 4, 1997, leading McKenna to conclude two things. One was that Bynum must have retired shortly after that last report. The other was that, like Tommy, Bynum had never even gotten close to identifying the killer. However, he had identified quite a few other people from the latent prints they had left in Harrison's car. Although Sara Reinhart had been the main woman in Harrison's life, she wasn't the only one. After questioning many of Harrison's friends, Bynum had come up with two others and matched their prints to the previously unidentified latents found in the car. One of the girls had even admitted to Bynum that Harrison had taken her to the same lovers lane a month before the murders.

Other latents belonged to Harrison's mother and father, a mechanic at the car dealership where he worked, and three of Harrison's male friends. It took him until almost a year after the murders, but Bynum had identified the owner of every latent fingerprint that had been found in Harrison's car. Unfortunately, none of those prints belonged to the killer.

McKenna had a lot to think about as he put the stack of reports back in his bag. Had Tommy and Bynum been chasing the same killer for years? he wondered. There were many similarities in the San Jose and New York cases, possibly more than could be reasonably attributed to coincidence, but there were obvious disturbing differences that had to be addressed and examined. Prime among these were the sex of the victim the killer had chosen to torture and the manner of torture, slashing to death as opposed to whipping to death. McKenna found that he could get by the dissimilarities in the cases by making one huge assumption—neither of the two giant differences mattered to the killer. If the same man had murdered all three couples, he derived his perverted pleasure from the pain he caused his victims, and it made little difference to him whether they were male or female.

The plane banked over the ocean and descended into San Jose from the west, passing over the golden hills that ringed the city. The hills looked familiar to McKenna, and he wondered if it was possible that he was passing over the spot where Sara Reinhart and Robert Harrison had suffered and died ten years before.

After landing at 12:40 P.M., local time, McKenna got to meet Randy Bynum sooner than he had thought he would. He was at the gate, holding up a sign with McKenna's name on it. Bynum was not at all what McKenna had expected, a tall black man, thin and in shape, sporting what McKenna guessed was a permanent smile and wearing the most outlandish garb Mc-Kenna had ever seen on a detective, active or retired, on duty or off.

Randy Bynum was a biker and appeared to be one of society's dropouts. Black leather was his thing; his ensemble consisted of a weathered leather jacket, high leather boots, and leather chaps worn over his jeans. Missing was the black leather Marlon Brando cap, but McKenna thought that would have looked better than the red bandanna Bynum had wrapped around his head to complete his deviant fashion statement. McKenna knew Bynum was in his sixties, but his costume and his ageless face placed him some-where in his forties. "I guess it's me you're looking for," McKenna said with some trepidation.

"Randy Bynum, at your service. It's a pleasure to meet you," Bynum said, offering his hand.

The two men shook hands and McKenna decided that he liked Bynum, whatever he chose to wear. Bynum had a firm handshake and a confident air about him. "I guess Tommy called you," McKenna said.

"About two hours ago, destroyed my plans for my eleven o'clock nap. He said you were going to call me sometime this afternoon, but I told him I could fit you into my schedule and show you around our burg. He also asked me to give you a message."

"Something about a lottery ticket?" McKenna guessed.

"That's it. He said he took it to Joe Walsh and found out he was right. The rollers in the Lotto machine smeared the scumbag's prints beyond recognition. Only good prints on the ticket belong to the bodega owner. That make any sense to you?"

"Yeah, it does. I was hoping for more, but it makes sense."

"You got a hotel picked out yet?" Bynum asked.

"No, but I'd like something close to your police headquarters."

"That would be the Fairmont if you don't mind old-fashioned and a little pricey. It's about a mile and a half from headquarters, but it's where I'd stay."

"Good enough. The Fairmont it is. I'll rent myself a car and follow you there."

Bynum rode his full-dress Harley-Davidson into town with McKenna fol-lowing in his rented Chevy Cavalier. Despite his appearance, Bynum was a cautious rider, but it still took only fifteen minutes to travel from the airport to the hotel downtown.

Bynum left his bike parked across the street from the hotel and joined McKenna in his Chevy for the trip to the crime scene. Following Bynum's directions, McKenna got on Highway 101. Within minutes they left down-town behind as the highway ran through miles of upscale single-family homes. "You know, in New York, homes like these would be in the sub-urbs," McKenna commented.

"I know, but here we're still in the city," Bynum said. "San Jose's spread out and still growing. Where we're headed used to be undeveloped and nicer, in the woods, but still part of the city. Unfortunately, a couple of years ago civilization finally caught up with it. The place where the two kids were killed is now in the backyard of a nice, rich family."

"You know them?"

"Sure, we're old friends now. See them all the time. They didn't know what had happened there before they'd bought the land and had their house built, and it still bothers them."

"Do they know we're coming?"

"Yeah. I figured you'd want to see where it happened, so I called them right after Tommy called me."

So, like Tommy, Bynum visits his crime scene all the time, McKenna thought. Obsessive behavior, but maybe that's the kind of behavior it'll take to solve this one.

Ten minutes later they left the freeway and the neighborhood changed from well-kept, middle-class homes to rolling hills with only an occasional house visible through the trees. All of the homes he could see were new, large, and expensive. "It's coming up on the right," Bynum said. "Silver Creek Estates."

McKenna made the turn into the development and saw at once that they had just entered the kind of neighborhood that would be touted as a gated community if it were in New York. There would be a guard shack at the entrance and a private security patrol, but in San Jose those precau-tions weren't deemed necessary. They had left the woods behind at the turn and the large homes were clearly visible from the road, each on about two acres and nestled into the grass-covered rolling hills.

"The road we're on now used to be a dirt track," Bynum said. "It's the one the kids took to the spot where they were killed."

"How much further is it?" McKenna asked.

"About half a mile. Last house in the development."

As soon as McKenna stopped the car at the front door, the owners came out to greet them. Rose and Joe DePraida looked like they belonged there. Both were in their thirties and dressed in jeans and brown shirts and both had deep tans that told of a love of the outdoors. Rose was carrying a boy about two years old and even he was tanned.

Bynum made the introductions as they stood in the driveway.

"Would you like to come in, Randy?" Joe DePraida asked.

"No. We're just going to hang out in back for a while, if you don't mind," Bynum answered.

"Not at all. Make yourselves at home back there."

Rose took her son into the house and Joe took Bynum and McKenna around to the back. The yard was unfenced and designed with the same respect for the landscape as the front of the house was. There was a pool, but the concrete under the water was brown so that it looked more like a swimming hole than a rich person's pool. A wooden swing set and playground were to the right of the pool and at the end of the brown lawn was a gazebo.

Even with the changes, McKenna recognized the spot from Bynum's crime scene photos. Shading the gazebo was the tree Robert Harrison had been tied to for his ordeal and the spot now occupied by the pool was where the Camaro had been found with Sara Reinhart's body inside. The view of the hills was spectacular and McKenna could easily understand why Sara Reinhart and Robert Harrison had used the spot for their romancing.

"I'll leave you two to your business. Holler if you need me for anything," Joe said and went into his house by the back door.

"I guess you come here a lot," McKenna commented.

"Every couple of weeks, but they don't mind," Bynum said. "It's a beautiful spot and they're sharing folks. They've taken quite an interest in this case, but they're too polite to be nosy about it. However, I break the rules and tell them everything that comes up on it."

"They know about the New York cases?"

"Sure. Matter of fact, it was Joe who told me about the latest one. He gets the *New York Times* delivered every day, so he gave me a call as soon as he read about it. You ready to begin?"

"Go ahead."

"Car was parked over there," Bynum said, pointing to the pool as McKenna followed him to the gazebo. Ten yards past the gazebo the ground sloped sharply down into a dry streambed.

"Is that where Harrison's body was found?" McKenna asked, pointing down to the gully.

"That's the spot and this is the tree where the poor bastard was tied," Bynum said, leaning against it.

McKenna took in the view for a moment, mentally reconstructing the crime. There was a stand of trees to his left. "Do you think that's where the killer was hiding while he waited for his victims to show up?"

"Certain of it, although they left nothing behind. They really policed up the area after they were done having their fun, even raked the ground to cover up their footprints. They had to be thorough bastards to think to bring a rake with them."

"They? You think there was more than one killer involved in this case?" McKenna asked, surprised at this new development.

"That's the way I'm looking at it now."

"I never saw anything in your reports that indicated that you thought there was more than one."

"That's because it only came to me about a year ago and I'd retired by then. I should have seen it sooner and I've been kicking myself since. There were two of them."

"What brought you to that conclusion?"

"Two things. First was that Robert Harrison was a real scrapper. Lately I've been talking again to just about everyone who knew him and they all tell me the same thing—he had a flash temper and he wouldn't go down without a fight. Besides that, he didn't scare easily. One of his friends told me a story last year about the time they were in Tijuana together in 1986. A couple of the locals tried to take them off at knifepoint and Harrison went into a rage. He wound up getting cut on his arm, but he beat the tar out of one desperado and then the other one took off."

"But he was up against a gun here," McKenna said. "That's different and he had to know he couldn't win."

"I don't think that would've mattered to him and this friend of his told me something else I didn't know. Ever since that time in Mexico, Harrison started packing a knife. Usually had his push-button switchblade in an elastic band on his leg. Once I found out about that, I talked to his folks again. They didn't know anything about a knife, but we went through all his things together. No knife, so now I think they used his own knife on him to slice him up—after he tried doing the same to them, that is. That's the only thing that makes sense to me now."

"Okay, give me the new scenario."

A roar interrupted Bynum, and McKenna looked up at a plane overhead descending for a landing and realized that he had been right about one thing. The DePraida home was on the approach path to the airport and just an hour earlier he had probably passed directly over the spot where they were sitting.

"Okay. Let's go through it," Bynum said. He got up and walked to the pool with McKenna following. Bynum looked around as he gathered his thoughts and McKenna did the same, taking in everything and imagining how it all must have looked in 1989.

"There was a full moon that night, perfect for talking and romancing at this spot. Harrison and Reinhart took in a movie, had dinner and a few drinks at the Bold Knight—one of our nicer restaurants—and then they came here. They left the Bold Knight around one A.M., figure half an hour to drive here, so they arrived at one-thirty. Our killers are already in place over there," Bynum said, pointing to the stand of trees. "They had everything they needed with them. Probably planned to do their whipping thing, but Harrison changed the plan on them."

"How did they get here? Do you still think they hiked in with all their stuff?" McKenna asked.

"Yes, that part hasn't changed. Found no sign that there'd been another car anywhere near here that night, but hiking in wouldn't have been a problem for them. It's not as rustic around here as it used to be, but there are still plenty of places within a few miles of here to hide a car."

"Then we'd have to assume that the killer or killers really know this area and have to be the outdoors type."

"Always knew that," Bynum said. "At least one of them has to be from San Jose to know about this place."

And if there are two of them, the other one has to be from the Washington Heights area, McKenna thought. If Bynum's right, knowing that should help us narrow the search. "Go on."

"They start sneaking up on the car, but it's bright around here at night when there's a moon. They get close enough to see what's going on inside, maybe wait until Harrison and Reinhart are going at it hot and heavy. That's their time and they close in on the car, probably one on each side."

"Are both armed?"

"I can't say for certain, but probably. In any event, they've done this before and they know how to handle it. They've agreed which one will do the shooting. The shooter is on the driver's side and the one on the passenger's side can't stay too close to the car because he doesn't want to risk getting hit by a ricochet."

"What's his part in this plan of theirs?" McKenna asked, then answered his own question. "They figure whichever one is left alive will bolt from the car on the passenger's side, trying to get away from the shooter. His job is to slow the survivor down until his buddy can make it over to help him out."

"Exactly."

"Does it make any difference to them which one they shoot?"

"I used to think so, but not anymore. They might have different sexual preferences, but I think the arrangement between them is that the shooter kills whichever victim he has the best shot at, the one closer to the driver's side. Whichever way it works out, one of them might be a little happier than the other, but they both left here content and probably sexually drained. The sex of the victim isn't that important to them, as long as they can subject him or her to excruciating pain. That's what gets them off."

Everything Bynum was saying had been previously theorized by McKenna, but he hadn't expected the old small-city detective to come to the same conclusion he had. "What are you basing this analysis on?"

"Research. I've been doing quite a bit of reading since I retired."

"Abnormal psychology?"

"No, heavy-duty underground smut. I've come up with a few publications that I think feature these guys. Filthy, perverted stuff."

"You mean, their pictures are in them?" McKenna asked, astounded.

"Can't be certain, but I'd say it's them."

"Have Rose and Joe seen it?"

"No, they're not the kind of pictures you can show decent folks. I told them about it, but they have no desire to see the pictures. They've done a lot of work with me and know there's two of them. They're quite willing to take my word on what's happening in the pictures."

"Where did you get them?" McKenna asked.

"Why don't we take this one step at a time?" Bynum suggested. "We've got a lot of work to do here before we're ready to talk about the pictures."

"Okay," McKenna said, but then his curiosity got the better of him. "I'm willing to follow your plan for me, but give me a break and tell me first. Randy, where did you get these pictures you're talking about?"

"Tijuana and the Internet," Bynum said patiently. "I've got them in my saddlebags for you and you're welcome to examine them when we get back to the hotel."

"Fine," McKenna said, excited, but also uncomfortable at the prospect of poring over the type of literature Bynum had in mind for him. "Let's get back to your scenario."

"Okay, let's. The first one the shooter sees when he shines his flashlight into the car is Sara Reinhart, and he lets her have it. Bang, one shot through the glass and into her head. Then he waits for Harrison to bolt, but they didn't figure on this tough guy with the knife on his calf. His girl's just been murdered and he's in a rage. Instead of bolting, he climbs over her body and out the broken window, trying to get at the shooter to cut his heart out. Caught them both by surprise."

"Does the crime scene evidence back this up?"

"Yeah, once you understand what happened. Harrison's left palmprint smeared with Reinhart's blood was inside the Camaro, on the ledge right under the broken window. It's his left because his switchblade was in his right by then. There were also fragments of glass in his hair and on his clothes, but it was only recently that I attached the proper significance to that. Until I smartened up, I had figured that those fragments got on him when that first bullet broke the window."

"I guess now you figure that he picked up the glass when he dove through the broken window, trying to get at killer number one," McKenna surmised.

"Maybe Harrison did get to him before number two finally got over to help out his partner. Sometime during the struggle was when Harrison got shot in the right arm by one of them, and that's when they had him. Poor Harrison lost, but now they're really pissed at him."

"Because one of them is cut?"

"That's a distinct possibility, but you tell me after you look at the pictures."

"One of them is cut in the pictures?" McKenna asked, hardly able to control his excitement.

"Yeah, the black one's showing a scar on his left forearm in one of the pictures. The other guy's white."

The black one? "His left forearm? God Almighty!" McKenna exclaimed. He wanted to drag Bynum out of there at that moment, race back to the hotel, and get to those pictures.

"Is there something you haven't told me?" Bynum asked calmly.

"When you talked to Tommy this morning, didn't he happen to mention that our killer has a three-inch knife scar on his left forearm?"

"He does?" Bynum asked. He was maintaining his calm, but McKenna could see that the news excited him.

"That's right. He does."

"No, Tommy didn't mention the scar. He gave me a general description of your New York killer, but the scar must have slipped his mind."

"But you knew that he was describing the black guy in your pictures, didn't you?"

"The description's close," Bynum conceded.

"Did it slip your mind to mention to him that you think you have a picture of the killer, or that you think there's two killers and you have pictures of both of them?"

"No. It didn't slip my mind, exactly, but I've already shown the pictures and explained my theory to another person who touts himself as a top investigator and all I got for the effort was ridicule and grief."

"Who did you show it to?"

"Not important right now, but nobody as famous as you. Since I knew you were coming here anyway, I figured we'd take it step by step. If you wind up agreeing with me, I guess I'll have the last laugh."

"Last laugh?" McKenna shouted. "If you're right and we get those two because of your theory and your pictures, I promise you that you'll have the first laugh, the last laugh, and all those pleasant little giggles in between."

Bynum looked pleased by McKenna's projection, but he wasn't yet ready to share his excitement. "Fine. Can we get on with this?" he asked, still calm and patient.

McKenna had many other questions he would have liked to ask first, but Bynum was in charge at the moment. "I'm sorry. Please continue."

"Like I said, Harrison was a tough piece of work and the shooter didn't want to kill him when Harrison came at him. First they had to have their fun, but whichever one is cut is now really mad."

"You mean, the black one?" McKenna asked.

"Yeah, the black one, if I'm right about this whole Harrison-with-the-knife theory," Bynum said, patiently enduring another interruption. "But I don't know if the black one was the shooter. Harrison was after the shooter, I'm sure, but in the struggle he wound up cutting Black, whether he was the shooter or not. Anyway, they're pissed, and that's when they came up with the knife-torture idea. How's that sound to you?"

"Plausible, but I don't have all the evidence at my disposal that you do," McKenna protested.

"I know, but one step at a time," Bynum said again, smiling and smug. "What I'm asking is, How does it sound so far?"

"The Harrison-with-the-knife theory or the Two-Killer theory?"

"Both."

"Let's examine it, piece by piece," McKenna suggested.

"I assure you that we'll do just that."

"Fine. Was any blood other than Harrison's and Reinhart's found here?"

"No, but right where we're standing is where the struggle took place. The grass was all matted down here, but the only blood was Harrison's from the gunshot wound. I think that if the black guy in my picture is one of the killers and he got cut here, he stopped the bleeding right away with a compress and a bandage. Then they washed away any of his blood that might've been on the ground before they left. Am I still sounding plausible?"

"Very. If they knew enough first aid to put a tourniquet on Harrison, then they certainly knew how to stop the bleeding on a cut of their own."

"Then so far, so good. There's a few other things to back up my theory. Have you studied the pictures of Harrison's body?"

"Yes."

"Well, take a closer look," Bynum suggested. "Maybe use a magnifying glass and you'll see some marks on his right calf that they didn't give him."

"Where he had his knife attached to his leg?"

"That's what I think. I bought one of those leg holsters for knives and wore it around for a day. Wound up with similar marks on my leg, but they're harder to see on black skin. I'll give you the holster and you can give it a try on yourself."

"Fine," McKenna said. "Is that it?"

"No, we're just beginning. First the talk, and now the work," Bynum said, smiling and even more smug. "Joe!" he hollered.

Joe DePraida had been inside awaiting his cue and he appeared at the back door. "You ready?" he yelled back.

"Bring him out," Bynum ordered, then walked back to the edge of the yard overlooking the gully. McKenna followed.

Joe entered his garage and came out pulling a child's wagon. Balanced on the wagon was a yellow dummy, the kind used in auto crash-tests. Around the middle of the dummy was a leather harness. Joe also stopped at the edge of the gully and dumped the dummy onto the ground. Still in the wagon was a long length of nylon rope.

"Joe, please give Brian the height and weight of our creature," Bynum said.

"He's five foot nine and weighs one hundred and seventy-two pounds," Joe stated.

"The same height and weight of Robert Harrison after the killers were through with him," Bynum said. "The weight of this dummy is also distributed in the same proportions as the weight of a human being is. I'm now going to stand in the exact spot where Harrison's body was found. When I'm in place, I want you to push or throw the dummy down the gully and try to reach me, anyway you can."

"Will I be able to?" McKenna asked.

It was Joe who answered. "On one try out of twenty-two, if you're strong enough and lucky enough to catch some great bounces."

Bynum tied one end of the nylon rope to the tree and McKenna understood one of the reasons for Bynum's leather costume. McKenna thought that it would be a tough climb down, and any other type of clothing would be ruined in the process.

As it turned out, nothing about the climb was tough for Bynum. He took a pair of leather gloves from his pocket, put them on and quickly rappelled down the incline, expertly sliding the rope through his hands as he descended. McKenna thought it was an amazing feat of agility for a man in his sixties, but Joe thought nothing of it. "He gets lots of practice," was his only comment.

When Bynum got to the bottom, he brushed himself off and walked to the center of the dry creek bed. For the first time, McKenna noticed

that the outline of the human form was painted on the ground in yellow
at the spot where Bynum was standing.

"Are you satisfied that this is the spot where Harrison's body landed
after it was thrown down here?" Bynum yelled up.

"Yeah, I'm satisfied," McKenna yelled back, then turned to Joe. "How
many times have you guys done this?"

"We've thrown that dummy down and pulled it back up a total of one
hundred and fifty-two times over the past two months. Usually we use a
winch to get it back up."

"But not today?"

"No, not today. Randy figured that, since there's three of us working
on it today, we might as well get some exercise."

"Good thinking. How many times have you managed to get that
dummy to land where Randy's standing?"

"By myself, never," Joe admitted. "But Randy's stronger than me and
he's two for forty-four."

McKenna took a good look at Joe and decided that he didn't appear
to be a weakling. "And how about when both of you heave it over the
side?"

"Almost every time. Sometimes we manage to throw it even further
than the killers did."

"When you do it by yourself, how do you get the best yardage?"

"Put it on your shoulders in a fireman's carry, go back to the pool for
a head start, then run back here and fling it off your shoulders," Joe suggested. "You just have to be careful that you don't go over the edge with
it."

"Fine," McKenna said. With some effort, he got the dummy on his
shoulders and did as Joe had suggested, running and stopping just short of
the precipice as he flung the dummy off his shoulders and into the gully.
He gave the effort everything he had, but was disappointed by the results.
He managed to get the dummy airborne for only a short distance and
watched as it rolled and bounced down the steep hill, finally coming to rest
ten feet from where Bynum was standing.

"Not bad," Joe said.

"Really?" McKenna asked, not sure whether or not Joe was putting
him on.

"Really. It's close to my record, and I've had lots of practice."

Without comment, Bynum snapped the rope onto the dummy's harness. Also without comment, Joe and McKenna then pulled it back up.
"Now what?" McKenna asked Joe.

"You take the legs and I'll take the arms. We swing it and let go on
the count of three."

McKenna followed the plan and, even before the dummy stopped rolling, he was satisfied that they had given it quite a ride. The dummy came to rest at Bynum's feet, but Bynum didn't gloat. He just bent down and again secured the rope to the harness.

"Randy!" McKenna yelled down.

"Yeah?"

"There were two of them."

FIFTEEN

McKenna was anxious to get back to the hotel, but Bynum was enjoying himself and was in no hurry. He was quick to point out that the amenities had to be observed. McKenna was forced to agree, so after leaving the DePraida's house, they drove downtown to the San Jose police station. The visit was short and perfunctory, just a courtesy call to the Homicide Squad to thank Gary Newell for his efforts.

As he said he would, Bynum did annoy the "kids." He questioned the four seasoned detectives there on the progress they were making on their cases. It was obvious to McKenna that Bynum, although retired, was familiar with all the active murder investigations in town and he gave at least one suggestion to each detective. By the time class was over, McKenna was certain that no one was sorry to see them go.

When they got back to the hotel, Bynum took the magazines out of his saddlebags. They were in the proverbial plain brown wrappers. McKenna thought their session was over for the day, but Bynum had other ideas. "You know, being single is okay, but it's got its drawbacks if you don't feel like cooking," Bynum said.

"Meaning?"

"Meaning this hotel's got a fine restaurant and all of a sudden I'm starving. Your smut session can wait a little while longer, can't it?"

What a ball-buster! McKenna thought. Well, two can play this game. "Of course it can. I'm in no hurry to see the faces of the men who've been torturing and murdering innocent victims for at least eighteen years. Matter of fact, I'm kind of hungry myself. Let's sit down and eat to our hearts' content."

They went into the hotel's restaurant, took a table, and ordered. Then

Bynum dropped another bombshell. "I hate to tell you this, but those pictures aren't going to help you much in identifying the killers."

"Why not?"

"Because they're wearing masks in the photos."

"Masks?"

"That's right. Leather masks and not much else."

That was a big piece of disappointing news for McKenna, but he was prepared to grasp at straws. "Beside the scar, are there any other identifying marks on them?"

"Black's got more old scars on his behind and back. Lash marks, I'd say, but I can guarantee that you'd be able to pick either of them out of thousands in any nudist colony. Nature has been very kind to Black and White."

Black and White. McKenna let his imagination run with that one for a moment, but Bynum had other concerns. "Since my magazines and what I've shown you so far isn't going to help identify them unless you do find them naked, would you mind telling me how you plan to proceed from here?" he asked.

"You mean proceed today?"

"No. Tomorrow would be fine."

"Depends on how far another commercial airport is from San Jose."

"That would be San Francisco International, about sixty miles from here."

"Then that's what I'll be doing tomorrow. It's close enough for the killer to have landed there and then showed up here to use the ATMs, so I'll visit the car rental agencies there to see if the black one rented a car in San Francisco. Just to be sure, I'll also check with every car rental agency in town."

"Long day, but even if you come up with nothing, you'll still learn something about the killers," Bynum said. "We're assuming that one of them comes from here, so if the New York guy didn't rent a car here, then the other one is still living in the San Jose area. It's that one's car that they're using."

"So in your San Jose case, at least, we're looking for a couple of bi-coastal killers."

"And in the New York cases?" Bynum asked with raised eyebrows.

"We've been working on the assumption that it's been one man, only because our witnesses only saw one man. That still might be correct. Maybe Black killed our two people by himself this time."

"He didn't," Bynum stated with conviction. "They're a team and they always have been."

"You're probably right, but I've got some work to do when I get back to make sure."

"Throwing dummies around?" Bynum asked.

"For openers. I'll start throwing a Cindy dummy around all by myself. If I can make the distance to the spot where her body wound up, fine. In that case, I'll say that just one of them threw her down the hill."

"But there still could have been two of them there," Bynum objected. "And no matter how you make out with your dummy, I'm telling you there were."

"I'm more than ready to concede that because it answers a big question that's been bothering me. Like I told you, our witness just saw Black and he was alone in the car. More than two hours later, he's alone again in Nassau County where he uses Cindy's cards at an ATM. But the trip to Nassau County should have only taken him an hour, and I'm pretty sure he was in a hurry to get there."

"So what's your assumption now to account for that missing hour?" Bynum asked. "Do you think that maybe he went back to the park to pick up White after he got the car, and then he dropped him off someplace in Nassau County before he used the ATM?"

"Not exactly. Black lost the hour before he got to Nassau County. He gassed up in Queens with one of Cindy's cards more than an hour and a half after he picked up the car. The trip from Washington Heights to that gas station should have only taken him a half hour, at the most."

"Even if he drove back to the park to pick up White first?"

"Yep. The spot in the park where the murders took place is only about fifteen blocks from where Black picked up the car, and I bet White was waiting even closer than that. I don't think he would have hung around the park, so maybe they arranged to meet a couple of blocks from it."

"I like your thinking now, but let me play the devil's advocate for a moment," Bynum said. "If there were two of them and Black dropped off White, that would've been in New York City somewhere, right?"

"That's the way it looks."

"And where do you think he dropped him off?"

"If I knew that, I'd be on a plane back right now. But if one lives in New York and the other lives in San Jose, two good guesses would be at a hotel somewhere or maybe at Black's house."

"Black's house? If there's two of them doing the killing, isn't it possible that Black's the one who lives in San Jose and White's the one in New York?"

"Good point, especially since Black was also the one who was running around at your ATMs here. I hadn't been looking at it that way, but I guess it's possible," McKenna conceded.

"Thank you. Now for the big question from the devil's advocate. If the two of them did your murders in New York, then why didn't they save themselves some trouble and go pick up the car together?"

"Maybe they didn't want to be seen together on the subway or in Washington Heights."

"Why not?"

"Because they didn't want to be remembered. A black guy and a white guy traveling together on the subway or walking around together in Washington Heights attracts more attention that a black guy traveling alone."

"I don't know the area, but you're probably right. These two are put together rather well and that makes them noticeable. Black and White would be bound to attract more attention if they were together than if they were alone."

"So they're staying in character if only one went to pick up the car," McKenna said.

"In character?"

"Being real careful in everything they do."

"Not everything," Bynum said. "They're either very greedy or they like showing off. Maybe both."

"What am I missing?"

"Nothing, yet. You just haven't seen everything I have. But you will."

"You mean your porn collection?"

"Exactly. As soon as you finish your reading, you'll want to give me a call. I'll be home, waiting."

"What is it you think I'll be calling you about?" McKenna asked.

"I might be wrong, but you strike me as the kind of guy who gives credit where credit's due. If I'm right, then you'll want to call me as soon as you finish just to tell me how smart I am."

After dinner, Bynum did as he said and went home to await McKenna's call. He would be back in the morning to accompany McKenna to San Francisco. McKenna was at the hotel elevator when he saw him off, but once Bynum was gone he decided that he didn't want to wait for the elevator. He took the stairs and ran up four flights to his room with the wrapped magazines under his arm, and then he sat down to do some reading. It was time to see something of the men he was chasing.

The first publication was called *Serious*. It was a thin hard-core porn magazine consisting entirely of full-page glossy photos depicting bondage and torture scenes. Whips, leather, or chains, and frequently a combination of the three, were evident in every one of them. There was nothing subtle about it, and while some of the scenes were staged using models for the benefit of the camera, McKenna was sure that in others the camera was an afterthought. He thought that people were actually being tortured in those, that the marks on their bodies weren't evidence of the skill of an off-camera makeup man. The welts, bruises, and cuts on the bodies of those bound victims looked real, causing McKenna to wonder if the people in the victims' role were willing participants. If so, he concluded, the world was a stranger place than he had previously imagined.

Leather masks were a common fashion item in the photos, frequently worn by the person inflicting the torture. McKenna thumbed through the magazine until he got to the photos on pages 10 and 11, the centerfold. He saw at once that he had arrived at Bynum's theory.

The first one showed a young girl secured to a tree with her arms spread behind her. She was Hispanic, about eighteen years old, dressed only in white panties and a bra, and clearly terrified. Her jet-black hair was long and loose, reaching just past her shoulders, and her face was contorted into such a look of terror that McKenna couldn't decide if she was pretty or not. He figured that she probably wanted to scream, but she couldn't— she was gagged with what appeared to be a sock stuffed into her mouth.

Not visible in the photo was the means used to secure her arms because they were stretched around the tree behind her, but she was further fastened to the tree with a dog chain tied around it at her neck. The tree was at the edge of a cliff overlooking a mountain valley lush with small, well-ordered farms.

Although the sun wasn't visible in the photo, McKenna deduced that the picture was taken either shortly after sunrise or shortly before sunset. However, from the shadows cast he could tell that the sun was low in the sky and to the right of the scene.

Black and White were also in the photo, one on either side of her, ten feet in front of the tree and facing her at a forty-five degree angle. They wore leather masks on their faces, leather harnesses consisting of a wide belt fastened to straps that crisscrossed their chests, gladiator-type leather sandals, and nothing else. Black was on the right in the photo and held a coiled leather whip in his left hand. White was on the left and held an extended whip in his right hand, with the tip of the whip just inches from the young girl's feet. Both men were muscular, both appeared to be close to the same height, and both were sexually aroused, with their penises erect and at attention in front of them. The two were exceptionally well-endowed, so well-endowed that McKenna knew Bynum was right. Black and White could be easily picked out of a nudist colony lineup consisting of a thousand men.

The second photo was taken after the first, after Black and White had started their fun. The camera angle was lower, showing the three figures only from their knees up. As evidenced by the cuts and welts on the young woman's thighs and lower groin, her panties had already been whipped off her. She was obviously in pain and trying to spit out the gag to scream as the action shot captured the beginning of the painful process involved in removing her bra with the whips. By then her hair and the sides of her bra were drenched in sweat. Both men had their arms extended as they whipped her and the tips of the whips were a blur as each struck her bra at the same time, shredding the material on the side of each of her breasts.

McKenna closely examined Black's left arm in the photos and found the knife scar. It was wide, showing dark brown on Black's coffee-colored skin, and it looked like it had been there for years. He could also see the faint lash scars Bynum had mentioned and figured they had been there much longer than the scar on his forearm.

McKenna turned to page 12, expecting a continuation of the action, but Black and White were only featured in the centerfold. The page 12 photo showed another two leather-masked men shoving a stick up the rear of a bound and gagged third man. He continued thumbing through the magazine, but there weren't any more photos showing Black and White torturing the girl or anyone else.

McKenna closed the magazine and examined the cover. At first glance, there was just the title *Serious* emblazoned in dripping red letters on a shiny black background. Then he saw it under the first *S* in very tiny red letters: "Fall '97." He thumbed through the magazine again, searching for a publisher's name or the place of publication, but found nothing.

McKenna went to the second magazine Bynum had given him. That one was called *In Charge*, and like *Serious*, it was thin and consisted entirely of full-page glossy photos. Except for the title, the cover was almost identical to the *Serious* cover. *In Charge* was printed in bold, block red letters on the shiny black background, and this time McKenna knew just where to look for the publication date. It was there, under the *I* in small letters: "Spring '89," making the *In Charge* issue eight years older than the *Serious* issue. However, both magazines were in pristine condition and McKenna would have been hard pressed at a glance to tell which one was older.

Again McKenna looked for the publisher's name and got nowhere, but it was apparent from the content, style, and cover that the magazines had the same publisher. He knew just where to look for Black and White and they were there again, their two photos again occupying the centerfold.

The setting and action was by then familiar to McKenna, centered on a tree at the edge of a cliff that overlooked another green, tropical valley, and whips were again the implements Black and White used to torment their victim secured to the tree. However, there was one major difference between the *Serious* and the *In Charge* photos. The *In Charge* victim was an Asian male in his twenties dressed in shorts and a red T-shirt, but the sex of their victim didn't appear to make much difference to the men with the whips. Both Black and White again wore only the leather masks, the leather chest harnesses, and the leather gladiator sandals, but once again they were sexually aroused as they regarded their helpless victim secured to the tree in the same manner as the young Hispanic girl. He was also apparently terror-stricken and gagged with a sock.

Once again, the first photo served to set the scene and, once again, the lighting told McKenna that the photos were taken either shortly after sunrise or shortly before sunset. The second photo was the action shot, taken from a lower level so that the three men were only visible from their knees up as the Asian was whipped. By the time the second shot was taken, his shorts and shirt were in blood-stained tatters and he was trying to scream through his gag as the tip of each whip ripped at his chest. Black had apparently missed his target by an inch, but White hadn't; the photo captured the blood squirting from the Asian victim's left nipple as the whip sliced it.

Black's left forearm was clearly visible as he stretched his arm to whip their victim, and McKenna examined the forearm closely. There was no scar, and Bynum's Harrison-with-the-knife theory got a major boost in McKenna's eyes. The *In Charge* issue was published months before Harrison and Reinhart were murdered and Black didn't have the scar. Eight years later, the *Serious* issue was published and there it was, an old scar.

McKenna placed the *Serious* and *In Charge* centerfolds side by side and studied them for some time. The wounds and the terror on the victims' faces all looked genuine to him, forcing him to a conclusion: Unless extremely talented makeup and special effects people had been employed to create the lash wounds on gifted actors, he was looking at evidence of a crime that was only rumored to exist. McKenna was certain that the Hispanic girl and the Asian male were dead, tortured to death for the bizarre sexual gratification of Black and White as well as for the profit generated in deviant circles by the sale of the photos. If so, there had to be more. If they *were* snuff photos produced for profit, then there also had to be a snuff film that recorded the victims' horrible ordeal from beginning to end.

According to the persistent rumors, these films existed and were produced in South America, Russia, and Asia. However, to McKenna's knowledge, never had there been a single such film produced in evidence in any court in the world nor had any person ever been charged with the production, distribution, or possession of a snuff film.

That was going to change, McKenna promised himself, for he thought it likely that he was staring at the masked faces of the killers he had been chasing for three days, Bynum for eight years, and Tommy for eighteen.

Cruel and greedy killers willing and eager to exhibit such a depraved in-difference to human life had to be captured and made to pay for their crimes, no matter what. Like Tommy and Bynum before him, the case had been transformed into an obsessive mission for McKenna.

By the time McKenna finally closed the two magazines, he was certain that he had caught two mistakes Black and White had made by selling the photos, mistakes that linked the murders of the Hispanic girl and the Asian male to Tommy's murders, Bynum's murders, and the murders of Cindy Barrone and Arthur McMahon.

Mistake number one had to do with the lighting in the second photo in each magazine. Those action photos shot from the knees up were brighter than the first photos, and McKenna now understood why. A covering had been spread at the feet of all the victims, but it wasn't the tar-paulin initially thought to have been utilized to collect the blood of the victims as well as the semen and sweat of the killers. True, the covering incidentally served that purpose, but it wasn't a simple tarp. The increased lighting and reduction of shadows in the second photos convinced Mc-Kenna that the killers had spread a light-reflecting material at the feet of their victims to improve the quality of the pictures and better show the torture they were administering.

Mistake number two convinced McKenna that Randy Bynum was more than a smart guy. Owing to the three-inch scar visible on Black's left fore-arm as he tortured the Hispanic girl, McKenna was ready to publicly ac-knowledge that Bynum was a genius and right in all things.

So McKenna dialed Bynum's number. "You are my hero and one of the best detectives I've ever met. Given your permission, I'm ready to follow you anywhere," he stated as soon as Bynum answered.

"So kind of you to say so, and yes, you have my permission," Bynum answered graciously.

"Now it's time for you to tell me. Who was that top investigator you went to with these photos and your theory?"

"I went as far as I could. I brought them to our chief of police. He was our chief of detectives when I retired."

"When did you go to him?"

"Eight days ago. It was Tuesday, June first."

"And when did you get these photos?"

"About two months ago, but it took me a while to understand them properly. I wanted to be sure I knew what I was talking about before I went to see the chief."

"And what was this top investigator's reaction?"

"He brought them to our Photo Section. According to our august expert, it's possible that the injuries depicted in the photos are the result

of some superior and very expensive special effects wizardry. Even probable, given the graphic nature of the photos and the apparent ruses used
in some other pictures in the magazines. End result, the chief told me to
go home, stay home, and stop bothering him with my far-fetched nonsense."

"Your chief is a moron," McKenna concluded.

"I know and, fortunately, so does our city manager. Nothing to do with
my case, but that chief was sent packing last Friday."

"Where did you get those two magazines?"

"Through the Internet, I got connected with a porn dealer in San
Diego who, believe it or not, is an ex–San Diego deputy sheriff and a very
nice guy. I had wondered for years if the killer had photographed his fun
in order to have a fond remembrance of his wonderful evening. I was
betting he did and—"

"Wait a minute," McKenna said. "You saying that you didn't come up
with your two-killer theory until you saw the photos?"

"Hate to make you feel better, but that's almost right," Bynum admitted. "Before that, it was merely a suspicion—not a full-blown theory complete with proofs, just like in geometry. But with one suspicion came the
other, which accounts for my knife theory after I found out that Harrison
usually carried."

Thank God! McKenna thought, suddenly feeling not so dumb. "I do
feel a little better," he admitted. "But you're still my hero. Go on."

"Anyway, we now know that there were two of them and that there
was a profit motive attached to their fun, but it took me a lot of asking
around in filthy places in order to come up with that knowledge. After that,
it took quite a bit of exercise on my part and Joe DePraida's before I was
finally able to understand exactly how and why Robert Harrison was tortured the way he was—with the knife instead of the whip."

"So how did this San Diego porn dealer come up with those magazines
and how is it that we now have them?"

"Figuring there *were* photos and hoping that the killer was greedy
enough to sell some copies, I was on the Internet in a private chat room
frequented by quite a few apparently depraved individuals interested in
bondage and sadism. Stories and rumors were swapped and photos of mutual interest were traded and sold, but it took me a while to find out that
many of the people in those chat rooms weren't in it for the fun."

"They were porn dealers?" McKenna guessed.

"Yeah, some were legitimate porn dealers, if there is such a thing, but
it took me quite a bit of legwork and more out-of-pocket cash than I'd care
to admit in order to learn that."

"And one of them was the San Diego ex-deputy."

"Yep. My new friend Ed Gallagher, although it took me some time to find out who he really was. You have to understand that most of the people in those chat rooms disguise their identity, something that's rather easy to do on the Internet."

"Including you, I presume."

"Yeah, including me. I set up a cash account under a phony name and rented a box from Mailboxes, Etc. in order to receive my filthy goodies anonymously."

"How long were you involved in this deception?"

"Years."

"And you paid for it all yourself?"

"I tried to get backing for the scheme when I was still on the job, but the moron wouldn't hear of it. Told me my scheme would taint the department's sacred reputation and he absolutely forbade me to go through with it."

"But that didn't stop you?"

"No, it just meant that I was on my own and paying the bills, without being able to tell anyone else about it."

"Okay, back to Ed Gallagher."

"He offered me one of those interesting publications for two thousand dollars and I asked him to describe them. He did, and I was very interested."

"Because the description of the torture in those centerfold photos matched Tommy's case?"

"Partially, but it also matched mine in a lot of ways. I told him I wanted them and he agreed to meet me in Tijuana. It was secret-agent stuff, all designed to make sure I was a legitimate rich pervert and not a cop setting him up in some kind of sting. I was to wear a green shirt and go to a certain phone booth down there at a certain time on a certain date. I did, and he called and directed me to another phone booth. When I got there, he was watching me from a bar across the street when I answered his call and he told me to come in. Gallagher's a big guy and he had another bruiser with him. They took me to the men's room and searched me to make sure I wasn't wired, then we sat down in a booth and did the deal."

"You gave him your two thousand dollars?" McKenna asked.

"Sure did."

"So what makes Gallagher such a nice guy?"

"Once I saw the photos, I knew what I had. I also knew that I had to try and find out where he had gotten them, and I saw only one way to do that under the circumstances. I came clean with him, told him who I was and what I was doing. Explained my whole case to him."

"And his reaction to that?"

"He was shocked. He told me he thought that the photos had been staged, that the whole running around to different phone booths was just his way of keeping my interest up because he knew that the deviants he deals with are only willing to pay big money for things that take them a lot of trouble to get."

"Because then they'll think the photos aren't staged, that there's real torture going on?" McKenna guessed.

"Of course, but they're already predisposed to believe that because they either fantasize about that kind of thing constantly or, maybe, they practice it in their own sex lives on a smaller scale."

"So what did Gallagher do then?"

"He came clean with me, told me who he was, and gave me back a grand."

"So you still wound up paying a thousand?"

"Yeah, but that's all right. A thousand is what Gallagher paid for them and I saw no reason for him to lose money on my case."

"Where did he get them from?"

"At a trade show in Las Vegas the month before."

"Porn dealers have trade shows?" McKenna asked, amazed.

"Sure do, lots of them, but the guy he bought the magazines from wasn't a legitimate porn dealer."

"How did Gallagher know that?"

"He knew simply because he doesn't know the guy, and he knows all the legitimate dealers. He heard from another dealer at the show that there was a guy at the bar who purported to have some great S and M stuff, but he wanted big money for it. Gallagher had already pulled his scam in Tijuana a few times and saw a chance to turn a good profit, so he met the seller in the bar and made the deal."

"Without knowing who he was dealing with?"

"Money's money, so he didn't really care. Like I said, he thought that they were just well-staged photos."

"Did Gallagher give you a description of him?"

"Asian male, thin, five foot six, in his forties, dressed gaudy, lots of gold jewelry."

"Think he'll remember enough about him to provide us with a sketch?"

"I think so, if you can provide us with an artist."

"Sure can. I've got an artist who'll be more than happy to help us out."

"In San Diego?" Bynum asked.

"No, he's in New York right now. But once I tell Tommy McKenna about Gallagher's Asian acquaintance, nothing on Earth can prevent him from meeting us in San Diego."

———

McKenna's request went through the chain of command, sort of. He called Tommy at home and filled him in. Tommy was excited and ready to go to San Diego, but he knew that Greve was shorthanded since he had sent a team to Puerto Rico to search for the 25th Precinct killer. Tommy called Greve at home, and Greve agreed to send him—provided Greve could get a few temporary replacements for the manpower he had spread around the continent. So Greve called Brunette and told him about the progress being made in California, Tommy's travel request, and the manpower problems he was experiencing.

The big case was quickly getting much bigger and the end result was that an hour after McKenna had called Tommy, Tommy called him back. "Ray thought that Greve needed even more manpower than he had requested, so Greve's gonna have plenty of people to throw your dummy around. When do you want me in San Diego?" he asked.

"Wait a minute! Ray gave Greve people just to throw a Cindy dummy down the hill?"

"That's right. Promised him three real bruisers in addition to people to replace me, you, and the team in P.R. Impressed the hell outta Greve when he saw how much importance Ray attaches to this case."

"We could've done the dummy thing when we got back, but it's just gonna prove that Randy was right and I'm already convinced he is."

"So am I, and it's something we should have come up with on our own," Tommy said.

"Why's that? Cindy's broken neck?"

"That and four broken ribs. One man throwing her down the hill probably couldn't cause that much damage to her body, but two men giving her a good toss could. We should've seen it," Tommy stated, but he was quick to change the subject. "When do you want me there?"

"Anytime Friday morning would be fine. We'll pick you up at the airport."

"The day after tomorrow? Why so long?"

"Randy. I knew that there's no way I could get our job to pay for his airfare, so he insists on driving himself down on his motorcycle. Besides, we have to check the auto rental agencies in San Francisco tomorrow and that's going to take us some time."

"How long will it take him to ride down to San Diego?"

"He figures about ten hours, more or less."

"And how are you going to get there?"

"I'm going to follow him in my rental. When we're done with it, I'll turn it in at the airport in San Diego."

"Driving all the way down there is rather inconvenient for you, isn't it?" Tommy asked.

"I guess."

"So I take it you really like this Randy Bynum, don't you?"

"He's good, and a real nice guy to boot. Dedicated almost beyond belief, considering that he's still working his case without being paid for his efforts."

"I liked him and I'm sure he's as dedicated as you say, but aren't you asking yourself one thing by now?" Tommy asked.

"You mean, Why didn't he tell you about this bombshell he's been sitting on?"

"Exactly. How long has he known that we're all chasing the same snuff killers?"

"From what he's told me, he's been sure for only a couple of weeks. But in his defense, he did go to his chief with the pictures and his theory."

"And?"

"The chief blew him off."

"Then his chief's a moron, but Randy knows me and I hope he recognizes that I'm not," Tommy said. "Granted, I didn't know it was two killers and we didn't attach the proper significance to Cindy's broken neck and ribs, but didn't Harrison also have some broken ribs?"

"Four, I think."

"Aha!" Tommy exclaimed. "Four broken ribs, yet Randy didn't attach the proper significance to that fact, either. He didn't figure out it was two killers until he saw his filthy pictures. Right?"

McKenna didn't think it was time to mention that it was only through extraordinary effort and expense on Bynum's part that anyone working the cases got to see the pictures. To keep things running smoothly, there was only one answer to Tommy's question. "That's right."

"Yet Randy doesn't come to us, and *our* boss *isn't* a moron. If Randy had cut me in on this two weeks ago, Greve and I would have already had the entire resources of the best detective division in the world working hard on this. We might've had those two scumbags in irons by now, maybe even before they would've gotten a chance to do Cindy and young Arthur."

McKenna thought that Tommy was stretching it a bit, but he knew Tommy, knew Randy, and knew that he was in a delicate situation. Big-city detective Tommy was famous and nationally recognized; small-city detective Randy was not, but he should be and maybe he knows that. Considering that in a nice, low-crime city like San Jose, the big case comes along only once in every career, if at all, how would Randy feel about handing over his work to someone else in another department on the other side of the country? McKenna asked himself. Better yet, how would I feel about it if I were Randy and I had continued dedicating myself to this bombshell case after I had been forced to retire without proper recognition?

McKenna didn't want to answer that one for himself, but he did have an answer for Tommy. "Since he's gotten this far on his own without help from anybody, maybe he thought he was going to carry the ball into the end zone unassisted. Then I showed up with a couple of more murders, killings much more explosive than the ones he's been working on all this time, and he decides for some reason that he likes me and trusts me. Maybe he's decided now to take the assist on his play, which just happens to be a very lucky break for us."

"Wait a minute!" Tommy insisted. "I was always ready to admit that Randy is pretty good and a sensible kind of guy. But are you saying that he thought he could capture these scumbags without us, without using the big guns to get two depraved-but-clever killers who've apparently been successfully operating internationally for years?" he asked incredulously.

"Maybe that's what he thought," McKenna said, knowing what was coming next.

"Then he must think he's better than us at solving homicides," Tommy stated, sounding even more incredulous.

"Silly idea, isn't it?" McKenna asked lightly in an attempt to calm Tommy down.

It worked. "Silly idea?" Tommy said, then chuckled. "It's patently preposterous, that's what it is."

The competition's really brewing now and maybe we'll all get a chance to see just how preposterous it really is, McKenna thought, but didn't say.

SIXTEEN

McKenna was awakened at 11:10 P.M. by his cell phone ringing on the pillow next to his ear. It was Bob Hurley. "Ten minutes ago, a 7-Eleven in Tempe, Arizona, at 109-14 McDowell Avenue, total of nine hundred dollars."

"Thanks, Bob. Can you stay on the line?"

"I'm here, but I expect I'll be getting another call on my other line in a few minutes."

"I know. He's probably in another 7-Eleven right now," McKenna said.

Using the hotel phone, it took him three precious minutes to call Arizona information and reach the Tempe Police Department.

"Sergeant Rausch. How can I help you?"

"Sarge, this is Detective McKenna of the New York City Police Department and I need a big favor in a hurry. Are you ready to write?"

"Wait a minute! Who's this?" Rausch asked.

"Detective McKenna of the New York City Police Department. It's important and it's got to be done now."

"Okay, Detective McKenna. What do you need?"

"A serial killer just used a stolen credit card at an ATM in a 7-Eleven at 109-14 McDowell Avenue and he's probably on his way to another 7-Eleven close by to do the same thing. You got another one near there?"

"Yeah, we've got one on Indian School Road, but the McDowell Avenue 7-Eleven is only a few blocks from the city line. There's a closer one in Mesa, about two miles up the road on McDowell."

"Fine. I need a unit right now at every 7-Eleven you've got, and I also need you to call the Mesa PD and ask them to do the same. I'm looking for two men, one black and the other white, both in their forties, both about five nine, hundred and seventy pounds and both in good shape. The black one is either bald or has his head shaved. I don't know if they're together there, but consider both armed and extremely dangerous."

"Any description of vehicle?"

"Sorry, no," McKenna said, then heard Hurley screaming on his cell phone. "Sarge, I'll be back with you in a minute. Can you get on it and please stay on the line?"

"You got it," Rausch said.

McKenna put down the hotel phone and picked up his cell phone. "I'm here, Bob. Where?" McKenna asked Hurley.

"Another nine hundred from another 7-Eleven on McDowell Avenue, but this one's in Mesa, Arizona."

"Got it, Bob. Stay on the line, please," McKenna said, then got back to Rausch. "You there, Sarge?"

Rausch wasn't, but he came back on the line a minute later.

"Either one or both of them were just at the McDowell Avenue 7-Eleven in Mesa," McKenna said.

"I've got the Mesa PD notified and our units are on the way to ours. What next?"

"I don't think they'll be hitting another ATM tonight, but I need the clerks interviewed at both the McDowell Avenue 7-Elevens right away. I need the best description they can give on whoever used those machines. Can you do that and get back to me?"

"Sure, but I'm going to need some verification on this first. You've got us pretty busy on just a phone call and I've got to know you are who you say you are," Rausch insisted.

"That's reasonable," McKenna said. "I'm in San Jose, California, right now on this case, but you can call the Manhattan North Homicide Squad office in New York for verification. Fair enough?"

"You've got it. Give me some phone numbers."

McKenna gave him the phone number for the Homicide Squad and for the Fairmont Hotel.

"Fine, I'll be calling you back," Rausch said. "When I do, are you going to tell me what this is all about?"

"That's a promise," McKenna said, then got back to Hurley. "Thanks for waiting, Bob. Can you give me a rundown on the cards they used?" he asked.

Hurley did. All of Cindy Barrone's cards had been used in either Tempe or Mesa for the maximum daily amount permitted by the credit card companies.

"Will they be able to use them again after midnight?" McKenna asked.

"What do you mean *they?* Is there more than one now?"

"Yeah, it looks like there's two of them."

"So which one killed my wonderful new client's son?"

"Either one, but probably both."

"Can I be the one to keep Mr. McMahon up to date?"

Fair enough, McKenna thought. Barrone and McMahon are paying the bills, which is the only reason I know that one or both of the killers are now wandering around Arizona while I'm looking for them in California. I put them on to Hurley, so why not make him look good? "You can be the one, as long as they understand that everything about this case is now very sensitive and highly confidential."

"Don't worry about that. I've already got McMahon dazzled into my corner and it won't hurt my business having Barrone for a friend. Give me the scoop."

It took fifteen minutes to fill Hurley in. By the time McKenna was done, Hurley was very interested and certainly more excited than McKenna had expected.

"Let me get this straight," Hurley said. "Are you telling me that the daughter of the speaker of the city council and the son of a very rich and powerful ex-congressman were killed to make a snuff film?"

"That's the assumption, but I don't think the killers knew what they were getting into when they did those two."

"But they sure do now, after all the press it got. Do you know what that means?"

"Yeah, it means they wouldn't dare try to peddle it. If they're smart, they've probably already destroyed the photos and the film, if there is one."

"*Au contraire, mon ami.* If they're smart they'll do no such thing," Hurley countered. "They *are* smart, aren't they?"

"They've been at it a long time and they're still out there."

"And greedy, too?"

"Apparently. Selling photos of torturing anyone puts them in some danger of capture, so they must be greedy."

"Then look at it this way. I don't know the market for snuff films, if there is one, and I don't know what deranged, wealthy-beyond-belief pervert could afford to buy this one, if it exists. But sooner or later, if those two filthy knuckleheads have any brains at all, it's going to dawn on them that they have in their possession the most valuable photos and/or videotape in the world today. Think about it and then tell me, am I right or am I right?"

McKenna's other phone was ringing, so he didn't have time to think about Hurley's premise. However, he did recognize that very few knew better than Hurley the art of making illicit money without going to jail. "I'm sure you're right, Bob, but I've got to go. Remember, please, confidentiality when you're talking to McMahon."

"Got it."

McKenna ended the cell phone call and answered the hotel phone. "It was the white one, both places," Rausch said. "Just came in, used the ATM, and left."

"Description?"

"Just like you said. Forties, five eight or five nine, about a hundred and seventy pounds, great shape. What you didn't tell us is he thinks he's Garth Brooks."

"He was singing?" McKenna asked.

"Not exactly, but he was dressed like a rich cowhand with the Garth black hat. Then, when he was getting money from our ATM, he started humming a Garth song."

"Are you sure?"

"No, but the clerk is. According to my officer, the clerk's a good old boy and looks like he really knows his Garth."

"Which song was it?" McKenna asked.

" 'I've Got Friends in Low Places.' You know it?"

"I've heard it, and I'm sure your clerk is right. I'm just beginning to understand that man must have friends in the lowest places imaginable. How about the Mesa store?"

"Not as good on the description. Clerk says that a cowboy came in and got a lot of money from the ATM. Aside from the fact that he was white and in his forties, she doesn't remember too much else about him."

"But it was just minutes ago," McKenna observed.

"I know, but those 7-Elevens are always busy and we've got a lot of cowboys or folks who'd like to be."

"Either clerk get anything on the vehicle he was in?"

"Ours did. The Garth getup grabbed his interest, so he naturally wanted to see what kind of pickup your man was driving. Watched him after he left the store, but no pickup. A four-by-four was parked at the end of the lot with the engine running. The cowboy got into the passenger seat and they took off."

"Did he get a look at the driver?"

"No, couldn't see him. They backed out of the spot and pulled straight out onto McDowell, headed toward Mesa."

"Anything better on the four-by-four?"

"Maybe a Cherokee, maybe a Blazer, white, big, kind of new, Arizona plates. Sounds like a lot of the cars around here. Folks like running around the desert in their four-by-fours and white's the best color to beat the heat."

"Then it wouldn't be a rental?"

"Not likely. Don't often see a four-by-four rental."

No rental car in New York, California, or Arizona? Can Black and White have cars in three places? McKenna wondered, but he didn't have time to dwell on it. "Does your department have an Artists Unit?"

"No, but the sheriff's got a deputy who's pretty good. When we need a sketch made, we ask permission to use her."

"The sheriff?"

"Yeah, Joe Arpaio, the Maricopa County sheriff and Lord High Mucky-muck around here."

McKenna had heard of Arpaio, a man who was becoming famous in law-enforcement circles for the tough way he managed his jails. However, McKenna hadn't known that Tempe was in Maricopa County. "Sounds like you're not a fan of his," he observed.

"I wouldn't go that far," Rausch replied. "Let's just say I like the way he does his job and leave it at that."

McKenna did. "Could you get Arpaio's artist to those 7-Elevens for me as soon as possible? I need a sketch while Garth is still fresh in those clerks' memories."

"Depends. I'm sure that Sheriff Joe wouldn't mind, but I'll have to go through channels and ask my captain first. He's nowhere near as accommodating as I am and I'll need a story for him, so I think it's time you tell me what's going on."

"Okay, here goes." After talking to Hurley, McKenna thought it unwise to mention anything about the snuff film theory until he had thought out the implications of going public with that. He told Rausch only about the six lovers lane sex murders over the years, sketching out the four in Fort Tryon Park and the two in San Jose. Rausch was sharp and not satisfied with the brief outline, so McKenna had to tell him how the killers happened to be in possession of Cindy Barrone's credit cards and her PIN numbers.

"How'd you work it so those cards are still good?" Rausch asked, still not satisfied.

"Connections," was all McKenna was willing to say.

"And how can you be sitting in a hotel in San Jose calling me five minutes after those cards are used and then tell me *where* they're being used?"

God, sometimes I hate sharp guys, McKenna thought. "Same connections is all I can say."

"Detective McKenna, I must say that you seem to be exceptionally well connected."

"Thank you."

"Just one more question before I can put your request through."

"Sure, go ahead," McKenna said, bracing himself.

"How is it that you can give us such a great physical description of these guys, but you need an artist for an idea on the white one's face?"

Sometimes I *really* hate sharp guys, and now is one of those times, McKenna thought. "We got the description of the black one from a witness who saw him use the cards in an ATM in New York. We have a sketch of him and a pretty good idea on how he looks."

"And the white one? Where did you get the physical description on him?"

How can I answer that without telling him that I saw photos of the guy close to naked, but that he just happened to be wearing a leather mask at the time? McKenna wondered, frantically searching his mind for something else that might satisfy Rausch. He came up with nothing, so he tried the old standard. "Got it from a confidential informant."

That didn't—couldn't—work with a guy like Rausch. "Oh yeah? So it's the old confidential informant, is it?"

"Yes, it is," McKenna answered, crossing Tempe off his list of places to visit maybe someday. He absolutely never wanted to look Rausch in the eye after that one.

But Rausch wasn't done with him. "And I suppose this observant confidential informant of yours only saw the white guy from behind?"

"Yes, that's it exactly."

"I see," Rausch said, chuckling a bit so that McKenna knew that he really did see. "I'll bring this artist request to the captain and give him your story. Matter of fact, I'll call him at home right now."

"Thank you. Think he'll buy it?"

"Probably. He's an arrogant bastard, but you got lucky."

"He's a dopey arrogant bastard?"

"Exactly. I'll be talking to you."

McKenna hung up, drained by his conversation with Rausch. He climbed back into bed and lay there with his eyes open. It had been a good day and he had learned a lot, but he didn't want to get caught short again with another sharpie like Rausch. The day's and night's events required some serious thought leading, he hoped, to a plan.

The good news was that Bynum was absolutely right. There were two of them and it was always easier to capture two people who committed crimes together than it was to capture one who kept his mouth shut.

But Hurley's premise had to be addressed. What value could be attached to photos and a video showing Cindy Barrone being tortured to death? Could they possibly be the most valuable photos and video in the world today?

After seeing the *Serious* and *In Charge* centerfolds, he was sure that snuff films existed, but why hadn't a single one ever been produced in a court of law anywhere in the world? Although making such a film would be against the law anywhere, the mere possession of one wouldn't be illegal in many countries. Of course, if such a film were to surface, the owner would at least be questioned closely by the authorities, his precious film would be confiscated as evidence of murder, and he would be publicly marked as the degenerate he was.

That had never happened because the snuff films weren't made to be sold to run-of-the-mill sadistic degenerates, McKenna concluded. To do so would subject the seller to a substantial risk of being charged with complicity in murder. Snuff films were made to be selectively sold to fabulously wealthy collectors who were only incidentally degenerates. McKenna thought them likely to be the same type of people who had stolen Renoirs hidden in a secret room behind the wall in their auxiliary wine cellars and was sure that they wouldn't risk showing their films to anyone else. Like the collectors of stolen art, the snuff films would be for their own private pleasure. They paid good money for them and told no one.

Then McKenna imagined the scenario in the case of the Cindy Barrone film. All of a sudden a new masterpiece is offered for sale on this highly selective market. What makes it a masterpiece isn't the quality of the film, although McKenna was sure it had been reasonably well made; nor is it the beauty and physical endowments of the victim, although Cindy had certainly been nice enough to look at before the film was made; nor is it even the especially sadistic type and duration of torture she had been forced to endure before she died. What made Black and White's film a masterpiece, possibly *the* masterpiece, was the identity of the victim and the widespread publicity, outcry, and public concern caused by her death.

It would also be remembered by any wealthy snuff film collector out there anywhere, McKenna figured. This man (or woman?) already has one or more snuff films, possibly even some made by Black and White, is rich enough and well traveled enough to have heard about the Cindy Barrone murder, and might even be astute enough to recognize her torture and death as a snuff film production. If so, he has already spoken to only one person about it, and that would be the intermediary who sold him his best film.

In any event, McKenna thought, the snuff film collectors' Mona Lisa will soon be on the market, and the bids were bound to be extreme. But have Black and White figured that out yet? he wondered. Have they figured out yet that they stand to make enough money to retire in luxury, obtain new identities, get plastic surgery, buy themselves an island somewhere, and make themselves more difficult to find than Joseph Mengele or Martin Borman?

Probably not, McKenna thought. Not yet, anyway, because if they had figured it out and knew how rich they were going to be, then why would they be subjecting themselves to even a minimal risk of capture by using Cindy Barrone's cards to steal amounts that should be chicken feed for men possessing that film?

So what do I do next? McKenna asked himself, realizing that if he was going to capture them, it had to be before they sold that film. He closed his eyes and reexamined all the conjectures and suppositions he had made to arrive at his interpretation of events.

The phone rang, breaking McKenna's concentration. "Your artist is on her way now," Rausch said.

"Thanks so much. When will I get the sketches?"

"Probably sometime tomorrow. She's got your number."

After hanging up, McKenna began searching for a plan. He came up with one after making a few more assumptions about Black and White. They were good and very careful, he reasoned, but they've been at their murderous business a long time, have probably had lots of practice, and yet they're still making mistakes—three of them that he knew about, so far. One big one was selling those photos to *Serious* and *In Charge*, one was letting Robert Harrison get into a position to cut Black, and the last was using Cindy's cards three times.

So they're good, but they're not perfect, McKenna decided. But were they always this good? Probably not, if they're like most professional crim-inals. They probably made lots of mistakes before they perfected their present routine, but they got away with them and that was a long time ago. I'm going to find those old mistakes, but where do I look?

Before he turned out the light and finally dozed off, McKenna knew that he would have to search far and wide for those mistakes. According to rumor, snuff films were made primarily in the Third World and the *Serious* and *In Charge* photos conformed with the rumor. He believed that the spectacular background vistas in the four photos weren't in the United States, but scenery that spectacular was bound to be recognized by some accomplished traveler.

There was a lot of work to be done and it would have to be done quickly, so McKenna planned to enlist the FBI's aid. Inquiries would have to be made with police agencies worldwide, and the FBI was in a better position to do that than was the NYPD. Bringing the FBI into the case wasn't a problem for McKenna since he had many connections in that agency, and one heavyweight in particular was a good friend of both his and Brunette's. Gene Shields headed up their New York office and had worked with them on a few big cases in the past. Once Shields was on board, the foreign aspects of the case would be done quickly and done right.

There was one more positive note, something that would give him a little more time, and he was grateful for the instinct that kept him from telling Rausch about the photos as he had fudged his way through the astute sergeant's questions. McKenna was certain that any publicity on the snuff film aspect of the case should be delayed as long as possible. Publicity or even informed speculation about the existence of the film would be bound to increase interest among collectors, raise the price, hasten the sale, and get Black and White quicker into the wind and out of reach.

SEVENTEEN

The sketch of White had come through the fax machine in McKenna's room and was his first order of business when he woke up. The trooper had drawn him wearing the cowboy hat, so McKenna could tell nothing about the man's hair. Worse, he thought there was nothing remarkable about the face—no moles, no mustache, no beard, no long sideburns, nothing that would make him stand out in a crowd. It was a face easily forgotten, and McKenna's optimism faded a bit.

Bynum showed up at nine o'clock wearing what McKenna had come to regard as California formal. In New York, suits were considered the uniform of the day for detectives, but every detective McKenna had met at the San Jose police station had been dressed as Bynum was, wearing cotton slacks, a nondescript sports coat, a no-iron shirt, and a preppie tie at half-mast. Still, McKenna considered Bynum's J.C. Penney look to be a vast improvement for him.

After McKenna relayed the night's events, Bynum was optimistic that the case was close to being solved. He didn't think much of the sketch of White, but it didn't dampen his optimism. "No rental car, so one of them must live in Arizona," Bynum stated. "After all, those two galoots can't have cars stashed in all three cities."

A galoot? The last time McKenna had heard anyone call anybody else a galoot was when he was a kid watching Roy Rogers on TV, but he liked the sound of it. "Maybe there's three galoots," McKenna countered.

"Three?" Bynum asked, smiling, but he said it in a skeptical tone of voice that put McKenna on the defensive.

"Sure," McKenna said. "Maybe the third galoot is their cameraman. Maybe they need three to carry all their equipment when they have their fun."

"You mean their camera, their video recorder, and the tripods? They wouldn't need three people just to carry that stuff. Two could do it easily."

So Bynum thinks they're making snuff films, too, McKenna realized. The fact that he had reached the same conclusion as the sharp San Jose detective made McKenna feel even more sure of himself. "Don't forget, they're shooting in low light, so they're probably also carrying light screens with them. I don't think the tarp alone gives them enough light."

"The tarp is a light screen?"

Bynum's implied question brightened McKenna's mood considerably. "Sure. You didn't know that?"

"No, but you're probably right. Now let me show you something that you didn't notice that might convince you that there's only two of them. Where's *In Charge?*"

McKenna hadn't wanted the maid stumbling across the magazines, so he had put them in his carry-on bag. He took *In Charge* out and handed it to Bynum.

Bynum opened it to the centerfold and gave it back to McKenna. "Take a good look and you'll see I'm right."

McKenna did, but he saw nothing of the kind. "What am I looking for?"

"Shadows."

Then McKenna saw it. The sun wasn't visible in the photo, but from the shadows cast by Black and White McKenna knew that it had been low in the sky, behind and to the right of the camera. Black and White both cast long shadows in front of them and angling to their left as they whipped the Asian man, but there was another shadow visible in the lower left corner of the photo. It was thin and rectangular and also slanted to the left. "The camera?" McKenna asked, pointing to the shadow.

"Close, but no cigar. The camera was mounted on a tripod at waist level when that shot was taken and it threw a shadow, but not long enough to be captured in the shot. Now take a look at this." Bynum took two photos from his pocket, glanced at them, and handed one to McKenna.

It was a picture of Bynum and Joe DePraida standing fifteen feet in front of the camera in DePraida's back yard. They cast shadows identical in length and at the same angle as the shadows of Black and White in the second *In Charge* photo. Also in Bynum's photo was a shadow in the lower left corner that was identical to the shadow in the *In Charge* photo.

"That photo was taken ten minutes after dawn and we used a timer to shoot it," Bynum said.

"And what's this?" McKenna asked, pointing to the mysterious shadow.

"That's the tip of the shadow cast by a video camera mounted on a tripod at chest level. It's two feet to the left of the still camera. Now take a look at this one," Bynum said as he handed McKenna the other photo.

Bynum's second photo was almost identical to the first. The only difference was a small shadow in the shape of a elongated semicircle on top of the video camera's shadow. "What's this?" McKenna asked.

"The shadow cast by the top of Rose DePraida's head as she stood behind the video camera. She was bent over, but the tip of her head is still caught in the photo."

"So there are only two of them, unless the third guy's a midget," McKenna admitted.

"Good thinking," Bynum said, patting McKenna on the back. "If there was a third standing behind either the camera or the video recorder, we'd have his shadow."

"You're the one doing the good thinking," McKenna said.

"Not that good, not all the time. You might find it hard to believe, but I looked at those magazines for two weeks before I saw that little shadow."

"Not hard to believe at all," McKenna said as he wondered how long it would have taken him to see the shadows. "Shadows are in every photo, but our minds are programmed not to see them. We focus on the action, not the shadows."

"Then maybe I'm not so dumb. It took me a while to figure out it was a video camera, and that's when I decided to take my own pictures with Rose and Joe."

"So now we're both certain about what we're dealing with here," McKenna said.

"That's right. What we're dealing with is two, and only two, murderous galoots who've been torturing and killing for years for fun and profit. We know that they're both probably AC/DC, that one might be from New York and the other's probably from San Jose, and we know that they like to travel a lot to make their films and take their pictures. In addition to all that, they have an eye for scenery and are pretty good photographers, all of which leads me to believe that we're going to get them soon."

"Because we know so much about them?"

"That's right. It's only a matter of time before we find out who they are."

McKenna hoped that Bynum was right, but he wasn't so sure. A lot more work would have to be done to put him in Bynum's state of mind.

The trip to San Francisco was a bust. No one fitting the description of the black killer had rented a car on Wednesday or Thursday at the airport rental agencies or anywhere else in town, but both Bynum and McKenna had expected that and it reinforced their belief that Black was originally from New York, White was from San Jose, and they had been using White's car while they were in town. They also agreed that the four-by-four in Arizona could mean that Black had moved and was living there.

"Are you going to Arizona?" Bynum asked McKenna on the way back from San Francisco.

"I don't think so. The Tempe police seem to be doing a pretty good job and I don't know what I could do there that would improve things."

"I'd like to go," Bynum said.

"Why?"

"Just because they're there."

Good point, McKenna thought, but didn't think Greve would be crazy about sending him to Arizona for that reason alone. They were there, or had been, but that fact alone wouldn't justify the expense of sending a detective on another trip.

McKenna's next phone call came as they crossed the San Jose city line and it changed his mind. "Detective McKenna, this is Lieutenant Eddie Taggart of the Maricopa County Sheriff's Department, Homicide Squad. I hope you don't mind my running up your phone bill." The drawl was slow and Western, bringing a picture in McKenna's mind of a tall, lean town marshal.

"Not at all, Lieutenant. What can I do for you?"

"What I can do for you is more like it. I heard about the ruckus you raised in Tempe and Mesa last night and I've got your VICAP request sitting in front of me."

"You've got an unsolved homicide with a .380 Colt Commander involved?"

"Got me a dandy."

"When?"

"Two years ago. January ninth, 1997."

"A lovers lane killing, two victims?"

"Might be, but can't say for sure. We've got one male victim found in the trunk of his car, shot dead in the head by the .380 Colt. The car had been pushed over the edge of a cliff on the Apache Trail near Superstition Mountain. We had some time getting down there and getting him out, had to use our helicopter and the car's still there."

"And the second victim?"

"Victim or suspect," Taggart said. "We know that his girlfriend was with him the night before we found the car and she's been missing ever since."

"Are there any lovers lanes located near the spot where the car was found?"

"Plenty of them, I imagine. It's pretty country."

"With high cliffs and great scenery?"

"I like it."

"Where is your office located?"

"We're in Phoenix, but that don't mean much. Maricopa County is about the same size as New Jersey, so I could be anywhere at any given time."

"What's the closest town to the place where the car was found?"

"Tortilla Flats."

"Tortilla Flats? I know there was a movie by that name, but there's really a town called Tortilla Flats?"

"It's not much of a town really, but it's been called Tortilla Flats as long as I can remember."

"And how far is that from Phoenix?" McKenna asked.

"About sixty miles southwest. The Apache Trail starts at Apache Junction."

"Southwest? So I'd have to go through Mesa and Tempe to get there?"

"If you're coming from California or the airport, you sure would. Why? You coming here?"

"I expect I am. Are you available the day after tomorrow?"

"Ah'm at your disposal. You have no idea how much that pesky murder and that girl's disappearance have been bothering me."

McKenna had to steal a glance at Bynum. "I believe I do. If it's the same killers, they've been bothering a lot of cops for a long time."

"Killers?"

"It's complicated and I'll explain when I get there. How about we shoot for eight o'clock Saturday morning at someplace in Tortilla Flats?"

"Fine. I'm sure we'll have a lot to talk about if you think it's *killers*. I'll meet you at the general store."

"Can you tell me how to get to the general store once I get into town?"

"The general store is the town. Not much to it."

"Then I should be able to find it. See you on Saturday."

McKenna relayed Taggart's information to Bynum and the rest of the trip passed in uncomfortable silence. McKenna knew that Bynum was waiting to be invited along on the trip to Arizona, but he didn't want to do that without getting Tommy's opinion first. Although McKenna liked them both, there was a competition developing between Tommy and Bynum and he was afraid that the two might not make good traveling companions on a long trip.

They got back to the hotel at four o'clock, later than he had expected. It had already been a long day and a long night of driving was in store. McKenna had to call Tommy, not only to tell him about the Arizona development, but also to find out what time his flight was arriving in San Diego the next morning. Sometime after ten would be better because Bynum wanted to leave at midnight for the drive down and McKenna had agreed.

"I need a favor before we leave tonight," McKenna said.

"The bullet used in my murders?" Bynum asked.

Sharp! McKenna thought for the umpteenth time. "Yeah, I'm going to need it for comparison in Arizona."

"I'm a civilian, so I can't get it, but I'll make a call. It'll be waiting for us at headquarters when we're ready to leave."

As soon as McKenna got up to his room, he called Tommy at home and brought him up to date. Tommy was happy to be going to Phoenix and he would bring the two bullets used in the four New York murders for comparison with the bullet in the Arizona murder. "Have you told Greve yet what's going on?" Tommy asked.

"He's my next call."

"Don't bother, I'll fill him in. I'll also tell him thay we may have those scumbags in the can before long."

"You're sounding very optimistic all of a sudden," McKenna observed.

"That's because I am mildly optimistic. If they did the Arizona killing, it's a large variation from their usual procedure," Tommy said. "We just have to find the spot where they killed them."

"I agree," McKenna said. "Something must have went wrong on them to make them vary their routine and they might've made a few mistakes."

"I've learned by now that they always make mistakes. We just have to be sharp enough to find them. See you tomorrow."

It didn't take McKenna long to learn that Greve had filled in Brunette. He had just finished eating his room service dinner when Brunette called. "I hear you're stirring up a hornet's nest quite well out there," Brunette said.

"I've had some very competent help."

"So I've been told, but I've got some bad news for you. We can't afford to have that Bynum character going with you two to Phoenix."

"No Randy?"

"Not on this one. I'm sure I'd love the guy, but your big case is quickly getting to be a humongous case. Think about how it would look to the press if they got wind of it, some retired small-town detective there to help out my own two best detectives. They'd have a ball with us."

McKenna did think about it and a caricature cartoon flashed into his mind. In it a little Randy was leading around the two big McKennas by the ropes through their noses. Both McKennas had buttons on their chests saying "New York's Finest" and Randy was pointing out to them magazines spread on the ground in front of them, each marked "Clue." It wasn't a pretty picture, but there was a problem. "He'll still want to come."

"But he won't, as long as you don't invite him."

"That's going to be awkward."

"I'm sorry, but that's the way it has to be. If it makes you feel any better, I'll make sure he gets plenty of credit at the appropriate time."

"When would that be?"

"When the headlines finally die down after my detectives catch those two. Then I'll fly him to New York, put him in a nice hotel, have a grand press conference, and give him a big medal."

"That would be nice, but it's still not fair now."

"I agree, but it's politics. I can't have Barrone thinking that there's even a remote possibility that there's anybody better than us right now or I'll have to put up with him troubleshooting us on a daily basis."

McKenna understood Brunette's reasoning and saw his predicament. "Okay, you're right. We leave Randy in San Diego, but we're still going to need some federal help on this."

"I've already spoken to Gene Shields and he's with us. He suggested we use his Behavioral Science Unit for a profile on your two killers and I agreed, so you'll be going down to Quantico as soon as you get back. He's also having his people go over all the old VICAP reports to pull anything even remotely similar to your case."

"Thanks. Anything else you can think of that I should be doing?" McKenna asked.

"No. Just keep digging, buddy."

EIGHTEEN

Bynum had called Ed Gallagher to let him know they were coming. According to the arrangement Bynum made with him, they would meet at Gallagher's home at noon.

Picking up the bullet at the San Jose police station was as easy as Bynum had said it would be, only because Bynum had arranged it. Ordinarily, subpoenas or court orders were required before one department would release its evidence to another department, but the San Jose PD settled for a promise from McKenna to ship the bullet back when he no longer needed it.

By 1:00 A.M. McKenna was following Bynum south on Interstate 5, possibly one of America's most boring highways. Randy was once again wearing his leather getup, but he didn't ride like an outlaw. The 70 mph speed limit was apparently also his personal limit and he never exceeded it. The road was wide, straight as an arrow, and everyone else on the road was doing eighty or better.

McKenna whiled away the time by counting the number of dirty looks he received from passing motorists and had reached ninety-three by the time they passed Los Angeles. Then his phone rang; it was Hurley. "An interesting situation has developed here, but I don't know how you'll take it," he said.

What now? McKenna thought. "Go ahead."

"My client has just instructed me to hire a Randy Bynum."

"To do what?"

"Whatever he likes, as long as he spends eight hours a day thinking about the case."

That was an interesting development, McKenna admitted to himself. "Then he'll have to cut down. He's already thinking about it at least twelve hours a day."

"That's too bad. I'm getting my cut on his salary for only eight hours a day. Do you think fifty an hour plus expenses will do it for him?"

McKenna quickly did the math. He knew that Hurley charged one hundred and fifty dollars an hour for investigative services, so that meant that he would be making eight hundred dollars a day profit on Bynum. "Not enough for a man of his talents. How about seventy-five an hour plus expenses?"

"Good God Almighty! I don't mind him grabbing a taste, but more than half? Don't forget, I've got payroll taxes and insurance to pay, not to mention sizable office expenses. Have a heart, will ya?"

"Okay, sixty," McKenna offered.

"Fine. Sixty it is," Hurley said quickly.

"Plus expenses."

"All right, plus expenses. Would you have him give me a call as soon as you can?"

"We're going to be busy for a while. Sometime tonight be all right with you?"

"Fine, but there's more. Hold onto your seat for this one. McMahon was wondering if having a snuff film featuring your two desperadoes would help you at all."

"Sure it would, but how would he go about getting one?"

"Through me, of course. I've got some connections with a few mobsters, so he's authorized me to make some discreet inquiries about obtaining one. Being a great guy, I told him that I'd only do it if my pal Brian approved the idea. Your approval would be unofficial, of course, and you never heard a thing about my efforts."

"How much is he willing to spend?"

"Whatever it costs, which teaches me one thing."

"You never want to piss off Arthur McMahon?" McKenna guessed.

"You've got that right. Do I have your approval?"

"Give me a couple of days to think about that one. We're picking up speed in this case. If we get a lucky break or two, I might be able to save him a bundle."

"Fine by me. Here's the last, another whopper. Cindy's funeral is a couple of hours from now and the press is gonna be there in force. Barrone's going to make a statement right after the funeral and the mayor is going to join him. It's my understanding that His Honor is going to authorize a hundred-thousand-dollar reward for information leading to the arrest and conviction of the killers. McMahon's gonna be at his own kid's funeral in Virginia today and he wants to up it another hundred-fifty thousand for a quarter mil total."

"Is he asking my approval on that?"

"More like your opinion, I'd say."

"Then get in touch with him and ask him to hold off. Hearing that there's a quarter-million-dollar reward for them would have to shake up these killers. I don't want them getting nervous and going to ground just when we might be getting close to them. I want them out there brazenly using those cards like there's nothing wrong."

"Whatever you say. I'll express your feeling to McMahon and try to save him some more money for now."

"Thanks. See ya."

McKenna found something disturbing in each item of Hurley's news. He was glad that Bynum was finally going to be getting paid for his efforts, but his starting work that day would be inconvenient for McKenna. He was afraid that Bynum might consider a trip to Arizona to be part of his new job, whether he was invited or not.

That would never do, McKenna decided, only because Brunette didn't want Randy in Arizona with them. It might come to that unless something underhanded was done, he realized, but he hoped it wouldn't because he thought that a man like Bynum should always be treated fairly.

His elation at the prospect of having a snuff film as evidence had also diminished substantially. If he needed an actual snuff film only to prove that they existed and that Black and White were the killers, he would be content to let McMahon buy one if that were the only way to do it. But it wasn't.

The more McKenna thought about it, McMahon spending a fortune on a snuff film served little purpose. Under the court rules and trial procedures currently in place in most U.S. states, the only film the prosecutor would be permitted to show to a jury would be at Black and White's trial for the murder of the victim killed in that film, and McKenna couldn't guarantee that he would be able to identify that specific victim or even the country in which he or she was tortured and killed. In New York, any attempt by the prosecution to show the film at Black and White's trial for the murders of Cindy Barrone and Arthur McMahon Jr. would be judged prejudicial by the court and denied—unless, of course, Hurley managed to somehow purchase the film of Cindy's murder and then persuade the judge that he had obtained it without police approval or complicity.

Both possibilities were remote, McKenna believed, but he had an even better reason to discourage McMahon from buying a film. If he were lucky enough to get Black and White soon, he felt that he would also get the very film he needed to convict them easily for the murders of Cindy

Barrone and Arthur McMahon—his case—and that would be the film of her murder. Better yet, he would get it for free because, if they didn't have it with them when he grabbed them, he would somehow get them to talk.

As for the rewards, he wished he had it in his power to dissuade the mayor from offering even the $100,000 reward. That reward was bound to make the killers more careful and McMahon's substantial addition to it would be sure to push them over the edge. They're travelers and they know their way around the world, so it's possible they'd run, McKenna believed, maybe run to a place where he couldn't get them.

Bynum and McKenna got to the San Diego Airport at eleven o'clock and went in to meet Tommy's flight. Walking out of the gate at eleven-thirty, Tommy greeted both men warmly and complimented Bynum profusely for his work on the case. To McKenna, it didn't appear as if there was the slightest hint of competition between the two, but he knew better. For years, each man had regarded the capture of the killers as his personal mission in life.

Tommy had only his carry-on bag, so they went straight to the car. Bynum knew the city and had an approximate idea of the location of Gallagher's house, so McKenna followed him. En route, Tommy studied the photos in the two magazines. Only minutes later Tommy was once again complimenting Bynum's ingenuity and powers of observation, and Bynum wasn't even there to hear it.

McKenna could easily see that it wasn't an act; the best homicide detective in the city of New York was genuinely impressed with his small-city rival. "I've got a little problem coming up with your hero," McKenna said. "He hasn't said so yet, but I'm sure he's expecting to be invited to Arizona with us."

"Then he should be invited," Tommy said.

"Ray doesn't want him there."

"Then he shouldn't be invited."

Tommy apparently thought that was that, but McKenna felt compelled to explain the situation. He told Tommy about the publicity angle Brunette feared, and then he told him about Hurley's offer.

"I understand Ray's concerns and I see your problem," Tommy said. "You think that once Randy's on Hurley's payroll, he'll see it as his obligation to go to Arizona?"

"That's right, whether he's invited or not."

"Then I see no way out but to play a dirty trick on our pal. I take it we're gonna stay here in town tonight?"

"Yeah, we've got to get some rest and it's a drive to Arizona. I figure we should get a hotel room and leave around midnight."

"Fine, that's late enough. Just before we go, give Hurley's number to Randy and tell him to call in the morning," Tommy suggested. "Tell him you don't know what it's all about, but you think Hurley's got some kind of job in mind for him."

"That really *is* playing filthy," McKenna observed.

"You see another way?"

"Can't say I do."

"Then listen to your uncle Tommy, kid."

Bynum's "approximate idea" of where Gallagher lived turned out to be fairly exact. He led the way to the large, stately, obviously expensive house on the water overlooking Coronado Island, making only one wrong turn along the way. It was a minor mistake, quickly remedied by a U-turn after traveling two blocks in the wrong direction.

It was apparent that Gallagher was a man who liked the good life. The lawn was deep green and lush, the shrubbery and flowers lining both sides of the circular driveway appeared to be professionally maintained, one of the doors of the three-car garage was open to reveal his cherry-red Jaguar XKE roadster parked inside, and there was a thirty-foot sailboat tied to the dock in back of the house.

McKenna was impressed, but not Tommy. "Smut must be paying pretty good these days," was his only comment. He put the magazines back in the plain brown wrapper and took them with him when they got out of the car.

Gallagher was at the door to greet Bynum as he got off his bike. He was a tall man, about six foot four, well built, bearded, and his long hair was tied in a ponytail. He was younger than McKenna had expected, maybe thirty-five, and he had a way of making casually dressed appear to be impeccably groomed. He looked happy to see Bynum, but McKenna suspected that Gallagher always looked happy and he could see why. Owing to the lifestyle he had established for himself, Gallagher could be a man without a problem in the world.

During the introductions McKenna noticed Gallagher's New York accent. "How long have you been out here, Ed?"

"Almost twelve years. My brother moved here before me, so I visited him and found nothing not to like about the place. A little boring at times, but I liked being bored here. Gives me time to focus on clean, healthy living."

Gallagher said it without a hint of sarcasm in his disarming, friendly manner, leading McKenna to believe that Gallagher had come to terms with the paradox he was living. He seemed to be a nice guy in a filthy business.

Unfortunately, Tommy wasn't content to let it rest there. "Considering the business you're in, I'd be interested to know how you stay focused on clean living."

McKenna winced, but Gallagher didn't seem to mind the question. "I get asked that all the time. C'mon in and I'll explain it to you."

They followed Gallagher inside and down a wide hallway to a spacious sitting room in the rear of the house. It was a comfortable sanctuary with a small wet bar on one wall, two enormous leather couches, and a spectacular view of the harbor through French doors that led to a deck and the pier. Family photos framed in silver were arranged on a long table on the wall opposite the wet bar.

"Can I offer anyone something to drink?" Gallagher asked.

All declined, so Gallagher took a seat on the couch and everyone followed suit. "It's like this," he said. "I was very happy in my job as a deputy sheriff here, but then my brother drowned in a diving accident in Cozumel. Left a wife and three kids, had only a small insurance policy because everything he had was invested in an adult book store he'd bought. It had been doing fairly well, but after he died it started going downhill. His wife was desperate, so she asked me to go partners with her and run it. The way I saw it, I had no choice."

"Did you know anything about the business?" Tommy asked.

"Not a thing. I had never even been in the place, but I had to learn quick. Found it's just like any other business. Find out what sells, try and get it at a cheap price, charge what you can, treat your customers nice, be fair with your employees, and pay your taxes. Anything that's left over is ours."

"I take it your business is doing fairly well now," Tommy said, pointedly looking around the room.

"It's doing great. We've got three stores now, so we can buy in volume at a discount. My sister-in-law's happy and well taken care of, and my nieces can all go to Ivy League schools, if they'd like."

"So it's worked out, as far as you're concerned," McKenna said.

"I guess. Mind you, it's not the kind of business I ever pictured myself going into because I've always thought of myself as a bit of a prude. If I only had myself to think about, I would've preferred to stay in law enforcement. However, I've managed to make this business work out better for everyone."

"Are you still a prude?" Tommy asked.

"I guess I am, in just about everything. I've had the same wonderful lady for seven years and wouldn't think about cheating on her. I drive at the speed limit, I don't cheat on my taxes, and to tell you the truth, half the time I don't know what the people are doing in the pictures in those books we sell. Whatever it is, it's sure not my idea of fun."

The more Gallagher talked, the more McKenna liked him, but apparently Tommy was slower to form an opinion. "Then tell me, what is fun?" Tommy asked. "Sneaking around Tijuana to sell degenerates some torture books with that secret agent routine of yours?"

"That's right. I guess I'm no damn good after all because I sure do enjoy it," Gallagher admitted, shaking his head and smiling to himself.

"Pretty profitable fun, too. Probably all tax free, I imagine," Tommy said.

"There's a profit to be made, I'll admit, but it gives me a problem. You see, Mexico's a strange place in some ways. Prostitution's legal there, but pornography isn't, so I can't declare the profits in Mexico and pay the taxes there. Uncle Sam winds up being the winner."

That was too much for Tommy. "Wait a minute!" he insisted. "Are you trying to tell me that you pay U.S. taxes you don't have to pay on cash money, just because you can't pay them in Mexico?"

"I'll show you my tax returns right now, if you like," Gallagher answered calmly. "There's a profit, pure and simple, and profits should be taxed. I'm sure the IRS doesn't know what to make of it, but last year I listed over thirty-two thousand dollars under 'other income.' Paid the taxes and they cashed the check, no questions asked."

Even with the offer on proof, Tommy still looked dubious. But not McKenna. Gallagher had information they needed and McKenna was ready to believe anything the man told them. "Okay, it's not the money," he said. "What's the fun in running the degenerates all over Tijuana before you overcharge them for the magazines they want?"

"Simple. I personally detest anyone who likes reading that torture-and-degradation stuff, but in my stores business dictates that I smile at them and treat them nice. No matter, the people who come into my stores aren't the worst degenerates. I sell the widely available trash there, so the worst of them are doing their shopping on the Internet. That's where the so-called good stuff is peddled, and that's where I find them. Find them, get some laughs running them all over Tijuana, and then I sit down with them and enormously overcharge them with a straight face. Makes me feel good inside, and you know what?"

"They always go for it," McKenna guessed.

"That's right, they almost always do. All the hocus-pocus convinces them I've got something really hot and illicit. If they have enough money to be able to come to Tijuana for the stuff in the first place, making them work for it clinches the sale."

"I'd have to agree with that," Bynum said. "I've read all sorts of stuff in the Internet chat rooms about going to Tijuana for the good stuff."

"I didn't know it at the time, but as it turns out in your case, you really did get the good stuff they're all looking for," Gallagher added.

"You didn't know it?" Tommy asked skeptically. Then he took the magazines from the wrapper, opened them to the centerfold, and spread them on the floor in front of him. "Couldn't you see that the people in these pictures are really terrified and in pain?"

"I thought it was possible, but I couldn't be sure. When I first got into this business, I was routinely fooled by photographers using good actors, good makeup, and good special effects. Cost me a sale one time when a Tijuana customer got pissed after I showed him what I had to offer. He told me the pictures were fakes, showed me the tricks that were used to make them, and told me how it was done."

"So all you can sell at your really high Tijuana prices are pictures of real pain and suffering, or stuff that looks like it is," McKenna said.

"That right. I've sold lots of good fakes to happy degenerates, but I'm sure that I've also sold them the stuff they really wanted. I guess stuff like that," Gallagher said, pointing to the magazines. "However, I never suspected there was murder involved."

"Don't they look scared enough and aren't they obviously in pain?" Tommy asked.

"Sure, but for enough money you can hire models to torture while you take your pictures. I've been in this business long enough to guess that there's models and actors out there who would probably enjoy it. Probably happens all the time."

"But you don't see it all the time?" McKenna asked.

"No, I don't. I'm a legitimate porn dealer."

"Why don't you tell us what that is, exactly," Tommy said.

"Sure. In addition to books and videos, I sell what we call adult toys and marital aids, all of which is legal. As far as staying legal when it comes to books and videos, that means no sex with children, no sex with animals, and no sex with dead people. Stretching the rules a bit, S and M bondage and torture is all right, as long as it's just pain they're simulating or showing in the pictures. But anything that would cause scars or permanent injury is definitely out for a legitimate dealer."

"But we know there are illegitimate dealers, and for them there are no rules," McKenna said. "For them, trading in snuff films and photos is good business."

"I guess it is, but before this I wasn't sure that snuff films existed. Like everybody else, I heard rumors about them, but they're something that wouldn't come a legitimate dealer's way."

"There's no shady legitimate dealers?" Tommy asked.

"There's some willing to stretch the rules, but certainly no one I know would risk everything by getting involved in something like that. Why would a guy like me who's doing pretty good already take a chance on blowing it all for one score? Forget legitimate porn dealers, what you're looking for is a well-connected guy in the shadows."

"And you don't know anyone like that?" Tommy asked.

"Honestly, no I don't."

"What about the guy you bought these from?" Tommy asked, pointing once again to the magazines.

"I don't really know him. Saw him twice at trade shows and met him once, but I don't know him. But I'm not sure he's the guy you should be looking for if it's snuff films you want."

"Why not?"

"Because he's probably a peripheral character selling a peripheral product. Snuff films would be big-money items made for the tastes of a very selective market. I think those magazines you've got are just a form of advertising."

McKenna got it, and he thought Tommy had as well, but both felt better to hear Bynum ask, "What do you mean, advertising?"

"Simple. The people who make those films can't advertise in the open market, so I think that their customers know that whatever's coming on line is advertised in the centerfolds of those two magazines, and maybe a few others. Since the customers' tastes probably vary widely when it comes to the victims, the torturers, and the methods used, they get a couple of sample preview scenes in the magazines. Whoever distributes those films does what the Hollywood studios do when they advertise movies."

"Teaser shots?"

"I think that's the term used. They put them in the theater lobbies wherever their film's playing or due to play. The photos in those magazines are like the coming attractions photos."

"And how do the customers get these magazines?" Randy asked.

"I imagine they're probably delivered to them directly by the people who market the movies. When the customer sees something he likes, he contacts the dealer, gathers together a bundle of cash, and orders it."

"Then how is it that you were able to get your hands on them?" Randy asked.

"Because I'm not a customer-in-the-know and I sell it to the same kind of people. We don't recognize it for what it is, but there's still a substantial profit to be made by just distributing a limited number of copies. Selling to us through their peripheral dealers probably offsets the advertising and production expenses."

"Then we still want to meet the guy who sold them to you," McKenna said. "If we don't get lucky soon, we'll squeeze him and he'll lead us to the main dealer. Squeeze that guy even harder, and maybe we get Black and White."

"Fine. What do you want me to do?" Gallagher asked.

"First of all, how well do you remember his face?" Tommy asked.

"Perfectly. I was with him for more than a half hour while we did business."

"Then you're going to help me make a sketch of him. Next, is there any way we can get into those trade shows?"

"You have to be a legitimate dealer and a member of whatever organization is sponsoring the show, but I can fix that. On paper, I'll make you one of my managers and sponsor you."

"Is it that easy?"

"Not exactly. If you go to a show, you have to appear legitimate or you'd be exposed in a minute. That wouldn't look good for me."

"So what do I do?" Tommy asked.

"You probably wouldn't believe it, but there's a lot to know about in this business. If you could spend a couple of days with me at one of my stores, I could probably teach you enough to pass a cursory inspection."

Tommy looked aghast at that prospect and very sorry that he had been the one to bring it up. But he had a way out. "It's your case, partner," he said to McKenna. "I guess you're the one slated to become the smut expert."

"I agree. I should be the one to do it, except for one thing."

"What's that?"

"You remember our pal Ray, our supreme commander, the guy we hate to disappoint?"

"Yeah, what about him?"

"Well, he's busy lining up federal help on this case as we speak. He's got Gene Shields on board and Gene has suggested that I get down to their Behavioral Science Unit in Quantico as soon as I get back. It's a political thing, so how would it look for Ray if I tried postponing so I could hang around in San Diego and learn about smut?"

Tommy knew he was had, but he wasn't prepared to go easy. McKenna watched as Tommy searched his mind for a way out, so he thought it was time to throw in the clincher. "Especially since my partner, who's been involved in this case much longer than me, is already right here in San Diego anyway."

Tommy was beat. "Okay, it's me. I'll run it by Greve, but not another word about this to another living soul. Agreed?"

"Agreed."

"Boss, is it all right with you if I start Monday?" Tommy asked Gallagher.

"Monday will be fine."

"Glad that's out of the way," McKenna said. "Now let's talk about the people who may be buying these films. You hear any rumors on that?"

"I hear lots of them," Gallagher answered. "According to the rumors, it's Saudis, nouveau riche Russians, this sultan or that, but one name that keeps cropping up is Chou Son Yee. Makes sense since he's reputed to be the largest mass purchaser of hard-core pornography in history."

"Chou Son Yee? Who's that?"

"One of the world's most powerful criminals. He controls the Golden Triangle in parts of Thailand, Laos, and Burma and is responsible for growing and exporting most of the heroin sold in this country. One of the last real warlords left in the world today, runs his territory like a feudal fiefdom."

When McKenna had been in the Marine Corps in Vietnam, he had spent five days in Thailand on R and R. He hadn't heard of Chou Son Yee, but knew the name didn't sound Thai. "Isn't Chou Son Yee a Chinese name?" he asked.

"Sure is, and he's got a Chinese history. During the Chinese civil war, his father was the commander of one of the nationalist Kuomintang divisions fighting in the south. After Chiang lost and evacuated to Taiwan, Chou's father's division was stranded along the Thai border and in big trouble. He wasn't a nice guy and the commies wanted him bad, so he took his division across the border and set up there. Made a fortune growing poppies and processing heroin, and Chou took over when the old man died."

"Doesn't it bother the Thais to have a foreign army running part of their country?" McKenna asked.

"Maybe, but there's not too much they're willing or able to do about it. The hill people who live where the Kuomintang division took over were always a troublesome bunch for the government. Bandits and revolutionaries, mostly, and Chou keeps them in line and low-profile. He also pays plenty of taxes to Bangkok, although our government contends it's mostly in the form of tribute and bribes. Since his men are well trained and well armed, and since he's developed a form of export income for the country, the Thais are content to leave him alone."

"Even though he's a national embarrassment?"

"That's right, but you have to understand the Thai nature. They're a very proud and a very polite people who've developed a way of dealing with embarrassments. They simply pretend that Chou Son Yee doesn't exist."

"I see," McKenna said, although he really didn't see at all. "Where does his mass purchases of porn fit into all this?"

"He buys most of it for his men, and over the years they've become real connoisseurs. They're a well-paid bunch of rogues, but Chou doesn't let them travel much to have fun spending their money. They're Chinese and don't consider the local women to be especially attractive, but they're not alone in that. The Thais don't think the hill people look too good, either."

"So they're happy with pornography?"

"For the most part, and it's probably built into their culture by now. But Chou's smart and he does provide a release valve every once in a while, sends his men in small groups on supervised jaunts to Bangkok. They come back from there ready and willing to do whatever he says for the chance to go again."

"And the snuff films? Would he would show them to his men if he had them?"

"Maybe, but I doubt it. I think he buys them for his exclusive use and enjoyment. He can't afford to leave his kingdom without risking capture, but a little about him has filtered out. It's said that he's one of the cruelest and most sadistic bastards the world's ever produced. Sex and torture are the same thing for him."

"How do you know so much about him?" Tommy asked.

"Have you ever been to Bangkok?"

"No."

"Well, I have. They have lots of trade shows there and I went to one, once. That's where the snuff film rumors were strongest and that's where I first heard about Chou. Anyone in this business who hangs around Bangkok long enough will hear about him and his tastes, so often that after a while the rumors begin to sound credible. If there are snuff films, then Bangkok is certainly one of the places where they'd be sold."

"Is it that bad a place?" Tommy asked.

"Over the past ten years it's developed into the sex and sin capital of the world. Tourism's growing by leaps and bounds and seventy percent of the people who go there are on sex junkets."

McKenna didn't think it was the appropriate moment to volunteer to the two prudes that he had been there. It had been long ago and he was afraid they might not understand.

———

With Gallagher's help, Tommy spent half an hour drawing the sketch of the "peripheral" dealer and then another half hour perfecting it until Gallagher could say with absolute certainty that the sketch was the man.

"What are your plans now, if you don't mind my asking?" Gallagher said when Tommy was finally satisfied.

McKenna didn't want to say that he and Tommy were going to Phoenix while Bynum was going back to San Jose.

Tommy didn't want to answer it either, so he just looked to McKenna. Unfortunately, so did Bynum and he seemed to be particularly interested in hearing the answer.

How do I sidestep this? McKenna asked himself. "We've all been up all night and we've all got a lot more driving to do, so we're gonna get some hotel rooms and get some sleep." Then he turned to Tommy and Bynum. "You guys ready to roll?"

They both took the cue and held a discussion on hotels when they got outside. Bynum suggested the Holiday Inn, so once again it was the McKennas following Bynum on his bike. "What a nice guy that Ed Gallagher is," Tommy said as soon as he got into the car.

"If he's such a nice guy, why did you just spend an hour breaking his balls?" McKenna wanted to know.

"Habit, I guess."

McKenna was exhausted, but Tommy and Bynum both said they felt fine. They went to the hotel's restaurant for lunch while McKenna went up to his room to get some sleep. He woke up at 11:00 P.M., showered and dressed, and then called Tommy's room. There was no answer, so he tried Bynum's. Again no answer, so he went downstairs and found them together at the bar having a beer. Bynum had changed from his leather look into one of his no-wrinkle, no-iron sports-coat-and-pants combos he must have had stuffed into his saddlebags.

"You guys get any sleep?" McKenna asked.

"Plenty," Bynum answered for both. "Are you finally ready to eat?"

"I'm starving."

"That's good, because I'm hungry myself."

"The restaurant here okay?" McKenna asked.

"It was fine for lunch."

Tommy ordered just soup and a salad, but both Bynum and McKenna ordered full-course dinners, causing McKenna to wonder if Bynum had a tapeworm.

"By the way, I told Randy that he's not coming to Arizona with us," Tommy said after they had ordered.

"Did you tell him why?" McKenna asked.

"Couldn't help myself. Had to let him know that he doesn't dress well enough to hang out with the big guys."

"You didn't really tell him that, did you?"

It was Bynum who answered. "I promised to improve, but he says I'm a hopeless case. He explained to me that he had his pride, told me that he wouldn't even walk around Brooklyn with me the way I dress."

McKenna didn't know what to say as he looked at Tommy in disbelief.

Tommy just shrugged. "Somebody had to tell him."

McKenna didn't want to see Bynum's reaction to that, but then he glimpsed a hint of a smile on Bynum's face. It was then he knew that he'd been had by experts. "What did you really tell him?" he asked Tommy.

Bynum answered. "He told me that you guys would love to have me along, but that your boss didn't want me there."

"And?"

"And what? I understand. No reason you two or your department should have to put up with any negative publicity over me being there. After all, you've got a job to do and I'm just a civilian now."

"Thanks for taking this so nicely, but we don't think of you as 'just a civilian.' Whatever happens, we sure wouldn't have gotten this far without you," McKenna said.

"Nice of you to say so."

"While we're all being so nice to each other, I need another favor from you."

"Anything."

"I know you paid good money for them, but I need your magazines."

"You've already got them," Bynum said.

"I mean to keep."

"You've already got them."

McKenna spent the next half hour smiling, but he was feeling miserable as he ate and made small talk with Bynum and Tommy. He wanted to tell Bynum about Hurley's job offer right then, but something Bynum had said prevented him from doing it. Bynum understood that he wasn't going because it wasn't his job to go. But what would he do if it was his job? McKenna wondered. He didn't know, so he reluctantly decided that the dirty trick would still have to be played in order to keep Brunette happy.

McKenna and Tommy were ready to head out after dinner, but Bynum decided that since his room was paid for, he would sleep the night there and ride back to San Jose in the morning. He went out to the parking lot with McKenna and Tommy to see them off, and then it was time. "By the

way, I think I've got a pretty good job for you, if you're interested," Mc-
Kenna told Bynum.

"Really? Sure I'm interested."

"I told a PI friend in New York about you and he wants to hire you."

"To do what?"

"He was kind of vague, but from what I gather he wants to pay you to
just think."

"That is kind of vague," Bynum observed.

"Yeah, but he's a real character. It's late now and even later in New
York, so why don't you give him a call in the morning?"

"Will do. Give me his number."

McKenna did, and he felt worse than he had in a long time as he and
Tommy pulled away, leaving Bynum in the parking lot scratching his head.
He couldn't get it out of his mind as he drove. Tommy let him stew in
silence until McKenna felt he had to say something. "What a nice guy that
Randy is," he said, more to himself than to Tommy. Then he realized his
mistake and hoped that Tommy hadn't heard.

Tommy had. "If he's such a nice guy, why'd you have to break his balls
like that?" he asked.

Touché.

NINETEEN

Tommy took over the driving at a rest stop at the Arizona border, but
McKenna was reluctant to give him the wheel. Although it was a bright,
moonlit night, he had been driving for hours across the California high
desert without enjoying much in the way of scenery and he saw that the
character of the landscape was about to change to something more interesting. The skyline on the Arizona side of the Colorado River was punc-
tured by craggy mountains dotted with saguaro cactus. Although he had
never been to Arizona before, he recognized the tall, fork-shaped cactus
as the background in many Westerns and knew that the only place they
grew in the U.S. was in Arizona and along the California bank of the Colorado River.

Tommy had a heavy foot, so it wasn't long before they met their first
state government representative, an Arizona highway patrolman. In most

places in the country when a person is stopped by the police, he or she is either treated to a lecture or given a summons, rarely both. Apparently it was to be a lecture, so Tommy gave the big, tough-looking, polite-in-a-cranky-kind-of-way cop his license and he saw no reason to further identify himself as he smiled and nodded his way through the lecture, learning along the way that they were in Arizona now, not loosely run California where people generally did whatever they felt like doing, and that Arizona was the kind of place where decent folks lived with restraint and obeyed the law.

"Yes, officer, you're right," Tommy said as he prepared to get his license back and be on his way. "We've heard that Arizona's a wonderful place, always wanted to come here, and we couldn't wait to get out of California."

Then the unexpected happened. The cop turned and walked back to his car with Tommy's license still in his hand. Tommy immediately feared the worst, believing that Arizona was running a two-for-one sale for folks driving cars with California plates, a rare special that entitled them to both the lecture and the ticket. Tommy got out of the car and went back to speak to the highway patrolman with his shield held high in his hand.

McKenna turned in his seat and watched as Tommy handed the cop his shield. The cop didn't look happy with it, but then a five-minute conversation ensued and both of them returned to the car, back-slapping and hand-shaking, the best of friends. As Tommy got back in the car, the cop bent over, gave McKenna a friendly wave, and asked, "You boys sure you got everything you need?"

McKenna was sure he had, but Tommy had a question. "Just one more bit of information, Roy. How long do you think it'll take us to get to Tortilla Flats?"

"If you step on it, you might be able to make it there by dawn."

"Well, I'm willing to give it a try."

"Go for it. Don't forget to say hello to Big Ed for me."

"Don't worry. I'll be sure to let him know that you're thinking of him," Tommy said as he pulled away. He brought it up to eighty and kept it there.

"You gonna tell me what happened back there?" McKenna asked. "It looked like things weren't going too well, and then you come back to the car with your long-lost cousin."

"Yeah, old Roy's a nice fella. However, I do have to admit that he wasn't too impressed with my shield and place of residence, at first."

"He wasn't? What did he say?"

"You want his exact words?"

"Please."

"What he said, exactly, was, 'Oh no, not another foreign cop. Why do I always get them?' "

"Foreign cop?"

"New York," Tommy explained. "I don't think we're the best-liked folks in the country."

"I see. And then?"

"Then I told him that we were on our way to see Lieutenant Eddie Taggart. That changed everything."

"That would be 'Big Ed'?"

"The very same, monster of a man. According to Roy, he must be more than six foot six and built like Tarzan."

McKenna wasn't surprised. Taggart was just how he had pictured him, only bigger. "I take it that old Roy really likes Big Ed?"

"Yep. Big Ed's real well thought of in these parts, him and his daughter."

"What about his daughter?"

"According to Roy, she's the prettiest little thing you've ever seen. Great cook, too, and real friendly-like. Roy says that Ed will probably invite us to dinner tonight to show off Peggy's cooking."

"Really?"

"I think it's worth a shot," Tommy said. "You had to hear Roy talk about her apple-rhubarb pie."

Although McKenna had never had a slice of apple-rhubarb pie in his life, for some reason he couldn't get it off his mind as they headed east.

The Apache Trail was a winding, tortuous road—narrow, poorly paved, hugging the side of a large, craggy mountain on the right with a sheer drop on the left. The going was slow, but since it was the only road to Tortilla Flats, getting there didn't cause the McKennas much of a problem. Tortilla Flats wasn't even a wide spot on the road on the one-lane mountain road. They were driving east into the blinding desert sun and had expected to see a sign that told them they were ENTERING TORTILLA FLATS, but instead the first sign they saw told them that they were LEAVING TORTILLA FLATS. Tommy did a U-turn and drove back a quarter mile to the only building they had seen in a while.

"How'd you miss that?" McKenna asked, pointing to the sign that on the front of the building that read TORTILLA FLATS TRADING POST AND GENERAL STORE.

"I don't know, but why don't you tell me something?" Tommy asked, pointing to the shaded front porch of the general store. "How'd you miss that?"

McKenna took one look and knew there was only one answer. "I dunno. Blind, I guess," he said, for there was Randy Bynum, sitting in a chair next to another man on the front porch. Both had their chairs propped back against the wall of the general store and their feet on the porch rail, and this time it wasn't Randy the Biker in his leather getup or Randy the Cop in his wash-and-wear costume. This time it was Randy the Cowboy. Bynum was dressed just like the man sitting next to him, wearing hand-stitched brown cowboy boots, faded jeans, a wide leather belt, a white two-pocket work shirt, and an old straw cowboy hat. Both had a bottle of Coke in their hands and they gave the impression that they were old friends.

The worn cowboy outfit reinforced McKenna's belief that Bynum had expected to be invited along on the Arizona trip since he had stuffed the clothes in his saddlebags in San Jose, along with the wash-and-wear sports coat and pants he had worn in San Diego.

Bynum gave them a smiling nod and a friendly wave, but that only increased the guilt they both felt. They stood outside at the porch steps, not knowing what to say.

The man with Bynum stood up. He had a large revolver in a holster on his belt. "Why don't you fellas come up and get outta the heat?" he asked. "We got a case of cold Cokes setting here waiting for you."

The heat *was* intense, maybe ninety degrees and it was still early, so the offer sounded great to McKenna, but he was confused and so was Tommy. "If that's Big Ed, we've been had good by Roy Forlino," Tommy whispered.

"Consider it your speeding fine," McKenna whispered back, but he had other thoughts on the subject. If the man with Bynum was Big Ed, then McKenna was certain that his daughter was the homeliest woman in the state. He was also sure that he never wanted to be even in the same room with her apple-rhubarb pie, a pie that was probably famous throughout Arizona for its vile taste and smell. Bynum's pal was no more than five foot eight, and although he was muscular enough for a man in his fifties, he had a large gut and was certainly no Tarzan.

"Hi. You must be Big Ed. Heard a lot about you," Tommy said.

"That's me," Big Ed said as the McKennas climbed onto the porch. "Who's been talking to you about me?"

"We happened to run into Roy Forlino," Tommy said.

"Old Roy? How'd you run into him?"

"By spoiling his fun. He thought he'd hit the jackpot last night, stopped a speeding car with California plates and then finds the driver with a New York license. Turned out to be just us."

"Oh yeah, you sure spoiled old Roy's fun all right. That was a trophy combo all in one car stop," Big Ed agreed. "Speaking of fun, old Randy here was just telling me about the joke you two played on him last night. That 'Call that PI fella in New York in the morning' business was a real hoot. We've been chuckling over that one for the past hour."

"Yeah, it was a regular side-splitter," McKenna said.

"Yeah, sorry it didn't work out. I'm the one to blame," Bynum said. "You guys forgive me?"

That was an unexpected development. "You want us to forgive you?" McKenna asked.

"That's right," Bynum said. He got up and placed one hand on Mc-Kenna's shoulder and the other on Tommy's. "You forgive me and I'll forgive you. Is that a deal?"

"That's a deal," Tommy said.

"You've got my vote, too, but what exactly are we forgiving you for?" McKenna asked.

"For being here, of course. I know you were ordered to leave me in San Diego and I would have stayed there last night and went home this morning if it wasn't for my new job. I hope you understand, but this is where my case is right now. I don't want you gentlemen mad at me, but I'd be remiss in my duty if I wasn't here."

"We know you and we knew you'd see it like that," McKenna said. "I guess you called Hurley last night?"

"Yep, about ten minutes after you left."

"How'd you know to do that?"

"I've seen a lot of guilty people in my time and knew you both had something on your minds when you pulled out. That really got me thinking, so I gave him a call."

"And you flew here?"

"Why not? It took me a while, but I finally got Mr. Hurley to agree to pay my expenses as well as my salary."

McKenna knew Hurley and immediately smelled a rat. "You work out a good salary with him?"

"I'd say so."

McKenna and Tommy waited for more, but Bynum wasn't offering.

Now how would Hurley have handled this so I wouldn't find out right away? McKenna wondered. "I guess it's over scale, more than he usually pays his investigators?" he tried.

"Considerably more."

"And he wouldn't want word getting back to them, so he's sending you a contract with a nondisclosure clause?"

"That's right. I can't tell anyone how much I'm being paid."

"Including us?"

"Mr. Hurley did mention that you both know most of the retired cops who work for him," Bynum said, hedging.

"We know them all, but we won't give them the number," Tommy said. "We could both retire tomorrow and we're just interested in what the current market is for investigators with our skills. We've heard that he usually gives his people twenty-five an hour to start."

"You're right," Bynum said. "At first he offered me twenty-five to do nothing more than think about the case. That was money for nothing as far as I was concerned, so I told him I couldn't do it. But I did tell him that I'd actually work the case for a little more and he agreed."

"How much more?" McKenna asked, afraid of the answer.

"It took a little haggling, but your friend Mr. Hurley is a very generous man. I got him up to forty an hour to do stuff I would've done for free," Bynum said proudly.

"Yeah, old Bob's the salt of the earth," McKenna said, and left it at that for the moment.

Tommy couldn't. "Yeah, he's a real spendthrift," he added. "I'll be sure to thank him for you when I see old generous Bob again."

"I'd appreciate that. Let him know that he'll get his money's worth with me."

"More than his money's worth, even," Tommy said. "I'll be sure to tell him that as soon as I can find him."

McKenna knew Tommy and recognized the anger under his calm exterior, but he didn't expect Bynum to see it.

He was wrong. "I guess Mr. Hurley is another guy who's playing a little joke on me?" Bynum said.

"That's a nice way of putting it."

"There's a nicer way, and it's probably true," McKenna added. "I know Hurley and it's not the money. He would've given you the full number, eventually. The joke's on us, just his way of telling us that he's in charge when it comes to setting his salaries."

"What *is* the number, if you know?" Bynum asked.

"Sixty plus expenses," McKenna said.

Big Ed whistled and said, "That's a hunk of change. From what I can see, you New York fellas are all a bunch of pranksters."

"Yeah, we're a riot," McKenna said. "I'm sure it's more comfortable inside, so let's go in, have a Coke or two, and get started on this case."

"We can if you want, but it's more comfortable out here," Big Ed advised. "Old Carl keeps that place like a freezer in there, air conditioner humming all the time."

"Really? How cold is it in there?" McKenna asked.

"Must be eighty. Much too cold for people around here," Big Ed said seriously.

McKenna and Tommy just stared at him, unbelieving, but Big Ed couldn't keep it up. He broke into a wide grin, opened the store's door, and said, "You fellas are good, but you're minor league around here. Until satellite TV came along, folks didn't have much to do for fun except torment each other with some of the craziest pranks you could imagine. Let's get in before we all melt out here like lard in a skillet."

Just what I needed, McKenna thought. Another one. It's gonna be a long, hot day.

TWENTY

The large, comfortable, air-conditioned room in the rear of the general store served as one of the many informal offices Big Ed borrowed around his district. He had brought with him the bulky case folders on the murder of Greg Norman and the disappearance of Glenda Anderson. It took him more than an hour to explain the work done in those investigations, and to illustrate his points as he spoke, the pertinent reports from the case folders were passed around the room. By the time he was done, Bynum and the McKennas had a fair idea of the way things worked in Arizona and how Big Ed operated.

For the past ten years Big Ed had been in charge of the Homicide Squad. He had eight detectives working for him, so none of the reports had been prepared by him. His job was to supervise the investigations, not work them.

Big Ed's presentation and the reports told McKenna that the rural lawman's easygoing manner and country charm disguised the fact that Big Ed was dedicated to his job and he knew the business of murder—he was experienced, highly trained, well read, extremely knowledgeable about the latest scientific detection and identification techniques, and he had taken a very active role in the two cases.

Attached to the top of most of the reports that had been submitted to Big Ed was a handwritten note. Some of these Big Ed had written to himself and contained his thoughts about the information stated in the report. They told McKenna that Big Ed was organized, intelligent, and perceptive. Other notes attached to the reports detailed the instructions Big Ed had given the detective who had prepared it or they listed Big Ed's comments concerning the quality of the work documented in the report.

The notes made it clear to McKenna that Big Ed was a demanding supervisor who didn't tolerate lack of initiative or sloppy police work from his detectives.

The cases had commenced on the morning of January 9, 1997, when Glenda Anderson's mother reported to the Mesa PD that her eighteen-year-old daughter hadn't returned home the previous evening. She had forbidden her daughter to go out that night, but found that Glenda had slipped out anyway sometime before 8:00 P.M.

The police weren't surprised. They knew Glenda as a girl who had frequently been in minor trouble over the years for truancy, shoplifting, fighting, and possession of marijuana. As a result, when she was sixteen she had been expelled from the local school and placed by the courts in a reform school. After a year there, she had been released under the supervision of the Department of Probation and she had reenrolled in Mesa Regional High School.

Glenda had done well there for a year. According to her probation officer, she was a pretty girl with an angelic face who looked young for her age. She had a tendency to respond with aggression to any taunts about her young looks, but she was struggling to keep these violent impulses under control. After returning to school, she had maintained a B average in her junior year and had also joined the track team and the volleyball team. She had excelled at both sports, and according to her probation officer, she had been hoping to get an athletic scholarship to attend college after she graduated from high school.

Then came the summer of 1996 and Glenda's troubles with the law had resumed after she got off probation and started going out with Greg Norman, another character well known to the Mesa PD.

Greg was twenty years old, a high school dropout but an excellent auto mechanic. He had been employed in his brother's service station and was a good worker who had loved his job, never missing a day unless he had been prevented from going to work because of his other interest in life— Greg Norman loved stealing cars, usually four-wheel-drive vehicles which he used to carouse around the desert. Unfortunately for Greg, while he was good at stealing cars, he wasn't an expert at keeping them. He was a wild driver who was frequently stopped for some traffic infraction or other while he was enjoying the capabilities of his new stolen car. As a result, before he had started dating Glenda he had already spent a three-month and an eight-month stint as a guest at the Maricopa County jail.

There was neither coddling nor amenities at Sheriff Joe's place. Greg had been assigned a bunk in a Gulf War army surplus tent in Tent City, a place where there was no coffee, no smoking permitted, no weight room, no recreation program, no conjugal visits, no pornography, no movies, and only one hot meal a day. What Sheriff Joe's jail did offer was 120 degrees Fahrenheit in the summer, close to freezing temperatures at night in the winter, sandwiches and Kool-Aid twice a day, and an opportunity to clean the county's parks and roads while closely shackled to four other prisoners under guard on a chain gang. Rewards for good behavior consisted simply of permission to watch either CNN or the Disney Channel on TV for one hour an evening.

Sheriff Joe's hospitality program wasn't much appreciated by Greg. In fact, he hated the place and had been heard to state many times that he would never go back there, but that didn't mean that Greg had changed his ways.

In August of 1996 Glenda and Greg had been arrested together in a Mesa shopping center for breach of the peace and simple assault after they had become involved in a dispute with each other which turned violent. They had been heard arguing loudly over the choice of movie they were going to attend that night and there was a definite winner and a definite loser in the resultant physical confrontation. Surprisingly, the winner was Glenda.

During the struggle, Greg had knocked out one of her lower teeth and had bruised her left ear, but when the fight was finally halted by two mall security officers, Glenda was on top of Greg. His shoulder had been dislocated and she had already blackened his eye and broken his nose by that time. She had obviously also intended to cauliflower his ears and ruin him for other women as she was still punching both ears when she was finally pulled off Greg by the security officers, who also suffered some minor injuries in the process.

When the police had arrived, both were arrested and taken to the hospital. Glenda had been treated and released, but Greg had spent two days there under guard. Each had charged the other with assault and the cross-complaint was processed through the courts, along with the breach of the peace charge and the assault charges made by the security guards. They had both pleaded not guilty and told the judge that they had made up and wanted to drop the charges they had made against each other.

The judge noted their previous arrests and didn't buy it. Their trial had been scheduled for January 12, 1997. Neither of them made it.

The Mesa detective assigned to investigate Glenda's disappearance visited Greg's brother's gas station and was told that Greg had not reported for work and wasn't home. His brother used the occasion of the detective's visit to file an additional missing persons report with the Mesa PD, but it wasn't taken seriously. The investigating detective noted the upcoming trial in his second report and stated it was likely that the couple had fled to avoid their likely prison sentences. He recommended on January 11th that the missing persons cases be marked closed, pending further developments.

His boss hadn't bought it. After Glenda and Greg failed to appear in court for their trial, he sent the detective to their residences to see if substantial amounts of their clothing were missing. As far as Glenda's mother and Greg's brother could tell, most of their clothes were still there, along with their suitcases. In addition, $240 was found in one of Greg's dresser drawers, and wrapped with the money was a receipt the detective found curious. Greg had purchased a half-carat diamond engagement ring from a Mesa pawn shop for $500 on January 8. Both missing persons cases were left open.

On January 13th a man piloting his small private plane reported seeing a car upside down in dense underbrush in a ravine at the bottom of a cliff off the Apache Trail. A sheriff's unit was dispatched to investigate, but the deputy couldn't get down the steep cliff to examine the car. A sheriff's helicopter was sent, landed near the car, and found that it was a 1985 4x4 American Motors Eagle sedan that had been reported stolen from the long-term parking lot at Sky Harbor International Airport. It had been left at the airport by its owner on January 8, but he had returned to Phoenix to discover and report the loss only that morning.

The roof of the car was smashed as a result of the drop off the Apache Trail, 200 feet above, and all the windows were shattered. Their noses told the cops that something dead was in the trunk, so they popped the lock and the body of a young, fully clothed, white male spilled out. He had been shot once in the side of the head and his face was battered. The Homicide Squad was notified and Big Ed arrived by helicopter with his crime scene technician and two detectives.

Big Ed estimated that Greg had been dead for approximately three days. He guessed that the facial battering had occurred postmortem, prob-ably as a result of the ride in the trunk down the cliff face. In addition to murder, he also classified the case as a robbery since Greg's wallet was missing.

There was much blood on the front seat of the car and in the trunk and samples were taken from both places for analysis. Thirty-six separate latent fingerprints were lifted from the interior and exterior of the car, but no further evidence was uncovered.

That afternoon Big Ed himself identified eight of those latent prints as belonging to Glenda Anderson. As a matter of procedure, he issued an all points bulletin for her apprehension, but he feared that she was also dead or the victim of a kidnapping. Dead was more likely, he thought, so he ordered that a search be conducted for her body in the Superstition Mountain area.

The way Big Ed saw it, Greg had stolen the car on the night of January 8 and had picked up Glenda at a prearranged location with a proposition in mind. Big Ed had figured there were two possible scenarios that could have developed after that, depending on where it was that Greg had proposed marriage after offering the ring he had bought that day.

Big Ed had thought the first possible scenario to be remote, but it still had to be investigated and the results examined before it could be discarded. In it, Greg takes Glenda parking somewhere on or near Superstition Mountain to enjoy a little romancing before their impending trial and incarceration. Once there, he offers her the ring and proposes. She rejects his offer, one of their violent arguments ensues, and Glenda kills Greg. She then put his body in the trunk, drives a few miles and pushes the car off the cliff, and then somehow makes it out of the area since she was facing time there anyway.

After two days of investigation by his detectives, Big Ed completely discarded the Glenda-kills-Greg theory. During that time his people had questioned every resident living in or close to Tortilla Flats. That process took two men less than three hours and no one had seen Greg, Glenda, the stolen car, or anything else on the night of January 8 that they considered suspicious or out of the ordinary.

So it was the second possible scenario, the one where Greg proposes to Glenda and she accepts. Then they go to Superstition Mountain to celebrate their engagement with some final romancing before their impending incarceration. There, tragedy overtakes them.

Big Ed figured that they had been ambushed by two killers who had sneaked up on the car while Greg and Glenda were really enjoying each other's company. They had shot Greg right away, and then they had done whatever to Glenda. After they were finished with her, they had either killed her or they had taken her with them for future enjoyment.

The location where Greg's stolen car had been found was the reason Big Ed was certain that there had been two killers. The Apache Trail winds along Superstition Mountain at that point, hugging the side for miles in either direction with a steep wall of rock on one side and a sheer drop on the other. There was no place to park, and certainly nothing within a few miles that could be considered a lovers lane.

So, Big Ed reasoned, after they had killed Greg and finished with Glenda at the lovers lane, they must have put Greg's body in the trunk of his stolen car and driven together to wherever they had their own car. Then one killer had followed the other to the spot on the Apache Trail where they had pushed the car off the cliff and they had made their escape in their own car. Maybe Glenda had still been with them at the time, but Big Ed figured it more likely that she had also been murdered and left on the mountain.

The search of Superstition Mountain proved to be a difficult task. Even though the terrain on the mountain area and anywhere near it is rugged, as a result of the Lost Dutchman Mine legend it is crisscrossed by paths and deeply rutted roads made by both amateur and professional prospectors who have been searching for the gold bonanza for a hundred years. After two weeks the entire mountain had been searched using dogs, police reservists, and over one hundred members of the sheriff's posse, and Big Ed was sure of two things: Glenda's body had not been left in the open and there was no Lost Dutchman Mine.

But Big Ed still hadn't been satisfied. If Glenda was on the mountain, the last remaining possibility was that the killers had thrown her body off a cliff whose base was inaccessible to the volunteers who had searched on foot. Big Ed had used the highway patrol's helicopters for two days before he was able to discount that possibility. If Glenda hadn't killed Greg and escaped, he was forced to conclude that the killers had taken her with them and killed her in another jurisdiction. Those two remote possibilities, the only ones left to him, mandated that thousands more investigative hours would be spent by Big Ed and his men on the case.

Meanwhile, the autopsy and laboratory analysis of the blood samples proved Big Ed right in both guesses he had made at the spot where the car was found. Greg Norman had been dead for three or four days when his body had been discovered, meaning that he had been murdered on either January 8 or 9. The battering Greg's face had endured had been incurred postmortem, probably as a result of the wild ride in the trunk. The autopsy disclosed that death had been caused by a single .380 caliber bullet to the head. A ballistic examination of the bullet had revealed that it had been fired from a Colt Commander and the laboratory report on the analysis of the blood samples taken from the car confirmed that it was all Greg Norman's.

Over the next two years Big Ed had his detectives investigate the finding of any unidentified female remains found anywhere in Arizona and the surrounding states. None turned out to be Glenda.

Big Ed figured that he was dealing with serial killers, so he sent one of his people to every conference on serial killers held anywhere in the West. They had at times returned with similar cases from other jurisdictions and Big Ed had examined them all. Not the same men, he had concluded, sometimes after conducting a lengthy investigation of his own.

On the chance that Glenda was alive and in hiding after killing Greg, Big Ed periodically had her mother and all her friends reinterviewed. Negative results, always. No one had heard from her.

Big Ed had also entered the case into the VICAP program, but the form only permitted him to list the known facts, not his suspicions. What it came down to was that the body of one male, a person with a criminal record, was found in a stolen car in a deserted rural area; the subject had been killed with a single bullet to the head fired from a .380 Colt Commander; there were two killers and the subject's girlfriend was missing, but her body had not been discovered.

End of report, but the FBI computer spit out five murders that had significant similarities to Big Ed's case. The basis for the match in most of them was the .380 Colt Commander and two suspected killers, so Big Ed spent hundreds of additional investigative hours before determining that the cases the FBI sent him didn't match his after all.

In desperation, Big Ed ended up asking that he be notified any time a VICAP request was made in a case in which a .380 Colt Commander was the murder weapon. The FBI complied and Big Ed continued wasting countless hours examining those cases.

So that request is the only reason we're sitting here, McKenna thought as Big Ed wrapped up his presentation. Tommy's first case was long before the VICAP program started and I can see quite a few reasons why Randy's case didn't pop up. He had originally thought that he was looking for a single killer in a torture double-murder case. The only thing that matches is the .380 Colt Commander, but there might even be another reason Big Ed didn't find out about the San Jose case. "When did your department get into the VICAP program?" he asked Bynum.

"About a year after my killings. 1992."

So that's it, McKenna thought. But I still don't understand why Big Ed's so obsessed with getting these killers. McKenna decided that he had to ask. "Big Ed, mind telling us what there is about these cases that had you so worked up for the past couple of years?"

"You think I'm crazy, don't you?"

"Not yet, but you're getting there."

"Unfortunately, by now my captain thinks I've already arrived. Spent well over a million dollars of our taxpayers' money to get nowhere," Big Ed admitted.

"So what is it? The victims?"

"Yeah, it's the victims. Once I got deep into this case, I found myself really liking them. Thought they might have been able to make something out of themselves."

Big Ed's statement had aroused Tommy's interest, if he wasn't interested already. "I can see liking them. Hell, I've locked up lots of people I've wound up liking, some of them even for murder," he said. "But these two kids were headed for the can. Hard to make something out of yourself after that."

"Maybe, but I think maybe they both needed another year with our sheriff to set them straight. They weren't real bad kids, just wild with a touch of larceny. But they never hurt nobody but each other and both were real polite when we got them the last time, gave nobody no trouble once they were finally in custody. I gave them a chance because they both came from good, hard-working stock, had people home who love them and want to set them straight. Let me tell you something about Greg you might find hard to believe."

McKenna noticed that Big Ed had everybody's attention. Tommy and Bynum were both leaning forward in their chairs, straining to hear every word.

"Greg worked like a dog at his brother's gas station. Made some money, but never enough to buy the four-by-fours he loved driving around the desert. Not a real bright kid, but a real good mechanic anyway. So he borrowed cars, usually without the owner's permission, which was bad. But he always got them started without causing lots of damage by breaking the steering column like every other mope out there does. Then he'd have his fun for a couple of days. If he wasn't caught, he'd leave it close to where he found it. Never a part missing, always washed and vacuumed, and always with a full tank of gas."

Big Ed's account was met by three unbelieving stares. None of the 'foreign cops' were ready to indicate that they were ready to fall for some rural lawman's wild yarns and then be laughed out of town.

Big Ed didn't seem to notice. "I'll go you one better," he said. "One time he put a ding on the fender of one of the cars he stole and he left it with $100 in an envelope in the glove box. Now, tell me. Do you fellas have any car thieves like Greg back where you come from?"

"No, we don't," all said simply, not sure whether or not the proper response should be: "Of course we don't, and neither do you."

"You don't have to believe me," Big Ed said, not fazed a bit by the response he was getting. "Ask any cop in Phoenix, Mesa, or Tempe. Whenever a four-by-four turned up missing, first person that came to mind was Greg. Of course, he wouldn't be around just then to answer their questions, but if it was found parked in what they've come to call 'Greg shape,' they'd know that they were right. Of course, they'd ask Greg about it first thing and he'd deny everything with a smile, but they knew. Word among those

cops used to be, 'If your four-by-four is dirty and you don't feel like clean-
ing it, run it low on gas and leave it in front of Greg's house. If you're
lucky and living right, maybe he'll steal it for a couple of days.' "

With one exchanged look, the McKennas and Bynum made a mutual,
silent agreement to do just that. The first Mesa, Tempe, or Phoenix cop
they ran into was in for some close questioning.

"Now that Glenda, she was another story," Big Ed said. "She'd had
her share of problems, but she was basically a good kid. Except for being
dirt poor, she had it all. Pretty, smart, tough as nails, and good at everything
she tried. Kind of tiny, but a real natural athlete and not afraid to give.
Her neighbors all loved her and she was always running errands for them
and doing this or that for those that needed it. Unfortunately for her, in
addition to all the good things she had, she also had Greg. A real love-hate
thing, but the general feeling around here is that they would've made a
good go of it once they got out of jail. If they didn't kill each other first
along the way, that is. Because of that, the other general feeling around
here is that whoever killed those kids has to pay, no matter how long it
takes and no matter what it costs."

They all paused to think about the two young people Ed Taggart had
brought to life in his description. Ed broke the silence."Let's get back to
work. You fellas now know almost as much as I do about this case. So tell
me, do you think we're all looking for the same killers?"

"Can't be certain, yet," McKenna said. "It depends on two things. First
is, Do you think it's possible that your ballistics people missed something
when they examined the bullet that killed Greg?"

"They might've. Most of our ballistics people are good, but I can't
vouch for all of them. What is it you think they could've missed?"

"Traces of paper burned into the sides of the bullet. The killers don't
want to leave us a spent cartridge casing as evidence, so they fire through
a brown paper bag. If you don't think you've got at least one exceptional
ballistics expert here, we've got one I can show it to."

"Would that be Brady Wilson?" Big Ed asked.

"Yeah, it is. How'd you know?" McKenna asked, shocked that the rural
Arizona lawman would know the name of the NYPD's leading ballistics
expert. At the same time, he hoped Big Ed didn't catch the surprised look
on his face and feel insulted by it.

Big Ed did catch it, but rather than feel insulted, he decided to have
some fun. "It's a well-known fact that us country folk aren't much on reading, but every once in a while the Pony Express rider screws up and drops
off a magazine at my humble sod shack. Once he dropped off the *American
Forensic Journal* and later on it was the FBI's 1998 *Advancements in Scientific Procedural Techniques Annual Update Report*. Took me forever, but

I was able to get through them and happened to notice that Brady Wilson had contributed an article to each of them. Did you happen to catch them?"

"Probably, but I can't say for sure," McKenna said with a straight face. "Do you happen to recall what Brady was writing about in those articles?"

"Now you're going to make me put a whole passel of hard words together, but as it so happens, I do recall. One had to do with calibrating changes in the refractive index at low temperatures in order to properly judge the trajectory of bullets fired through windshield safety glass and the other had to do with new measures being used by your Ballistics Section to analyze bullets fired by smooth-bore homemade guns."

"Oh yeah, I read those. They were pretty good," McKenna said as he promised himself that he would never ask Big Ed another question. It was time to change the subject. "The other thing that will tell us whether or not we're dealing with the same killers is the location where the murders took place. You haven't found it yet, but I'm going to tell you what it looks like and maybe you'll be able to show us where it is. Ready to give it a try?"

"*Maybe* show you? I was born and raised in these parts and been working here most of my life," Big Ed said proudly. "If your description is accurate and if the place is within a hundred miles of where we're sitting, I don't deserve this job if I can't take you straight there."

Wow! This description of mine better be detailed and it better be accurate, McKenna thought. "There will be a seldom-used road that leads there, but the road will have to be good enough to drive on. It will probably end at the spot and it will be high up, on top of a cliff, and the view will be magnificent. This place will be a lovers lane known only to a limited number of locals. There will be a tree near the edge of the cliff where the killers can tie their victim while they torture him or her, but they have a problem with sunlight since they're photographing and videotaping the whole thing. They need natural sidelighting, so the view must be either north or south of the tree, never east or west because then the sun would interfere with their photography. They wait in ambush, so there has to be a spot within a few miles where they can hide their own car so that the victims don't see it as they approach the spot. Take some time and tell us if the spot I just described rings any bells."

"I don't need any time. It doesn't," Big Ed stated at once. "We've got trees in ravines and along dry creek beds, but they usually don't grow at altitude in these mountains. It's hot and dry here most all the year and the soil high up is either rock or sand."

McKenna was crestfallen, and he could see that Tommy and Bynum were feeling the same.

"Does it have to be a tree?" Big Ed asked after a minute.

"I guess so. I mean, it always has been."

"How about something as big as a tree, but not a tree?"

McKenna got it at once. "You mean a saguaro cactus?"

"Yeah, that's what I mean. Could it be a saguaro cactus those filthy, murdering perverts tied Glenda to?"

"Yes, it could be."

"We'll be going there in about half an hour," Big Ed said, sounding absolutely sure of himself.

"Why not now?" Tommy asked.

"I figured that we'd be doing a lot of talking today, and after that we'd be covering a lot or territory. I didn't want to waste a lot of time, so I arranged for one of our helicopters to pick us up at noon."

That was bad news for McKenna. He enjoyed flying, but only in planes. Two near-fatal crashes in helicopters in the past years had completely removed the thrill of riding in them. He felt a knot start to form in his stomach.

"In the meantime, I'm done talking," Big Ed said. "It's somebody else's turn, and when I leave here I want to know why those kids are dead. More than that, I want to know exactly what those filthy, murdering perverts did to Glenda."

"There's quite a bit to tell," McKenna said. "We know what they are, but we don't yet know who they are. Eventually we will, and then they'll have to pay. I can promise you that."

TWENTY-ONE

The helicopter arrived on schedule and landed in the small parking lot across the road from the general store, but there was a problem. McKenna knew that the NYPD had the same type of four-seat helicopter in its older inventory; it was in such a machine that he had suffered through one of his near-fatal crashes. The other was that there were five of them, counting the pilot. McKenna wouldn't have minded staying behind.

It was easily resolved. "Ain't room for but four in that machine, so give me the keys and take a break," Big Ed told the pilot. "Got some cold Cokes left in the back room."

"Sure, Big Ed." The pilot handed Big Ed the keys, but then had a question that tightened the knot in McKenna's stomach. "You remember how to fly that rickety old thing?"

"I think so. It's like riding a bicycle, isn't it?"

"Somewhat, I guess," the pilot conceded. "Though you can fall a little harder in that thing."

McKenna had already resolved not to ask Big Ed any more questions, so the task fell to Tommy as the four men walked to the helicopter. "Guess you use helicopters quite a bit," he said.

"Often enough. Our department's got vast distances to cover, so we've got a great helicopter pilot training course. Send one of my people to it every couple of years, so I've got me three good pilots."

That made McKenna feel a little better, but only for a moment. "Matter of fact, been meaning for some time to get to that course myself," Big Ed said as he climbed into the pilot's seat.

Tommy and Bynum got into the backseat and strapped themselves in while McKenna stood outside thinking and watching Big Ed through the front passenger window. The lieutenant seemed to know what he was doing as he peered at some gauges, flicked some switches, and finally started the machine up. With the rotor blades stirring up the sand around him, McKenna made his decision. He climbed into the passenger seat next to Big Ed and fastened his seat belt tight.

Big Ed pushed the stick down and the engine revved up, but nothing else happened. He reacted by leaning over and placing his hands under the seat, searching for something.

"What's the matter?" McKenna asked.

"I dunno. Seen this done hundreds of times and the machine always goes up," Big Ed said as he continued searching without finding what he was looking for. "Do me a favor, would ya? Take a look in the glove box and see if the instruction manual for this thing's hiding out in there."

In a terror-stricken trance, McKenna did as he was told, frantically rummaging through the many papers, maps, and maintenance logs. No instruction manual, so he closed the glove box.

"Not in there?" Big Ed asked, sounding concerned.

"No. Now what?"

"I don't know, but I've got an idea. Let's see what happens when we do this and this at the same time." Big Ed did something with the stick and something with his feet and the helicopter took off, rising at a steep angle as it rapidly accelerated forward.

When McKenna's stomach finally dropped from his throat and returned to its proper place, he happened to notice from the corner of his eye that Big Ed was smiling at him and having a grand old time. It was then that McKenna knew he'd been had once again—Big Ed was an excellent pilot. "Didn't you say you've never been to that training course?"

"Haven't been, but I always wanted to go just to see how good it is. Trouble is, Sheriff Joe sees no need to send me."

"Because you already learned to fly this thing just by watching?" McKenna asked.

Big Ed got another laugh out of that question. "Not exactly."

"Then how?"

"I was a helicopter pilot in the army, flew two tours in 'Nam. Now I'm in the Air Force Reserve over at Luke Air Force Base, CO of the Eleventh Rescue Squadron."

McKenna sat back and tried relaxing, but it was difficult. He had every confidence in Big Ed, but saw no reason to be flying along less than two hundred feet from the ground at more than a hundred miles an hour. Worse, McKenna felt that he was losing his orientation since they were flying away from the big mountain he had assumed was Superstition Mountain and they were heading toward the desert.

Big Ed noticed McKenna's discomfort. "Don't worry, I'll be grabbing some more sky in another minute," he said. "The side of the mountain behind us is all part of Tonto National Forest, not where we're going. There's no vehicles permitted on that side."

"Not even helicopters?"

"No, but not for the reason you think. This side of the mountain is under the approach lanes for both Scottsdale and Sky Harbor airports. Got to stay low and make a wide U-turn around the mountain to the side we're headed for or I'll be risking getting flack from some overcautious, wise-ass pilot."

McKenna searched the skies overhead and found that, this time at least, Big Ed had been on the level. A commercial aircraft was headed their way from the south, but the big plane was going to pass thousands of feet above them and a mile behind them.

Once Big Ed had completed his low, wide circle around the mountain, he started the helicopter in a gradual climb and McKenna finally was able to relax a bit, watching the desert pass rapidly below them as they closed on the mountain. It appeared to be steep, craggy, and forbidding, rising sharply from some small foothills on the desert floor. From a distance, there was very little vegetation visible on the mountain itself, and certainly no trees. However, as they got closer McKenna could make out a saguaro cactus here and there, most of them growing near the base or on top of the mountain's many minor promontories.

Big Ed was flying a straight course toward the mountain and apparently knew exactly where he was going. "That's the Apache Trail, the part of it you didn't get to see on your way into Tortilla Flats," he said, pointing down and to his right.

McKenna looked down and saw the one-lane road snaking along the side of the mountain, but it wasn't paved on this side of Tortilla Flats. Far below the road was a dry creek bed, but the trees and bushes crowding its banks told McKenna that it wasn't always dry. They were over the foothills by then and he also saw that this side of the mountain wasn't as forbidding as it had appeared at first, at least not to those owning a dirt bike, an ATV, or a good four-wheel-drive vehicle. From high in the air, he counted four such vehicles. They were miles apart, running along four of the many winding, torturous dirt paths now visible in the foothills and even on the mountain.

Big Ed slowed the forward motion of the helicopter as he started descending, and after a minute McKenna saw where he was heading. One of the winding dirt paths ended at a cliff about halfway up the mountain. The path in spots was fairly wide and even wider at the ledge, wide enough to permit a careful U-turn close to the massive, solitary saguaro cactus perched at the top of the cliff at the path's end. There was another spot on the path just as wide, about a hundred yards from the end, and there also the mountain pitched steeply downward at the edge of the path. There were three saguaro cacti growing here, but they were much smaller than the massive one at the end. In places all along the side of the path the soil was sandy enough to also permit the existence of the sagebrush and other small desert plants growing there.

"That look like the killing spot to you fellas?" Big Ed asked, pointing down at the end of the path.

"The exact place," McKenna answered. Both Tommy and Randy agreed.

"I thought so. If it is, let me show you where the perverts hid their car while they watched and waited," Big Ed said. He banked the machine sharply to the left and followed the path down for a mile to a spot where it forked with another. The second path turned left toward the mountain and it disappeared between two high rock formations.

Big Ed hovered over the fork in the road. "That's where they hid their vehicle while they watched and waited," he said, pointing forward to the slit between the two rock formations. "You can't tell from up here, but the road from the Apache Trail up to this point isn't too good. Got to have a four-wheel-drive to get here."

"Not inconvenient for them because they've got one," Tommy said from the back. "Let's get back to the spot, put her down, and we'll take a look."

Big Ed acknowledged Tommy's suggestion with another steep, banking turn and he followed the path back up until he was over the wide spot before the end. He descended straight down, kicking up sand as he gently landed the machine among the three cacti at the edge of the cliff. As soon as he turned it off, all got out and started walking quickly up the path toward the end.

McKenna felt excited, but maybe not as excited as Bynum. Bynum broke into a trot and pulled ahead. So did McKenna, and it developed into a race. Bynum was certainly fast for a man his age, but no match for the younger McKenna, a man who ran at least two marathons a year. They were both headed for the cactus and McKenna got there first, skidding to a stop at the top of the cliff. He would have liked to stand there and enjoy the spectacular view of the desert below, but there was something else he had to see first.

It was there, but the saguaro was scarred in only one spot, a light gouge on the cliff side of the cactus, about two feet up. He had expected another gouge higher up, a mark left from the chain the killers used to tie Glenda to the cactus at her neck, but it wasn't there.

Bynum arrived, slightly winded, but he was oblivious to physical discomfort as he also examined the cliff side of the cactus, running his hand along its prickly sides at the place where the neck-chain marks should have been. He pulled a few spines from his hand as he stood there, looking at the cactus and thinking.

"She got away from them," McKenna stated. "Somehow, when they were tying her arms to the cactus with the chain and the handcuffs, she got away. That's why there's only one scar, and it's not very deep."

"You mean, they didn't get a chance to whip her?"

"Not here," McKenna said. He pressed his finger into the cactus at a spot between some spines and left a small indentation in it. "If they had whipped her while she was tied here, she would have been struggling like mad and the chain behind her would have left a much deeper gouge than this one."

Big Ed and Tommy arrived. Tommy was breathing normally, but Big Ed's extra weight had him huffing a bit. As they examined the cactus, McKenna explained to them what he thought had happened.

"So how'd she get away and what happened to her then?" Big Ed asked.

"I don't know how she did it, but the answer's here somewhere. They left something here that they don't want anyone to see. That accounts for the break in their procedure, why they went to the trouble of getting Greg and his car out of here and dumping it off the Apache Trail miles from this spot. They didn't want us to find out where they had killed him."

"So you think they left something here because they didn't leave his body here?" Big Ed asked.

"It's the only thing that makes sense to me. It's something that would help us identify them or give us a clue as to what they're up to."

"And Glenda?"

Because of the way Big Ed asked it, for some reason McKenna didn't feel comfortable telling him the rest. He ran his tongue around his lips, but by then Tommy had figured it out and he was tougher. "Glenda's dead, of course," he said. "She's fast and she took off down the road as soon as she broke free. They chased her, but they couldn't catch her. Otherwise, they would have just brought her back here and continued with their fun. In that case, we'd have our two marks."

"So what happened?" Big Ed asked, then he answered his own question. "They saw they couldn't catch her, so they shot her while they were running after her."

"Right," Tommy said.

"So what did they do with her body?"

"Either buried it close by or took it with them, I guess," Tommy said.

"They didn't bury it around here," Big Ed countered. "I had the dogs up here a few times and they would've found her if they did."

"And they didn't take her with them, either," McKenna added. "Why should they when they could have just as easily dumped her in the trunk with Greg? Then it would've been just a double-homicide for you, two people shot on the mountain, but nothing to give us an indication of where or what they were up to."

"So what happened to her?" Big Ed asked again.

"I don't know yet."

"Maybe they threw her off the cliff," Bynum said, peering over the edge.

"No, that's not it," McKenna insisted. "If they threw her over the edge, sooner or later her body would be found and it would lead us right back to this spot. Like I said, they wouldn't have wanted that, went to some trouble to prevent it."

Bynum didn't appear to be listening. He continued peering over the edge, squinting, and then he got down on his belly with his head over the edge of the cliff.

He had everyone's total attention and all crowded the edge. McKenna saw nothing but the desert and foothills far below.

"Mind telling us what you're looking at?" McKenna asked as he bent over Bynum.

"Nothing much. Just the thing they didn't want us to see," Bynum answered calmly.

That did it. Seconds later there were four men prone on the ground, getting their clothes dirty and not caring a bit as they peered over the edge of the cliff. "Is it that white-and-metal contraption in those rocks down there that you're talking about?" Big Ed asked Bynum.

"That's it," Bynum, McKenna, and Tommy answered in unison.

"Fine, but what is it, exactly?" Big Ed asked.

"It's a portable light-reflecting screen," McKenna said, getting up. "It looks almost like those old portable screens we used to show our eight millimeter home movies on. That's why they didn't leave the bodies up here."

"Because we might've seen that screen and figured that they were filming and photographing whatever they had intended to do to Glenda up here?" Big Ed asked.

"That's one reason. Another is that they had intended to take it with them when they left, so there might be quite a few of their fingerprints still left on it."

"After two years? It don't rain much up here, but it does from time to time and then it really pours. We'd have to be pretty lucky if there's still prints left on it."

"Aren't we lucky?" McKenna asked.

"I don't know how lucky I am, but I'm sure I'm not as lucky as you fellas," Big Ed replied.

"Nobody is," Tommy said. "Do you think we'll be able to get it today?"

"It's still pretty high up and it would be a tough climb up those rocks for even an experienced climber," Big Ed said. "However, I could use the chopper and lower one of you fellas on the hoist to pick it up."

"Then we'll get it," Randy said.

"Yeah, Brian will get it," Tommy said. "He's the youngest one here, so I think it's only fair that we lower him down to pick it up." He got up and brushed himself off and so did Big Ed, ignoring the look they were getting from McKenna.

"Now who's gonna explain to me how it got down there?" Big Ed asked. "Seems to me, they'd have to be pretty careless to have dropped it down there by accident."

"They were uncharacteristically careless, but only a little," McKenna said, trying to put his next proposed adventure out of his mind. "Big Ed, what's the weather like in January up here?"

"Much the same as now, except maybe twenty degrees cooler."

"How about wind?"

"Oh, yeah. Sometimes gets windy up here, usually in the morning," Big Ed said, and then he got it. "Matter of fact, in the winter the wind usually starts gusting around dawn, maybe a little before."

"And where does it come from?"

"Usually from the west," Big Ed said, pointing away from the mountain and toward Apache Junction.

"So that's south," McKenna said, pointing past the cactus to the desert far below. "And the sun rises in the east on the other side of this mountain, but that's not much of a problem for them. The sunlight reflects off the desert. They need only to catch that light for their early morning photo project, so I figure they placed their light-reflecting screen . . ." He walked to a spot ten feet west of the saguaro and tapped the ground with his foot. "Right here."

"I see," Big Ed said. "After they set it up, along comes a gust of wind that blows it over the cliff."

"It's just speculation on my part, but maybe more than that happened," McKenna said. "Maybe that screen is how Glenda got away on them."

Big Ed thought that over for a moment. "I see what you're getting at, but go ahead and give us your version," he said.

"Okay. One of them is setting up the light screen right here and the other one is with Glenda, tying her to the cactus over by you. Now, they just shot Greg and she might know what's coming, so she's terrified—just the way they want her. What they can't know is that although she's small, baby-faced, and looks like a pushover, she's tough enough to knock Greg around and real fast to boot. The one with Glenda might have a light meter with him, trying to tie her in just the right place, when up comes the gust of wind. It picks up the screen and maybe the screen whacks that guy before it tumbles off the cliff. Glenda sees her chance, breaks loose, and takes off."

"Plausible," Big Ed said, with Bynum and Tommy nodding in agreement. "But runs off to where? Have you figured that out yet?"

McKenna had, but he didn't want to be the one to tell Big Ed. Fortunately for him, Tommy was looking down the path and then he turned and gave McKenna a nod. He knew, and he wasn't afraid to say it. "I'd say she's at the bottom of one of these cliffs, probably at the bottom right near where the chopper is parked."

"So they did shoot her?" Big Ed asked.

"Yeah, they did. Otherwise she was fast enough and she would've got away from them," Tommy said.

"Then, if you're right, Brian's wrong. They threw her body off the cliff after all."

"Not true. I'm right, and so is Brian."

That got Big Ed really thinking, but McKenna could see that Bynum also had the answer. "They shot her while they were chasing her, but they didn't kill her. She was hurt, but still able to move," Bynum said.

"She jumped?" Big Ed said, not sure if he believed it. "Could that be it? Suicide?"

"Only in a manner of speaking," McKenna explained. "It's difficult for us, but try putting yourself in her head for a moment. Even before the killers showed up, she had to be depressed because she knows she's going to jail in a couple of days. Then she saw them kill Greg, the guy she loves, and she's figured out that they're going to kill her—only her death is gonna be much slower and much more painful. She's hit and hurting, and now they're gaining on her. She knows she can't get away, so she takes the only option she sees left. She breaks for the cliff and jumps."

"I wouldn't call that suicide," Bynum said.

"Neither would I." McKenna was quick to agree as he watched Big Ed staring at his helicopter, lost in thought.

"But she can't be at the bottom," Big Ed said. "If she was, her body would have been found by now."

"Then she didn't make it all the way down," Tommy stated impatiently. "Let's go see how far she got."

Big Ed didn't like that, but by then he knew the three foreigners were right. "Okay, let's go," he said.

"But maybe we can save ourselves some time if we fan out and search the ground on the way down. Maybe we'll stay lucky," McKenna suggested.

"Search for what?" Big Ed asked.

Once again, it was Tommy who answered. "Spent shell casings. They wouldn't have been firing through their paper bag when they were chasing Glenda. She was fast and pulling away from them, so they would've needed their sights to hit her. Ergo, no paper bag, and who knows how many shots they fired on the run before they finally hit her?"

"Nobody knows except them," McKenna said. "I'm sure they searched the ground after Glenda jumped and spoiled their fun. They picked up as many of their shell casings as they could find, but maybe they didn't find them all."

"Here's hoping," Big Ed said.

The four men formed a line across the path and slowly made their way down, searching the ground as they walked. It took them fifteen minutes to get back to the helicopter, and they arrived there empty-handed and feeling down. Then came the next depressing task. They each took a spot fifty feet apart on the edge of the path at the cliff and, lying prone, scanned the ground far below. It took fifteen minutes before they were ready to concede that Glenda wasn't below them, so they moved past the helicopter further down the path and repeated the process for another fifteen minutes. Still nothing.

By that time McKenna was beginning to feel foolish and even more

depressed as he questioned his own version of events. They were just getting ready to try searching the cliff even further down the road when
Bynum's sharp eyes brought McKenna back up and proved him right. "I
think I see her," Bynum yelled.

"Where?" three voices yelled back at once.

"About a hundred feet below Brian."

McKenna looked straight down and still didn't see any sign of Glenda.
However, although it had to be three hundred feet to the bottom of the
cliff, there was a rocky outcropping about a hundred feet down. The path
curved away from the mountain at the point where Bynum was lying, so
McKenna realized that Bynum had a better view of the outcropping than
he did.

McKenna pushed himself a little further over the edge. In the rocks
of the outcropping, close to the cliff face, something metallic was reflecting
the bright western sun. Even from that distance, McKenna recognized the
handcuffs, and looking closer he could see the bones of the arm and wrist
still inside the loop. Scattered among the rocks close to the cliff were more
bones, and then he saw the skull, ten feet from the handcuffs.

By then, Bynum, Tommy, and Big Ed were standing over him. "Looks
like the vultures and the buzzards got her," Bynum said.

McKenna knew Bynum was right, but he didn't answer and he didn't
move. He just kept staring down at what was left of Glenda Anderson,
piecing together what had happened to put her remains in the state they
were in. By the time he finally stood up, he had played the whole picture
through his mind's eye. Glenda had hit the rocks after she jumped and she
had died instantly. Unfortunately for Big Ed, her body had taken a bad
bounce on the rocks, bouncing in toward the cliff face where she couldn't
be seen instead of out and down to the desert floor below to a place where
she would have been found.

But it was a good bounce for the local vultures and buzzards. They
had probably started on her right after she jumped, McKenna figured. They
had been able to feast on her, undisturbed by coyotes and other desert
scavengers. By the time Big Ed had brought his dogs up here two weeks
later, there wasn't enough meat left on her bones for the dogs to get even
a whiff of her from this distance.

"I'll call our Rescue Squad to go down and get her," Big Ed said.

"Didn't you say that you've got a hoist on that helicopter?" Bynum
asked.

"Sure do. Got a basket, too."

"Then don't bother the Rescue Squad. I'll go down and get her."

"No, I'll go," McKenna said. "After all, like Tommy said, I'm the youngest."

"You might be younger and we both know now that you're faster, but do you really think you can climb down this cliff better than me?" Bynum asked pleasantly.

McKenna remembered the time he had watched Bynum rappel down that cliff at the end of the DePraidas' back yard. "No, I'm sure I can't."

"Nice of you to say so. Let's get ready."

"Before we do, I've got a thought," Tommy said. "Since it gets windy up here and it's sandy in spots, who's to say that Mother Nature hasn't covered up whatever cartridge cases the scumbags might have left here? Now that we're here with our own wind machine . . ."

Big Ed finished the thought. "We should put it to good use before we start blowing everything around haphazardly while we're bringing Glenda up. We've got nothing but time and she can wait a little longer."

All agreed and Big Ed got back into the helicopter, leaving the McKennas and Bynum standing down the path. He started it up and rose twenty feet. First he guided the machine slowly down the path to the spot where Glenda had jumped, blowing up sand with the rotors as he went. Then he turned the helicopter 180 degrees in place and flew slowly up the path, still blowing up sand. He continued past the saguaro cactus, swung out over the desert, turned, and landed back at the same spot from which he had taken off. He shut off the engine and the four men started walking slowly in line up the path, searching the ground in front of them as them walked.

A half hour later they hadn't found a thing, so Big Ed repeated the sand-blowing process. Tommy found it on the second trip up the path. Lodged among the exposed roots of a small sagebrush was the .380 brass cartridge case. He picked it up by inserting a key in the hole and held it up for all to see.

They didn't need an expert to see that there, on each side of the cartridge case, were the fingerprint lines left by whoever had loaded the cartridge into the magazine two and a half years before—prints visible to the naked eye because the heat of the exploding gunpowder as it had propelled the bullet after Glenda had also seared the loader's prints into the sides of the cartridge case.

Tommy took his handkerchief from his pocket and gingerly placed the sacred object in it. "Now we can get Glenda," he said.

McKenna stood on the path, watching the operation in the sky above him and on the outcropping on the cliff below. It was a dangerous undertaking and every one of his nerves was on edge.

Tommy was up in the helicopter with Big Ed, operating the winch and hoist. Big Ed kept the machine hovering twenty feet over the top of the path and a hundred and twenty feet above Bynum on the rocky outcropping protruding from the side of the cliff face.

The sun was setting as Bynum finished putting the last of Glenda's bones into the body basket attached to the end of the long cable connected to the helicopter's winch. He gave the machine a wave and Tommy started the winch.

Guided by Bynum, the body basket swung from the cliff face and started rising as the cable was electrically wound on its spindle in the helicopter. When it rose a hundred feet and cleared the path, Big Ed guided the helicopter a little closer to the mountain so that McKenna was able to unhook the body basket from the cable. Once he had the basket safely on the ground, he waved.

Big Ed again swung the helicopter over the cliff face and Tommy let the weighted cable down in order to bring Bynum back up to the path. When it was close enough Bynum grabbed it and attached it to the harness he was wearing. Tommy started the winch pulling him up and two minutes later Bynum was on the path, being helped out of the harness by McKenna.

Big Ed again landed the helicopter on the wide spot in the path. He shut the machine down and both he and Tommy came down the path to meet Bynum and McKenna. Once there, the four men stood silently looking down at Glenda's remains.

Bynum must be something of an amateur anthropologist, McKenna figured, because he had managed to arrange Glenda's bones into skeletal form in the basket. Her skull and every bone was approximately where it should have been if she had been lying face up in the basket and had died there long ago, but that didn't help matters much. She had been picked clean by the buzzards and vultures and the natural process of decay had done the rest.

McKenna thought that her sun-bleached bones were a sad testament to the young life cut short. He struggled to keep his anger under control. He had his hands in his pockets and inadvertently felt Cindy's earring on his key ring. That did nothing to help his control.

Bynum had found more than Glenda's bones on the outcropping. One pair of handcuffs was there, attached to a long dog chain. Glenda's clothes were tattered and bloodstained as a result of the sharp-beaked scavengers' quest for food; she had died wearing a pair of white slacks, a red blouse, and white or light pink panties and bra.

McKenna dared a glance at Big Ed's face. He saw what he had expected there and more. Big Ed's face was flushed and red with anger, but his eyes were also filled with the tears that he made no effort to hide or wipe away.

"Found these things down there, too," Bynum said, reaching into his pocket. He took out a spent and deformed .380 bullet, a cheap gold-plated necklace with a pendent nameplate attached that proclaimed "Glenda" in fancy script, and the half-carat diamond engagement ring that Greg had given her the night they both had died. "You'll notice that her pelvis bone is broken and chipped on the right side, so I think that's where she got hit," he said, holding up the bullet. Then he offered the bullet, the necklace, and the ring to Big Ed.

Big Ed disregarded the bullet, but he took the diamond ring and the necklace and placed it in his open hand for all to see. "Those filthy bastards," was all he said, softly and to himself as he wiped his eyes on his sleeve.

Self-consciously, the McKennas and Bynum looked at each other, looked down at Glenda, looked everywhere but at Big Ed as they each marveled at the way the tough and experienced supervisor of homicide detectives was taking the discovery of the remains of a girl he had known was dead for years.

The silence was beginning to get uncomfortable when, without another word, Big Ed put the ring and necklace in his pocket. Then he turned and walked back toward the helicopter.

As he stared at Big Ed's back, McKenna was sure of one thing. When they got the killers, and they would, it would be much better for them if they weren't captured anywhere near the State of Arizona and Big Ed Taggart.

Since Bynum was already wearing the harness, he volunteered for the mission to retrieve the light screen from the base of the cliff, but McKenna wouldn't hear of it. It was his job and he would do it. Nevertheless, he felt foolish as he put on the harness in the helicopter with both Tommy and Bynum grinning at what McKenna knew was his boyish show of bravado.

Once Tommy attached the harness to the winch cable, Big Ed took the machine up and over the cliff face. The sun was just disappearing behind the mountain as McKenna began the descent from the helicopter. He kept his vision focused on the desert floor as the rocks below him went from shadow to darkness, but he could still see the white light screen. Then a gust of wind slammed him into the cliff face. He was startled but unhurt as he once again swung over the desert floor suspended on his cable. It happened again fifteen seconds later when he was just twenty feet over the light screen, but this time McKenna was ready and he easily pushed himself off the cliff face.

McKenna was surprised when he felt himself rising when he was so close to his objective. Big Ed was taking no chances with the wind and

McKenna was being pulled back into the helicopter, empty-handed. Big Ed slowly flew the machine away from the mountain as McKenna rose.

"Too gusty up here at sunrise and sunset," Big Ed yelled from the controls as soon as McKenna was in. "Tomorrow's another day."

TWENTY-TWO

The McKennas and Bynum took rooms for the night in a Super 8 motel in Apache Junction and all caught up on their sleep. After breakfast at Denny's the next morning, the three were ready to get the light screen.

It wasn't to be. By ten o'clock Big Ed had them in the helicopter once again approaching Superstition Mountain and McKenna had the harness on. But they were too late: It was gone.

Big Ed landed the helicopter alongside a dirt track a half mile from the spot where the light screen should have been. Even before he had finished shutting it down, the McKennas and Bynum were out and looking for tracks on the ATV rough road. It took them half a mile of walking and searching the ground in the hundred-degree heat to discover that there were none. Although the road had been used by the killers the night before and had almost certainly been used by other people in their ATVs in the past week, there were no tire tracks at all on the dirt road.

"They're still thinking and being careful. They dragged something behind their vehicle to obliterate the tire tracks," Bynum observed, stating the obvious.

Neither of the McKennas felt like answering as the three walked slowly back to the helicopter to rejoin Big Ed, each man silently mulling over the other implications made obvious by the absence of the light screen.

"Nothing?" Big Ed yelled as the three men shuffled up to the helicopter.

Silence gave Big Ed his answer, but he was ready to bounce back. He started by putting the obvious into words. "They were somewhere in the area yesterday and saw a police helicopter land at a spot they knew was real hot for them. Since our shenanigans yesterday were visible to anyone within ten miles of the mountain, that doesn't make them geniuses."

"No, it doesn't make them geniuses," Tommy agreed. "What it does make them is god-awful lucky murdering bastards. They're killing people all over the country and they just happened to be here when we thought we were getting lucky."

"It's not that they're so lucky," McKenna countered. "Let's face it. We figured Black lives here and it's just our bad luck that one or both of them were around to see us yesterday. They must've whooped it up big time when they saw that we couldn't get their light screen. Then they simply knew what they had to do and they did it, spent the night retrieving their long-lost property before we did. Left us all dumb and wondering if it still had their prints on it."

"Prints, hell!" Bynum said. "By now I'm ready to swear that light screen had both of their names, their addresses, their phone numbers, and even their social security numbers embossed in gold on the frame."

"We're still not in bad shape, so let's get back to basics and see what else this really tells us," McKenna suggested.

No one objected, but Bynum and Tommy still looked unhappy. Big Ed had a straight face on, but McKenna thought there was a smile tugging at the corners his lips. "You know something we don't?" McKenna asked, his curiosity aroused.

"No, nothing I can think of," Big Ed answered good-naturedly. "Why you ask?"

"Because you don't seem to be sharing the mood of my compadres here."

"Well, I have to admit I'm disappointed that we didn't get what we were after this morning, and I'd be the first to say that's mostly bad news."

"Mostly?"

"Yeah, mostly, meaning it's total bad news for you gentlemen. However, we did find Glenda, and Sheriff Joe will make sure she'll have quite a funeral."

"And that will make him happy?"

"Yeah, and me too. I generally find that I'm happy whenever he's happy. Life's like that on this job."

"I imagine it will be a very public funeral?"

"Politics demands that it be a whopper," Big Ed said, shaking his head and chuckling. "Mayors from every city in the county and probably even the governor there in the first row, all with their best crime-fighting speech in their pockets ready to go in case anyone asks them to say a few words."

"I don't get it," Tommy said. "Why all the press attention for a nobody's funeral?"

"To understand that, you have to understand the way things work in this county, meaning, you have to understand a few things about Sheriff Joe's posse system. The search for Glenda was pretty big news a couple of years ago, generated a lot of press because of all the posse members involved in looking for her. Spent a lot of time and energy on it and the search got good press coverage."

Tommy still didn't get it. "Why's that? They got nothing else to write about?"

"Sometimes no, but the posse is always news around here. It's an innovative idea and a lot of influential people are working members—including some civic-minded millionaires in the habit of contributing to political campaigns. Since Sheriff Joe enjoys a local approval rating that fluctuates between eighty-five and ninety percent, you have to add in that every politician with any hope of being reelected has to be a working posse member. They all spent a lot of time looking for Glenda and that's why finally finding her is gonna be big news."

"So Arpaio's going to shine," McKenna said.

"He sure will. He took some heat because of the money and manpower he let me spend on Glenda's case over the past couple of years, but now it looks like he was right all along. He'll be sure to say so, especially since Glenda and Greg's murder is now part of a much bigger case."

How does that affect us? McKenna wondered. Do we need our big case becoming bigger still?

Before McKenna could come up with an answer, Big Ed cut his ruminations short. "You were saying, Brian?"

"What?"

"Saying something about we're not really in bad shape and getting back to basics?"

"Oh, yeah," McKenna said. He took a moment to put his thoughts in order before continuing. "Black and White might still be close, might even be watching us right now. After all, they knew we were coming back here today."

Each man had already realized that the killers could be watching them from countless places within five miles from their location in that open country, but McKenna's statement still caused all to glance around.

"They've figured out by now that we've connected them to a bunch of killings, and because of the light screen, they must realize that we know they're photographing their fun," McKenna said. "But we still know a lot that they can't know we know."

McKenna surveyed his audience and received three passive stares in return. He then realized that each of them already knew what he was going to say, but he felt obliged to continue. "They don't know that we found the shell casing they couldn't find after they shot Glenda, so they don't know we've got two fingerprints from one of them. And, maybe more important, they don't know that we know there's two of them. There's plenty of work we still have to do to make up for this setback."

"They're gonna figure now that there's a chance we'll think they're photographing and filming their murders as part of a commercial venture," Bynum said.

"Maybe," McKenna admitted. "But if they do, how does that hurt us? Their work isn't exactly mainstream and hasn't been made public after all the years they've been operating. I think they'll assume we won't be able to find their stuff no matter how hard we look."

"I disagree," Tommy stated. "They've been operating successfully for at least eighteen years that we know about. Now, all of a sudden, two days after they use Cindy's cards in Arizona, we're here recovering a body they left two years ago. That's got to get them wondering, and whatever conclusions they draw, it's got to make them nervous—maybe nervous enough to run."

"Maybe, maybe not. Depends on how smart they are," McKenna said. "I think they were watching the mountain because they knew their cards were hot. The question is, When did they know?"

"You mean, was it after they used the cards here or after they used them in San Jose?" Tommy asked.

"Exactly. Suppose they've suspected we've been tracking her cards since they used them in San Jose. After all, it was uniformed units that checked out the 7-Elevens. They might've hung around after they got their cash and saw the activity. They're still not sure it's the cards, but they're still greedy. So what do they do?"

"Come here and use the cards again. Then they see the Tempe and Mesa cops show up right after they leave and they know for sure that the cards are hot for them."

"If you were them, would you have taken a chance on using those cards again here? Or would you have been smarter than them and just have gotten rid of the cards?"

"I'd have gotten rid of them right after San Jose," Tommy stated.

"And what does that tell you?"

"Either they're nowhere near as smart as we thought they were or they have absolutely no respect for us."

"Wouldn't that make them downright stupid?" Big Ed asked, but he didn't expect an answer. "Everybody ready to go downtown to ballistics?"

"There's somebody working there on a Sunday?" McKenna asked.

"This Sunday there is. I called Wade Barton at home this morning and asked him to come in. Told him we'd be needing him and asked him to take another look at the bullet that killed Greg."

"He doesn't mind?"

"Not at all. When I said we thought that bullet might've been fired through a paper bag, I got the impression that he was in a hurry to get in. He's the dedicated kind, takes a lot of pride in his work."

Big Ed set the helicopter down on the landing pad behind his office on Durango Street in Phoenix, then drove the McKennas and Bynum to the sheriff's headquarters building downtown. Wade Barton was waiting for them in his corner of the lab.

"You were right about the paper bag," he said, not sounding at all thrilled. "I found a minuscule burnt fiber imbedded in one of the grooves on the bullet. Can't tell what color it was, but the only conclusion to be drawn is that the bullet was fired through a paper bag."

"Don't beat yourself up over it. No harm done," Big Ed said. He took the bullet from his pocket that had been found with Glenda's bones. "Can you do a comparison on this bullet and the Greg bullet?"

"Sure." Barton took the bullet from Big Ed and held it at eye level for a moment. "For starters, it's a .380 caliber. I've already got the Greg bullet under the scope," he said. There was a comparison microscope on his desk with two small, padded vises on the stand under the eyepieces. He placed the bullet in the empty vise, bent over, and peered through the eyepiece. "Are you thinking that both these bullets were fired by the same gun?" he asked a minute later without looking up.

"That's what we're figuring," Big Ed said.

"Then you'd better start figuring different. Both were fired by a .380 Colt Commander, but different guns."

"Are you sure?" McKenna asked, trying not to sound offensive.

Barton stood up straight and faced him, not appearing at all offended. "Certain. Same make, model, and caliber, but different guns."

"Or different barrels for the same gun?" McKenna asked.

"Yeah, could be different barrels."

Unlikely this time, McKenna thought. Why would they change barrels on a gun after killing Greg? They didn't plan on killing Glenda, they were just going to torture her to death. No, it has to be that they had two guns with them.

Tommy was on the same track. "It's not surprising. They had a backup gun with them, one that they never intended using until Glenda bolted on them," he said, then took from his pocket the bullet that had killed Arthur McMahon. "Mind comparing this one against the bullet we just gave you?"

"Not at all." Barton took the Glenda bullet from the vise and replaced it with the McMahon bullet. It took him only a minute to draw his conclusion. "Same gun."

"We outsmarted those cheap bastards," Tommy said proudly. "When

Glenda's body wasn't found after the search, they figured it probably would never be found. They felt safe using the same barrel on their Barrone-McMahon caper, and that's gonna hang them for four murders."

"Yes, these bullets officially link your cases and ours," Barton said. "But when you say *them*, are you saying that there's more than one man doing these killings?"

"Yeah. They're a team, but keep that under your hat," Big Ed said.

"How many murders you got so far?"

"Eight that we know about for sure, but we're certain there's many more we haven't found out about yet."

"Anything else I can do for you?"

"Just one more thing," Bynum said. He gave Barton the bullet that had killed Sara Reinhart. "Can you check this one against the other two?"

"Certainly. You think your luck will hold?"

"No."

Bynum was right. His bullet matched neither the Glenda nor the Greg bullet, which made sense to McKenna. They had made a mistake, but Black and White were not to be underestimated, he thought. Using the same gun barrel to shoot both Glenda and McMahon was an aberration from their usual, well-planned, murderous procedure, something they had probably never done before.

"What's next?" Tommy asked.

"I figure we should drop in on Sheriff Joe," Big Ed said. "Might need you gentlemen to help me convince him on a few things that might be important to us down the road."

"What things?" Tommy asked.

"It would make wonderful press and Sheriff Joe likes that, so we'll have to convince him not to hint to his favorite reporters that there's two killers, that they're making movies, and that we have some fingerprints."

"Is it going to be hard to do that?" McKenna asked.

"Could be, but he's a sensible sort. He'll see things our way, eventually."

TWENTY-THREE

TUESDAY, JUNE 15, NOON, NEW YORK CITY

Greve wasn't paying his high-priced detectives to go to funerals in Arizona, and that was that. Neither McKenna had really wanted to go to the affair, so Greve's policy had been the perfect excuse to give Big Ed. Bynum would represent the three of them at the services, and he didn't seem to mind.

On Monday morning McKenna had driven Tommy to Sky Harbor to catch his flight for San Diego and his new porn career. Then McKenna had turned in the rental car and caught his own flight back to New York.

It had been a busy morning. It had taken McKenna his first four hours in the office to document the progress made in the case in Arizona and California, all the time sidestepping questions from very nosy detectives about what Tommy was doing on the West Coast. True to his word, McKenna managed to avoid telling them the true nature of Tommy's current duties. He left them all with the impression that Tommy was searching for the intermediary who had sold the *Serious* and *In Charge* magazines to a San Diego porn dealer and he didn't elaborate.

Next, Greve had to be satisfied. McKenna brought his reports into the boss and sat there while Greve read through them. There were a few things in the reports that appeared to make Greve unhappy and he wasn't the kind of man accustomed to being unhappy alone. "You're proposing to give that cartridge case to the FBI for identification of the fingerprints? Why?" Greve asked.

"Because they're better equipped to do the search and they've got countless times more fingerprints on file. With our equipment, we could take much more time and come up with nothing if we don't have their prints on file."

"I'm not disagreeing, but the feds are a little peculiar sometimes. They're helpful if you approach them right, but they have the habit of thinking they're in charge when things start looking good."

McKenna knew that he shouldn't, but he couldn't bear to miss the opportunity to needle Greve a bit. "Am I understanding you correctly, Lieutenant? Are you inferring that this case is beginning to look good to you and might even be solved before you're ready to retire?"

"I'm ready to admit that it's going a little better at this point than I thought it would. But remember this. There are ups and downs in every big case and it appears that you're enjoying the ups right now. Enjoy it while you can because I'll be here to guide you through the downs when things aren't looking quite so peachy to us."

A mistake and enough said on that point, McKenna realized. No more ribbing Mr. Life-of-the-Party.

Greve still had a few other points on his mind. "When you bring them that cartridge case, make it easy for them to remember where it came from," he said. "Marked NYPD evidence, tagged, and sealed in one of our evidence bags."

"It's not one of our bags that it's in."

"It's not?"

"Nope, because it's not our evidence." McKenna took out the clear plastic evidence bag containing the cartridge case and placed it on Greve's desk. Stamped across the bag was MARICOPA COUNTY SHERIFF'S DEPART-MENT. "I had a tough time convincing the sheriff there that I should be the one bringing it to the FBI. Fortunately, the sheriff used to work for the DEA and he's met Gene Shields. The only reason I've got it is that I told him I'd be dealing directly with Gene and his department wouldn't be getting cut out of the loop when we get the killers ID'd."

That news seemed to set Greve's mind at ease a bit. "Good policy, go right to the top if you can. Now to the final thing I'm worried about. You think Tommy has a shot of finding the guy who sold Gallagher the magazines?"

"It's an outside shot."

That put the scowl back on Greve's face. "How long is he planning to spend on it?"

"He'll be back in three or four days, after he learns enough about the business to pass as a porn dealer. After that, he'll just go to whatever trade shows Gallagher thinks he should attend."

"Meaning he'll be flying all over the country, staying at nice hotels, and maybe even renting cars while he gets material for his new book at the taxpayers' expense."

"Probably."

"Geez" was Greve's only comment. He leaned back in his chair and closed his eyes.

McKenna was wondering if the interview was over when Greve's cat surprised him and jumped on his lap. McKenna didn't know how to handle that, so he stroked the cat's ears and the animal began purring so loudly that Greve heard him and opened his eyes. He appeared to be shocked. "Never saw him do that with anyone else before," he said.

"Maybe he likes me."

Then Greve shocked McKenna when he said, "Then I guess you must be okay. It appears that you're doing a good job on this case, so I'm gonna go out on a limb. I'm mildly optimistic that you're gonna solve it soon."

"All that because your cat likes me?"

"He's a highly intelligent animal. A wonder, really. When are you meeting Shields?"

"At his office at two."

"And then?"

"I'll probably be off to Quantico tomorrow."

"If that's the way it works out, don't bother coming back to the office tonight. Give me a call and let me know what Gene has to say, then go home and get some rest."

How absolutely decent of him, McKenna thought. I'm really beginning to love this cat.

McKenna had one stop to make before seeing Shields, but it was on the way downtown. Bobby Bluteau was an old retired detective who loved to travel. During his time with the NYPD he went just about everywhere on his vacations, and after he retired, he found that the least expensive way to indulge in his favorite pastime was to become a travel agent, a profession with many travel perks. He operated a Liberty Travel franchise at East 27th Street and Second Avenue and he was the most likely source McKenna could think of for the information he needed. Better yet, Bobby was sharp, discreet, and had worked for years in the Brooklyn Sex Crimes Unit, so he wasn't easily shocked.

Bobby was at a computer terminal talking on the phone at a desk in the rear of the busy agency when McKenna walked in carrying a large manila envelope. He saw McKenna at once, waved to him, and motioned him to a chair at the side of his desk as he continued his conversation and worked his keyboard, booking someone on a Caribbean cruise.

McKenna sat, waited, and looked around. There were four other travel agents in the office working for Bobby and all were on the phone or talking to customers who had come in. It was easy to see that Bluteau was doing just fine in his business.

"Just give me a minute to close out this sale and I'll send you wherever you want to go, Brian," Bluteau said after he hung up. He made a few more entries on his keyboard, then printed out some tickets and put them in an envelope. "Okay, Brian, what can I do for you?"

"I've got something to show you that'll only take a few minutes of your time, but it's got to be on the q.t."

"Something to do with the Barrone case?" Bluteau guessed.

"Uh-huh." McKenna took the *Serious* and *In Charge* magazines from the envelope, opened them to the centerfold pictures, and passed them to Bluteau. "I'm hoping you can tell me where in the world these photos were taken."

Bluteau quickly looked back and forth from one magazine to the other. "Are these photos real?" he asked.

"Unfortunately, yes."

"Good God Almighty, I thought I'd seen everything. Then these people were tortured to death like the Barrone girl?"

"That's the assumption I'm making. They're dead, but I have to know where they were killed."

"I've got one for you for sure," Bluteau said, passing *Serious* back to McKenna. "I've been to that very spot. Beautiful place, as you can see, but not many people get there. It's about ten miles outside a little town called Herradura, about half an hour from San José, Costa Rica."

San José? This case is becoming even stranger, McKenna thought. Two McKennas and now two San Josés.

"Is the spot a lovers lane?"

"Could be at night, but I was there in the daytime for the view. There's a dirt road that ends at that cliff, as I recall."

"Is the road in good shape?"

Bluteau chuckled. "You've been to Costa Rica, haven't you?"

"Yeah, sorry. Stupid question. Most of the roads there are in horrible shape, even the main highways."

"And the road leading to that place is worse than most. I had a guide and he got me there in one of those old Land Rovers everybody's got down there, but I remember thinking at the time that we weren't going to make it."

"How about the place in the other magazine. Recognize it?"

Bluteau studied the *In Charge* centerfold, then shook his head. "Not specifically, but it looks like a place I'd like to visit. The scenery looks like either Thailand or Cambodia, but the poor guy at the end of the whip is definitely Thai. That help you out?"

"I don't know, but it sure gets me to thinking."

The FBI's offices in New York are located downtown at 26 Federal Plaza, a modern building close to the courts and police headquarters. McKenna was escorted to Shields's spacious office by a pleasant receptionist. He felt honored that Shields was waiting for him at the door, and he could see that the receptionist was certainly impressed.

Gene Shields had been one of New York's big shots for years, a well-respected man and the top federal law enforcement officer in town, and he loved the job enough to have turned down many higher federal positions just to keep it. He was a man-about-town who traveled in the society circles, a devotee of the theater, the better restaurants, the museums, and all the other things New York had to offer. Originally from Baltimore, Shields was that rare breed of person who came to visit and found he could live nowhere else. New York wasn't for everyone, but it was for him. McKenna shared his viewpoint, and having worked with Shields before, considered him a stand-up guy and a good friend.

McKenna started by giving him the clear plastic bag containing the cartridge case.

"The latents look pretty good to the untrained eye," Shields said after examining it for a moment.

"They look pretty good to me, too, but I'm reserving judgment until I hear what the experts have to say."

"And we've got experts aplenty. Matter of fact, it might be a very good thing for you that you decided to include your federal cousins in your present caper," he said with a smile.

"Why's that? You come up with something already?" McKenna asked, trying to keep the excitement out of his voice and sound as nonchalant as Shields.

"Not me, personally, but a source of mine in the Behavioral Sciences Unit filled my ear when I called down to make an appointment for you and explain what you've been up to. He's been around forever and he remembers an old case from one of your favorite countries."

"Costa Rica?" McKenna asked at once.

"Yeah, surprised?"

"Why would I be surprised?" McKenna asked.

"Because I seem to recall you going on and on telling me what a wonderful, crime-free country it is."

"I used to think so until about half an hour ago."

"You knew?"

"Yeah, I knew. Want to see a picture of the crime taking place?" McKenna asked. He opened his manila envelope, took out *Serious*, opened it to the centerfold, and passed it to Shields.

McKenna had gotten used to the reaction people showed when they first saw the photos, but Shields surprised him. He appeared detached and clinical as he studied the photos. He closed the magazine, gave it back to McKenna, then shook his head. "Just horrible."

"Was it a double torture-murder there?" McKenna asked.

"Two of them. Four murders eight years apart. I understand that there's a few differences from your present case, but one big similarity you wouldn't expect."

"The weapon?"

"A .380 Colt Commander."

How can that be? McKenna wondered. Airport security then wasn't as tight in the Third World as it is today, but it still should've been very

difficult for Black and White to smuggle a gun into Costa Rica. Unless . . .
"There haven't been any more recent cases in Costa Rica, have there?"

"Don't know yet, but I'll have the answer for you soon."

"Why the delay?"

"Because we were never really involved in their cases. Only reason we
know about them is because twelve years ago the Costa Rican government
sent the poor cop who had those cases to Quantico to get a psychological
profile on his killer."

"Can you get me a copy of that profile?"

All of a sudden, Shields didn't look so self-satisfied. "You'll have it when
I get it, but I don't think it's gonna make me comfortable."

"Because it's so wrong?"

"I guess it has to be if we gave them a profile on one killer and there
have always been two of them."

"I'm not here to throw any stones. Tommy's one of the best and he
thought there was only one of them for eighteen years," McKenna said.
"When were the last murders in Costa Rica?"

"Around 1985, I believe."

"I'm willing to bet there haven't been any new ones down there. At
least, not with the .380 Colt."

"I see you're on the right track. You got it figured out yet?" Shields
asked, once again smiling smugly.

"I think so, but give me another minute."

"Take your time."

McKenna did, taking a full two minutes before he had everything
worked out in his mind. The conclusion he drew was the only one that made
sense to him, and it also explained quite a few other things about the way
Black and White operated. "They work for the airlines, probably crew members," he stated. "Matter of fact, either one or both of them are pilots."

"I don't know about them being pilots, but we're on the same wave-
length."

"Believe me, one of them is a pilot. It was staring me in the face and
I should have figured it out sooner. I've been operating with a lot of wrong
assumptions about them. Back in eighty-five airline crew members never
had to wait around to go through the metal detectors at the airports in
most countries, and especially in some of the sleepier parts of the Third
World. But they have to now at every airport I know of, so they wouldn't
risk bringing the .380 in to do another set of murders there."

"True, but why are you so certain that one of them is a pilot? I'd have
thought that they were both flight attendants."

"Because of the places where they do their killings. All secluded places and hard to find. We were going under the assumption that one of them must have grown up in New York and the other one in San Jose, but then the Arizona murders popped up. Another secluded place, so secluded that you'd have to swear that they grew up in the desert out there."

"But that's not the case at all?"

"Nope. They might not be from any of those places, but they know them well because they see them from the air on their landing approaches. The California murders were under the approach to San Jose International Airport and Superstition Mountain is under the approach for all the airports in the Phoenix area. And you know how quite a few flights come into LaGuardia early in the morning when the weather's good?"

"Sure do, and it's the best view of this town you'll ever get," Shields said. "Right up the Hudson, then they do a wide turn over Westchester County and come into the airport from the north."

"And before they start that turn, they're flying right past the Cloisters. There are always commercial aircraft in the sky there, and I should have seen that sooner. Unfortunately, we're so used to seeing planes in the air that we don't see them when we see them. We should, but we don't."

Shields took a minute to mull over McKenna's theory before he commented. "Let me see if I've got this straight, as you see it. When they're flying in early in the morning, they're searching the ground and looking for what? A solitary car parked in a secluded spot with a view?"

"You've got it. It might take them dozens of flights before they find a place they like enough to investigate it on the ground, but that's what they do."

"Sounds plausible, but not entirely convincing," Shields said.

"I'm not a betting man, but I'm ready to go out on a limb on this one," McKenna said, sitting back in his chair. "I'll bet you dinner and a show that I'm right. *The Scarlet Pimpernel*, soup to nuts—tickets, taxis, everything."

"How are you gonna finally convince me that you are right? Do I have to wait until you're in a position to ask them how they picked their spots before we can take in the show?"

"Not at all. You're a reasonable man, you just need one more substantial piece of proof to see that I'm right. Matter of fact, I'll be big about it and give you two pieces of proof."

"Which would be?"

"I'm willing to bet that every one of their murders in Costa Rica was beneath the approach path to Juan Santamaría International Airport. That should do it."

"Juan Santamaría? Is that the airport in Costa Rica?"

"That's the one the American airlines use. It's right outside of San José and close to some real pretty country."

"Okay, that's one if it works out for you. What's the other piece of proof you mentioned?"

"This, but it's going to take some work on your part," McKenna said. He removed *In Charge* from his envelope and passed it to Shields. "Open it to the centerfold."

Shields did. He had no reaction, only a question. "Where is it?"

"I can't be certain on that one, but I'd say someplace near Bangkok, Thailand. You're gonna have to make a color copy and have it shown to somebody influential in the Thai police. But before you do that, whoever talks to them will have to convince them that they have to keep it under wraps until we give the okay."

"I don't know if we'll be in a position to do that. I understand from the DEA that they've become pretty independent when it comes to dealing with us. They just smile politely, yes us to death, and then do whatever they feel like doing—usually nothing."

"If you can't have somebody convince them, then don't show it to them," McKenna said. "We've got enough to go on for a while. Have we got a bet?"

Shields held up the magazine. "You're saying that poor guy was also tortured on an airport approach path?"

"That's what I'm saying."

"Give me a minute to think this over before I commit." Shields poured them both another cup of coffee while he pondered McKenna's rather expensive proposition. "No bet," he said at last, then was quick to change the subject. "You know who you need on this to help you out?"

McKenna knew exactly who he needed. Timmy Rembijas was a smart, well-liked, hard-working agent assigned to the FBI's JFK Airport Task Force for so long that he even bowled in the baggage handlers' and the maintenance workers' leagues. He had contacts with people in all the airlines and knew everybody at the airports, but most of them had long since forgotten his real, hard-to-remember name. To all he was simply Timmy JFK.

Even if the fingerprints on the cartridge case were as good as they looked and either Black or White could be identified from them, countless hours of plodding, boring investigative work would have to be done with the airlines to learn the identity of the other one. Since there were no witnesses to any of their crimes, the case against them would rest entirely on circumstantial and scientific evidence. For starters, it would have to be demonstrated to the jury that Black and White were together in the area of every murder, and that was where Timmy JFK and his airline contacts would really come in handy. Black and White's flight schedules would have to be obtained in order to match them against the dates of the murders, and Timmy could get them faster and easier than anyone else.

However, McKenna felt that it would be inappropriate for him to ask Shields for Timmy JFK's services. He knew that Timmy JFK already had a heavy schedule infiltrating and exposing organized crime's many larcenous activities at the airports. "I know who I'd like, the guy who could do the job I've got in mind better than anyone, but I don't know if he's available."

"I'm making him available," Shields stated. "I'll explain it to him and you've got Timmy JFK for as long as you need him."

It was a gracious move on Shields's part. He was asserting no control over the case, but was still lending his manpower and resources freely. Of course, there was a catch and both men knew it. McKenna thought it would be amusing to put it on the table. "Okay, I've got Timmy JFK and I really appreciate it. Now what can I do for you and yours in return?"

"The usual. Gracious acknowledgment and kudos to the Bureau and Timmy JFK at your press conference after you get these guys. The standard, 'I couldn't have done it without the professional assistance and resources freely rendered unto me and my humble department by those dedicated FBI agents,' would be nice."

"Fine. And if it turns out that we don't get these guys?"

"Then don't mention us at all and forget we ever talked, of course."

TWENTY-FOUR

The idea of another trip didn't sit well at first with Angelita, especially when McKenna told her he would probably be making many more of them before the case was over. Besides spending a couple of days in Quantico, he expected to be going to Costa Rica and any other country where the FBI inquiries uncovered more of Black and White's activities. So, once the kids were in bed, McKenna spent a few hours explaining the case to her. Although she wanted him to retire and leave New York and its problems far behind them, once she was fully versed on Black and White's long murder spree she was solidly in his corner and agreed that they had to be stopped.

Angelita also had more faith in McKenna's abilities than McKenna thought he deserved, so she was quite certain that if anyone could get Black and White into irons, her husband was the one to do it. He left home the next morning, packed for a two-day trip, and with Angelita's blessing to go wherever the case took him.

McKenna considered it a plus that Costa Rica was one of the countries where Black and White had operated. He had spent weeks there before on another case, knew the country well, and also knew some of the local cops, but he was somewhat puzzled by the fact that the tropical paradise had experienced a rash of unsolved serial killings and he hadn't heard about it while he had been there. Serious crime was a fairly rare phenomenon there and the type of spectacular double murders Black and White pulled should have come up in conversation somewhere during his dealings with the local police. It hadn't and McKenna wondered why.

McKenna made a call before leaving town and John Harney was waiting for him near the Lincoln Tunnel entrance when he pulled up. As Harney got into the car, one look told McKenna that he was anxious and annoyed.

"I hope you've got something for me to bail me out," Harney said. "My editor doesn't appreciate reading about *our* story in some out-of-town paper."

"Sorry, John, but I had to make a deal with Sheriff Arpaio to keep us on track here. We agreed that he would be the one to break the story."

"He broke it pretty good," Harney said, then gave McKenna a faxed copy of the *Arizona Republic*'s coverage of Glenda's funeral.

It had been exactly the affair Big Ed had predicted, with the mayors of Phoenix, Tempe, and Mesa in attendance along with, of course, Sheriff Joe Arpaio. Arpaio had been interviewed after the service and stated that the discovery of Glenda's body was one result of a two-year investigation by his department. He also said the murders of Glenda and Greg had been linked to the 1989 murders of Robert Harrison and Sara Reinhart in San Jose and the recent murders of Cindy Barrone and Arthur McMahon in New York and that his department was conducting a joint investigation with the NYPD to identify and apprehend the killer.

McKenna found nothing objectionable in Arpaio's statement and appreciated the fact that Arpaio had referred to the *killer*, not *killers*, and he had made no mention of snuff films.

"I need lots more than the *Arizona Republic*'s got," Harney insisted when McKenna finished reading.

"I'll give you what I can," McKenna said, then briefly outlined the California murders, emphasizing Randy Bynum's role and telling Harney he had been put in touch with Bynum by Tommy. However, he said nothing about Cindy's credit cards, nothing about Black and White, and nothing about snuff films. That would have to come later.

"So how did you wind up in Arizona?" Harney asked.

"Can't tell you that, yet. To be honest with you, there's still a lot I'm not telling you, but you'll have the whole story as soon as I can give it."

"I guess I'll have to accept that for now. Was Tommy in Arizona with you?"

"Leading the charge."

"Is that how we're still gonna play it?"

"Exactly."

"Suit yourself. So somehow you and Tommy mysteriously wind up in Arizona. And then . . . ?"

"Except for what you read in the *Arizona Republic*, the only thing I can add is that Bynum found a bullet that was fired from the same gun that killed Arthur McMahon."

"Are you going to come up with any more murders?"

"Already have, through the kind services of the FBI."

"They're in on this, too?" Harney asked.

"They're being most helpful, and you can print that."

"How many more murders?"

"Can't tell you that yet, and I can't tell you where."

"Care to comment on where Tommy is?"

"How do you know he's still gone?" McKenna asked.

"Called him at home. Wife told me he'll be back in town soon, but she wouldn't tell me where he was."

Harney's got Tommy's home number? That's a big indicator of how close Tommy keeps his pals in the press, McKenna thought. "Then let's leave it at that. Tommy's out of town pursuing other aspects of this investigation."

"Mind if I make it sound mysterious?"

"Not at all."

McKenna got to Quantico at five o'clock and checked into a motel. He wanted to catch Shields before he went home for the day, so he called him before unpacking. "I was just about to call your cell phone," Shields said. "I've got some news, some of which isn't going to come as a surprise to you."

"Costa Rica?"

"Yep, Costa Rica. Spoke to the cop who has all the cases, been working them for years. There was another one after he came to Quantico for the profile, two more bodies but a different gun. They used a .25 caliber Astra."

"An Astra? It figures, a cheap Spanish gun. They bought it down there when airport security tightened up and they couldn't risk bringing their Colt Commanders in anymore. When was the last one?"

"January of ninety-seven."

"On the airport approach path?"

"Glad I didn't take your bet. All of them were, at a cliff in the woods outside a pretty little mountain town called Herradura. The people there have been going through a reign of terror for twenty-two years, although none of the victims were locals. The agricultural extension of the national college is right outside town, so they've got a lot of students living nearby."

"All the victims were students?"

"Can't say for sure, but I believe so."

"I've got to get down there and see what the Costa Rican cops have come up with," McKenna said.

"You can if you want to, but you don't have to. Miguel Morro said he'd be happy to come up and bring you everything he's got."

"That's the cop?"

"That's him, Inspector Miguel Morro. Sounds like a nice guy, but he's got some venom in him when he talks about this case."

"Showing signs of obsessive behavior?" McKenna asked.

"Exactly. You going down or is he coming up?"

"When can he be here?"

"He was willing to come today, right after I got off the phone with him. Tomorrow be okay with you?"

"Here in Quantico?"

"He says he'll meet you anywhere. Where are you staying?"

"The Sheraton Motor Inn, Room 206."

"I'll tell him and call you back with the details."

Shields was fast. McKenna had just finished unpacking when he called back. Morro would be flying into Washington and would meet McKenna at his motel at six o'clock the next evening, which suited McKenna just fine. He wanted to get home as soon as possible and thought he might be able to wrap up his meetings with Morro and the profiling experts in one day.

After dinner at McDonald's, McKenna returned to his room to prepare himself for the next day's meetings. He knew that the FBI's profilers would probably have many questions for him and he wanted to have the answers at his fingertips, so he sat down for a boring evening spent studying his case folders.

Then came two calls that changed his plans for the evening. The first was from an irritable Tommy with a piece of mildly surprising news: Randy Bynum had just joined him as a fellow employee at Gallagher's porn shop. The second was from Arthur McMahon, and he sounded faint and ill as he requested a meeting.

McKenna hadn't told McMahon he would be in Virginia, so it was obvious to him that McMahon had a spy in the FBI. By then, that neither surprised nor disturbed him. He liked McMahon more every time he talked to him and had planned to fill him in completely anyway.

By eight-thirty McKenna had taken the bypass around downtown Richmond and was close to McMahon's house on River Road on the outskirts of town. He was in estate country, with one magnificent home larger and prettier than the next—and older. Most of the homes were set on five acres or more of manicured property.

McMahon's directions had been precise enough to allow McKenna to find his driveway with a minimum of difficulty. There was no name at the entrance, but the estate was surrounded by an old, eight-foot-high brick wall, the only one on River Road. McKenna drove in, expecting to immediately see the house, but he wasn't there yet. The asphalt driveway was under a canopy of tall magnolia trees that bordered it on both sides. Most of the property was rolling pasture dotted with an occasional stand of trees. The hay had been recently harvested, but McKenna saw no bales of hay, no farm machinery, nor livestock of any kind. He also passed a well-preserved old barn with a corral in back, but he saw no horses. The sun had just set, but there was still enough light to enable McKenna to catch a glimpse of the brick wall in the distance on one side or the other as he drove. By the time he had traveled a mile, he had already calculated that there were enough bricks in that wall to build a fair-sized town.

Then the house came into view and it wasn't at all what McKenna had expected. It was large enough and pretty enough, but certainly not one of the grand homes owned by McMahon's neighbors living on much smaller plots. By disregarding the acres and acres of property surrounding it, McKenna could easily imagine that the house belonged to a middle class family—certainly upper-middle class, but not Old Money. McKenna was also surprised that it was by far the newest house in the area, maybe ten years old.

The road ended in a circular driveway at the house. The outside lights went on and the front door was opened by a middle-aged, thin black woman in a white, starched nurse's uniform as McKenna pulled up. He straightened his tie before he got out of the car, then reached into the backseat for his briefcase containing all the things he intended to show McMahon.

The nurse was smiling so broadly as McKenna approached that he felt as if he was visiting relatives. "So good to finally meet you, Detective McKenna," she said, extending her hand. "I'm Ginny."

McKenna took her hand and noticed that she had a strong grip. "That wouldn't be Virginia, would it?"

"Yes, Virginia from Virginia. Not very imaginative on my folks' part, was it?"

"It's fine, a very pretty name anywhere, and I'm Brian."

"I know. That's what Mr. McMahon calls you whenever he talks about you, which is most of the time since, since . . ."

McKenna saw that Ginny couldn't bring herself to say it, and he liked her even more for it. "Since his son was killed?"

"Yes, since then. It's always Brian this or Tommy that. He knows all about you and I've been learning quite a bit myself."

"How are the both of you getting so smart about us?"

"Newspapers. He's got copies of every article either of you have ever been mentioned in. He studies them, knows about every big arrest you've ever made and every famous case you've ever won."

"How about the arrests we didn't make and the cases we lost in court?"

"He knows about them, too, but he's happy there haven't been any of those in years. He thinks it's because you're both getting older and wiser."

"Certainly older. How has Mr. McMahon been feeling?"

"Not well this morning, but better this afternoon. He had a mild heart attack after the funeral and it's always bad the first couple of days."

"This wasn't his first heart attack?"

"Good Lord, no. He gets heart attacks like other people get colds. C'mon, we better get in or he'll think I'm out here blabbing stories about him." Then Ginny laughed and shook her head. " 'Course, he'd be right, same as always. Lord, that man sure knows my foolish ways."

McKenna was sorry to see the informal interview end and suspected that Ginny, with very little prodding, could give him more insight into the way Arthur McMahon thought than anyone else could. But he followed her in, closing the door behind them.

The house was a center-hall colonial with ten-foot ceilings that made it appear bigger from the inside than it did from outside. Ginny led McKenna to a parlor in the rear of the house, off the kitchen. McMahon was there, dressed in pajamas, slippers, and a robe. "Good to see you, Brian," he said as he hobbled to the door to meet McKenna.

Ginny brushed past McKenna with her arms raised. She made a move to help McMahon, but he waved her away. "I'm fine," he insisted. "Besides, haven't you got anything else to do besides hiding my cigars, watering down my brandy, following me around like a baby, and filling poor Detective McKenna's head with nonsense?"

The words were harsh, but said with a smile. Ginny shook her head, gave McMahon a condescending look, and lowered her arms, but she kept pace with him, at his side and ready to catch him if he faltered.

McKenna got the impression that, despite appearances, the two were buddies and had been for years. He felt it was time to get the conversation back on track. "How are you feeling?" he asked.

"Not as good as I'd like, but well enough, considering. Have you eaten yet?"

"Yes, thanks."

"Then just coffee, or would you care for something else?"

"Just coffee would be fine."

"Good. Let's make ourselves comfortable, shall we?"

McMahon walked back to his chair, closely followed by Ginny. As soon as he was settled in, she left for the kitchen.

McKenna sat on the sofa and placed his briefcase next to him. Ginny returned with coffee for McKenna and brandy for McMahon, then left again.

"What do you expect to get accomplished at the Behavioral Sciences Unit?" McMahon asked.

"A psychological profile on the killers, and it'll probably be pretty good. They've got a track record when it comes to profiling serial killers, good enough so that more than once local cops were able to zero in correctly on a suspect using just the FBI profile."

"But you shouldn't need such a profile on them, should you?"

"No, not if we get an ID from the prints on the cartridge case. Then we'll know who one of them is, and after that it'll be just routine investigative work to find out the identity of the other."

"So why get profiles on them at this point?"

"Two reasons, number one being politics. The FBI is lending us substantial assistance on this case, and they're going to be doing even more to help us before this is over, so it's payback of a sort. You have to understand that their Behavioral Sciences Unit is one of their pride-and-joys. Always getting national exposure of one kind or another on those sensational magazine-type TV shows. I'm sure they'll be right on the money with these profiles and they'll get plenty of exposure on it once this is over. You know, taking what they tell us our killers will be like and why they do the things they do and comparing it against what we find out they really are like once we get them."

"You're right, and that's bad."

"Bad? Bad for who?"

"Oh, it'll be good enough for the FBI, give their Behavioral Sciences Unit plenty of good exposure. But it'll be bad for us and the prosecution once you arrest those two and it comes time to bring them to trial."

McKenna had a glimmer of understanding on where McMahon was

going with his reasoning, but he also recognized that sitting in front of him was one very smart lawyer who should be heard fully whenever he felt inclined to talk about trials. "I'm listening."

"Please do, because I think this is important to us. Quite naturally, those TV shows you've talked about will spend plenty of money with people like our Bob Hurley for an investigation into their backgrounds for comparison against the FBI's profiles. For starters, these PIs will uncover their horrible childhoods and all the mindless abuse they sustained. Then they'll go on to that early, mind-altering and behavior-changing sexual rejection they experienced at the hands of some unreasoning person they loved. These are all things I predict will be outlined in the FBI profile. Agreed?"

McKenna had no choice. While he had personally handled only one serial killing case in the past, he had followed every other known case with interest, reading everything he could get his hands on. He had read enough to know that, in most instances, serial killers aren't born, they're made, and McMahon had just described the typical production process. "Let's say you're right."

"Let's. Now here comes the real focus of the show, the kicker for the ratings, that aspect of the case the producers will use to generate controversy and sympathy where really there should be none. What I'm talking about is controversy about the killers and sympathy for them—not for their victims, who will be all but forgotten in the ratings scramble. They'll go into these monsters' present lifestyle and employment, and what will they find for the viewers of America?"

McKenna had the answer. He was reluctant to state it, but McMahon had left him no choice. "That they appeared to be normal, respected members of their communities—a hardworking duo, probably well educated, apparently socially adjusted, and certainly intelligent. So intelligent, in fact, that they were able to perpetrate the most horrible crimes throughout the world for at least twenty-two years without the police anywhere even linking their crimes together or suspecting what they were up to."

"Exactly. The producers will leave at least some of our sensation-seeking viewers with a type of respect for those two—a grudging respect, at best, but respect is respect. After respect comes a certain understanding, especially among those whose mommies were mean to them, whose daddies beat them with the belt, and all those who have loved hard and lost so badly that it affected their lives forever after. The men who killed my son will be portrayed to them as people who had experienced abuse no ordinary person could possibly stand, and yet they still managed to become successful pillars of the community, hard-working taxpayers with an unfortunate dark side."

McKenna knew McMahon was right and he would have been happy

to let the matter rest there. But McMahon wasn't. "Have you seen any of the shows we're talking about?"

"Yes," McKenna admitted.

"Sensational, biased, and distorted enough for you?"

"More than enough."

"Well, I've also seen some of them and I'm led to an inescapable conclusion: quite a few of the regular viewers have to be dimwitted enough to classify the program content as news, not entertainment. Then for the wrap-up, which the writers always end with a statement in the form of a question for our not-so-bright viewer. In our case it will probably go something like, 'We've tried to show you what happened and, in depth, why. Now the questions we all must ask ourselves are Who's at fault? Is society to blame for the horrors we've just witnessed? And finally, what should we all be doing to ensure that, in the future, men like X and Y, two apparently successful, upstanding members of their communities, aren't propelled to these unthinkable acts of violence. Goodnight.' "

McMahon looked to McKenna for a review of his performance. "Well, am I on the money?"

"It seems you've thought this whole thing through, but I'm amazed that it could all go down that way simply because I went to the FBI for profiles on them."

"That's because you didn't understand broadcast journalism, my boy. It's not news that's important, it's ratings. Controversy sells, so that's what they generate. I don't have to tell you what we wind up with after that program airs, do I?"

"No, you don't. It's gonna leave our prosecutor with the difficult task of finding twelve people for a jury who haven't seen one of those shows. Otherwise, he'd have to figure in the back of his mind that he might wind up with a nit-wit on his jury who's already answered for himself just those questions the writers asked at the end of the show."

"Precisely my point," McMahon said. "Only one stubborn nitwit who's been made to see things from Black and White's perspective could leave us with a hung jury."

"Especially in a death penalty case," McKenna added. "If he's been made to feel any sympathy at all for them, he might be more likely to vote for acquittal rather than have them executed for crimes he thinks he understands."

"Which brings to mind another point, one I'm afraid you'll find objectionable," McMahon said. He waited a moment, staring at McKenna, but then he shook his head. "I'll get to that later. Do you have any thoughts on this matter you'd like to add?"

"Just one. Even without a prime-time show, every motivating detail of

Black and White's lives will be probably brought out at a trial anyway. Their attorneys will try to get every sympathetic factor they possibly can before the jury, and they might be allowed to do it."

"Possibly, but at whose expense?" McMahon asked, smiling.

McKenna got McMahon's point. "Black and White's. They'd be the ones paying the PIs to look into every filthy aspect of the lives, not the networks."

"And that's something I can live with. That's fair enough and they'd be operating within their constitutional rights. I just don't want the networks subsidizing their defense and doing a better job on it than the best defense lawyers could possibly hope to do in court."

McKenna realized just then that no matter what his personal stake in Black and White's fate, McMahon was still a constitutional lawyer through and through. He would use every means at his disposal to assure their capture, including some of questionable legality. However, once they were in court and their case was before a jury, that sense of fair play he lived his life by would prevail.

McMahon had given McKenna something to think about, but he wasn't through yet. "You told me that you had two reasons for your visit to Quantico. Politics and . . . ?"

"And the worst-case scenario. The prints on that cartridge case looked pretty good to me, but I'm not a fingerprint expert. Maybe they aren't that good, or maybe they are and whoever put them there doesn't have his fingerprints on file anywhere. If the worst happens, those FBI profiles will come in pretty handy for me once I begin narrowing down suspects."

"From Timmy JFK's work with the airlines, I presume?"

God, this man really does know everything! McKenna thought, getting annoyed in spite of himself. "Yes."

"Then I hope you won't get mad at me, but let me put your mind at ease somewhat. The prints are quite good."

"How could you know that?" McKenna blurted out.

"Because I've had a high-ranking federal official make a discreet inquiry on my behalf. Your cartridge case arrived at the FBI Laboratory in Washington at three-forty-five this afternoon. It was immediately examined by their top two fingerprint experts, and they're optimistic that an identification will be forthcoming from those prints."

It was good news, but McKenna's annoyance intensified. Not only did McMahon know everything he did about his case, he knew more. McKenna decided to slow McMahon down a bit, if he could. "Then they'll get the identification, if the prints are on file."

"I'd say there's a ninety-nine-point-something chance that the prints are on file somewhere, if they look in the right places. You see, I agree wholeheartedly with your airline theory. I've made some inquiries and learned that commercial pilots are fingerprinted as part of an FAA background check required for their pilot's license, and other crew members are usually fingerprinted by their airlines for identification purposes, just in case their plane goes down."

"So the FAA and the airline fingerprint records should be the first place the FBI looks for a comparison."

"Yes, it should be, but it won't. They'll go through all the criminal files first. Maybe our killers will be there and maybe they won't."

"Why not go right to the place where we know their fingerprint records are?" McKenna asked, then answered his own question. "Legal procedure and constitutional safeguards. Prints taken for administrative purposes are kept separate from criminal prints. Since it's certainly crimes we're investigating, they have to search through the criminals before we can venture a peek at the good-citizen fingerprints."

"Yes, unless we want to take a chance on our fingerprint identification being suppressed in court on a technicality. We wouldn't want some high-minded and well-intentioned appeals court judge setting new law and establishing additional constitutional safeguards for the citizenry-at-large, thereby protecting them from overzealous government agents while he releases our killers to emphasize his point."

"No, we wouldn't. You wouldn't happen to have a legal and proper time frame for all this comparison work, would you?" McKenna asked.

"Just so happens I do. If he's got a criminal record, we'll know who he is by tomorrow. If not and he's a pilot, we'll know the day after. Worst case is if he's just a crew member. Then the airlines will have to be subpoenaed for their fingerprint records, an unusual procedure with inherent risks for us."

"Because the word might get out?"

"Yes. The FBI will have to articulate why they need to examine the airlines' fingerprint records and the word might get out. Remember, this case is national news, and the press would be very interested in hearing from any airline personnel manager with a story about the unusual things the FBI is asking him to provide."

McMahon was sitting back in his chair, sipping his brandy and eyeing McKenna shrewdly, waiting.

The implications were clear to McKenna. McMahon had laid out his case and it was time for McKenna to announce his decision. "Maybe tomorrow's not the exact right time to have these two profiled. Speaking for myself, I'd opt to wait and I could probably convince Gene Shields to see it our way. But there's a problem, and he'll be here tomorrow with two new murders for us. The FBI will be anxious to profile those cases—so anxious that even Gene Shields might not be able to prevent it."

For the first time that evening, McKenna was telling McMahon something he didn't already know and it gave him a small, perverse pleasure. "You don't know about the new cases from Costa Rica?" McKenna asked.

"No, I didn't know about them. Please enlighten me."

"I'm meeting the Costa Rican detective tomorrow at six and he'll fill me in then."

"Does that mean two additional victims?"

"No, six. Three double murders."

"Bringing the known body count to sixteen?"

McKenna quickly did the math and initially came up with only fourteen before realizing that McMahon was also counting the two people pictured in *Serious* and *In Charge* as the other two murdered souls. "Yes, sixteen that we know about so far."

"I'm hoping you have some pictures to show me in that briefcase."

"Do you feel up to it?"

"Without wanting to sound perverted, I can honestly tell you that I've been looking forward to seeing what my son's killers look like since you called me."

"Okay, it's your choice." McKenna removed the magazines, opened them to the centerfolds, and passed them to McMahon.

A minute went by as McMahon glared at the photos. Then it became two and McKenna felt uncomfortable staring at McMahon and imagining the thoughts going through McMahon's head. By the time four minutes had passed, McKenna didn't know where to look. Then McMahon closed the magazines and passed them back. "Thanks for your patience, Brian. I was considering for a minute or two asking your permission to make a copy of those photos, but then I decided that it wouldn't be good for my mental health having them around."

"Wise decision, I think."

"I'm afraid we're at the unpleasant part of the evening, but it's something I feel I must discuss with you. I know that you and Tommy have been working very hard on this case and I'd be remiss if I didn't tell you how exceptionally pleased I am with the results you've achieved in such a short time. I also realize that the both of you will enjoy a large amount of personal and professional satisfaction when you arrest those two, which makes this even harder for me to say." McMahon leaned back in his chair, for once uncomfortable and searching for words.

"Please get on with it," McKenna said impatiently.

"All right, I will." McMahon leaned forward and stared intently at

McKenna. "When the time comes, I would prefer that the men who murdered my son be arrested by the Arizona authorities and prosecuted there for the murders of Glenda Anderson and Greg Norman."

"What?" McKenna shouted, keeping himself glued to the sofa by sheer force of will. He managed to calm himself down and return McMahon's measured, dispassionate stare. "Do you realize what you're saying? Better yet, do you realize what you're asking?"

"Yes, I know what I'm saying, I know what I'm asking, and I know it will be difficult for you to accept."

"Difficult? Try impossible, and I'm not speaking entirely for myself. I can't even begin to imagine the prospect of relaying this idea of yours to Tommy and my boss."

"Are you willing to listen to what I have to say?"

"I'll listen, but from my perspective it's an impossible idea."

"I'm usually not cursed with impossible ideas," McMahon said softly and sounding contrite.

"I believe that, but if you ever had the unwelcome opportunity to spend five minutes in a closet with your idea and our Lieutenant Greve, you yourself would come out admitting that it's an impossible, foolish idea."

"Okay, given, it's an impossible idea. However, you said you'd listen, but I'm asking more than that. Could you listen *with an open mind* to how a foolish old man came up with this impossible idea?"

Foolish old man? You're anything but that, pal, McKenna thought. You're quickly becoming the enemy, but you'd also be one powerful enemy I don't need. "Okay, my mind's open. Go on."

"Okay, let's say for the sake of argument that they've been arrested by you and Tommy for the murder of my son and Cindy Barrone, a crime that occurred in Manhattan. Let's go even further and presume that you have an airtight case against them, something I'm sure that you and Tommy will have before you make any move to arrest in a case this big. Now the ball passes out of your hands, and goes where?"

"The Manhattan DA."

"Right. Upstanding old-timer, very professional, extremely well regarded, and in possession of an excellent conviction rate, especially when it comes to cases where the press is very interested. However, this fine old gentleman exhibits one astonishing quirk. Since the death penalty was reinstituted in New York, do you know how many times he's asked for it in the cases that fell under his jurisdiction?"

"None."

"Correct. Let's forget the Manhattan DA for a moment and look at the whole state of New York. How many prisoners do you currently have on death row?"

"None."

"Correct again, and the death penalty had been back on the books for five years there. Now back to our immediate concern, the Manhattan DA. Do you know how many times he could have legally asked for the death penalty, and I'm talking about perfectly heinous crimes committed by uncaring, depraved individuals?"

"I don't have the exact figure, but I'd guess that the number is somewhere around five."

"The number is exactly eleven. Now, to his credit, he got convictions in all eleven cases and some of them resulted in sentences of life without parole, but that's not what I'm looking for. Worse yet from my point of view, I'm told there are people doing life sentences in New York prisons who are actually enjoying their time there. That's not what I want for the people who murdered my son."

McKenna understood McMahon's feelings so clearly that, for the moment, he could think of nothing to say.

"Now let's wander to Arizona," McMahon said. "How many people has the state of Arizona executed since the Supreme Court permitted them to reinstitute their death penalty, which is, incidentally, something they never wanted to abandon in the first place."

"Six."

"And how many people does Arizona have on death row?"

"I don't know."

"Okay, no more questions because I'm being patently unfair. I didn't know either before I had it investigated, but they've got twenty-six on death row. I'd like to make it twenty-eight before I die."

"I see your point, but I can't go along with it."

"Because if you did, you'd be committing political suicide in your police department?"

"First would come the misery, then the suicide."

"I understand, but tell me this honestly, looking at things from my viewpoint. Do you still think it's a foolish idea?"

"Not foolish, but still impossible."

McMahon smiled, and McKenna didn't like it. "Impossible?" McMahon asked.

"Close to it, and I'll tell you something else. You're gonna have the big guns arrayed against it if you try engineering it."

McMahon said nothing, but the smile faded. He was apparently lost in his own thoughts for a few minutes and McKenna was content to leave him there because he had his own thinking to do, examining the weaknesses in his own position if he had to go to war with McMahon over this one. There were many, so many that he was forced to admit that McMahon had quite a few big guns of his own arrayed in the prospective battle if it came to that. McMahon might win if he tried.

McKenna looked up to find that McMahon was staring at him, waiting. "Well, are you gonna try it?" McKenna asked.

"You understand my position?" McMahon countered.

"Perfectly, but the question remains. Are you gonna try it?"

"Are we friends?"

"That depends, but I'd say we were getting there."

"I'll settle for that because I would value having a man like you for a friend. Going further than you'd like for the moment, I would like to think of us as two friends who admire and respect each other, but we're two friends who have unfortunately become involved in a squabble over a principle that affects us both."

"So you're gonna try it?"

"Yes."

"And you think you'll win?"

"I'm not accustomed to losing political battles of this nature, so yes, I think I'll win."

McKenna chuckled, then found himself wondering what was so funny. Then it came to him, the irony of his own position.

"I hesitate to even think it, but if they run to someplace we can't get them, I'd have a better shot at continued happiness in the NYPD."

McKenna had expected his statement to shock McMahon, but it didn't. Instead, McMahon just mulled it over for a minute. "I think I understand your position. If they run, your department gets credit for exposing them, identifying them, and stopping the killing. Taking it a step further, you're a municipal police department that can't be expected to arrest criminals who've fled to places where even our powerful federal government can't touch them, no less bring them back for trial."

"Yeah. Nasty thought, isn't it?"

"No, not so nasty. In the long run, that might even work out better for the both of us."

McMahon had McKenna's total attention. "Give me a clue on that, would you?" he asked, but McMahon didn't. He just returned McKenna's gaze with a trace of a smile on his lips.

"Are you saying that there's nowhere that you can't get them?" McKenna asked.

"Not exactly. First I'd have to know who they are and then I'd need some idea on where they are."

"And then what? You'd have them killed?"

"That's all I'm prepared to say for now unless we can go off the record and be very candid with each other."

"Why not? We've been off the record before talking about matters that could put us both in jail."

"This is different by a matter of some degrees. Then we were talking about evading privacy laws, now we're talking about something infinitely more serious that can never go further than this room."

Do I really want to know about this? McKenna wondered. Then, for reasons he couldn't quite fathom, he put his hand in his pocket and rubbed Cindy's earring between his fingers as he thought. He had made himself a solemn promise that he'd get Cindy's killers and he would, one way or the other. "I'd like to hear what you have in mind, but before you tell me you should know that it will leave this room."

"How many people?"

"Three."

"Just three?"

"Exactly three."

"And you trust them?"

"Enough to assure you that, counting me, there's only four people who are ever going to hear what you have to say right now."

"That's good enough for me, but before I begin I feel compelled to tell you how I look at this. I believe in the law of this land and I also believe in lawful treatment for those who break the law, no matter how horrible the crime. However, when a person charged with violating our laws flees to a place where there is no law or where the law can be bought by him for his own purposes, then our fair system of justice is effectively neutralized. I would prefer justice under the law, but in a place with no law there still must be justice."

"And you would administer that justice if they fled beyond the reach of our laws."

"Not personally, although I must confess that I wouldn't mind doing so. But there will be justice of the eye-for-an-eye variety if they should flee, even if it takes all the means at my disposal."

Your considerable disposal, McKenna thought as he examined McMahon's intentions. And why couldn't he do it? We'll identify them, and if they flee, the federal government will investigate. If their investigators are good enough, and in this case they certainly will be, they'll pull out the stops and soon be able to give us some idea where they fled to. Then the ball's in McMahon's court and he'll feel free to do what governments have done for years, including our own in the not-so-distant past. If he can't have them brought before the law and then legally executed, he'll have them assassinated. Easily accomplished, if enough money is thrown into the pot and the right people are sitting around the table. "Do you have any idea who you'll use?"

"Not yet. I won't think about that unless they flee. In that event, I'll give it a great deal of thought and come up with a viable, professional, competent personnel decision."

"I imagine our government will make some extradition demands to whatever country they flee to."

"Of course, and they'll be ignored. Those two have considered their eventual residence carefully and probably long ago made contingency plans about where they'd go if things got too hot for them here. It would have to be a country that would ignore or rebuff our government's demands for their extradition."

"But wouldn't it embarrass our government and make it suspect in the event those two were killed soon after their government rebuffed or ignored our government's demands?"

"Yes it would, and I'd never do anything to embarrass our government's reputation in the international community. If necessary, I'd be prepared to wait years for the opportune moment before taking the appropriate action."

"Years? You probably don't have years left."

"Probably not, but that makes no difference to me."

"But didn't you tell me you wanted them dead before you died?" McKenna asked.

"What I actually said was dead or under sentence of death. If they flee, they've placed themselves under sentence of death."

"Pronounced by you?"

"Yes, unfortunately."

"And these death sentences of yours will remain in effect even after you're dead yourself?"

"Yes, I assure you that they will remain very much in effect if I should die before they do," McMahon answered calmly.

"And who's going to see to that?"

"Ginny."

"Ginny?" McKenna said incredulously. "Your nurse is going to make sure those two are killed if you die before they're caught?"

McMahon smiled. "My nurse? Ginny's a lot more than that. I've known her since she was born, brought her and her mother home from the hospital."

"Her mother worked for you?"

"For my family from the time she was a teenager until she retired in eighty-five. Feisty lady, just like her daughter, and a good friend to my wife besides. She stayed around for a few years after my wife died, but she's living in Florida now. She comes up every year for her church picnic and we have a good old time sitting in the kitchen with a bottle of brandy and telling each other the same old family stories we've told a thousand times before."

McMahon's mood had changed for the better since the conversation had shifted to Ginny, so McKenna decided to stay on the subject. "Does Ginny work for you full-time?"

"Lord, no. I'd go out of my mind. She works for an agency, only works here when I'm sick. Runs the place and keeps everything straight, which isn't easy. You might've noticed on the way in that the hay's just been harvested."

"I did."

"Ginny took care of that," McMahon said proudly. "Got some dirt-poor farmers to harvest it for themselves and take it away."

"For free?"

"Of course for free, but there's a bonus involved. There's a substantial tax break for me, as long as I can keep this place on the county's books as farmland."

"Farmland? I also noticed that you've got lots of pasture, but no horses or any other livestock."

"Had plenty of horses when the kids were growing up, but they lost interest in them. Too much trouble to keep around, so I sold most of them off."

One thing McMahon had said didn't jibe with the information McKenna had. According to Andino, Arthur was McMahon's only child. "Who do you mean when you say the *kids*?"

"Arthur and Ginny."

McKenna said nothing and tried to keep his face straight, but something must have passed across it and McMahon caught it.

"It's a Southern thing, something you might not understand," McMahon explained. "She's not my blood, of course, and her mamma was in charge of raising her, but she was always here, one of the family. When they were growing up, Ginny and my Arthur were so close that her mamma and I used to worry that one day they'd run off together and ruin us both."

McKenna accepted that at face value, and realized that Ginny's starched white uniform was another Southern thing, displayed for his benefit to keep up appearances. "So Ginny's the only family you've got left?"

"In a manner of speaking," McMahon said, and then he laughed for the first time that evening, maybe for the first time in weeks. "Once I'm gone, it's gonna really disturb some of my highfalutin neighbors when they come to find out who owns half the property along their precious River Road, as well as a few of the mortgages on their pseudoplantation estates."

McMahon took his first sip of brandy, then made a face and held the snifter up to the light. "That color look right to you?"

"A little light. I'd say she watered it down a bit."

"Damn! It's tough to be sick around here," McMahon said loudly, but he was smiling at McKenna. "She wouldn't be happy unless she heard me complaining," he whispered.

"Is she in on your plans for Black and White if you die and the law can't get them?"

"Course she is. It's *our* plan."

"Is she tough enough to see it through?"

"Don't let that down-home country charm of hers fool you. She's smart as a whip and tough as nails, but we view this matter differently. Ginny's a good person, but she doesn't think much of all my legal niceties. If those two flee, they should pray they die before I do because I believe that executions should be as painless as possible."

"And what would be Ginny's plans for them?" McKenna asked. "Have them tortured to death?"

"She'll pay to have them killed, but she'd pay a lot more to have them captured. She wants a video in which they die like Cindy Barrone did, an eye for an eye."

"Does Paul Barrone have an inkling on any of this?"

"Not yet, but we talk" was all McMahon was prepared to say.

Just then Ginny came in carrying a medication tray. "Time for your pills, Mr. McMahon. Matter of fact, well past time."

McMahon looked disdainfully at the pills on the tray, then pointed at one. "That the pill that makes me groggy?"

"Yes, but it's the one you need the most. You'll be going bye-bye very soon, so say goodnight to Brian."

McKenna was mentally exhausted after his session with McMahon. Bye-bye and goodnight was good news as far as he was concerned.

TWENTY-FIVE

McKenna woke early and his first unpleasant chore was the call to Greve. The lieutenant was predictably enraged by McMahon's intention to have Black and White prosecuted in Arizona, but eventually McKenna was able to convince him that there was no way around it. If it came to a battle, McMahon would prevail for two reasons. One was that the bullet that would lead to either Black or White's identification was the sheriff's evidence. Greve might have been able to figure a way around that, but he didn't have the weight to get around McMahon's ace in the hole. With Barrone as a secret ally, McMahon was in a position to make the battle not worth the price for the NYPD and even the Manhattan DA, if he elected to get into the fray.

Unless Black and White were arrested in New York, an unlikely event, McMahon would win and they would be tried in Arizona. Greve was a realist and he decided he would call Arpaio to get his best deal before the sheriff learned how strong his position had suddenly become.

Brunette and Shields were McKenna's next calls, and they concurred with his assessment of the situation. Finally he called Tommy on the West Coast to fill him in, possibly the call McKenna had been dreading most, but it turned out to be the easiest. Surprisingly, Tommy shared McMahon's feelings and relished the prospect of Black and White suffering through the heat on death row.

McKenna spent the rest of the day as a tourist, visiting the Marine Corps Museum and treating himself to a good lunch in a nice restaurant. He was back in his room by five to prepare for his meeting with Miguel Morro.

McKenna's first impression was that Morro looked too young to have been assigned that first double murder in Costa Rica in 1977, twenty-two years before. But despite his young appearance, he appeared extremely professional, wearing a tropical seersucker suit that fit his trim frame just right, even with his jacket buttoned. His wing-tipped brown shoes were buffed to a high gloss, and what appeared to McKenna to be a Madison Avenue tie was snug at his neck. Even his thick briefcase was a quality stitched leather model that perfectly matched his shoes and, McKenna was sure, his belt.

"It's a pleasure to meet you, Detective McKenna," Morro said in clipped, unaccented English as he expended his hand. "I hope I'm not late."

McKenna doubted that Morro had ever been a minute late for any appointment in his life. "No, I think you're pretty much on time," McKenna said as he shook Morro's hand. "The pleasure is mine, and it's Brian."

Morro put his briefcase on the table, right next to the three stacks of case folders McKenna had placed there, but Morro showed no interest in them.

"Who's first?" McKenna asked.

"Since I understand that you have some answers to many of the questions I've been asking myself over the years, why don't I begin? I'll tell you what I've done and you can tell me where I went wrong."

McKenna found Morro's suddenly humble attitude a bit disconcerting until he noticed that the Costa Rican's face didn't match his words. Morro looked confident, like a man who knew he had done everything right. McKenna was eager to provide enlightenment to the dapper, self-assured Costa Rican, but he still felt the need to say something polite. "I've got some answers for you, but only because I've been very lucky since I got this case."

"Just lucky? Really? I remember when people used to say that I was a lucky detective, but that was a while ago," Morro said, but he said it with a smile.

"When did it end? When you got these cases?"

"That's right. April twelfth, 1985, the end of my luck."

If Morro had always had all the Costa Rican cases, the date didn't jibe with McKenna's information. "I thought these murders have been going on in your country since 1977."

"They have been, but we didn't know about it. The first victims were Sonia de Angeles, age nineteen, and Jesus Melendez, age twenty-four, two students at the University of San José's agricultural extension college in Herradura. They were last seen on Friday, June twenty-second, 1977, when they left to go camping together. When they didn't show up for their classes the following Monday, they were reported missing by the dean. I found their bones in 1985."

Something didn't make sense to McKenna. "They were just listed as missing for eight years, and that was that?"

"Incredible, I know, but Sonia and Jesus were Nicaraguans known to have Sandinista sympathies. The Sandinista revolution was in full bloom then, so the local detective who had the case took the easy way out."

"What did he say? That they probably sneaked back home together to join their revolution?"

"That's exactly what his report said. Our people never cared much for the Sandinistas, so that was good enough at the time."

Something on McKenna's face must have indicated to Morro that his explanation wasn't good enough. "A classic case of incompetent and uncaring police work, I'll admit," Morro added, but he wasn't offering an apology. He was just stating a fact.

"Where is that detective now?"

"Gone."

"Retired?"

"No, just gone. I found the bones when I found the bodies of the next set of victims, and there was quite a bit of public criticism over the way he'd handled the first case. The heat was too much for him, so he just quit and left."

"How were you assigned?"

"The dean at the college is a man of some influence. When another two of his students failed to return after a camping trip in 1985, he by-passed the local police and went directly to the minister of justice. Unfortunately, the minister assigned me and my life has never been the same."

"What agency are you with?"

"The *Policia Nacional*, something like your FBI on a much smaller scale."

"Why were you the one assigned, if you don't mind my asking?"

"Because I used to be thought of as one of our hot shots. Maybe too young, but always lucky."

"I've found that the sharp guy who works the hardest usually has the most luck," McKenna offered.

"That would be nice if it were always true, but nobody's ever accused me of being a dummy and I've been breaking my ass on this case for fourteen years. No luck and not much to show for my efforts. Worse yet, the heartless, murdering animals kept on killing."

"Animals?" McKenna asked, surprised.

"Yeah, didn't you know? There's two of them."

All of a sudden, Morro looked even brighter to McKenna. "Yeah, I knew that. But how did you know?"

"I figured out years ago that there had to be two of them. I knew I was right when I saw them, but we're getting ahead of ourselves."

Way ahead of ourselves, but he can't be as unlucky as he's led me to believe, McKenna thought. "One black and one white, pretty good shape?"

"That's them, but I'd say they're in excellent shape. I should know, since they were naked when I saw them."

"Right after one of their murders?"

"As they were throwing a body off a cliff, but I was too far away to see their faces clearly."

"How far away?"

"Too far, even with the fancy equipment I had. Three miles, more or less."

"Is that why they got away?"

"No. They got away because they were lucky and I wasn't. I got close, but they got away," Morro said, but without remorse. Again, it was another fact he was stating, not an apology.

"How long ago was that?"

"January twenty-eighth, 1997. Right after they killed Esteban and Cecilia Santiago."

"A married couple?"

"No, brother and sister. Argentine backpackers on vacation. He was twenty-three and she was just seventeen."

"Were those the last murders they did in Costa Rica?"

"Yes, thank God. They didn't know how close I was to them at the time, but I couldn't keep it away from the press. Must've given them quite a shock when they read the papers the next day, but it's not all bad. I like to think that I slowed them down and saved some lives."

Maybe in Costa Rica you did, just a part of the picture, McKenna thought, but he saw no reason to burst Morro's bubble. Besides, the surprises were coming too fast and he wanted to put them in context. "Let's get back on track," he suggested. "The 1985 murders?"

"Maria Castellana and Tomas Vega, ages twenty-two and twenty-three. Went camping together for the weekend in Vega's Toyota Land Cruiser. I was assigned when they didn't show for classes and I started out by doing all the things you'd expect, I hope."

"Interview family and friends of the victims, check with all the camp-sites in the country, search the area around Herradura, and put an alarm out for the Land Cruiser," McKenna surmised.

"Exactly. Got me nowhere and took the better part of a week, but I did find out that Maria and Tomas usually camped locally. It's a beautiful area, but pretty rugged. I had about three hundred student volunteers and the local cops for the initial search, but not much more help than that back then. I felt that Maria and Tomas were dead, probably murdered by the same man who had killed Sonia and Jesus, but I had to find the bodies before I could get really serious with the investigation. Saw no other way to find them quick, so I went to the press for help."

"And they ran with it?"

"Big time. I believe you're familiar with our newspapers?"

"Yeah, I've had some experience with them. Not much in the way of news, read a lot like *Soap Opera Digest*."

"That's because there usually isn't much news in Costa Rica. Not bad news, anyway, but this was different. Double murders are rare there, and they played it to the hilt. Ran front-page interviews with Maria and Tomas's families, real tearjerkers with the mothers pleading for help to find their children. The day after the articles ran I had over ten thousand people show up in Herradura to help me with the search."

McKenna found the number astounding. "Ten thousand?"

"Maybe more. The latecomers had to park more than two miles from town, but I used them all. Stretched them in a line and we found the Land Cruiser at the end of an old logging road about six miles east of town."

"Where'd you find the bodies? West of town?"

"You're thinking like me. I didn't know there were two of them then, but I figured that whoever had killed Tomas and Maria was cagey enough to dump the Land Cruiser on the other side of town from where he'd killed them and dumped the bodies. I started the searchers going west in as much of a line as they could manage. At one o'clock I got a message that there was a bad smell whiffing up from the bottom of a cliff near the end of another old logging road about seven miles west of town. Rough road, tough going even in my four-by-four. By the time I got there, there were thousands of people at the edge of the cliff."

"Was there a clearing there?"

"You mean, was it visible from the air?"

The question was another surprise for McKenna, one that led him to believe that he wasn't going to be giving Morro that many answers after all. "Yeah, that's what I mean."

"A nice clearing, about an acre. The area at the end of the road had been heavily logged, almost to the cliff. I looked over the edge and couldn't see them, but the wind was blowing our way and the faint odor told me that Maria and Tomas were there in the woods at the bottom, three hundred feet straight down."

"Was it a beautiful spot?" McKenna asked.

"Breathtaking. Forested mountains on all sides and the valley below covered with small farms."

Time to give him a surprise, McKenna thought. He took *Serious* out of the manila envelope, opened it to the centerfold, and passed it to Morro. "Are those the killers, is that Maria Castellana, and is that the spot?"

Morro studied the photos for a moment, but his reaction disappointed McKenna because there was none. No surprise, no shock, no excitement, nothing that told McKenna that Morro was impressed and learning from his smarter northern neighbors. Morro closed the magazine, examined the cover for a moment, and passed it back to McKenna. "Yes, I'm sure that's them. But no, that's not Maria and no, that's not the spot. But you're close."

"Do you know who the girl is?"

"Cecilia Santiago and the spot is on top of the same cliff, but about a half a mile south."

"The Argentine girl, the one you almost caught them on in ninety-seven?"

"Yes, Cecilia and her brother, but you're missing some pictures. They shot Esteban in the leg, but that's not what killed him. They also tortured him to death."

Another variation on their usual procedure, McKenna thought, and Morro is right. There are more pictures and film somewhere recording

Esteban's death. "Do you know what this means?" he asked, pointing to the magazine.

"Sure," Morro answered at once. "It means they were out of the country before the newspapers came out the next day, so they didn't know they were hot. Otherwise, they would never have risked selling those pictures."

"Did you know they were photographing their murders?"

"Not for sure, but I suspected they were. However, we're getting ahead of ourselves again."

McKenna didn't like it. He had expected to be the one giving the answers, not asking the questions. Morro's blasé attitude disturbed him, even though he realized the Costa Rican was right—they were getting ahead of themselves once again. "Okay, back to Maria and Tomas."

"With all the professional help I had there, it wasn't a big problem getting down the cliff. My four victims and their camping gear were all there on the forest floor, pretty close together—Tomas's and Maria's bodies along with most of Sonia's and Jesus's bones."

"Most of the bones? What happened to the rest?"

"Carried off by scavengers, but both Sonia's and Jesus's skulls and their clothes were still there. Sonia still had hers on, but they had been shredded by the scavengers. She'd been shot once in the head and the bullet was still there, inside her skull. Gun used to kill her was a .380 Colt Commander."

"Burnt paper residue embedded in the bullet?"

"Yes, gun fired while held in a paper bag."

"And Jesus?"

"Clothes spread all around, so he was naked when they threw him off. Skull crushed, but I'm assuming that was from the fall. Our pathologists couldn't give an exact cause of death from the bones I was able to give them, but we both know how he died."

"Yes, horribly," McKenna said. "How about Tomas and Maria? Which one of them got the full treatment?"

"Maria. She was naked and lying face up, but at the time she was in such horrible shape that I couldn't tell how she died. Her body was bloated and black because of the natural decomposition, there was the feedings of the scavengers to consider, and the damage caused by the fall down the cliff, but I could see hundreds of what I thought were cuts from her nose to her knees."

"What were they, lash marks?"

"That's what our pathologist thought, but even he couldn't be sure at the time."

"Any evidence of sexual intercourse?"

"Couldn't tell. Too much time had passed and her vagina was torn pretty badly."

"How about her back? What kind of damage there?"

"Very strange. Buttocks lashed, probably postmortem."

"Evidence of restraining devices?"

"Horrible bruises on her neck and wrists," Morro said. "I'm assuming this is matching your cases?"

"Exactly what I expected. How about Tomas?"

"Fully clothed, cause of death one shot to the head. Colt Commander, .380 caliber, burnt paper fiber embedded in the bullet. Different gun than the one they used to kill Jesus, or the same gun with a different barrel."

Looks like this guy's got everything just about figured out, McKenna thought. "Any hope of a crime scene on top of the cliff?"

"None. By the time I was pulled back up, there were thousands of people there. I figured that any evidence left there had been trampled and destroyed by then. I wasted time for the next ten years doing all the routine things."

Just like Tommy and Bynum, McKenna thought. He could see that Morro was reliving those years and suffering every one of them.

"Were you able to get information on similar cases?" McKenna asked.

"None. Officially, I wasn't even allowed to make requests."

"Why?"

"It might be hard for you to understand, but these crimes are sort of a national embarrassment for us. We like to project ourselves as an egalitarian, family-oriented, and relatively crime-free democracy, a friendly tropical paradise where tourists don't have much to worry about as they spend their money and boost our economy."

"What does that mean, publicity-wise? Is there a lid on these murders?"

"An unofficial lid. Our newspaper editors understand how important tourism is to the nation, and they've been told about the many phone calls the ministry of tourism received from concerned travel agents all over the world after the spectacle involved in the discovery of the first four bodies. Their policy has become: the less said about the murders, the better."

It was time to change the subject, McKenna thought. "Did the press keep the lid on even after the Argentines were killed?"

"No, the story was too big. The coverage wasn't explosive and it wasn't picked up by the wires, but it still affected our tourist flow from Argentina."

"Badly?"

"About twenty percent down, a disaster as far as the ministry of tourism was concerned. Argentina, Canada, and the U.S. provide the bulk of our tourists, so our policy of understating the problem was reinforced," Morro explained, but he didn't sound happy to McKenna.

"I take it that you don't agree with that policy."

"I hate it as much as everybody else when tourism goes down, but that policy might be responsible for the deaths of Esteban and Cecilia Santiago."

"Because they had no idea that they were camping in the woods a mile away from the site of four horrible, unsolved murders?"

"Yes," said Morro with a grimace.

McKenna paused in sympathy, then asked, "How did you know they'd come back to the same spot to kill again?"

"I didn't, but I figured they liked the setting. I found an abandoned shack on top of a mountain across the valley from the cliff and I was provided with some high-powered optical equipment for both night vision and day use. Then I had some of the trees on top of the cliff at the murder site cut down so we could see it clearly from our observation post. Hid some sensors in the woods around the campsite and set up a plan with the police in Herradura and the surrounding towns to capture them if they hit again. Then came the hard part."

"Waiting?"

"For nine years of my life. I was in that shack with a telescope pressed against my eye almost every night from 1988 to 1997."

Now that could certainly create an obsession, McKenna thought. "Why every night? I'd think that the site was used by campers only every once in a while. No campers, no reason to man your observation point."

"True, but there were two people camped there almost every night. Hard to believe, but after the murders the site had become popular among the more daring students at the college. I guess the sense of danger spurs romance, because we had couples there almost every weekend. On weekdays I supplied most of the campers."

"Undercovers?"

"Yes, from the *Policia Nacional*. Matter of fact, that spot was responsible for two marriages and one divorce in our department and I can tell you one thing—whether it was cops or students camped there, nobody got much sleep."

"Complacency never set in over all those years?"

"Not with my people. No matter how many times they'd been there, every night I showed them the pictures of what those monsters did to Maria Castellana. That kept them alert and ready. Unfortunately, when the killers did hit again there were legitimate students camped there."

"Otherwise you would have gotten them?"

"I like to think so. My people were well trained, well armed, and in good shape. Getting them was all that they'd thought about for years. There was a hiking path that ran along the top of the cliff, so it would have been no problem for my people follow it to the place where they'd just killed Cecilia and Esteban."

"How long would it have taken them?"

"It was a rough path, so maybe fifteen minutes of tough running. But we had no luck, my people weren't there, and Murphy's Law ruled that morning. What could go wrong did go wrong."

Although the Costa Rican's words were calm, his face showed a hint of rage. "Sooner or later, it happens to everyone on a big case," McKenna said.

"So I've heard," Morro said evenly. "But if it didn't happen to me this time on my big case, only God and those monsters know how many young people would still be alive and enjoying their lives for years to come."

He's right, but what do I say to that? McKenna wondered. If he had caught them in ninety-seven, for starters Cindy Barrone and Arthur Mc-Mahon would still be alive and I wouldn't be here talking to him.

"Sunday, January twenty-eighth, 1997, just after eight in the morning. I was manning the shack with Diego Feliciano, one of my men," Morro said without preamble. "Diego was looking through the telescope, watching a student couple at the campsite preparing breakfast. Out of the corner of my eye I thought I saw a movement on the cliff across the valley, a half mile south of the campsite. At first I thought a naked person had just jumped off the cliff, but then I knew it was *them* and that they had just murdered another two young people."

"They killed another two people just half a mile away from the place you'd been watching for nine years? That sure was bad luck," McKenna commented. "What did you do then?"

"I got behind the telescope and trained it on the spot just in time to see them swing another naked body off the cliff. While Diego was setting up the camera on the spot, I got the Herradura cops on the radio, broadcast the killers' description, and activated the plan. They set up roadblocks and called Rincon Hermosa and Ariete for reinforcements."

"Ariete?"

"Another small town, nine miles south of Herradura."

"Where were the roadblocks set up?"

"On the Herradura road, two miles on either side of the beginning of the logging road going to the campsite."

"How many cops are we talking about?"

"Not many. Herradura has a five-man department, but Rincon Hermosa and Ariete only have two each. I called San José and got more help on the way from the *Policia Nacional*. By that time, my killers had thrown all the camping gear off the cliff and were already gone. Diego and I took off for the campsite."

"Did you manage to get any pictures of them?"

"Diego shot a roll. Thirty-six exposures."

"Any good?"

"Not bad, considering the distance and the morning haze. Used a filtered one thousand millimeter Nikon telephoto lens set up on a tripod-mounted, motorized thirty-five-millimeter Canon."

Morro opened his briefcase, removed a folder, and casually pushed it across the table to McKenna.

The 8x10 enlargements *were* good, McKenna had to admit. As in all telephoto 35mm shots taken at great distance, they were grainy, but Black and White were center frame in most of them as they pitched the wrapped bundles of camping gear off the cliff. Of course, the photos weren't as good as the *Serious* and *In Charge* centerfolds, but in these they were completely naked—no masks or leather harnesses. Their faces were blurry, but Mc-Kenna could see that Black was smiling in quite a few. He closed the folder and pushed it back toward Morro.

"Usually," Morro continued, "it takes twenty-two minutes to drive around the north end of the valley from the shack to the logging road. We made it in eighteen that morning, but Diego swore that he'd never again get into a car I was driving. We passed our northern roadblock along the way, then drove up the logging road straight to the campsite. Told the students to get out of there quick as they could, and we started running the hiking path. Saw nothing along the way to Cecilia and Esteban's campsite, and not much when we got there—just the remains of their campfire. Couldn't even see them when we looked over the cliff."

"Was there a clearing there?" McKenna asked.

"No, but it was still a beautiful spot."

"And did the hiking trail end there?"

"No, and don't bother asking your next question. To my discredit, I didn't know where it ended. I had always assumed that the killers took the logging road to the campsite to do their murdering."

"Maybe they did, the first two times."

"Maybe, but not when I'd thought I was ready for them. More bad luck, mine and those two kids. This time the killers used that trail and were on their way into my trap when they came across Cecilia and Esteban, two perfect targets of opportunity they couldn't resist."

"How far ahead of you were Black and White when you finally got to Cecilia and Esteban's campsite?"

"They had about an hour on us, so Diego and I took off down the path running for all we were worth. After another mile, the trail forked. It looked like the left branch was leading to the Herradura highway, so we split up. Diego took the left branch and I had all our units move to cover the highway south of Herradura. If that was the way they had come in, we still might have gotten them. But it wasn't."

"Where did the right branch lead?"

"Down to the valley, but it took me another hour of hard hiking to find that out. The trail ran right down to the Pan American Highway. I don't know how far behind them I was by the time I got there, but they were gone."

"Real bad luck, but nothing more you could have done at that point," McKenna said.

"Yes there was, and I tried doing it. I called the airport police, gave them the killers' descriptions, and had all flights out delayed and all passengers prevented from boarding. Then I hitchhiked to the airport and helped look for them for an hour. As you know, they weren't there—at least, not the black one."

"You think it's possible that White was among the passengers waiting there?"

"Not now I don't, but I did at the time. I questioned a few well-built white passengers traveling alone—a Cuban, a Canadian, and an American. I was specifically interested in what they'd been doing immediately before arriving at the airport, and they all had stories for me that sounded good. Unfortunately, I didn't have enough to hold them and I didn't have enough time to check out their stories."

"Why not?"

"Because the minister of tourism countermanded my orders and let the planes go. It seems that I had infuriated the airlines. Many of the passengers delayed at our terminal had connecting flights to catch in places like Miami, Mexico City, and Havana. I was disrupting schedules and creating quite an expense for the airlines, so they complained to the minister and he folded."

"No big thing," McKenna said. "You didn't see Black and White in the terminal because they were already on board their plane. They're crew members."

"I know that now, but I didn't then," Morro lamented.

"How do you know?"

"Esteban's autopsy. The bullet removed from his leg had been fired from a .25 caliber Astra. That made me ask myself, Why a different gun? I asked about changes in our airport security arrangements and came up with the same answer as I assume you have."

"You have, but what made you think they'd be going to the airport in the first place?" McKenna asked.

"Three things. For one, the Pan American Highway runs right by it. Two: They'd had lots of practice killing and I knew it hadn't been in Costa Rica, so there was a good chance they were foreigners. And three: While watching that campsite for nine years, I'd seen thousands of planes fly over me on the approach to the airport and that had made me wonder if the killers had discovered the campsite from the air. I knew that if they didn't go to the airport right after the killings, they'd soon be there."

"Then I think we're both right."

"We are, and I've got a little present for you," Morro said. He reached into his briefcase and passed McKenna an envelope.

"What's in this?" McKenna asked.

"The names of our killers, somewhere. It's a list of the airline crew members who flew in and out of San José from January twenty-fifth to January twenty-ninth, 1997."

"You couldn't get a list of the crew members who were there for the weeks of the first two murders?"

"No, our procedures were different then. Nobody checked crew members' passports, they were just waved through Immigration and Customs. However, you'll notice from that list that many changes have been made since Esteban's and Cecilia's murders."

McKenna opened the envelope and pulled out the three-page list. It contained rows of names of pilots, copilots, and flight attendants, along with the numbers of the flights on which they had arrived and left San José. Neat lines were drawn through the names of all the females and most of the males. "Do these crossed-out male names belong to the crew members you've checked out?"

"Yes. At one time or another they've all flown back into San José and received a good look from me. You'll find that there's only eight male crew members who haven't returned. If we're right, two of those eight are our killers."

"Have you been able to find out if any of them are black?"

"I could've made inquiries to the airlines, but thought that unwise. I didn't want to take a chance on an official inquiry from me getting back to them."

"I agree. I'll be able to find out, and it won't be an official inquiry to the airlines."

"And you'll let me know the results?" Morro asked.

"At once, of course."

"Good." Morro took a business card from his wallet and handed it to

McKenna. "Feel free to call me anytime, day or night," he said. "Now, is there anything I've missed that you'd like to know?"

It was the question McKenna had been dreading. "As it turns out, not much."

TWENTY-SIX

McKenna had planned to call McMahon before going to bed, but McMahon called him first. "I have a message from our police commissioner," McKenna said. "He wants you to know that he admires your ability to get things done your way. Arizona's fine by him."

"Good, but that's not the reason I'm calling. I've just learned that the FBI's linked your fingerprint to a name."

Isn't it funny that McMahon's got the news before Shields does, McKenna thought. "Is he an air crew member?"

"Currently he's a pilot for American Airlines. James Hillman, age fifty-one. Lives in San Francisco."

McKenna was going through Morro's list as McMahon talked. James Hillman was there, one of the names that hadn't been crossed out, and McKenna's heart skipped a beat. He had been right, which meant that he was also looking at the other killer's name and he had a good idea who it might be. Right under Hillman's name was Jason Robles, another name that hadn't been crossed out. Robles was the copilot on the same flight Hillman had flown in and out of San José. Morro's list didn't state the date and departing time of American Airlines flight 307, but McKenna was willing to bet it had left just hours after Hillman and Robles had murdered Cecilia and Esteban. "Which one is Hillman? Black or White?"

"Black."

"There's some things we should talk about," McKenna said.

"Exactly what I was thinking. You want me to keep Hurley from tracking Hillman and let you do your job."

This guy's a mind reader! McKenna thought, but he said, "That would be appreciated."

"Done. Just keep me posted, will you?"

"I promise." The phone rang again just after McMahon hung up.

"Got some good news for you, buddy," Shields said.

"I know. Black is James Hillman, an American Airlines pilot."

"God! That McMahon's really well informed."

"I know. A shame, isn't it?"

"Not as long as he's on your side," Shields said.

"I'm also glad we've got Morro on our side. He's good, and thanks to him, I've got a pretty good idea on who White is. It needs checking, but it looks like he was Hillman's copilot when they flew into Costa Rica to murder the last two victims there."

"When are you going to need Timmy JFK?"

"As soon as possible. How about tomorrow, starting with lunch at the Wicked Wolf?"

"I'll take care of it. He'll be there at noon."

After Shields hung up, McKenna thought he would go over the reports documenting Esteban's and Cecilia's murders. He opened up the first folder and, on top, saw Morro's crime scene photo of Cecilia's horribly mutilated body lying on the forest floor. He merely glanced at it before deciding that reading the reports and studying the photos could wait.

To avoid the Washington traffic, McKenna had left the Quantico Sheraton at 6:00 A.M. He made good time and was at a table in the Wicked Wolf at eleven-thirty, consulting one of New York's premier personalities. Chipmunk was a bartender there, but he was much more than that. He was a friend to reporters, prosecutors, detectives, and federal agents, so the Wicked Wolf was the place where they got together to work out unofficial deals, squash rumors, and air gripes in a congenial atmosphere. It was a neutral zone where Chipmunk was the moderator and final law.

How Chipmunk arrived at this exalted position was a mystery to anyone who bothered thinking about it. For the more astute, his role was simply accepted as a fortunate and long-established fact, a case of the right man for a difficult job requiring diplomacy, an extraordinary share of common sense, a pleasant personality, a knowledge of the inner politics and protocol of the various law enforcement agencies working the city, and—above all—connections.

Chipmunk knew everybody in town worth knowing, an issue complicated by the many wannabes who listed him as their best friend when, in fact, Chipmunk had no idea of their existence.

McKenna had known Chipmunk for twenty-odd years, since his drinking days. Although McKenna had long ago realized that he shouldn't, couldn't drink, he was still among the many who counted Chipmunk as a reliable and trusted friend, and sometimes more. He thought of Chipmunk as his oracle, the person who always knew somebody who could provide a

crucial missing piece whenever McKenna had trouble developing information on one of his cases.

After the amenities had been observed, it was Chipmunk who first
turned to business. "Heard your case involves snuff films."

"That's right."

"Interesting, considering how those films have been the topic of some
other inquiries I've heard about," he commented.

McKenna wasn't surprised at the depth of Chipmunk's knowledge on
what was supposed to be one of the most confidential aspects of his case.
He had seen most of the Manhattan North Homicide Squad in the Wicked
Wolf at one time or another and Chipmunk considered many of them
friends. They knew they could tell him about any case without worrying
about word traveling down the bar to the reporters usually seated there.
"Interesting? What else did you hear?" McKenna asked.

"That Bob Hurley is looking to procure one of those films for his new
client, and money's no object."

Could McMahon be double-crossing me and going behind my back
after I asked him to hold off on looking for a film? McKenna wondered.
"How old is this information?"

"About a week."

That put McKenna's mind at ease. "Then it's too old. He might've
been looking for one then, but he's going to hold off."

"Maybe on buying one, but he's still trying to get a line on where to
get one if he needs it. I understand he's had his people out trying to locate
Johnny Nolan."

McKenna had known Nolan for twenty years, but hadn't seen him in
some time. Nolan was a retired detective, a sharp, debonair, personable
man-about-town who was generally well liked—but not by McKenna.
Years ago, they had both worked in the Manhattan South Robbery Squad
and McKenna had noticed that rather than work his cases, Nolan had
spent most of his time planning his second career—the one he would
pursue after his retirement from the NYPD. The only cases he had put
any energy into were those robberies involving influential or wealthy victims.

Nolan's planning had paid off for him when he learned a Saudi prince
had been the victim in a hotel-room robbery. The prince had ordered a
high-priced call girl to his room, but the price had turned out to be higher
than the prince had anticipated. Sometime during the entertainment, she
slipped the prince a mickey and then let her two male accomplices into
the room.

When the prince awoke to a pounding headache, he also found himself
poorer by one hundred and forty thousand dollars in cash and jewelry and

in a dilemma the robbers had anticipated. For years many Saudi princes visited New York to enjoy themselves in sinful pursuits that would not be tolerated in their puritanical Muslim society at home. The prince couldn't report the robbery without risking some embarrassing and pointed inquiries from the Saudi religious authorities that could result in his beheading, so the only person the prince had mentioned the robbery to was the hotel's chief of security, a retired lieutenant and also, coincidentally, Nolan's brother-in-law.

News of the prince's plight quickly found its way to Nolan's ears and he had gone to work feverishly and competently. Although no report of the crime had been reported to the police, within two days Nolan had the call girl and her accomplices in handcuffs in a townhouse owned by another Saudi prince, but they weren't under arrest. Nolan convinced the trio that it was in their best interests to return the prince's jewelry and cash. To obtain their freedom they returned what they had left of the loot and the prince emerged from the affair only eight thousand dollars poorer and forever in Nolan's debt.

Rumors of Nolan's unsanctioned and unofficial efforts on the prince's behalf had eventually reached the Internal Affairs Bureau, but it was too late in arriving. Nolan had already retired to become the trusted friend, bodyguard, and consort of every Saudi prince visiting town with debauchery on his mind, a very profitable and comfortable position for a retired second grade detective. Nolan excelled in his work, ingratiated himself with many of the higher-priced call girl rings and the owners of the city's more exclusive clubs, and many times, accompanied this prince or that on their fun jaunts around the world.

A real sleaze, McKenna thought, as he pondered the question inherent in Chipmunk's information: What would make Hurley think that Nolan might have access to a snuff film? McKenna waited and looked to Chipmunk for the answer.

"About six months ago Nolan was in here with his load on, talking about a film one of his princes had just bought in Brooklyn with his help," Chipmunk said. "Quite a horror show it was, according to him."

"A film, not a video?"

"He says it was old, probably made before videos came around. It was a film shown on a screen."

"Were Black and White in it?"

"I don't know. I didn't ask any questions, just let him ramble on."

"Is it possible he was bullshitting?"

"I don't think so. The film was so graphic and horrible that it even shook up Nolan, and he's a hard-ass. He was close to slobbering in his drink, so I don't think he was exaggerating a bit."

"Did he mention anything about the victim or the setting?"

"Nothing about the setting, but he did say the victim was a young Spanish girl, one of those dark South American types. Looked like a teen-ager to him."

"Type of torture?"

"Whips and knives. He also said that the kid was beheaded at the end of the film, just to show that it was all real. Said his prince got a real charge out of that."

"If Black and White did the killings in that film, the beheading angle is something new for them," McKenna observed. "Any idea on where No-lan might be found?"

"None. I do know that he's not in town, hasn't been in weeks. Hurley's people have talked to his ex-wife and she had nothing to say except that she's very happy. Nolan's got her alimony paid up two years in advance."

I've got to get to Nolan and find out where he got that film, McKenna thought. But can I find him if Hurley can't? Unlikely. If Nolan is to be found and induced to share his information, Hurley's probably the one to do it.

Chipmunk had given McKenna plenty to think about. Timmy JFK came in and was warmly greeted by both men. When Timmy sat down, Chipmunk took his cue and went back behind the bar to serve the three patrons patiently awaiting his return.

Timmy was a large man, six foot four and stocky, about forty years old with a full head of black hair, single, and happy, as evidenced by the smile always fixed on his face. He reminded McKenna of a large, friendly teddy bear. Apparently, many women also thought so, and those who knew Timmy JFK thought that he might be the most hugged man and cuddled man in town. Timmy did great with the ladies, but he was a perfect gen-tleman and never bragged or talked about his love life.

McKenna got right down to business, outlining the progress made in the case while Timmy JFK seemed to be listening with half an ear. Mc-Kenna knew that Timmy's manner was one of the things that made him the perfect undercover—Timmy JFK remembered everything he heard and saw without seeming to take an interest in anything.

"So what's my mission?" Timmy JFK asked when McKenna was through with his explanation.

"Find out everything you can about Hillman and Robles, especially their work histories. I need to place them here, in San Jose, in Arizona, and in Costa Rica on the dates the other four murders there were com-mitted."

"No problem."

"For now, can you do it unofficially and discreetly so word doesn't get out that we're looking at them?"

"For now?"

"Until we find out whether or not they've skipped the country. If they have, my job gets harder but yours gets easier. If they've gone, I'll get you subpoenas and you can make all your inquiries official."

"Fine. I've got a few friends in personnel at American Airlines, so I'll start snooping and asking around this afternoon. Should be able to tell you sometime tonight whether or not they've skipped. What else?"

"Nothing else, at the moment."

"Want my thoughts about a few things that must be bothering you?"

"Like what?"

"You know they're not renting cars, so haven't you been asking yourself how they always seem to have a car available for their use wherever they go?"

"Yeah, that's been bothering me," McKenna conceded.

"Pool houses and cars. Airline crews spend about three nights a week away from their domiciles, so groups of them get together and rent houses close to the airports. Usually keep an old car or two at the house for use by the pool members when they stay at the house. Very convenient arrangement, and pretty cheap when the cost is spread out over a large enough pool of members."

"What's the domicile? Their home city?"

"Not necessarily. Their domicile is just the city they're based out of, but that doesn't mean they have to live there. Don't forget, air crews are gone from home a lot, but they don't actually work a lot of hours. They can fly to their domicile from just about anyplace in the country for next to nothing with their employee discounts. Matter of fact, I know pilots who are domiciled in New York but still live in Florida. Airlines charge them something like twenty dollars to fly up to work."

"But why would they spend for pool houses? Don't the airlines pay for them to stay in hotels when their flight schedules take them away from their domiciles?"

"Yeah, but they also pay them something not to use the hotels. Most would prefer to get into a pool, have a car available, and make a few bucks extra in the process."

"I see. Seems like a sensible arrangement."

"There's other benefits to being in a pool if you like to travel when you're not working or if your flight schedule takes you to a particular city only every once in a while. It's a bit complicated, but there are reciprocal arrangements between pools in different cities. Pool members can stay in a pool house just about anywhere for a nominal fee on a space-available basis."

"Would you be able to find out if Hillman and Robles are in any of those housing pools?"

"I'll give it a shot," Timmy JFK said. "You'll be hearing from me soon."

TWENTY-SEVEN

After lunch, McKenna went to the office. There had been a homicide in the 34th Precinct that morning, so the place was empty. He spent three hours preparing his reports on his meetings with Morro, McMahon, and Timmy JFK, then began reading the reports Morro had given him on the murders of Cecilia and Esteban Santiago. That took another depressing hour, and at the end of it, McKenna couldn't decide which of the two had suffered more. As in all the other torture cases, Cecilia and Esteban had finally bled to death and their buttocks had been whipped postmortem.

Greve came in with six detectives at five-thirty and McKenna was surprised to see Tommy among them. All appeared to be in a good mood. Greve nodded to McKenna on his way into his office, then closed the door behind him.

"When did you get in?" McKenna asked Tommy.

"Eight this morning. Caught the red-eye from San Diego last night."

"And you went right to work?"

"There was a murder," Tommy said, considering that explanation enough.

"How did it go?"

"Good. Dominican drug-related killing, sixteen-year-old drug-dealing victim, nineteen-year-old drug-dealing shooter. Found out he went straight to his crib after knocking off the competition and packed himself a suitcase, so we'll get him. Got Monahan and Nigel at JFK and a few Port Authority detectives at Newark Airport waiting for the kid to show up for his flight to the Dominican Republic."

It sounded like a closed case to McKenna if the shooter followed the typical routine—kill the competition, then relax out of reach in the home country and wait to see what develops in New York. "Whose case is it?"

"Monahan's, a ground ball. Let's go out for coffee."

The coffee pot was on and full, so McKenna knew that Tommy wanted to talk to him alone. "Fine, but let me get my paperwork signed first."

"Mind if I take a look, first?"

"Not at all." McKenna gave Tommy the reports and waited while Tommy read them.

"Good enough job," Tommy said, giving the reports back to McKenna. "I'll be downstairs in the car."

Something's on Tommy's mind. Looks like a tough night shaping up, McKenna thought. He found Greve at his desk with his cat on his lap, both the picture of contentment. He gave Greve the reports, then spent ten minutes filling him in on the recent developments. "Sounds like you're getting close to wrapping this one up for the sheriff and me," Greve commented.

"I hope so. I take it you were able to work out a deal with Arpaio?"

"Like you pointed out, had to. Unless we get them in New York, he gets them for prosecution in Arizona. The benefit for us is that the credit will be spread all around. Once those two scumbags are in his tender care, the deal is that Arpaio's people, us, and the FBI will all be happy dancing together in the spotlight."

"Not a bad deal, considering the bind McMahon had us in," McKenna commented.

"No, not bad. While we're talking about deals, mind telling me what your plans are after this case is over?"

"Go back to the Major Case Squad, I suppose."

"Given any thought to staying here?" Greve asked.

It was an invitation and an endorsement, the stamp of approval McKenna had been hoping for from the taciturn squad commander, but it caught McKenna by surprise. He didn't know how to answer, and Greve saw that.

"Think about it," Greve said, then gave McKenna the ultimate compliment. He signed McKenna's reports without reading them and placed them in his out basket.

"Thanks, I will."

McKenna found Tommy downstairs behind the wheel with the motor running. On the seat next to him were the previous day's copies of the *News* and the *Post*. McKenna got in and Tommy took off without saying a word, but McKenna then knew what was on his mind. As requested, Harney and Messing had made Tommy the leader in their papers' box scores for his work during the California and Arizona adventure.

Ten minutes later they were in Fort Tryon Park at the spot where

Cindy Barrone and Arthur McMahon had been murdered. Tommy shut off the engine and passed the newspapers to McKenna. "Time we got a few things straight," he said.

"You don't like what you've been reading?" McKenna asked without opening the papers.

"It's entertaining, but no, I don't like it. I never needed a press agent before and I don't want one now."

"Okay."

"That's it? Just *okay?*"

"That's it. I've publicly made our point and Barrone should be feeling a little chastised and stupid by now. Next time something pops on this case, I'll even up our score in the press."

"Your turn to be the hero?" Tommy said.

"If I am the hero."

"I don't foresee anything major coming from me in this case, do you?" Tommy asked.

"Not really, but we're still a team."

"Yes, we are," Tommy said. The two shook on it, got out of the car, and walked to the spot where Black and White had tossed Cindy Barrone's battered body down the hill. Each was lost in his own thoughts for a while, and then McKenna's phone rang.

"Got some news, but you're gonna have to move fast," Timmy JFK said. "Where are you?"

"The Cloisters."

"Too bad. Robles isn't running. He's the copilot on American Airlines flight seven-oh-one. San Francisco to JFK, gets in at six thirty-two."

McKenna checked his watch. Ten after six, not enough time to get to the airport and take a look at Robles. "What about Hillman?"

"Looks like he's running. He was scheduled to pilot the flight with Robles, but he called in sick last night. My bet is that he's long gone."

"But Robles is still working? Doesn't make sense, unless . . ."

"I know. Doesn't make sense unless Robles isn't White," Timmy JFK said, completing the unwelcome thought. "Were you able to get a description on Robles?"

"Sketchy. When he started with American eight years ago, he listed his height as five foot ten and his weight as one seventy on his application, but he is a white male."

"How old is he?"

"Forty-seven."

"He fits White's physical description pretty closely. Does Robles always fly with Hillman?"

"Haven't been able to find that out yet."

"Where are you?" McKenna asked.

"At our airport office, but I'm here by myself. Want me to go take a look at Robles?"

"Can you?" McKenna asked, and then he realized that luck was smiling on him. "We've got two men at the airport right now. Can I call you back in five minutes?"

"I'll be here."

Next McKenna called Greve and learned that things were still going his way. Monahan and Nigel had just captured their shooter at the Air Dominicana ticket counter as he had tried to purchase his escape ticket. Greve would have them drop off their prisoner at the Port Authority Police station house in time to be at the American Airlines terminal when flight 701 arrived.

McKenna called Timmy JFK back and relayed the news. "What if Robles fits the White description to a *T*? Want us to grab him?" Timmy asked.

"Not yet. I want you to follow him and see if he's in on a pool house."

"You got it. What if he doesn't match?"

"Follow him anyway. If he's been flying a lot with Hillman, they might be in on the same house. Tommy and I will be headed for the airport as fast as we can, so tell Monahan and Nigel to put the surveillance over the radio."

"We've got him under observation," Monahan transmitted as the McKennas sped east on the Long Island Expressway. "About ten pounds overweight, but he looks like a body builder. Could be your man if he went off his diet since his last starring role."

"Where is he now?" McKenna asked.

"Waiting for a bus outside the American Airlines terminal. He's got the pilot and two of the flight attendants with him. One suitcase apiece and he looks like he doesn't have a care in the world."

By the time the McKennas were on the Van Wyck Expressway headed south to the airport, the flight 701 crew had boarded a bus. With Monahan and Nigel following in one car and Timmy JFK in another, the bus made its round of stops in the airport and exited on South Conduit Avenue, headed east. Tommy caught up to the caravan as the bus left the city limits and entered Nassau County on Merrick Road in the village of Valley Stream.

Two stops later, the flight crew got off together and McKenna got his first look at Robles. He didn't like what he saw; Robles was a bit overweight, and worse, he looked like a nice guy. Robles was the center of conversation as the flight crew turned off Merrick Road and walked up a residential street, wheeling their suitcases behind them.

Tommy parked in the bus stop and the McKennas stood on the corner, watching the backs of the flight crew. It was a short wait. The crew left the sidewalk at the third house from the corner and stood on the stoop, waiting while Robles searched through his pockets for the key. He couldn't find it, so one of the flight attendants opened the side compartment on her suitcase, took out a key ring, and let them in.

"Not a very organized guy," Tommy observed.

"No, he's not," McKenna agreed. "But somebody was organized enough to have rented a house a half hour by bus from the airport. Let's get set up, and then we'll take a walk by that house."

"We looking for a car?"

"A dark red Oldsmobile or Buick."

Monahan and Nigel were parked on one end of the block and Timmy JFK on the other when the McKennas walked by the old, large house. They didn't find the car, but there was a garage in the rear of the house. They decided to wait until dark before taking a peek into the garage. They had more than enough manpower on hand for that simple mission, so they released Monahan and Nigel to book their prisoner. Timmy JFK also left to do whatever guys who get all the girls usually do.

At nine-ten a red Buick emerged from the driveway. Robles was at the wheel and he had one of the flight attendants with him. The McKennas followed them to the Schooner, a restaurant on the water in Freeport fifteen minutes from the house. Robles parked the car in a lot on the side of the restaurant and they went in. Both he and the flight attendant had changed from their uniforms into casual clothes. They took a table overlooking the canal in the rear of the restaurant and the McKennas watched them from the bar. They soon decided that if there was anything romantic going on between Robles and the flight attendant, it wasn't apparent from their behavior. The couple appeared to be all business, just two workers enjoying a nice dinner after a long day.

After finishing his salad, Robles got up and went to the men's room. Tommy followed him in and emerged with a report. "Robles definitely isn't White," he told McKenna.

"Little dick?"

"Stood at the next urinal and took a peek. Not tiny, but he'll never win any bets with what he's got."

Robles's anatomical shortcoming was bad news, but McKenna had expected it. If Robles was White, he shouldn't be working. Instead, he should be with Hillman, headed for a place where they wouldn't be easily found. "Let's get back to the office, make some phone calls, come up with a plan, and call it a day," McKenna suggested.

While Tommy typed up the report on the surveillance of Robles, McKenna ran the Buick's plate through DMV and found that the car came back registered to Jason Robles at the Valley Stream address. He next did a license check through the computer and learned that Robles didn't have a New York State driver's license.

It was what McKenna had expected. Robles didn't live in New York, but, since the car Black and White had used when they murdered Cindy Barrone and Arthur McMahon was registered in his name, it was reasonable to assume that the house was also rented by him. Sooner or later, Jason Robles would have to be interviewed and maybe squeezed a bit.

Then came the phone calls and the first one was to Arizona, a short conversation with Big Ed. The FBI had already told Big Ed that Black was James Hillman and Big Ed had acted on the information, obtaining an arrest warrant charging Hillman with the murder of Greg Norman. But Big Ed had a problem and he couldn't do much in the open with his warrant. Hillman lived in San Francisco and he had committed a double murder in California, so Big Ed didn't want to lose control of the investigation by involving the California authorities at that point. He would be sneaking north in the morning with two of his men to quietly check out Hillman's residence.

McKenna agreed with Big Ed's proposed course of action. Quietly was the way to go, just in case White hadn't yet skipped with Hillman—if, in fact, Hillman had fled. Next, McKenna beeped Timmy JFK and Timmy called five minutes later. "I need a few more things from you, as soon as you can," McKenna said.

"Robles not the guy you're looking for?"

"No, but I got seven more names from Morro I'd like you to check on, all crew members. I need to know if any of them quit their jobs recently or called in sick yesterday or today."

"All American Airlines?" Timmy asked.

"No."

"Then I don't know if I can do it tonight and tomorrow's Saturday. I might not be able to get you anything until Monday when the rest of my airline pals go back to work."

"I know, but see what you can do. If you can't get it until Monday, that will have to be good enough."

McKenna's last call was to Kennedy's restaurant. As expected, Hurley was there. "You making any progress tracking down Johnny Nolan?" McKenna asked.

"Who said I'm looking for Nolan?" Hurley asked defensively.

"Can't say, but I'd like to know how you're doing," McKenna answered, leaving Hurley to figure it out for himself.

"He used his Visa to charge a fortune at a cat house in Paris two days ago, but I don't have his exact location yet. When I find him, I'll let you know."

"Before you talk to him?"

"If you insist. You're not thinking I'm up to anything you'd consider underhanded, are you?"

"It did cross my mind that maybe you should have told me about Nolan and that snuff film."

"An oversight," Hurley offered. "It won't happen again, as long as you and McMahon stay in sync on your plans. Care to bring me up to date so I can tell him how you're doing?"

McKenna didn't feel like talking to McMahon just then, so Hurley's request fit his plans exactly. It didn't take long to fill Hurley in. Then McKenna had a question, one with answers he wasn't yet entitled to know, legally. "Did you find out anything on Hillman you'd care to tell me about?"

"You mean, did I find out anything before you interfered and stopped me from profitably spending my client's money?"

"Yeah, that's what I mean."

"James Hillman, age fifty-one, lives at 451 Decatur Street in San Franciso. Married, no children, wife's a high school teacher. They're doing very well financially, no mortgage on his four-hundred-thousand dollar townhouse. Owns two cars, a Mercedes and a Jag; been working for American Airlines since 1990. Lots of credit cards, all up to date with zero balances. That's all I got on him for now, but I'm itching to get into the details of his miserable, sordid, murderous life."

"Will you be able to tell me all the places he's used his credit cards?"

"As soon as I get the green light, I'll do much better than that. Given two days and enough money, I'll be able to tell you who his grandfather was boffing before he met his grandmother. That good enough for you?"

McKenna had heard it before. "Fine, Bob, but hold off for now."

"Mind telling me why?"

"Because I'm inclined for now to get what we need legally with subpoenas."

"There's no profit in that. Legal sucks and it takes too long."

"I know, but it's beginning to look like time is something I'm going to have a lot of on this case. Might as well keep it all aboveboard and cheap."

"You're hurting me, Brian. You're really hurting me."

"Sorry," McKenna said, but he wasn't. The last call of the night was another one to Big Ed to give him Hurley's information on Hillman.

TWENTY-EIGHT

SATURDAY, JUNE 19, NEW YORK CITY

At Angelita's insistence, McKenna stayed home on Saturday to enjoy his first day off in two weeks. Timmy JFK and Big Ed had his cell phone number and Tommy had also taken the day off, so McKenna couldn't think of any pressing reason to go to the office. He slept until ten, then spent the day playing with the kids and relaxing with Angelita. The kids were exhausted and in bed by eight, so McKenna and Angelita went into their bedroom. They talked and enjoyed themselves with the TV on in the background.

Big Ed called at eleven-thirty while Angelita was in the shower. "Hillman's definitely running and I'm having a hard time keeping a lid on this," Big Ed said. "I'm thinking about visiting the local cops in the morning and filling them in."

"Do we have to do that so soon?"

"I think so. I want to get a search warrant to do his house and also put a wire on the phones. His wife would've let us search the place today without the warrant, but I want to keep this whole thing on the up and up."

"You talked to her?"

"After ten hours of sitting down the block from the house, I saw no reason not to. She was in and out all day, went shopping a few times and then to the movies with another woman. The house is a hard place to watch, very residential and pretty exclusive with no great place for us to set up. Spent the afternoon ducking neighbors, the local cops, and their private security patrol and we couldn't keep that up, especially after I got a peek in her garage when she went to the store. The Jaguar's gone and I've got an alarm out for it."

"When did you talk to her?"

"About an hour ago, when she got back from the movies. Rang her bell, showed her the warrant, and put her in shock. Then I ruined her life when I showed her some pictures of her husband and his buddy having their fun. I thought she was going to faint on me, but she got a grip on herself. Felt real bad about it, Janet Hillman's a nice woman. Good looking and a class act to boot."

"Is Janet totally in the dark, you think?"

"I'm almost sure of it, but get this. She'd thought her husband was a pillar of the community and a good man."

"And now? Did she believe you when you told her all he's been up to?"

"Not at first, but the magazine pictures changed her mind. She knew that was him torturing those people and said so. She also admitted that she'd been worried all day and was expecting something when he left last night."

"What did he tell her?"

"Basically, nothing. He went up to the bedroom after dinner and packed a bag. Very abrupt, told her he loved her and that he'd be in touch. Bussed her on the cheek and he was gone before she could get a word or a question in."

"Are you going to be able to keep her cooperative?"

"I'm trying. I told her to prepare herself, but nothing would be going to the press from me unless I had to. We're pals now, so I think she'll be talking to us for a little while."

"Were you able to get any clue on who White is?"

"Someone named Ronnie, I think. According to Janet, Hillman never entertained at home and she didn't know if he even had any close friends. He rarely got calls at home, but yesterday morning somebody named Ronnie called and asked for her husband. She told him that her husband had just come in from a flight and was sleeping. Ronnie wanted her to wake him up, but she wouldn't. He insisted and she hung up on him."

"Did he call back?"

"Apparently, around noon. Her husband had just gotten up and he answered the phone. Took it into the den and closed the door behind him. When he came out a half hour later, she thought he looked worried. Then he asked her why she hadn't woken him up when Ronnie called and they got into a tiff, spent the rest of the day not talking to each other until he finally left."

"What else did you learn about Hillman?"

"Quite a bit. Born in New York, suffered some terrible abuse and beatings as a child. His mother and her boyfriend were arrested for it when he was three and he was placed in foster care. She says he's still got scars on his butt from being hit with belts, chains, whatever."

"Yeah, we've seen his old scars in magazines," McKenna noted. "What happened to his mother and her boyfriend?"

"They went to jail and he spent time in a few foster homes, might have got some more abuse along the way. The mother was still in jail, but she put him up for adoption at the urging of the state. He finally got lucky and was adopted by the Hillmans, a well-off Jewish couple active in children's causes."

"Where did the Hillmans live?"

"Where do you think?"

"San Jose."

"San Jose it is. The Hillmans did okay by young James, and apparently he turned out to be a bright kid with some athletic ability. Went to the University of San Jose, played football for them, and joined the air force ROTC. Went into the air force after he graduated with honors, and they made him a pilot. He got out in 1975 and went to work for Pan Am. When they got into some financial trouble in eighty-two he switched to United and then to American Airlines. Been with them since ninety."

"Did she mention where he usually flew to?"

"Yeah, everywhere. He liked traveling and preferred being a fill-in pilot. Prefered foreign travel, but he'd go with a smile on short notice to wherever they'd send him."

"So he usually didn't work with the same crew?"

"Apparently not, although he would fill a slot and work weeks with the same people."

"Are the Hillmans still alive?" McKenna asked.

"Father's dead, mother's in a nursing home in San Jose."

"Does he visit her?"

"Every week, without fail. According to his wife, Hillman's crazy about her. Says he's always been a real momma's boy."

"Figures," McKenna said.

Big Ed's phone call had been informative, but offered McKenna no encouragement as he searched through Morro's list. There was nothing close to a "Ronnie" on it, which perplexed him. Was it possible that only Hillman worked for the airlines and that his accomplice flew as a paying customer to their murders? That would have involved hundreds of trips before they found their victims in place at the lovers' lanes and campsites. Considering how greedy Black and White had shown themselves to be, McKenna thought that to be an unlikely prospect. White had to fly with Hillman, either as a crew member or . . .

McKenna was dialing the phone when Angelita came out of the bathroom. "Who are you calling?" she asked.

"Miguel Morro in Costa Rica."

"At this hour? Are you calling him at home?"

"Yep, and I don't think he'll care."

"Brian, so good of you to keep me in mind," Morro said pleasantly when he answered.

"Sorry about the hour, but there's something I need to know that only you can tell me."

"Anything."

"Do you have available the names of the three men you questioned at the airport after the murders of Cecilia and Esteban?"

"Not immediately available, but I can get them from my office in town. I take it this is important?"

"You tell me. If I'm right, you questioned one of the killers. He's probably already fled with his pal, but I've still got a slim chance of getting him."

"You know who the other one is?"

"Yes, James Hillman. He was the pilot of one of the planes sitting on your runway while you were questioning people in the terminal."

"Then I got close, didn't I?" Morro asked with regret dripping from his voice.

"Damn close, even closer than I am right now. You would've had them if your minister of tourism hadn't interfered."

"What makes you think that I talked to one of them? Have you given up the theory that they *both* worked for the airlines?"

"Not at all. When you questioned them, did you happen to examine their tickets?"

"Yes, just to confirm they were going were they said they were going. Why?"

"Because, if I'm right, one of them was flying on an employee discount ticket. He works for the airlines, probably off and on with Hillman, but he wasn't part of the crew that day."

"Give me your number. You'll be hearing from me in less than an hour."

McKenna had nothing to do while he waited, so he decided to see if Timmy JFK was still up and around. He beeped him, and as usual, Timmy called a few minutes later. "Did I wake you?" McKenna asked.

"You kidding? The night is still young and I'm single, remember? Matter of fact, I've spent most of the night working on your behalf. Still am."

"Really? Doing what?"

"Bowling and having a few beers with some influential pals of mine from the airlines."

"Anybody from American Airlines?"

"Only the assistant vice-president in charge of personnel."

"How about somebody who used to work for Pan Am?"

"I imagine so. Lots of people in management worked for Pan Am at one time or another and I've got quite a crew here with me."

"Where are you?"

"The Chelsea Piers. You know the bowling alley here?"

"You mean the new, high-priced, very fashionable bowling alley frequented by our beautiful people?"

"You know it. I've been making a lot of inquiries that have been making my executive friends very curious, and maybe a little nervous as well."

"Are you making any progress?"

"Not yet, but I will. When we leave here, my pals from American and United are going to tap into their personnel computers for me. In a few hours I should have everything you need to clear up most of the names on that list of yours. If one of those people didn't show for work, you'll know who White is."

"Not necessarily. How long you gonna be there?"

"A while."

"You want some more company?"

"It wouldn't hurt if you could explain how things are to these guys. Soothe their nerves a bit and tell them how they're not in for any bad publicity for their companies."

"Can't guarantee that for your American Airlines pal, but I'll do my best by them if they stay straight with us."

"I guess that's all they can hope for. We'll be waiting."

McKenna found Timmy JFK seated at a table in the upstairs bar overlooking the bowling alleys in Chelsea Piers. Seated with him were two middle-aged men who managed to look prosperous and successful while dressed in bowling shirts. Timmy JFK introduced him to Tom Girvin of American Airlines and Trent Stroh of United. Both airline executives looked apprehensive at first, and even more so after Timmy JFK made the introductions. They obviously recognized McKenna and had some inkling about what his sudden presence meant.

McKenna thought he would spend a couple of minutes on the niceties, but Girvin got right down to business. "Detective McKenna, does Timmy JFK's recent curiosity about our personnel have anything to do with your Cloisters case and all those other murders?" he asked.

"It does, and I'm sorry that there's no way to sugarcoat this. One of your pilots is one of the killers."

"A pilot?" Girvin said, visibly stunned. "One of our pilots? Are you sure?"

"Yes, I'm sure, and it's not going to get any better for you. The Cloisters killings are only the tip of the iceberg. I'm just as sure that your pilot and his partner have tortured and murdered at least fifteen people all over the world."

"Fifteen?" Girvin asked faintly as the color left his face. "He murdered fifteen people while he was working for us?"

"No. I don't know if you can take this as good news, but there's only six murders we know of while he was working for American. The rest of them were killed while he was working for United and Pan Am."

The news did't appear to do anything to lift Girvin's bleak mood, but he did give Stroh a small, sympathetic smile.

"Who is this pilot?" Stroh asked.

"James Hillman. You know him?"

"Yes, I know him. Excellent pilot, one of the best in the business," Stroh said. "I'm not doubting you, but it's hard to believe that he's a killer."

"I'm sure it is. That's why he's been so successful at it for so long," McKenna countered.

"Maybe, but I also find it hard to believe," Girvin added. "I would've characterized him as an exceptionally stable person. Unfortunately, I've done just that, officially and on paper."

"I guess you know him fairly well," McKenna said.

"I thought so before tonight, but now you might be able to add one more murder to his total."

"Yours?" McKenna guessed.

"Yeah, mine. I recruited him from United."

McKenna wasn't an expert on the intricacies of corporate politics, but he knew enough to recognize that Girvin was in trouble. If heads were going to roll, the odds were that his would be the first and the prospect obviously wasn't sitting well with Girvin. He was staring at McKenna, but McKenna got the feeling that Girvin was staring right through him as he contemplated his future.

Self-preservation was also on Stroh's mind. "How many murders did Hillman do when he was with United?" he asked.

"Four we know about. Two in Costa Rica and two in California."

"All the same type of murders they did at the Cloisters?"

"All sex-torture killings with some variations."

"Do you know who the other one is?"

"I think so."

"Please don't tell us that he's also a pilot," Stroh pleaded.

"That's what I need you to tell me. He works for the airlines, but I don't know which one," McKenna said. He let the tension build for a moment as Stroh and Girvin stared at him expectantly. "Jerome R. Dix. Flew to Costa Rica on an employee discount ticket to do some murders with Hillman. Know him?"

"Southwest Airlines, thank God," Stroh said at once. "And he's not a pilot, he's a cabin steward."

"How do you know?"

"Because he came to work for us after the Pan Am breakup. Only stayed for a year or two before he moved on to Southwest."

"Any problems with him while he was at United?"

"None I'm aware of. Model employee, good attendance record, and never a complaint from him."

"Any idea why he left United?"

"Job security, I'd say. Comparatively speaking, we weren't paying too well at the time and there were some major labor problems on the horizon for us."

"Do either of you know anybody in personnel at Southwest?"

"I'm sure we both do," Girvin said. "What do you need?"

"For now, I need to know his address and whether or not he called in sick today."

"You think he did?" Stroh asked.

"Yeah, they suspect we're on to them and we know that Hillman's running. It figures that Dix is running with him."

"So you need this information immediately?" Girvin asked with a faint note of hope in his voice.

So we've come to the negotiations, McKenna thought. Let's get this over with in a hurry. "I want to have it in the next hour or so, but I need lots more than that. By morning, American, United, and Southwest will be served with subpoenas for their personnel files and I'd like them packaged and waiting for me. I also need a complete list of the people either of them worked with on a regular basis."

"That would involve waking up some high-ranking people in our companies and getting them to their offices as quickly as possible," Stroh said.

"I'm aware of that, and I'd appreciate the effort. Appreciate it so much, in fact, that I won't be throwing any knuckleballs your way at the big press conference I'll be having sometime soon. After all, you guys are good friends of Timmy's, and he's a good friend of mine," McKenna said, nodding in Timmy JFK's direction.

"Knuckleballs?" Stroh and Girvin asked together.

"Yes, knuckleballs. In return for your immediate help and your complete cooperation in the future, I'll do whatever I can with the press to make the best out of the bad situation your companies are now in, publicity-wise."

"Can you give us some idea on how you propose to do that?" Girvin asked.

"Despite their quirks, I will characterize Hillman as one of the best pilots in the business and Dix will wind up looking like the most courteous and conscientious cabin steward ever to grace the skies. I'll emphasize that they passed through the most rigorous screening processes imaginable before your companies hired them. For good measure, I'll add that I'm as shocked as those wonderful executives in the airline industry that these two highly trained, thoroughly screened, competent professionals could do the things they did. Somewhere near the end of the press conference, I'll also be sure to thank American and United for all the help they've given me. How's that?"

"Is there anything else you'll be needing from us?" Girvin asked.

"It would be nice to know every place they flew and when, both on duty and off."

"You got it."

"Fine. Just one more thing. I don't know if it's possible, but I also need to get into Pan Am's old personnel files on them."

"For you, Detective McKenna, anything's possible," Stroh said. "Let's start waking people up."

TWENTY-NINE

McKenna called Big Ed's cell phone just after two in the morning. Big Ed answered on the fifth ring. "You asleep?" McKenna asked.

"Sure was, but something tells me that my day's beginning early today. What've you got?"

"White is Jerome Ronald Dix. He lives in Scottsdale and he's a cabin steward for Southwest Airlines."

"You sure he's White?"

"You tell me. He's been on vacation since June third, but on June fifth he flew to New York on United Airlines, one day before the murders of Cindy Barrone and Arthur McMahon. On the night of June seventh he took American Airlines flight seven-oh-one to San Francisco. I'll let you guess who the pilot was on that flight."

"James Hillman, of course."

"Correct, as always. He stays in town a couple of days while they bilk

Cindy's cards and plan their next move, and then he takes Southwest to Phoenix."

"And we know Hillman went with him to use Cindy's cards," Big Ed said.

"We know, but I can't provide proof on that yet. I won't have Hillman's flight records and his employee discount ticket purchases for another few hours."

"You having any trouble getting that stuff?"

"None whatsoever. The airlines are fully on board."

"Good, because we're going to need more on Dix. From what you've told me so far, we still don't have enough for an arrest warrant for him."

"I know, but I would have him tied up in a loose circumstantial package by morning if I were to show one of our judges that, besides being in New York together at the time of the Cloisters killings, Dix and Hillman were also in Phoenix, California, and Costa Rica when ten torture sex-murders were committed."

"But you're not going to do that, are you?"

"No, I think you'll agree that it's best that we keep all the paperwork in Arizona."

"I do. You don't expect Dix to still be home, do you?"

"He's had no employee discount travel after he returned to Phoenix, but no, I don't expect him to be home waiting for us."

"Then I'll have a detective go over, ring his bell, look in his garage, and talk to his neighbors. If he's gone, I think it's time to go public with what we've got before those two get too far away."

"I agree. There'd no longer be a reason for any secrecy. I'll have their employee ID photos, so I can soon have their faces plastered all over the front pages here," McKenna said. "I'll fax them to you and you could do the same in Arizona, if you like."

"And in California as well. First I'll tell Hillman's wife to get ready. She's got a tough time coming."

"I'd get out of town, if I were her. The press will be tripping all over each other to get an interview from her, and you know how obnoxious they can be."

"That's exactly what I'll suggest to her. Then I'll visit the San Jose cops, tell them what a genius Randy is, and have them get the warrants for Hillman's house and phones."

McKenna called Greve at home with a progress report and a request. To save time, he wanted to ask Brunette to arrange another visit to his friendly judge's home in Queens. Greve gave his blessing and by 6:00 A.M. Mc-Kenna was in the office with the court orders he needed for Dix's and

Hillman's personnel files from American, United, and Southwest Airlines. He called Girvin and Stroh at their offices for their fax numbers and was pleased to learn everything he needed from American and United was already on the way by messenger. The Southwest files on Dix were also on the way from their company office in Phoenix and would be arriving at the homicide squad office sometime that morning.

That was all good news for McKenna, but Stroh had a bonus for him. He knew the man who had been the personnel manager for Pan Am, and their records on Hillman and Dix would also be at the office as soon as possible.

McKenna caught a nap with his head on his desk, but he was more tired than he had thought. He awakened at eleven to find Tommy seated at his own desk, reading one of the files stacked in front of him. "Good morning and you owe me twenty bucks," Tommy said pleasantly.

"Good morning and what for?"

"Your share of the tips we gave the messengers who brought all this stuff," Tommy answered, pointing to the files.

"Very generous of us, wouldn't you say?"

"We always were good tippers."

"Good stuff?"

"Interesting reading."

"How long you been at it?"

"Couple of hours, long enough to get through it all once. Now I'm rereading the tough parts."

"Care to fill me in?"

"Buy me lunch, I'll tell you all about it, and we'll call it square on the tips," Tommy offered.

"Good deal, but isn't it a little early for lunch?"

"Maybe for you, but I already had breakfast."

"What time did you get here?"

"Quarter to seven, but you were already napping."

"Aren't you supposed to be off today?"

"Yeah, just like you."

Greve had called Tommy and told him that there had been some developments, McKenna realized, and he wasn't surprised that Tommy had come in on his day off. "Is Greve coming in, too?"

"He usually drops by on Sunday afternoons for an hour or so just to see how things are going, but we can push up his schedule if we need him."

"How about the team that's working the day tour? What time do they get in?"

"Sunday's a late day for murder. They'll start drifting in at noon, more or less," Tommy said as he picked up the files. "Let's get out of here before they do so I don't have to hear them bitching about me finishing the last of the coffee."

Big Ed called McKenna's cell phone as Tommy was parking down the block from Kennedy's. "Dix isn't home and his car's gone," he said.

"Any idea on when he left?"

"None."

"Did your detective talk to the neighbors?"

"Sure did, all rich, snooty people. Lots of space between houses and they all claim they mind their own business and don't bother with Dix. One says she saw him sometime last week, but that's about all I got from them."

"Is it a nice house he's got?" McKenna asked.

"*Nice* would be an understatement. He's in the hills where the real estate is high and he's got a lot of room for a single guy. Two car garage and four bedrooms, at least."

"Any idea on how much that would go for?"

"Much more than he should be able to afford. I'd say someplace in the neighborhood of half a mil. We got enough for a search warrant?"

"Hold on a minute," McKenna said, then turned to Tommy. "We got enough in our files for a search warrant on Dix's place?"

"Arrest warrant, search warrant, and any other kind of warrant you'd like. Get a fax number and tell him you'll be sending everything he'll need in a couple of hours."

McKenna did that, but he had one more question. "You find out what kind of car he's got?"

"Sure. Ran him through DMV and came up with a ninety-seven Grand Cherokee four-by-four, white in color. Same car they used to bilk Cindy's cards here and just the vehicle he'd need for tooling around Superstition Mountain in some comfort.

"Can he see the mountain from his house?"

"Great view from the front lawn. I'd bet Dix and Hillman sat right there, sipping suds while they watched us buzzing around looking for Glenda."

On their way to the back room at Kennedy's, the McKennas passed Harney and Messing sitting at the bar. The two reporters were sipping from enormous Bloody Marys, their traditional Sunday morning antidote for their traditional Saturday night festivities.

McKenna was happy to see them, figuring he would get two of his planned tasks accomplished while he was there. He brought them back to life when he told them he'd give them a good story in about an hour, after brunch.

Tommy led McKenna to a table in the rear. Then he ordered just coffee, telling the waitress that they would be ordering brunch in a half hour. Once they had their coffee in front of them, Tommy took two photos from his coat pocket and passed them to McKenna. "Their company ID photos," he explained. "Pretty recent. Hillman's was taken in ninety-seven and Dix's was shot last year."

McKenna studied the photos and was surprised at how unremarkable the two looked. Hillman's face was even-textured and coffee-colored. He wasn't bald in the photo, but McKenna could see why he might have shaved his head. His hair was short and receding past his ears. He was clean-shaven, wore a hint of a smile as he stared at the camera, and appeared to be about forty-five years old.

Dix was also clean-shaven. He had his dark brown hair cut short, his eyes were hazel, and he looked bored and slightly older than Hillman.

McKenna thought that neither had any distinguishing features that would make him stand out in a crowd and he took some time to commit their faces to memory before passing the photos back to Tommy.

Tommy opened two of the folders, took a document off the top of each, and handed them to McKenna. "Now here's where it gets a little interesting. Looks to me like they met in the air force in Vietnam."

The documents were copies of Hillman and Dix's air force separation papers, their DD-214 forms. The forms contained more than a little information McKenna found interesting.

Hillman was born on March 9, 1948, making him fifty-one years old. The form listed a San Jose address when he joined the air force as an officer candidate in August, 1970. He was discharged four years later as a captain with an occupational specialty listed as PILOT, SINGLE AND MULTI-ENGINE JET RECONNAISSANCE AIRCRAFT. His decorations were the National Defense Service Medal, the Vietnamese Service Medal, the Vietnamese Campaign Medal, and the Air Medal. His DD-214 listed one year of overseas service.

Dix was fifty, born on October 12, 1948. He lived in Levittown, New York, when he enlisted in the air force in July 1968. His occupational specialty was RECONNAISSANCE PHOTO PRELIMINARY ANALYST. He was discharged seven years later as a master sergeant in July, 1975, one year after Hillman. His decorations were the National Defense Service Medal, the Vietnamese Service Medal, the Vietnamese Campaign Medal, and the Good Conduct Medal. He had a total of four years, four months overseas service when he was discharged.

"This explains a few things about the business they've made for themselves," McKenna observed. "A photo expert and a pilot trained to closely observe things on the ground below him. Maybe they met while they were in the same unit, but you're off on one thing—odds are that it wasn't in Vietnam. Most of our troops were on their way out of there by the time Hillman joined up in 1970. Figure six months O.C.S., another year while the air force teaches him to fly, and it's 1973 before he's ready to fly any photo-reconnaissance missions."

"Then how do you explain his Vietnam medals?" Tommy asked.

"Easy. We were still helping out the South Vietnamese as much as we could, but not with combat troops. He was flying over Vietnam, doing reconnaissance, but I'll bet that he was based in Thailand."

"Thailand, you say? Now that's interesting."

"Why's that. You find that they did a lot of traveling there?"

"Sure did."

"Together?"

"Only twice, but we can talk about that after you answer one big question for me."

"If they were based in Thailand, then how did Dix get his Vietnam medals?" McKenna guessed.

"That's the one. Hillman might be in the air over Vietnam earning his medals, but that would leave Dix on the ground in Thailand doing his photo analyst thing."

"That's right, but he'd still be entitled to the medals. Besides, Dix went into the air force two years before Hillman did and he had more than four years overseas service listed on his DD-214. I'd guess that he did one tour in Vietnam while the U.S. was still active there and another tour in Thailand, if that's where he met Hillman."

"So I'm still right, partially. If Hillman was in Thailand, then that's where they met up and became pals," Tommy stated.

"I don't know about that. Maybe they met there, but pals? It's been my experience that captains don't usually pal around with master sergeants."

"You wouldn't think so, but our captain and our master sergeant did."

"How do you know?"

"Because when Hillman got out of the air force he went right to work flying for Pan Am. A year later, Dix gets discharged and Pan Am immediately hires him as a cabin steward based on this glowing letter of recommendation." Tommy took a letter from one of the folders and gave it to McKenna.

It sure was a glowing recommendation, McKenna had to admit after reading it, and Hillman must have been a good pal of Dix's by then. In his letter Hillman stated that he had been fortunate enough to have had the opportunity to observe Dix perform in an outstanding manner a tedious, demanding, and exacting job under intense daily pressure. He further characterized Dix as intelligent, hard-working, courteous, conscientious, punctual, and loyal. It was the type of letter McKenna wouldn't mind having in his own personnel folder. "Okay, you *are* right. The captain and the master sergeant were good pals in the air force because somehow they recognized that they had a lot in common."

"Could it be that they recognized way back then that they were both murderous, sadistic degenerates?" Tommy asked.

"It bears checking out. I'm gonna ask Gene Shields to look into their military records for us. What's next?"

"Next, they're both domiciled in New York when Dix starts with Pan Am. Hillman's already got an apartment in Freeport and Dix gets one in Valley Stream, so they're living pretty close to each other. Convenient arrangement for them, two bachelor apartments in Nassau County about half an hour away from JFK."

"Are they working together?"

"Sometimes, but not often. You have to remember that Pan Am was our big international carrier at the time and neither of them had seniority then. Hillman winds up flying as a co-pilot to Europe most of the time and Dix is usually assigned to their long South American run. New York to Miami, then on to Buenos Aires and Santiago, Chile."

"Because Dix speaks Spanish?"

"They both do, along with a few other languages. Quite a linguistic duo we have here. Hillman's major was Romance languages at the University of San Jose, so Pan Am's got him listed as speaking Spanish, French, and Italian. Dix is even more exotic. Spanish and Tagalog."

"The Spanish he might have picked up on his own, but I bet the air force sent him to school for the Tagalog," McKenna said.

"That figures. At the time, we had big air bases in the Philippines and Dix was a smart guy. The air force values that."

"You've got their IQ scores?"

"Pan Am had them tested when they first joined up. Hillman's got a one fifty-six and Dix isn't lagging far behind. One forty-six."

"Bad news for us," McKenna observed. "A genius and an almost-genius."

"What's the matter? You never took down any smart guys before?" Tommy chided. "Smart or dumb, they all make mistakes. That's what brings us to this point, dragging them to the ends of their murderous criminal careers."

"I hope so, but let's not be patting ourselves on the backs until we've got them standing in cuffs between us."

"For quite a few more murders than we know about at the present moment. Here's an interesting item for you."

"Employee discount travel?"

"That's right. Even back then, they did a lot of flying together while one was getting paid and the other was soaking up his employee benefits."

"Where are the murders?"

"Besides the 1977 murders we already know about in Costa Rica, I'd say we should start by looking into some murders in Barcelona, Spain, and Santiago, Chile, to round out their Pan Am experience."

"Have we got them together in Costa Rica when Sonia de Angeles and Jesus Melendez were killed?"

"Friday, June twenty-second, 1977. Dix is the cabin steward on a flight to San José. He's got a one day layover there before the return flight to New York. Sitting in coach on employee discount tickets for those flights was Hillman."

"How many times had they been together in San José before that?"

"Six. It took them six trips before they found Melendez and de Angeles at the spot. As for Santiago, they were a little luckier. They went there only three times together before they did whatever they did there on February second, 1978. For those flights, Dix was the cabin steward and Hillman was in first class enjoying the best of service."

McKenna was impressed that Tommy had digested the facts and dates and could quote them without notes after only one reading of the files. "And they never went back to Santiago after that February second?"

"Not together they didn't. February second was when they got lucky there."

"And Barcelona?"

"Tougher for them. Nine times together, Hillman the co-pilot and Dix in coach. The murders there must have been on August ninth, 1982. They never went there together again after that."

"That's after the first Cloisters murders," McKenna observed.

"Yeah, my case. They were both off and on the ground for those, meaning that they were both in New York for their first domestic murders."

"As far as we can tell, so far."

"So far, but it looks to me like Arizona, San Jose, and ours in New York were the extent of their domestic murders."

That's good, McKenna thought. The jurisdictional problems were already complicated enough without adding in another U.S. police agency. "Besides the other four we know about in Costa Rica, does it look like they did any more overseas?"

"After they left Pan Am, I'd say Singapore and the Philippines for sure, and maybe Hong Kong."

"But not Thailand?"

"No, not Thailand. I'm thinking that maybe Thailand was where they peddled their videos."

"Maybe. According to Ed Gallagher, Thailand *is* the sin center of the world. Give me the background on their move to United."

"Pan Am's running into some financial difficulty in eighty-two and United raids them for routes and personnel. Hillman leaves first when they offer him a promotion to pilot. Domicile him in San Francisco, closer to home, and he gets married a year later."

"Where's he flying to?"

"Mostly domestic and Hawaii, with an occasional flight to Asia. Dix goes to United in eighty-five, just before Pan Am goes under, and they leave him domiciled in New York. He's still going south, back and forth to Miami weekly and to Central and South America a couple of times a month, but he doesn't stay with United long. Goes to Southwest in eighty-six, domiciled in Phoenix and flying nothing but domestic."

"Any employee-discount travel between San Francisco and Phoenix?"

"Only three flights down by Hillman. Dix only flew to San Francisco when they were flying together to Asia."

"I'm assuming you have them both together in Arizona when Glenda and Greg were killed?"

"Sure do. January eighth to the tenth, 1997, Hillman's second trip down."

"And his third was last week, when he went down with Dix to bilk some more from Cindy's cards?"

"That's right. Gets some extra cash, sees us flying around their mountain, and helps his pal to finally recover their light screen."

"And plan their getaway after they saw us," McKenna said.

"I assume so."

"Tell me about their Asian travels."

McKenna was relieved to note that Tommy didn't have everything committed to memory. Tommy turned one of the files over and read from the notes he had written on the back of the folder. "They were both flying as passengers on all of them. One trip to Hong Kong ending October fourth, 1984, four trips to Manila ending February third, 1986, and three trips to Singapore ending September ninth, 1997."

"And Thailand?"

"There together in May of eighty-four and November of eighty-four. Seven trips before and after that, but never together. Hillman does four and Dix three."

"How long do they stay there, on the average?"

"Four days."

"That's interesting," McKenna said.

"Why's that?"

"I don't know, but it's interesting. Let's eat and then get our interviews with Harney and Messing out of the way."

"Good idea. I think it's time to tell them just about everything."

"So do I."

"And then?"

"And then back to the office for mounds of paperwork, I'd say. What you told me in fifteen minutes is gonna take hours of typing before it'll be fit for Greve to read with a smile."

"You think so?" Tommy asked. "I've always found him to be a pussy cat."

Greve dropped by the office at five o'clock, just as the McKennas were putting the finishing touches on their paperwork. He took the pile of DD-5s into his office and emerged fifteen minutes later. "We can't sit on this," he said. "I'm going to have to call Snyder at home."

McKenna had been afraid of that, but knew that Greve was right. John Snyder was the deputy commissioner of public information, a man charged with the task of keeping the press informed and happy. "He might want to schedule a press conference tonight," McKenna said.

"I imagine that's just what he'll want, especially once I tell him that you've already given everything to the *News* and the *Post*. He'll have the *Times* and the news networks screaming 'Foul!' and crawling all over him if he doesn't."

"We'd rather that Harney and Messing have the story for themselves for a day," Tommy said.

"An exclusive?" Greve asked with an eyebrow raised. "Did you two promise them an *exclusive?*"

"Not a promise, exactly, but we did tell them that we'd see what we could do."

"I can see how that would make them your friends for life, but it could make Snyder my enemy for life."

"True, if he didn't know about it," Tommy said. "But Synder's a politician, and politicians come and go. You'll be around long after he's gone, and I owe Harney and Messing a big favor."

All true, McKenna thought as he watched Greve think over Tommy's big request. Tommy did owe the two reporters for the way they handled his not being assigned to the case. And Snyder wasn't a cop, he was a politician who served in his cushy position "at the pleasure of the police commissioner." On the other hand, Greve was cadre; he was secure in his position, a competent and renowned favorite of the last three police commissioners. Snyder could be a nuisance to Greve, but he couldn't really hurt him.

"What do you think your pal Brunette would say about this?" Greve asked McKenna.

"I can't say for sure, but I know that he likes Harney and Messing. They've all been pals for years."

"Then we won't ask him," Greve said. "It's better that the *Times*, the wire services, and the TV reporters be mad at Snyder than Brunette be mad at me."

"So you'll go along with it?" Tommy asked.

"Okay, why not? Print reporters can be long-term, understanding friends when you need them. On the other hand, those TV glamour boys are ungrateful bastards with no memory. Maybe it's best to let Harney and Messing hog the story for a day and feed it to the wire services as their editors see fit."

"So you're not going to tell Snyder what we've got so far?" Tommy asked.

"That would be stupid. When he reads Harney's and Messing's pieces in the morning, he'd be sure to cause me some problems. I'm going to tell him, but then I'm going to make him see things our way."

"How are you gonna do that, if you don't mind my asking?" Tommy said.

"I'm going to call him at home and tell him about the recent progress. I'll also tell him that the *News* and the *Post* already have the story and then, of course, he'll want to schedule an immediate press conference to stay in good with the network reporters and *Times* reporters. Then I'll have to convince him that he should wait on his press conference because the mayor, Brunette, and Barrone will probably want to be there. That should do it."

"Because today's Sunday?" Tommy asked.

"That's right, everybody's day off and they'd have to come in. I'll have Snyder asking himself, 'Who would I rather piss off, the network people and the *Times* or the mayor, Barrone, and Brunette?'"

"Lieutenant, we're both learning," McKenna said. "When it comes to the politics of this job, you've got a genius for making whatever you want to do seem to be the only smart thing to do."

THIRTY

On Monday morning the McKennas primed themselves for their press conference at Police Headquarters by first reading Harney's and Messing's syndicated stories. Dix's and Hillman's airline ID photos were on the front page in both the *News* and the *Post*, filling the page under the headline. WANTED WORLDWIDE was the simple *News* headline; the more informative *Post* headline was CLOISTER KILLERS IDENTIFIED with the subcaption PILOT AND CABIN STEWARD THOUGHT RESPONSIBLE FOR LONG SEX-KILLING SPREE.

Almost everything the McKennas would want publicized was in the articles and both were relieved to see that the competition the papers had been promoting between them was a dead issue and that there was no mention of the snuff-film angle. That could come later, they had decided.

Then it was on to headquarters for the show at ten o'clock. The auditorium was jam-packed with reporters and cameramen from both local and national print and TV networks when the McKennas met Greve there. The mayor was in Washington, so it was Brunette who made the opening statements. Barrone, ever the politician, was standing behind him for the cameras from the national networks.

Brunette didn't take long. He identified James Hillman and Jerome Dix as "strong" suspects in the murders of Cindy Barrone and Arthur Mc-Mahon and said that it was likely that both were responsible for many other torture-sex killings around the world. He identified Hillman as a pilot for American Airlines, Dix as a cabin steward for Southwest Airlines, and he described them as fugitives who had been identified during a joint investigation conducted by the NYPD, the Maricopa County Sheriff's Department, and the FBI. He added that the Costa Rican National Police had also contributed substantially to the investigation before he turned the podium over to Greve.

Greve didn't take long, either. He took ten minutes to outline the investigation and describe the crimes in California, Arizona, and Costa Rica. Then he folded up his notes, put them in his pocket, and nodded to his audience.

The shouted questions began immediately and Greve responded to the first three by stating that "Detective McKenna will answer that for you." Then he looked in the McKennas' direction, smiled briefly, and walked away from the podium.

Both McKennas were left momentarily in a bind and smiling at each other in some confusion because Greve had not indicated which of them was to answer the questions. Brian McKenna ended it by giving Tommy a slight shove toward the microphones.

Tommy rose to the occasion, looking the confident man in charge as he answered questions for half an hour. There were no questions about Cindy Barrone's cards or the films and Tommy never mentioned them. At every opportunity he gave credit where credit was due to Big Ed, Miguel Morro, Randy Bynum, and the FBI. He stated that it was just a matter of time before Dix and Hillman were captured and was ambiguous and noncommittal in answering questions concerning where they would be initially prosecuted.

McKenna was especially pleased with the way Tommy handled the many questions about Dix's and Hillman's employment. The first reporter to ask about it was incredulous in his tone. "How is it possible that these two depraved, blood-thirsty murderers could have worked for so long in such responsible positions for the airlines without being suspected by anyone of anything?"

"Because they look so normal, normal enough to have passed through a rigorous screening process when they were first hired by Pan Am. By all accounts, they were very good and extremely professional at their jobs, so good that United Airlines, American Airlines, and Southwest Airlines were glad to have them. Sure, they used their employment to get to the places where they committed their crimes, but what they did for a living had nothing to do with what they did when they weren't working."

The same question came in another form after that, but Tommy simply said, "Already answered. I have nothing bad to say about the airlines and we find them faultless in their hiring practices. They're cooperating fully in this investigation, and we appreciate their help."

Tommy thanked the FBI and the Costa Rican police once again before turning the microphone over to Barrone.

Tommy went home after the press conference and McKenna visited Shields at his office. "Did you guys treat us nice this morning?" Shields asked.

"I think you'll like it," McKenna said. "Tommy and Ray mentioned the invaluable help we got from the FBI at least once every five minutes."

"How about you?"

"I didn't speak."

"Why not? Your case, you should've been the one doing the talking."

"Any other time, but not this one. Barrone was there, so we took another slap at him by letting Tommy do the talking."

"How did he take that?"

"Gracious enough, at least in front of the cameras. Naturally, the press had some questions for him. At the end he had to publicly thank Tommy and myself for the job we're doing."

"If I were you, I'd quit tugging his beard for a while," Shields suggested.

"We will. I think it's over and done with. He slapped Tommy by taking the case from him and Tommy slapped him back by producing anyway."

"Good enough. I take it you're here because you need more of our invaluable help?"

"Lots more. We need to get a look at their military records and we need you to check with the police in Spain, Chile, the Philippines, Singapore, and Hong Kong for similar cases."

"Dix and Hillman have been visiting those places?"

"Frequently," McKenna said. He gave Shields a list of the dates of Dix and Hillman's trips.

Shields studied it for a moment. "This shouldn't take long. The last time they went to a place should be the dates of the murders."

"That's what we think."

"Any idea where they ran to?" Shields asked.

"We think Thailand's a good possibility. For whatever reason, they go there a lot."

"It's probably too late, but I'll have the Thai immigration people alerted to keep an eye out for them."

"Couldn't hurt, but it probably is too late. If that's where they were going, they must be there already."

McKenna was in the office, watching the clock and waiting for his day to end when he got a phone call. "Detective McKenna, my name is Susan Hsu. This call is costing me a fortune, so I'm going to be brief. I'm certain that one of the men you're looking for is in Singapore, and I'm pretty sure the other one is as well. I'm a flight attendant for Air Canada and they were on my flight from Toronto to Bangkok. They got on at our stop in Vancouver on Friday and got off at our stop in Singapore."

"Which one are you sure of?"

"The black one. Hillman. He was in first class and I'm pretty sure the other one was, too."

"Were they together?"

"No, they were sitting in different rows and I don't think they said a word to each other for the whole flight."

"Where are you now?"

"Some place over the Pacific on our return flight. I'm using an Airphone and I think it's costing me about twenty dollars a minute on my credit card to talk to you."

"Over the Pacific? Then how did you find out that I was looking for them?"

"We supply the *Herald Tribune* to our first class passengers and I just finished reading it. Their pictures and the story are on page three."

Thank God the *News* and the *Post* syndicated Messing's and Harney's articles, McKenna thought. And thank God the *International Herald Tribune* ran with it. "Don't worry about your credit card, we'll be picking up the bill. Do you know what names they were traveling under?"

"No, you'll have to get to Air Canada for that, but that shouldn't be a problem for you. It was our Flight 134 and I can tell you that Hillman was in seat 6A and the one I think was Dix was in seat 3D."

"What drew your attention to them?"

"I couldn't help noticing that they were both in great shape for men their ages, thought it was strange that we had two types like them on the same flight in first class. Except for the movie stars, most of the people we get in first class on the Singapore run are old enough, but certainly not in the shape those two were."

"Did you have any conversation with them?"

"Nothing out of the ordinary, except for one thing. I served Dix a coffee after dinner and I saw that he had a carton of cigarettes in a bag from the Duty Free Shop. I told him that I thought it unusual that a man in the shape he was in would smoke."

"Marlboros?"

"Yes, I think it was Marlboros he smoked."

"What did he say to that?"

"Sounds funny now, knowing what I know now. He smiled at me and told me that smoking was his only vice."

"Yeah, I'd say that's funny. Anything else you can think of to tell me about them?" McKenna asked.

"No. Sorry, nothing really."

"Nothing to be sorry about. You've been a tremendous help. What time does your flight get into Toronto?"

"Eleven o'clock Toronto time tonight. Why?"

"Don't take this the wrong way, but I'm going to have a Toronto detective there to meet you and take a statement from you after you land. Short and brief, just tell him what you told me."

"Why should I have to do that? Don't you believe me?" Susan Hsu asked indignantly.

"I believe every word you said and I'm going to act on your information as soon as I get off the phone. However, in a case as important as this one, my boss would demand that I make sure that you are who you say you are and not some prankster filling my head with nonsense for a laugh. You can understand that, can't you?"

"I guess so, but does this mean that you'll be dragging me to court in New York if you get those two?"

"No, I don't think so. What it does mean is that you're probably in line to receive a piece of the reward offered for their arrest and conviction after I get them."

"Really?" Hsu said pleasantly, all trace of annoyance and indignation suddenly gone from her voice. "If that's the case, then don't trouble yourself about my phone bill. Consider this call my civic duty."

McKenna knew it would be a while longer before he would be going home, but he didn't mind. He beeped Timmy JFK as soon as he hung up.

By six o'clock McKenna had the information he needed from Timmy. According to Air Canada, the black man in seat 6A on flight 134 was named Reginald Johnson and the white man in seat was seat 3D was Marvin Grossman. They had made their reservations for the flight within an hour of each other on Thursday, the day before the flight. Both had paid cash for their tickets at the Air Canada ticket counter in Vancouver two hours before the flight had taken off and both were traveling on American passports. Each had checked in three pieces of luggage.

"Amazing! How do you get all this stuff so quickly?" McKenna asked.

"Wait a minute," Timmy answered. "You asking to peek up the magician's sleeve?"

"No, that's all right. Forget I asked. You think Shields is still in the office?"

"Of course. He's supposed to get off at five, but he never leaves before seven. He'll be there."

Timmy was right, McKenna found out a minute later. "Do you notice that we're talking quite a bit lately?" Shields asked. "Seems to me that maybe I should be on the city payroll and have my face splashed all over the evening news. What else can I do for you?"

"Plenty. They flew into Singpore, but I still think they're headed for Thailand."

THIRTY-ONE

McKenna had hurried to finish his paperwork and get home to see his family, but the kids had already eaten and were in bed by the time he got there. Angelita served him a roast chicken hot plate and he watched TV as he ate on a tray she had set up in the living room.

That morning's press conference was being rebroadcast on New York 1, the local cable news network, but McKenna's mind was elsewhere. He finished eating and turned off the TV as Barrone came to the microphone.

Angelita brought his plate into the kitchen, then returned and sat beside him on the sofa. "You look exhausted," she commented. "You're working too hard."

"Working long, baby, not hard. It's not like I'm digging ditches, sweating and getting dirty."

"Fine. When are you going to get those two so we can get back to what we call a normal life around here?"

McKenna appreciated Angelita's confidence in him, but When? was the crucial question in this case. It was the same question he had been asking himself while staring at the tube. "I really don't know, baby. Soon, I hope."

"You hope? Not good enough," Angelita said, then she tussled his hair and slapped him on the back. "Get to bed, hot shot. You're too tired and not thinking correctly."

"Not thinking correctly about what?"

"About whatever it takes to end this case, but it'll come to you."

McKenna thought she was joking. "Are we experiencing some marital discord?" he asked.

"Not yet, but it won't be long if this keeps up. I've been missing you and the kids have been missing you, so I want this case over with, those two in jail, and you home a lot more than you have been lately."

McKenna was exhausted, but he couldn't get to sleep before figuring out the three things that were bothering him. If Susan Hsu was right and it was them on her flight, then why did they leave from Vancouver, why are they going to Singapore, and what did they do with their cars?

McKenna decided to answer the last question first. He got up, dialed information, and got the phone numbers of the South San Francisco and Vancouver police departments. After calling them, he went to his computer, got on-line, dialed up CompuServe, and spent an hour brushing up on his Asian geography.

By midnight the South San Francisco and Vancouver cops had called him back and he knew that Susan Hsu had been right. Dix and Hillman had been on her flight from Vancouver to Singapore. By one o'clock Mc-Kenna thought he knew why and he had formed a theory concerning their intentions. He went back to bed and, finally, to sleep.

McKenna wasn't optimistic, but he held onto the hope that the Singapore police would find Hillman and Dix. He arrived at the office an hour early, but Greve was still there before him and he called McKenna into his office. McKenna saw that his DD-5s from the previous day were already signed and in Greve's out basket, so he knew that Greve was up to date.

"You're starting to look a little frayed at the edges, Brian," Greve said. "You need a full day off and a good night's sleep."

"Why? Is my paperwork suffering?"

"No, it's fine, but it's taking its toll on you. What time did you get out of here last night?"

"Eight-thirty."

"Get any sleep?"

"Not much, but you know how it is. Can't get those two off my mind and I lay awake searching for something I missed, all the time wondering how the police in Singapore were doing."

"Seems to me you didn't miss too much," Greve said.

"But I did miss something?"

"Just a little something that's been bothering me. I was hoping to find the answer in your reports, but it wasn't there," Greve said, treating Mc-Kenna to a small, embarrassed smile to show his disappointment.

This Greve's a sharpie, McKenna thought as he concentrated on keeping his face a blank. Glad I lost that sleep last night. "Go on."

"Why did they leave from Vancouver? They were right there in San Francisco and there have to be flights from San Francisco to Singapore."

"Vancouver because they didn't want to take a chance on being recognized while they were catching their flight. Hillman's been flying out of the San Francisco airport for years, so he must know plenty of people there. He doesn't need somebody to tell us down the road, 'Hillman? Yeah, saw him catching a flight to Singapore last week.' "

"Then how did they get to Vancouver?" Greve asked.

"They drove there in Dix's Cherokee."

"How do you know that?"

"Because Hillman's Jag is parked in the long-term lot at the San Francisco airport and the Cherokee is parked in the long-term lot at the Vancouver airport. They probably thought it likely that they'd be flying back in a week or so and driving home to resume their lives."

"You think they thought of this flight as a practice run?"

"Yes, I do," McKenna said. "They figured we were tracking them through Cindy's cards, but I don't think they expected we were close to learning who they were. They were just being careful, putting themselves out of reach while they waited to see what developed."

"Maybe, but they're sure running now," Greve observed. "You know for certain that the cars are at the airports?"

"According to the cops in Vancouver and South San Francisco they are."

"I didn't see that in any of your reports."

"It's not. I didn't think of checking the airport parking lots until after I got home last night. I should've thought of it sooner," McKenna admitted.

McKenna expected some gentle chiding, but he didn't get any. Greve stayed right on track. "So why Singapore?"

"They've been there three times that we know about, but Singapore's not their final destination. I'm inclined to believe that they got off the plane there to confuse pursuit, just in case we did somehow manage to track them."

"Are you sure? I understand Singapore's a civilized place where everybody speaks English. Why wouldn't they just stay there?"

"English is the official language there, but it's a predominately Chinese city-state—the kind of place where a black and a white American wanted worldwide would have to stand out after a while. It's also a hard place to escape from if you don't have a boat because there's only one causeway off the island. That wouldn't be for them."

"Where does that causeway go? Malaysia?"

"Yeah, but that's not where they're headed, either. Only six hours by train or car up the Malay Peninsula is Thailand. That's where I think they're headed, their home away from home. Matter of fact, I'd be willing to bet that they're already there."

"Makes sense," Greve said after thinking over McKenna's assessment. "They were stationed there and they've certainly been back there enough times. Lots of expatriates living there, so they might be able to blend in with the rest of the foreigners."

"Without too much of a problem," McKenna agreed. "It's also become a major tourist destination and there's plenty of Western companies setting up there. Once the heat's off, they could easily blend there and keep themselves quite comfortable."

"If they had enough money," Greve said.

"Which brings me to my next point. I believe they must have a ton of loot stashed, but wouldn't it be nice to know if any of it is in Thailand?"

"You're talking about asset searching?"

"Yes."

"You know how to do that?"

"I've got a little experience," McKenna said. "Worked on cracking a ring of fences about ten years ago."

"Not good enough. It's a whole new ball game with off-shore banking havens and computerized money transfers, and you're talking about finding loot stashed in the Third World. Nowadays, you'd have to be a expert PI with lots of experience to come up with anything there," Greve said pointedly.

Of course, McKenna knew that Greve was right and he knew what he had to do to find Hillman and Dix's stash. But before he did, he wanted to have the boss on board. "An expert like Hurley?"

"He's an expert, and he'd be free for us," Greve pointed out. "Wouldn't McMahon be more than happy to turn him loose and pick up the bill?"

"He would, but that'd give him another weight to hang over our heads. Sometimes I already feel like he's the boss."

"I know what you mean. I don't like it either, but I've learned to live with it."

"You know that anything Hurley gives us wouldn't be legally obtained, don't you?" McKenna asked.

"I don't care. I want those two murdering scumbags in irons, the quicker the better."

Nothing could be clearer than that, McKenna thought.

Greve's Mother Goose attitude had extended to Tommy. He had given Tommy two days off and had insisted that he stay home and get some rest.

It was only eight o'clock, still an hour or two before Shields got into his office, so McKenna typed his report about finding Hillman's and Dix's cars. Then he went out for some breakfast and was back in the office when Shields called at nine-thirty.

"Haven't heard anything from the cops in Singapore yet, but here's a surprise for you. According to the State Department, the passports they're using are valid."

"Stolen?" McKenna asked.

"Nope. Valid and never reported stolen."

"They set up false identities for themselves?"

"That's the way it looks."

"When?"

"Hillman was first issued his Reginald Johnson passport in June of seventy-six. Dix got the Marvin Grossman one a month later."

"Have you got their passport applications?"

"Right here. Both presented birth certificates and New York State driver's licenses. They both used 491 West Twenty-second Street in Manhattan as an address."

McKenna had seen it many times before when he had worked in the Special Frauds Squad and had once arrested a con man who had established nineteen separate identities for himself, but he still marveled at the foresight shown by Hillman and Dix. "When did they renew the passports?"

"Last year. Both used the same San Jose, California, address. 2048 Bird Avenue, apartment two."

"That one bears some checking out. I'll see if I can get the San Jose PD to do it for me. Anything back on our other inquiries, yet?"

"Just Hong Kong. They've got no unsolved murders committed during the time Dix and Hillman were there. I should be hearing from everyone else one way or the other sometime this afternoon. However, I do have Dix's and Hillman's service records. You were right about a few things there."

"They met in Thailand?"

"That's right, while they were both assigned to the 504th Reconnaissance Squadron at U Dorn Air Force Base."

"How about the Philippines?"

"Dix spent two years stationed there before he met Hillman."

"He didn't learn Tagalog just by being there, did he?"

"No, he's not that sharp, thank God. He learned it at the Defense Language School, Monterrey, California, courtesy of the air force and the American taxpayers. Graduated in the top third of his class."

"And Vietnam?"

"You were right about that, too. Hillman was never actually stationed there, but Dix was. Like in Thailand later on, he spent a year as a photo analyst in a reconnaissance squadron, 1969 to 1970."

"They really have been around," McKenna noted.

"Sure have, and it was our government that put them together and gave them the skills to get into their enterprise."

"No one's to blame but them. If they weren't killing together, they'd be doing it separately," McKenna stated with a conviction he didn't feel.

McKenna had to call McMahon to get his permission to use Hurley's services, but he wanted to be able to give McMahon an up-to-date report when he did. That meant calling Big Ed in California, something McKenna was reluctant to do just then. Due to the time difference, he figured that Big Ed would be sleeping and he didn't want to wake him up again. He decided to wait an hour or so before calling and was surprised when Big Ed called him first.

"Glad you're up and around," Big Ed said. "I was afraid it was a little early for you."

"Not for me, but how about you?" McKenna asked. "Have you been to bed yet?"

"Not yet, but soon. Thanks to that news conference of yours, I've been scrambling to stay one step ahead of the press. Had a gaggle of them camped out on Mrs. Hillman's front lawn by the time we finished executing the search warrant there. Real nosy, pushy, obnoxious lot they are."

"You had the San Francisco cops with you?"

"Yeah, sharp bunch. Wouldn't have come up with much without them."

"Anything helpful?"

"Certainly interesting, but I don't know how helpful. Nothing that tells us what Mr. Hillman has been up to on the side or where he's off to now, but we were able to substantiate that he is a bona fide degenerate."

"Whips and chains?"

"Photos and videos too, along with the tripods and cameras they used to record their home-entertainment sessions. I figure that Mrs. Hillman thought we'd never find it, but those San Francisco cops knew just where to look. They're the ones who found the treasure trove behind a false wall in her bedroom closet. Could have knocked me over with a feather when I saw that stuff."

"Did the photos and videos feature just her and him?"

"*Feature*'s the right word, but yeah, it's just the two of them working out in the ones I've had a chance to look at so far."

"Torture?"

"Nothing that would leave any scars, but certainly heavy-duty S and M. A real education for a country boy like me, I'll tell you that."

"Does it look like she was a willing participant?"

"Willing? Let me tell you this, Brian. It's nothing that I'd want the press to know because I still like that woman and we're going to need her down the road, but that pretty, sweet, polite, butter-wouldn't-melt-in-her-mouth little lady is one tarnaceous sexual freak."

A *tarnaceous* sexual freak? Don't know what that is, exactly, McKenna thought, but I take it to mean that Mrs. Hillman was a something more than a willing participant. "Does it look like she was in charge?"

"About half the time, as far as I can tell, but I'm no expert. She's got sexual ideas about what's fun that don't occur naturally in the minds of women where I come from."

"Was she right there in the bedroom while you were doing the search?"

"Right there with us the whole time, serving sandwiches to us all and being as polite as can be."

"What was her reaction when you found the stuff in the closet?"

"Same as the San Francisco cops. Nonchalant, like every vigorous, sex-ually active couple has those kinds of things hidden in their closets."

"Could you use any of the photos you have to identify Hillman as one of the whippers in the *Serious* and *In Charge* torture photos?"

"Could I? I've got photos of him in much the same leather getup and mask, highly aroused and big as life to boot. With that rare-sized equipment he's got tucked in his pants, it'd be no problem. Show some of these photos to any jury, then give them a look at those magazine spreads, and there's only one conclusion they could reach—that's got to be him."

"So you did do good on the search," McKenna said.

"Not as good as I'd hoped. Still no clue about where those two are headed."

"Don't need that from you. I know where they're headed," McKenna said. He took five minutes to tell Big Ed about Dix's and Hillman's flight to Singapore and his ideas on their eventual destination.

"Makes sense to me, but I'd have to say that you got real lucky with that flight attendant recognizing them and calling you," Big Ed said.

"I got lucky because they made a mistake. If they had flown with the crowd in coach, chances are they wouldn't have been noticed. But in first class, with their own flight attendant assigned to do nothing but pamper them, they were bound to be remembered."

"That's one way to look at it," Big Ed said. "It's like their greed, the thing that first put us on to them. Their love of creature comforts is another mistake they're bound to make again."

"Hopefully," McKenna said, then got back to Big Ed's activities. "Where is Mrs. Hillman now?"

"That's one good thing I got done. Got her away from the press and in your Fairmont Hotel in San Jose."

"Do you still think she didn't know what her husband was up to?"

"She's sure got some bizarre sexual quirks that must have suited him to a T, but I'm convinced she's a kind person. She's the kind of woman who couldn't hurt anyone except in her own playful way in the sack. She's wouldn't condone killing by anyone, including her husband."

"How about Hillman's mother? Did you get a chance to talk to her?"

"Yeah, went to the nursing home and we had a real long chat. Left as confused as she is."

"She's not mentally competent?"

"Let's just be kind and say that the old girl's getting on in years. She doesn't even know her husband's dead, and he passed on ten years ago. She does have a memory. Remembers her fifteenth birthday party right down to the dress she was wearing and the raspberry filling in the cake, but she's not much on current events."

"Were you able to get her to talk about her son?"

"A bit. According to her, little James is a good boy, smart in school, and real strong for a kid his age. She's pretty sure that he comes to visit her a lot."

"Okay, so that was a bust," McKenna said. "How about the search in Scottsdale?"

"Heard from my detectives late last night. Dix is another freak, for sure. Big house, but Dix apparently doesn't do much social entertaining in the usual sense. They didn't find any torture paraphernalia, but two of the bedrooms are decorated in classic dungeon and another is set up as a photo lab. Expensive equipment and lots of it, but Dix didn't leave any photos there. Just like Hillman, he's got all the weights and exercise equipment to keep himself in shape. My people didn't find anything they considered evidence, left the place just like they found it."

"No phone book?"

"No, but we've subpoenaed his telephone records. Should know sometime today who he's been talking to."

"Have you got Hillman's phone records subpoenaed, too?" McKenna asked, then instantly regretted the question.

"Goddamn, just when I thought I was doing so good. Forgot to do that," Big Ed said.

"You did?"

"Of course not. I'll pick them up this afternoon, then we'll be headed home. Stay lucky, big city detective. I'm counting on you to make us all look good."

McKenna called McMahon, took fifteen minutes to fill him in, and got his permission to use Hurley once again. "You want me to call him first?" McMahon asked.

"Please do. Tell him I'll be stopping by to see him."

"Remarkable man, your Mr. Hurley. Did he tell you about the film that ex-detective of yours saw?"

"In a roundabout way he did. To tell you the truth, it crossed my mind for a moment that he might've intended to pull an end run on me."

"Do you mean, attempt to negotiate the purchase of that film on my behalf without telling you?" McMahon asked.

"I guess so. Like I said, it only crossed my mind for a moment."

"I'll admit that I toyed with testing the feasibility of the idea, but you've already told me that we shouldn't need such a film. That's still the case, isn't it?"

"I hope so. You'll recall that I also told you that I didn't want you trying to buy such a film without my okay, don't you?"

"Yes, I do. I'm aware that you're in charge of this investigation, Brian. My role is simply to assist you in any way I can, as long as my wishes are considered."

"As far as your wishes are concerned, things have pretty much gone your way. Haven't they?"

"It would seem so, so let me put your mind at rest. I'm extremely satisfied with the job you've been doing, so nothing's going to happen on my end without your approval."

"Thank you, but I'd like you to honestly answer one question for me. We've been lucky so far, but suppose down the road I hit a dead end. Am I still the boss?"

"You don't foresee any dead ends, do you?"

"Can't tell. What I do see is some more progress forthcoming, but it's a big world and those two know their way around the darkest places. I can't guarantee that we'll find them anytime soon, so I'd still like an answer from you."

"My answer's the same. You're running it and nothing will be happening in the foreseeable future without your knowledge and approval."

THIRTY-TWO

McKenna knew too many of the retired detectives and bosses working for Hurley, so he didn't want to meet Hurley in his office. Gossip travels fast in those circles and McKenna figured that the fewer people who could directly testify about his dealings with Hurley, the better.

Hurley trusted his people completely, but he also understood Mc-Kenna's concern. Consequently, they arranged to meet at Kennedy's. Hurley said that he wanted a couple of hours to take a preliminary look at Dix's and Hillman's financial history before the meeting, so they decided on a late lunch at one o'clock.

McKenna had a few things to do, so the delay was fine with him. He wanted to check out the address Hillman and Dix had used when they last renewed their passports, but he didn't want them reading in the newspapers that the police knew the names they were traveling under. He decided that the mission was best handled through Bynum, so he called him at Gallagher's bookstore. Bynum wasn't in yet, but Gallagher was. "Could you relay a message to Randy for me?" McKenna asked.

"Sure, but he won't be in until ten. Mornings are slow in this business."

"Ten will be fine. Tell him that Dix and Hillman are traveling with passports in the names of Marvin Grossman and Reginald Johnson with an address at 2048 Bird Avenue in San Jose, apartment two. I need Randy to have a pal in the San Jose PD check out the apartment to see if they're still renting it, but it has to be somebody he can trust to be discreet. Randy will understand what I mean."

"Okay, but why bother checking out an address on a forged passport?"

"Because the passports aren't forged. They're legit. They've also got driver's licenses in those names, and I wouldn't be surprised if they've got bank accounts and credit cards as well. Complete false identities, a very handy thing to have if you're on the run."

"I don't want to sound stupid, but would you mind telling me how they did that?"

"A little expensive and not a hard thing to do, especially back in the seventies when they did it. No photo IDs and computer cross-checking then. They could've bought forged birth certificates, but I'd bet that they picked a name they liked off a gravestone. A kid who died young, born about the same time they were. Then they got an address in those names."

"Without ID?" Gallagher asked.

"Not hard if you check into a rooming house and pay a couple of months in advance. That's what they did in New York. Cash talks in places like that, very few questions asked, so they've got a legitimate address and a place to get their mail. Then they get phone service for Marvin Grossman and Reginald Johnson."

"Without ID?" Gallagher asked again.

"Without ID. They simply called up and ordered service. Since Grossman and Johnson didn't have a credit history with the phone company, they had to pay a two- or three-hundred-dollar bond before the phones were installed. After a month, they had phone bills in their new names, a necessary thing to have when they started out. Then they called the Department of Health for applications for certified copies of their Marvin Grossman and Reginald Johnson birth certificates."

"It's that easy?"

"Just about. The applications might've had to be notarized, but that was just a matter of having a notary stamp and seal made up. Then they mailed back the notarized applications with the fee and maybe a copy of the phone bills to establish residence. After the birth certificates arrived, they got their driver's licenses and maybe even social security cards for Grossman and Johnson."

"Wouldn't the driver's licenses have been difficult?"

"An inconvenience, but not difficult. They had all the documentation they needed, but they had to go through the hassle of learner's permit and a road test the first time. Then came the passports, another easy thing for them with the identification they've accumulated."

"Very good," Gallagher said. "If they kept those passports current for all these years, I'd bet that they've turned in their New York licenses for California licenses."

"I'm sure they've turned in all their New York licenses for California licenses."

"You think they've established other identities?"

"I'm sure of it, all apparently legitimate."

Hurley was seated in the back room and waiting for him when McKenna arrived. The PI was unusually effusive in his greeting, leading McKenna to suspect that he was being had, somehow. Hurley had a thick file folder on the table in front of him, another thing that made McKenna suspicious. "You seem to have managed to accumulate quite a bit of paper in only a couple of hours," he noted.

"Very good. You caught me, Brian. The boss didn't authorize it, but I've been working on Dix's and Hillman's backgrounds in my spare time."

"What did it cost you to come up with what you've got so far?" McKenna asked, nodding toward the folder.

"I could have gotten it cheaper with some simple negotiations, but I felt that time was of the essence. Maybe eighty thousand so far, my cost, give or take ten grand, and I'm only scratching the surface."

"That's a pretty big bill you've got brewing."

"That's not the bill, that's just my cost. The bill will be a work of art and it'll be well worth the price to my wonderful client and you." Hurley opened the folders, carefully aligned the pages, closed it, and patted it lovingly. "I've got stuff in here you couldn't get at any price from the run-of-the-mill shysters running around this town calling themselves private investigators."

"This information enterprise of yours could have turned out to be a rather expensive hobby. Like I told you, I had intended to get that stuff legally."

"Legally? Bupkus!" Hurley said, smiling to himself like it was a joke he had never heard before. "Even if you knew where to look and how to do it, it would take you hundreds of subpoenas and at least a year. By the time you got close, they'd have moved their money and gotten themselves a couple of new names in a different country."

"Are you telling me that there aren't people in the government who could do it in a reasonable amount of time?"

"Where in the government? The FBI? The IRS?"

"To name a few."

"If they could, they'd have had me in jail a long time ago. Rank amateurs operating without the proper motive."

"The profit motive?"

"Exactly. Those gumshoes run around tossing subpoenas and upsetting people who could help them. On the other hand, those same people look forward to hearing from me."

"Because you bribe them?"

"Let's just say that I give my old friends the proper respect their position deserves. I know you really don't want to hear the filthy little details of this business, so why don't we get off that subject and on to something I'd like you to tell good old Bob."

"Good old Bob? That would be you?" McKenna asked.

"Of course it's me."

"Okay, what is it that you want me to tell you?"

"I think it would be nice of you to admit that, in the back of your mind, you always knew that you'd have to come to your old friend Bob for the goods on those two."

At first, McKenna had to fight the impulse to laugh in Hurley's face. But Hurley was looking at him with such an earnest and expectant look on his face that McKenna did as Hurley had suggested. He searched the back of his mind. "Okay, enough! I admit it. Now, tell me. What have you got that's so good?"

Hurley smiled like a baby being tickled. "Wouldn't you rather talk over lunch? It's on me, a small way to show my gratitude for putting McMahon onto me."

Hurley springing? That's a new one, McKenna thought.

Hurley made small talk while ordering and didn't get down to business until the waitress left with instructions from Hurley to bring their meals in twenty minutes. "Dix is slightly more complex from a financial viewpoint, so let's start with him," Hurley suggested. "Legally, Jerome Dix came into existence in New York on January thirteenth, 1955, when he was adopted by Jerome and Martha Dix."

"Wait a minute," McKenna said. "He was adopted, too?"

"Yeah, in New York when he was six, just like Hillman. Interesting thing is that both their adoptions were handled by the same agency, the Good Samaritan Home."

"One of the biggest, and maybe the best, but is it possible they knew each other way back then?"

"Bears checking, but I'm not going to waste my time or my client's money doing it. There are plenty of agencies that specialize in that who-are-my-real-parents business and I'm sure that one of those TV exposé shows will hire one of them to do that for us before long."

"Was he abused like Hillman was?"

"Before he was adopted? Don't know, but there's no indication he suffered any after. Lived in Queens with his new family, then they all moved to Levittown just before he started high school. Good student, but nothing really exceptional. Got letters in football and track. Graduates fifty-second in a class of a hundred thirty-two, then goes into the air force. I understand you've already got the details of his service record?"

"Yeah."

"Good. I figured you would, so I didn't bother. He opens his first bank account after he joins the air force, starts saving regularly. Scrimps and saves up twenty-six thousand by the time he gets out. Lot of money for the time, but nothing unusual there. Also takes out a fifty-thousand-dollar life insurance policy naming his adoptive parents as the beneficiaries."

"Are they still alive?"

"Still alive and living in Tampa, Florida. They moved there in 1985, right after the father retired from the post office. Forty-five-thousand-dollar house, but their son treats them good. Bought them three new cars in the last ten years. The first two were Fords, but the one last year was a Lincoln. Not too shabby, considering they've got just under eight grand in the bank."

"Okay, his parents' finances don't support the purchases of those cars and, presumably, neither does Dix's. How did he do it?"

"I wasn't able to find out about the Fords, but I did learn that Dix's father paid for the Lincoln with a check drawn on a Cayman Islands' bank."

"Did the Lincoln dealer tell you that?"

"No, his bank did. Indirectly, of course. Happen to have a photocopy of the check right here." Hurley rummaged through his folder, produced a sheet of paper, and handed it to McKenna. "You can keep that. Matter of fact, I'm going to give you everything I've got in this folder to go through when you get the chance."

It was a enlargement of the microfilm photo of a First Cayman Bank check showing the front and back. The amount was $42,516 in U.S. dollars drawn on the account of Richard Freeman. "Chalk up another identity for Dix," McKenna said. "Marvin Grossman and Richard Freeman."

"Give Hillman another one, too. Besides Reginald Johnson, he's also the Justin Cox with an account at the same Cayman Islands bank as Dix. Dix, Cox, and Johnson. Cute, huh?" Hurley didn't look like he was going to say another word as he gazed at McKenna with the smuggest, know-it-all look on his face imaginable.

McKenna thought he could wait it out, but then Hurley browsed through the folder, whistling to himself as if he were alone in the room.

McKenna realized after a minute that it was time to fold and give the devil his due. "Good old Bob, would you mind sharing your wisdom by instructing me on how you managed to come up with that wonderful piece of information?"

Hurley looked up and gave McKenna a benevolent smile. "Glad to, Brian. After all, I'm here to help you through the tough points in this little investigation of yours. On April second, 1984, Dix had his Cayman bank wire four hundred thousand dollars to an account he had opened in a Hong Kong bank with this Justin Cox. I took a look at it and found that Justin Cox had also wired four hundred grand from the same Cayman bank into the same Hong Kong account the very same day. That interested me, so I compared the handwriting on Cox's wire transfer authorization with Hillman's mortgage application for his present San Francisco townhouse." Hurley extracted the documents from his folder and passed them across the table.

McKenna placed them side by side and it was immediately apparent to him that the blank spaces in both had been filled in by the same man. Hillman had crossed his *t*s with a slant and had dotted his *i*s with a circle in both documents. McKenna also noticed that he had purchased his home in 1985 for $260,000 with a $150,000 mortgage. "Okay, same man," McKenna said. "Is all their money still in that Hong Kong bank?"

"No, it went out in two-hundred-thousand-dollar dribs and drabs from eighty-four to ninety-one. Those funds were used to capitalize the Joy and Good Fortune Real Estate Management and Holding Company in Thailand. I have the incorporation papers in here for you," Hurley said, tapping his folder. "However, I haven't had a chance yet to have them translated into English. What I can tell you is that Hillman and Dix, operating as Cox and Freeman, are part of a three-way partnership with a Thai national named Tao Rai Mettakaruna."

"Which one is the president of this company?"

"Officially, Mettakaruna is. Hillman is the secretary and Dix is the treasurer."

"How much did Mettakaruna put up?"

"As far as I can tell so far, nothing. It's my understanding that under Thai law, Thai nationals must have a majority interest in many types of businesses operated by foreigners there. I'm assuming that Mettakaruna is their front man."

"What real estate does their company own and manage there?" McKenna asked.

"I don't know yet, but I'll find out. Like I told you, I'm still scratching the surface."

"Does it look to you like this business is successful?"

"Very successful. I don't know what kind of profit they've siphoned off and hidden in other places, but checks into their Hong Kong account from their Joy and Good Fortune enterprise have exceeded their original investment by almost four hundred thousand dollars."

"So those two dirtbags are just about millionaires."

"More than just about. Counting what they have as Hillman and Dix, they *are* millionaires a couple of times over. They've been building equity over the years with their houses, and their Cayman Islands accounts have also been growing in spurts. Dix has got roughly six hundred thousand in his and Hillman is hovering around three hundred fifty grand."

"How does the money go into those accounts?" McKenna asked. "Cash deposits?"

"That's right, presumably the cash they get from selling their videos."

"What's the usual deposit?"

"Started out between forty and fifty thousand apiece about once a year, but it looks like their recognition in the degenerate world has been rising steadily. Last cash deposit was seventy thousand apiece last December."

"Say about a hundred and fifty thousand a video? Peanuts for them in their present financial condition. They might've started out torturing and murdering for profit and fun, but now it's fun and profit."

"That's the way it looks to me," Hurley said. "If you don't get them, they'll never stop."

"How about their legitimate finances under the Hillman and Dix names?"

"Living good, but to the unenlightened eye it would appear that they would have to be on a tight budget to maintain that lifestyle on their airline salaries. They struggle by, for the most part, and rarely use their illegitimate funds to finance their legitimate lifestyle."

"Rarely?"

"Two big exceptions were Dix's house in Scottsdale and Hillman's Jaguar. Dix used a hundred thousand from his Cayman account and Hillman took fifty thousand to make those purchases. Both times they funneled the money through Dix's father's account."

"It's like I've been saying. Their love of comfort might be their undoing if I can catch them living it up with their pants down, in a manner of speaking."

"Maybe, but keep in mind that they're usually a very financially disciplined duo."

"I will. Just a few more questions before we chow down. Do they own any houses in Thailand?"

"Foreigners can't own property there under their own names, and they probably don't own any houses under their company," Hurley stated. "They have Joy and Good Fortune corporate American Express cards in their Cox and Freeman names, but the only time they use them is for restaurants and hotels in Thailand. If they had houses there, I figure they wouldn't be staying in hotels."

"I agree. Any chance they've used those AmEx cards recently?"

Hurley looked hurt by the question. "Without me knowing? None. I've got all their cards flagged under all their names. Wherever they are and whatever they're doing, they're operating strictly cash."

"Do they have any credit cards from their Cayman Islands bank?"

"Both have the bank's platinum Visa, both never used."

"What's their credit limit?" McKenna asked.

"Whatever they have in their accounts, which, practically speaking, means no credit limit. In most Third World countries it would be hard for even the great McKenna and McKenna team to back them into a corner they couldn't buy their way out of."

"Thanks for that insight, good old Bob. You're doing more than anyone else could, but I'm still wondering about something you haven't brought up."

"Johnny Nolan?"

"Yeah, what about Johnny Nolan?"

"Nothing. Zilch."

"C'mon Bob. Don't tell me you can't find an old buddy of yours who's charging a fortune and living like a king in the hottest spots on the planet?"

"Hard to believe, isn't it?"

"After seeing today what you can do, yes. It's hard to believe."

"Maybe he knows I'm looking for him and he doesn't want to talk to me," Hurley offered. "After all, Johnny keeps his ear to the ground."

"Why wouldn't he want to talk to you? He can't know that you want to grill him on his prince's snuff film."

"Maybe he does."

"How?"

"Quite a few of his other old pals are now working for me. I'm wondering if I've got a leak in my organization."

"That ever happen to you before?"

"Never, but you know how it is. There's always some mangy cur that will bite the hand that feeds it, and it would serve me right. I'm too good to my employees."

"Let's eat before you spoil my appetite."

THIRTY-THREE

Big Ed called an hour after McKenna got into the office the next day. "Got some good news for you," he said. "The San Jose PD helped me get a warrant and we did good on the search. We won't be needing Hurley to spoon-feed us anymore. That apartment's their office."

No longer beholden to McMahon and Hurley? That is good news, McKenna thought. "What've you got?"

"Complete business records on the Joy and Good Fortune Company, along with all the banking statements and income tax returns for Grossman, Freeman, Cox, and Johnson. We need a sharp accountant to go over all this stuff, but it looks to me like they were trying to stay square with Uncle Sam. Their alter egos showed a profit on their foreign enterprise and paid some taxes every year, but they do have two sets of books."

"So they weren't really square."

"Those greedy bastards? What do you think?"

"I think not, but income tax evasion will be the last thing they'll have to worry about if we can do our jobs. Any videos or pictures there?"

"No, almost nothing on that other business of theirs."

"Almost?"

"One letter was from someone named Tao."

"Tao Rai Mettakaruna?"

"I don't know how common a name Tao is in Thailand, but presumably."

"What did Tao have to say?"

"Short and to the point. 'Congratulations. The negotiations were difficult, but ultimately successful. I am pleased to confirm tentative sale of latest product for one million U.S. in cash. As in previous sales to client, he insists on viewing representative excerpts before making payment. I await your instructions.' He just signed it 'Tao,' but we know what it's all about."

"Sure. The front man for their Thai corporation is also the salesman for their torture-and-death videos. He just arranged the sale of the Cindy Barrone-Arthur McMahon video for the best price they ever got."

"That's my read on it. You'll also be interested to learn exactly what kind of business the Joy and Good Fortune Real Estate Management and Holding Company is actually engaged in."

"You're right about that."

"They own and manage two bars and hotels in Bangkok with an unusually large number of young female employees who are making quite a bit more than you'd expect."

"Whorehouses?"

"Whorehouses with some interesting names—Punishing Delight and the Leather Emporium. Unusual places for unusual tastes is my guess."

"Not unusual for them."

McKenna had been waiting for news of the FBI's inquiries into the other murders, and Shields called at one o'clock.

"No old, unsolved torture-murders in Singapore while Dix and Hillman were there, but the Philippines and Barcelona are hits," Shields said. "Two killings in the Philippines, one in Barcelona, and they were there for all of them."

"Only one in Barcelona?"

"Unusual for them. She was a prostitute who usually worked the Rambla in the downtown section, but they killed her in a park on their last joint visit to Barcelona."

"Parc Guell? Was that the park?"

"Yeah. How'd you know?" Shields asked, unable to conceal his surprise.

"Because I've been there and it fits their MO. It's a big park in the hills on the outskirts of the city. Great views of Barcelona and the Mediterranean beyond."

"You notice any statues while you were there?"

"Couldn't miss them. They're everywhere, classic sculptures of the Roman gods and others depicting action scenes from Roman mythology. Why?"

"Because they chained her to one of them and whipped her to death. Then they went back to their MO, threw her body down the hill in front of the statue. Wasn't found until noon the next day."

"Any physical evidence?" McKenna asked.

"Just the body, and you know by now what she looked like by the time they got through with her."

"Yeah, I know. Once young and pretty, but whipped in something you'd find hanging in a cannibal's butcher shop."

"What do you think about the variations in their MO?"

"They got bored. Went to Barcelona nine times without finding a suitable couple in the park, so they improvised. I'd say that one of them found the girl on the Rambla and talked her into coming up to the park with him. The other was there waiting, and that was it for her. What about the Philippines?"

"Just what we'd expect. Lovers lane on Mount Pinatubo in February of eighty-six, Dix and Hillman's last visit there. The guy executed in the car with a .45 Colt automatic, the girl tied to a tree and whipped to death."

"They weren't crew on that flight, so they couldn't bring their guns in," McKenna surmised. "Must have picked up the .45 automatic locally to do their killing."

"Must have. The bodies were discovered the next day and the local press made a big deal over it. No physical evidence was left at the scene, so the cops rounded up the usual suspects. No one was charged and the case was forgotten."

"How about Chile?" McKenna asked. "No results?"

"Can't say yet. Haven't heard anything back from them, but the immigration people in Thailand, Malaysia, and Singapore got back to me. You were right on all counts."

"They're in Thailand?"

"Looks like it. They flew into Singapore as Johnson and Grossman, then caught a train north. They entered Malaysia as Cox and Freeman. Six hours later they left Malaysia and entered Thailand, still as Cox and Freeman."

"Are they still there?" McKenna asked.

"According to the Thais they are. They haven't left the country under any of their names."

"Are the Thais looking for them for us?"

"Yes, but not officially yet. We're dealing with some high-level people there, people who I'm told can be trusted to keep this search under wraps for a while."

"What do we need to make the search official? Arrest warrants?"

"That's it. Have Big Ed fax me the warrants and I'll get the ball rolling through the State Department."

"And then?"

"Then take a couple of days off and relax. The ball's no longer in our court."

THIRTY-FOUR

WEDNESDAY, JULY 28, 1:00 P.M., NEW YORK CITY

After lunch, McKenna wasted some more time by shining his desk for the second time that day. The ball had been out of his court for over a month and he hadn't done anything significant on the case in two weeks. He was bored to tears waiting for the news that the Thais had finally located and captured Hillman and Dix. He would never say it out loud, but he was losing hope that they ever would.

Almost every loose end had been tied up by McKenna in the first two weeks following Dix and Hillman's flight. Robles had been interviewed and it had been established that Hillman was a member of the pool house in Valley Stream. Dix had also been a guest there the day before the Cloisters murders and Robles remembered that they had used the Buick registered to him the night of the murders.

Hillman's and Dix's phone records had been obtained and compared. Over the years, they had been in constant touch with each other. With that documentary evidence, McKenna could easily establish the connection between them in any court, anywhere.

Shields's inquiry had given the Chilean police quite a jolt, but they had finally gotten back to him. A teenage boy had been kidnapped and tortured to death in the hills overlooking Santiago during Dix and Hillman's last visit there. The crime generated predictable public outrage and the police there had worked fast to develop and arrest a suspect, but he didn't survive their interrogation process. The Chilean police had considered the crime solved until Shields's unwelcome inquiry showed them that they had killed the wrong man.

Investigators from Spain and the Philippines had come to New York for a conference hosted jointly by the FBI and the Manhattan North Homicide Squad. Investigators from Chile had also been invited, but the Chilean government, understandably, declined to send them.

After the conference and case review, Spain and the Philippines also lodged warrants with the Thai government requesting the arrest and extradition of Hillman and Dix. Costa Rica wasn't represented at the conference and didn't have diplomatic relations with Thailand, but they also lodged the same request with Thailand through the Spanish government.

More light had been shed on Dix's and Hillman's finances. During his search of the San Jose apartment, Big Ed had found two sets of books for the Joy & Good Fortune company. According to the set of books Dix and Hillman kept for the Thai government, the company was barely profitable, and the company paid very little in taxes in Thailand. However, according to the second set of books Dix and Hillman kept for themselves, the enterprise was enormously profitable, even after the political contributions Tao Rai Mettakaruna made on the company's behalf to many named Thai politicians to avoid overzealous examination of their clubs' activities and their other set of books.

Both sets of books had been thoroughly examined by a team of FBI forensic accountants and a report had been issued. The conclusion was that

Dix and Hillman were guilty of income tax evasion in both the U.S. and Thailand; furthermore, the company had made highly questionable political contributions in Thailand to avoid unwanted government inspection and regulation there. That report was forwarded to the Thai government for information and consideration, but it was never made public.

As both Hurley and McMahon had predicted, Hillman's and Dix's crimes and life stories had become a media sensation. Intense media interest and pressure could be resisted for only so long, McKenna knew from past and current experience. He himself was under daily pressure from the press for interviews and information and he would have been happy to fold if that was what it took for them to just leave him alone. But he couldn't fold and he couldn't tell the press any more than they already knew on the progress in the investigation because there hadn't been any progress made in three weeks. Under the terms of the arrangement that had been worked out with the Thai police, McKenna also couldn't tell the press that Dix and Hillman were hiding out somewhere in Thailand as Justin Cox and Richard Freeman.

Initially, that arrangement had been all well and good. McKenna had expected the Thais to locate and produce Dix and Hillman in short order, but that hadn't happened and the delay was becoming a source of major discomfort and embarrassment for him. Brunette and Greve had some patience left, but the press and McMahon were snapping at McKenna's heels.

Uncomfortable as it was, the press McKenna could deal with. There were reporters camped outside the office shouting questions every time McKenna entered or left, but he had developed a thick skin and simply pushed his way through them every time.

McMahon was another matter. He called McKenna at least once a day for a progress report, and McKenna's daily "Sorry, nothing new" had worn thin with McMahon and prompted some strong suggestions from him. McMahon wanted to go public with all the information known about Dix and Hillman and then mount a media campaign to embarrass the Thais into intensifying their efforts to locate and arrest the fugitives. Fine by McKenna, but McMahon's plan had met with disapproval from the State Department, disapproval so strong that even McMahon, despite intense lobbying efforts, hadn't been able to overcome it. The official U.S. government position remained intact; relations with Thailand shouldn't be jeopardized over a matter that was bound to be resolved eventually anyway.

So McKenna struggled through every day, reporting to the office through the crowd of reporters to do, basically, nothing. The boredom was wearing him down. He had asked Greve to assign him to other cases or at least let him help out any other detective in the unit by doing anything they wanted, but Greve wouldn't hear of it. As the detective assigned to the most newsworthy case ever worked by the Manhattan North Homicide Squad, the public perception had to remain that McKenna was hard at work solving that case, and only that case.

Tommy, of course, had also been initially hounded for information by the same reporters hounding McKenna, but he had quickly found a way to make himself unavailable to them. He told them that he had signed with a publisher to do a book on the case and there was, of course, an exclusive nondisclosure clause in his contract regarding any aspect of the investigation in which he was connected in any way. "Sorry, but you know how it is," Tommy said with a smile to any request for information. They understood completely and frequently wished him well.

Tommy's performance didn't require a great deal of acting ability on his part because he had, in fact, signed just such a deal. He and Randy had already completed the detailed outline for their project. They had received their nice advances, and they were also looking to McKenna for the final chapter. "But that could wait," they told him cheerfully once or twice a week. "Keep your chin up and it'll be okay for all of us. We'll get them, sooner or later, and certainly before our one-year contract deadline on delivery and acceptance of the completed manuscript expires."

McKenna was at his desk, enjoying his fifth cup of coffee while searching for the seven-letter answer to 39 Down to almost complete the *Post*'s crossword puzzle. He was surprised when his phone rang and it was Randy Bynum.

"I might have Tao under surveillance," Randy said.

McKenna stood up so fast that he spilled his coffee across his shiny desk. He knew that Randy was at a trade show in Atlantic City, but he hadn't expected to hear from him since Randy had been at another show the week before in Reno and had developed no more than a $600 losing streak at blackjack. "Where are you?"

"The Bally Park Hotel. Tao's in his room right now, room 618."

"Did he sell you anything?"

"Some moderately good stuff, paid him three thousand for it. I've got four stills with more to follow. Definitely torture, but not Hillman and Dix."

"Is what follows going to be a snuff film?"

"He wouldn't say that in so many words, but I think so. I promised him a hundred thousand for a legitimate snuff film, but he wants to check me out, first."

"Check you out? How?"

"I don't know, but my cover might not hold up. I had to give him my driver's license, my Visa, and my trade show credentials."

"He's calling a PI to have you checked out," McKenna said.

"That's a good possibility."

"Do you have enough right now to have the local cops grab him for questioning?"

"That's already in the works. I called McMahon and he's calling the New Jersey governor. I expect that I'll have some official company here pretty quickly."

"You called McMahon before you called me?"

"Brian, you better get the proper perspective on this," Bynum said. "McMahon's paying me, not you."

"So what's this? A courtesy call?"

"Yes."

Once again McKenna was headed south on the New Jersey Turnpike with the skyline of New York fading behind him. An hour later, after a stop for gas and coffee, he felt that he had finally calmed down enough to call McMahon. When he did, Ginny answered. "Hi, Brian. How are you?" she said pleasantly.

"Fine, thank you. I'd like to speak to Mr. McMahon."

"I know, but he's on the other phone."

"Then ask him to get off the other phone and come to this phone right now."

"Really?"

"Yes, really."

"I think it would be better if he called you back," Ginny suggested. "You seem to be terribly upset."

"I think annoyed and disappointed best describes my present state of mind, but please get him."

"If you insist, but try not to upset him too much. He hasn't been feeling too well lately."

It took McMahon another minute to get on the line, but McKenna thought he sounded just fine. "Hi, Brian. I guess you heard the good news."

"I've got some news, but what's the good news?"

"Tao Rai Mettakaruna is being held at the Atlantic City Police Head-quarters."

"Really? What's he being charged with?"

"Whatever you'd like, if anything. I'm assured that you will have full discretion in this matter."

"He can walk if he makes a deal with me?"

"The New Jersey authorities don't have a vested interest in this case like we do. At the moment, they're quite compliant."

"Who's spoken to him so far?"

"No one except Randy. Any interrogation will be conducted under your authority and any decisions regarding Mr. Mettakaruna's current and sudden legal problems, whatever they may be, will ultimately be made by you."

"Am I to understand that I've got a blank check with the Atlantic City police?"

"You understand correctly. Go to work," McMahon said, then hung up.

Maybe a little rash and impatient at times, but not a bad guy, McKenna decided. McMahon certainly knows how to get things done.

The Atlantic City police's detective commander met McKenna at the door to the squad office and escorted him in and through to his own office. On the way McKenna passed the cell with Mettakaruna sitting inside by himself. With just a glance McKenna saw that he was a small, slight man, just the person Gallagher had described. He was sitting erect on the bench facing the cell door and he nodded to McKenna as he passed by. McKenna thought Mettakaruna appeared concerned, but not alarmed.

Bynum was sitting at the squad commander's desk, but he was nothing close to the Bynum McKenna had seen last. Randy the Cowboy had transformed himself into Randy the Successful Sleazeball. His hair was slicked back, he wore a white silk open-neck shirt with two black dice embroidered on the pocket, there was a thick gold chain around his neck, from which hung a gold pyramid with a large diamond in its center, and he sported a ring on his right hand with a ruby so large that McKenna thought it should be in a museum somewhere. Completing the effect was Bynum's new smile with the two gold-capped front teeth shining through.

"I believe you know this *gentleman*," the squad commander said in a tone of voice that conveyed his impression that Bynum was considered anything but. That was all he said before he left, closing the door behind him and leaving McKenna and Bynum alone in his office.

"Touchy, isn't he?" McKenna asked.

"Understandably so," Bynum said. "We're breaking one of the great common-sense rules and we're getting away with it. I'm sure it's annoying him."

"Which rule is that?"

"Don't fuck with the bear in his cave."

We're sure doing that, McKenna realized. Nobody likes a naked display of power, and here we are in the squad commander's town, two politically connected interlopers taking over his office while we decide the fate of a prisoner his people had arrested. Certainly a touchy situation, but Bynum interested McKenna more at the moment. "Is that ring real?" he asked.

"I assume so. It's Hurley's, and so is the chain and medallion. A little gauche, but I've gotten used to it."

"Très gauche, I'd say. When did he give you those baubles?"

"Lent them to me a while back," Randy said, and left it at that.

Since it appears that Bynum isn't in a hurry to explain things, I guess it'll have to be later. "What did Mettakaruna sell you?"

"These," Bynum said. He picked an envelope up from the floor next to his chair and passed it to McKenna.

The envelope contained four 8x10 black-and-white photos shot in what looked to McKenna to be a torture dungeon. There were only two people in all the photos: a middle-aged, overweight Asian male, possibly Chinese, and a young, thin, darker Asian girl who McKenna was sure was originally from someplace in Southeast Asia. Neither of them was in good enough shape to be considered actors or professional models.

In the top photo the girl was stretched out on a large wooden wheel. She was in an almost-upright position, with her back arched and pressed against the wheel. Her feet were tied together at the ankles and secured to a rung at the bottom and her arms were stretched over her head with her wrists secured to a rung at the top of the wheel. She was naked, but the man was fully dressed as he whipped her breasts. Her face was contorted in pain and her mouth was open so that McKenna could almost hear her screaming.

The second photo showed the same scene as the first, but it had been taken minutes later. The girl was a bloody mess with long, wide gashes everywhere on the front of her body, but concentrated in the area around her breasts. The man was still whipping her and she was still screaming.

The settings of the third and fourth photos was still the dungeon and showed only the same tormentor and the same victim, but there had been a position change. She was tied face-down hand and foot to steel rings embedded in the floor, but her midsection was draped over something that reminded McKenna of a gymnastics horse. In her position her behind was the highest part of her anatomy and the part of her receiving the man's attention as he whipped her backside with a bamboo rod. Blood was dripping from her frontal wounds and had formed a pool on the floor under her, but she was very much alive as she turned her head to look at her tormentor, still screaming.

The last photo was taken after the third with the man and girl in the same positions. Her behind, her back, and the back of her legs were covered with welts. The man was still hitting her with the bamboo rod, but she was past caring or feeling, either unconscious or dead.

McKenna stacked the photos and replaced them in the envelope. "They look like surveillance photos to me."

"That's what I've been thinking," Bynum said. "Poor lighting and the camera isn't correctly positioned to catch all the action. I don't think the man was aware that he was starring in Mettakaruna's production."

"And the location? One of their S and M clubs?"

"Another good assumption."

"The girl's dead, of course," McKenna said.

"Of course. I think she's one of their employees, but I'm sure she didn't suspect what she was getting into that time with that client. But no matter, she's dead."

"What makes you think she was one of their employees?"

"Take a good look at the first and third photos. She's got some light scars on her breasts and behind from being whipped before that last session. Nothing nearly as severe as we saw in those photos, but she'd been whipped or beaten with the rotan before. Looks to me like she was a professional S and M plaything before they retired her."

"What's a rotan? The bamboo rod?"

"Uh-huh. Nice tool they use to inflict pain in Asia. When used by an expert, it can either keep the damage to a minimum or maim the victim for life."

"Or kill her with lots of pain, apparently," McKenna said. He didn't want to look at the photos again, so he took Bynum at his word. "Did Mettakaruna tell you something that makes you so sure she's dead?"

"Like I said, indirectly. While I was buying those photos, I naturally inquired if the video that went with it was available. He told me 'possibly,' if there was such a video, but he also said that it would be expensive if it existed. I offered him fifty thousand, but he didn't take me seriously at first. Then I took him to my room and showed him the fifty grand lying on top of my two-hundred-grand stash. His saliva's still on my carpet."

"Hurley's supplied you with that kind of cash?" McKenna asked, amazed.

"I'm not on a tight budget," Bynum said, brushing the question aside. "Naturally, I told Mettakaruna that I would be willing to pay more if that was a bona fide snuff film. That's when he took my ID and credit card to have me checked out, but he left me optimistic. Told me that the video, if it existed, had a beginning, more excitement than was shown in the photos, and a definite end."

"Was his room searched?"

"Not yet, but that's not where the video is. He's got a big package in the hotel safe. Managed to see it when they put my cash in, right after the locals threw the cuffs on him."

"Good work," McKenna said. "We'll take a look at it later on."

"You going to get a warrant?"

"Won't need one. Mettakaruna's gonna give it to us."

"Why would he? Wouldn't that hang him?"

"Get him a heavy-duty pornography charge in New Jersey, but not much more than that. Even if the film shows the girl being killed, New Jersey would have to prove jurisdiction for any accessory-to-homicide charge. Since we know the crime didn't even happen in the U.S., their jurisdiction problem would be a difficult one to overcome."

"Fine, but I still don't understand why he'd just give it to us."

"He'll do it if he's smart. If not, I'll make him smart and tell him why he doesn't want us to get a warrant."

"Why don't you explain it to me, first," Bynum said.

"Sure. I'll explain to him that us going to court to get that search warrant would potentially involve making a public record out of some of the elements of the deal he's going to make with us."

"You're certain he's going to deal with us?"

"Once he gets some prodding and a few guarantees, as soon as he can. He's desperate and probably very scared."

"He didn't look that scared to me," Bynum observed.

"That's because it's not us he's afraid of."

"Then who?" Bynum asked, then answered his own question after he thought about it for a minute. "Hillman and Dix, two guys he knows are stone-cold killers who'd be happy to snuff him after one of their long, hard fun sessions."

"Hillman, Dix, and who knows how many others? Depends on who he sold their videos to over the years, doesn't it?" McKenna asked. "Think about it. Dix and Hillman are the most wanted men on the planet right now. Everything they've done in their lives is now the subject of intense public interest and Mettakaruna could severely embarrass anyone he sold their videos to."

"You're right. I'm sure it's now apparent to Hillman, Dix, and many others that Mr. Mettakaruna has outlived his usefulness, but is it apparent to him yet?"

"I think so. Did you really expect that you'd find him here peddling his wares when everybody's looking for his partners, employers, or whatever his relationship is with Dix and Hillman?"

"I'll admit that I thought this would be a bust," Bynum said. "I should have figured it out as soon as I saw him, because he already has. He sent the letter confirming the sale of the Cindy Barrone and Arthur McMahon video before Dix and Hillman were publicly identified. He wrote them from Thailand and they're now in Thailand. He should be there with them helping to complete their big sale, but he knows now that he'd have been killed by them."

"So he fled, but he's also in need of cash to completely disappear in some comfort," McKenna added. "That's why he's here."

"I guess you've already figured out how to make that work to your advantage?"

"I'll be playing some things by ear when I talk to him, but I've got a basic strategy worked out."

"Would you like to let me sit in?" Bynum asked.

McKenna liked Bynum and didn't like hurting his feelings, but he felt it necessary to send another message to McMahon. "Sorry, Randy. You're good, but you're no longer a cop. I don't want to complicate things when I question him."

Bynum gave McKenna a smile that belied no hard feelings. "Understood. Just thought I'd ask."

McKenna had two phone calls to make before he could question Mettakaruna. First was the pleasant one to Gene Shields for approval. Then came the one that irked him, the call to McMahon for coordination and the necessary political influence.

When McKenna felt he had everything he needed in place, Bynum brought Mettakaruna into the squad commander's office and left him alone with McKenna.

McKenna's first impression was that, just like his handwriting, Mettakaruna was a neat, precise man. He pointed to the chair on the other side of the desk and Mettakaruna sat down, his hands folded on his lap as he stared at McKenna, waiting.

"Do you know who I am?" McKenna asked.

"I do. You're Detective McKenna of the New York City Police Department, the man charged with investigating the murders at the Cloisters," Mettakaruna answered without a trace of emotion.

"And, of course, you know why you're here."

Mettakaruna just nodded.

"Good. Saves us some time and some nonsensical, meaningless sparring. I'm going to put our cards on the table, we'll conduct some negotiations, and then you'll tell me without reservation everything you know about James Hillman and Jerome Dix. You'll also help us to locate them, and if I deem it necessary or convenient, you'll also cooperate in whatever scheme I might devise to bring them into custody."

Once again, Mettakaruna said nothing. He just stared at McKenna, but there was a slight, sardonic smile tugging at his lips.

"Richard Freeman and Justin Cox," McKenna said suddenly, but the only reaction he got from Mettakaruna was a small, almost-imperceptible nod.

"Good. No need to answer now or commit in any way I can hold you to. Let's just have a little case review to see where we're at. Let's try the Joy and Good Fortune Real Estate Management and Holding Company, Tao Rai Mettakaruna, president."

Another small nod from Mettakaruna.

"Snuff films made in California, Arizona, Costa Rica, Chile, Barcelona, and the Philippines?"

Yet another nod.

"S and M magazines sold by you containing photos that depict torture killings?"

There was no reaction from Mettakaruna, exactly what McKenna had expected since possession of such magazines were the only crime Mettakaruna could be charged with in New Jersey, and conviction for that crime could be a long shot. Mettakaruna obviously realized that and he wasn't committing.

"*Serious* and *In Charge?*"

Again, no reaction.

"A letter from you addressed to Cox and Freeman, aka Dix and Hillman, at 2048 Bird Avenue in San Jose. In that letter you confirmed the sale of a video they made while they tortured Cindy Barrone to death."

McKenna was rewarded with the slight nod and the sardonic smile.

"And last but not least, the underlying basis of our little chat—a video now in the Bally Hotel's safe that documents the torture and murder of a girl in a premise in Thailand that is owned and managed by a corporation nominally headed by you. How am I doing?"

Mettakaruna sat thinking for a moment before he answered. "You know, Detective McKenna, that nobody has informed me of my constitutional rights since I was arrested and brought here."

"That's correct, and I would be willing to sign a statement to that effect."

"Might I ask exactly how that statement would affect my current legal difficulty?"

"It means that nothing you tell me until I do advise you of your constitutional rights could ever be used in court against you. With that in mind, I'll ask you once again. How am I doing?"

"On the face of it, Detective McKenna, you seem to be remarkably well informed."

"So nice of you to say so. Now, on to more pressing matters that concern you personally. Besides your legal problems in New Jersey, I think you've got other things to worry about. I think that you're under the perception that your life is in danger and I also think that you presently find yourself in precarious financial condition."

"As I said, you seem to be remarkably well informed."

"Thanks again. Have you heard, Mr. Mettakaruna, that the first rat to leave a sinking ship is sometimes the only rat to survive?"

"Yes, I've heard that and I emphatically believe it's true."

"Then I've got some solutions for your problems, if you believe that you can trust me."

"You've got a good reputation," Mettakaruna said.

"A reputation I value. After we chat here for an hour or two, we'll go over to the Bally Hotel where you'll pack your stuff and give me whatever interesting things you've got there. Then we'll come back here and one of the nice detectives outside will read you your constitutional rights. You will then be arrested under whatever name you like for the crime of Promoting Obscenity."

"I don't see the benefit in that for me."

"But there are benefits for both of us. Mind if I explain mine first?"

"Go ahead."

"There's a judge sitting in an empty courtroom in Trenton right now who is waiting to hear you plead guilty to the charge. He will then sentence you to five years in some horrible, maximum security prison, but the sentence will be suspended and you will be paroled in my custody. Do you understand what that means?"

"I assume it means that you'll slap me into that prison if you find my cooperation lacking."

"Very good. That's my hammer over you, but here's the good news. You will be enrolled in the Federal Witness Protection Program and you'll remain in it until one year after you testify at Dix's and Hillman's trials. You'll be given a new identity that you can keep. You'll also get a living allowance and a monthly stipend."

"How about any legal problems that might develop for me in other countries as a result of Dix's and Hillman's activities?"

"Nothing I can do about that, but the fact that you are in the U.S. and in the Witness Protection Program won't be revealed to any of them."

"Including Thailand?"

"Especially Thailand, as far as I'm concerned. The cops there don't seem to be breaking their asses for me."

"Would you term this monthly stipend you mentioned 'comfortable'?"

"Livable, but you can do better than that for yourself. There's also a considerable reward for the arrest and conviction of Dix and Hillman, and there's a possibility that the amount can be increased by a party who's very interested in this investigation."

Mettakaruna had a lot to think about, but it didn't take him long. "Detective McKenna, we can do business."

THIRTY-FIVE

It was dawn by the time McKenna and Mettakaruna got to the Gramercy Park Hotel in Manhattan. Mettakaruna would be guarded around the clock by detectives from the Homicide Squad until the case was resolved and he was placed in the care of the feds who supervised the Witness Protection Program.

Tommy was waiting for them in the lobby. They checked Mettakaruna in and accompanied him upstairs to his large, comfortable three-room suite. Mettakaruna excused himself and went to bed, closing the bedroom door behind him. It had been a long day and night for both of them, but longer for McKenna. He had been awake for all of it while Mettakaruna had slept in the car during the drive back from Trenton.

"You look like shit," Tommy said cheerfully.

"Thank you, but I'm holding up. Nothing wrong with me eight hours in the sack wouldn't cure."

"Is what you got worth the cushy deal you gave that scumbag inside?"

"Only time will tell."

"What've you got?" Tommy asked.

"Mettakaruna can't say for certain, but he thinks it likely that Dix and Hillman are out of our reach. Out of everybody's reach, for that matter."

"In Thailand?" Tommy asked.

"Maybe northern Thailand, maybe northern Burma, maybe northern Laos, but someplace in the Golden Triangle. He thinks they're hiding out as guests of their old pal, General Chou Son Yee."

"I guess that would put them out of reach."

"Far out. The general is the law in the Golden Triangle. It would take a major, coordinated military operation to get them, something the governments of Thailand, Burma, and Laos are presently unwilling or unable to do."

"How did the general, Dix, and Hillman get to be old pals?"

"Dix's and Hillman's clubs basically serve as R and R centers for the general's troops."

"They're all S and M freaks?"

"Just the way he wants them—vicious, cruel, and totally insensitive to human life. Also keeps them totally loyal to him, ready to torture and kill anybody he'd like."

"Okay, Chou's got his system and he's got good soldiers as far as he's concerned. Loyal, depraved killers," Tommy said. "Do you have any idea how this R and R system works with Dix and Hillman?"

"Simple. The general shows his favor with the people who please him by sending them to Dix and Hillman's clubs in Bangkok. When they arrive, usually in small groups, they're supervised by Mettakaruna's people while they shop, spend money, and do the town without attracting too much attention from the local police. But it's at the clubs where the real fun happens. They're lodged, fed, and entertained, doing almost anything they like with and to the employees, within reason—and the bounds of reason are stretched pretty thin there."

"Stretched to include murder, I suppose?"

"Rarely, and then only for Chou's real favorites. Buying somebody to torture and kill is expensive and entails a certain amount of risk, even in Thailand."

"Is the film you got from Mettakaruna a snuff film?"

"Definitely."

"Shot in one of their clubs?"

"Yes, the Leather Emporium in Bangkok. It shows Ne Woo torturing a Cambodian girl to death. Woo runs the general's operation in Laos for him. A real favorite, so he's been allowed to kill three girls at that club in the past five years."

"Can you be sure from watching the film that she's really dead?"

"There's two copies of the video and one's slightly longer than the other. In the shorter version that Mettakaruna was going to sell Randy, Woo beats her until he's too tired to hit her anymore. She sure looks dead by the time he's finished with her, but a great lawyer might be able to convince a dumb jury that she's not."

"But he wouldn't have a chance if the jury saw the longer version, would he?"

"The second video's the clincher. The camera's still running after Woo leaves and one of the club's supervisors comes in with a Samurai sword. He's apparently had lots of practice because he chops her head clean off in one stroke. Then he picks it up by the hair and brings it right up to the camera lens to show whoever's buying the video that he's got the real thing."

"The video wasn't shot for Woo as a souvenir of his visit?" Tommy asked.

"He doesn't know that there was a video made that documents his visit, and neither do Dix and Hillman. They always strive to keep their relations with the general perfectly correct, and he sure wouldn't like this."

"I'd think he wouldn't," Tommy agreed. "A video like that could be very bad publicity for him."

"Mettakaruna says he's got three more videos like the one he's given us," McKenna said, "all showing one or another of the general's top hench-men torturing Cambodian girls to death in the Leather Emporium."

"So what's the plan? We embarrass Chou into giving up Dix and Hill-man?"

"More like blackmail him into doing it, but it's gonna be tough to do."

"Why? Because the State Department doesn't want us embarrassing the Thais?"

"There's that to consider, but the State Department's position is going to change. Chou demands loyalty, but he knows it's a two-way street. He owes Dix and Hillman, and all his men know it."

"For running great whorehouses? Not much of a debt."

"No, for doing one of their torture-murders and giving the general's men a lesson in discipline for him," McKenna said. "Remember the victim in the *In Charge* centerfold?"

"Never forget it. Asian male, mountain setting."

"According to Mettakaruna, he was a DEA informant sent to spy on the general's operation in Thailand. Poor devil was caught when he tried to buy the cooperation of one of Chou's men, so Chou decided to give his people a lesson on the dangers inherent in talking bad about him. Dix and Hillman happened to be around, so they did the general a favor and had a little fun while they were at it. It was a good show, as far as they were concerned, so all his men know that the general owes Hillman and Dix."

"I see. Chou would lose face with them if he turned them over to us?"

"Yes, he certainly would. However, there could be something good for us in this. If it was a DEA informant they killed, that could make the Justice Department cranky—maybe cranky enough to affect the State Depart-ment's don't-upset-the-Thais policy. That'll put more pressure on Chou to turn them over."

"Where are those other videos?" Tommy asked.

"That's going to be a bit of a problem."

"You don't have them?"

"No. Mettakaruna's got them hidden somewhere."

"So we'll make him give them to us."

"Can't do that. Cagey bastard didn't tell me about them until after I closed the deal with him."

"So what? Put the screws to him."

"Tommy, are you trying to tell me that a deal's not a deal if the guy we're dealing with turns out to be a sharp piece of work?" McKenna asked.

Tommy had to stop and think about that one for a minute. "What do we have to do to get them and keep Mettakaruna happy?"

"We have to buy them from him. Three videos, three hundred thou-sand."

"Whaat? We have to make that complicitous, murderous, double-dealing scumbag that happy?"

"I think we do, but it won't be up to us."

"McMahon?"

"Uh-huh. We could try pressuring the Job to come up with it, but I think McMahon would insist on covering the cost to get things rolling in a hurry."

"You'd better hope so, because three hundred thousand would take quite a bit of the shine off your golden-boy status. They'd be chuckling in squad rooms for the next twenty years over this great deal you've worked out."

"I know."

McKenna was taking a nap on the couch in the sitting room of the suite while Tommy sat in the chair, reading the paper and watching the bedroom door. At eight o'clock Greve came up, surprising them both. The squad commander rarely left his office unless there was a fresh murder. "First day, and already I've got a coverage problem," he explained. "Got three men going to court this morning, so I can't get anybody else up here 'til noon."

"So what's the plan?" McKenna asked.

"You'll explain this deal to me, and then you'll go home and get some real sleep. I'll stay with Tommy until I can get somebody else up here."

Both McKennas were shocked. An NYPD squad commander helping to guard a witness, that most menial of detective duties? They realized they were watching history in the making.

"Bring yourselves under control and keep this under your hat," Greve said curtly. Then he called room service and ordered up a large pot of coffee.

It took McKenna the better part of an hour to recount his New Jersey activities. "Three hundred grand?" Greve said, shaking his head as he stared at McKenna. "Three hundred grand counted against my budget? I don't mind getting into the record books, but they'll be laughing about this one in squad rooms for the next twenty years."

"I guess you had to be there," McKenna offered.

"Don't think it would've made much difference. A deal's a deal and I know these things happen when you're dealing with slippery pricks like the guy inside."

"If it turns out we need those videos, we'll work him down," Tommy said.

"Way down, and we'll bring the sheriff into it, too. No sense in giving him a free ride if it's gonna be prosecuted in Arizona."

"Are we forgetting about McMahon?" McKenna asked.

"I'd rather," Greve said. "I already feel like he's holding the mortgage on my house."

"But if worse comes to worst, we let him spring?"

"I guess so," Greve answered. "Enough of that. How's the quality on the videos we've got?"

"I've just seen one of them run on fast forward, but it looked okay to me," McKenna said. "A little dark, but you can certainly see what's going on."

"You haven't sat and watched it through?" Tommy asked.

"No. I was pressed for time and, quite frankly, I've already seen enough of it," McKenna explained.

Greve and Tommy just looked at each other, and McKenna knew they were thinking his attitude wasn't appropriate for a homicide detective. McKenna was prepared to agree, if asked. He knew the girl was long dead and there had been nothing he could do to help her as he had watched her suffer and die, but he didn't want to see it again.

That made no difference to Greve. "Sorry, Brian, but you're not going home quite yet." He called the front desk and had a VCR brought up. The girl's murder had to be endured and studied, and it was.

Greve and Tommy sat on the sofa, watching the tape. McKenna was in the armchair across the room, watching them and noting the horror, disgust, and anger reflected on their faces. They're not so tough after all, he thought.

As the girl's head was being chopped off, the bedroom door opened and Mettakaruna came in, wearing a silk robe and looking dapper and refreshed. He was the focus of everyone's attention. "Good morning. Any coffee left?" he asked pleasantly.

McKenna looked back to Tommy and Greve. From the look on their faces, he thought for a moment that he would have to do something quick to save his star witness's life, but it didn't come to that.

Greve was the first to regain his composure. The tape had ended, so he got up and turned the TV off. "No, it's gone. We'll order some more if you'd like, but I've got a few questions for you first."

"And you are . . . ?" Mettakaruna asked.

"Lieutenant Greve, my boss," McKenna said before Greve could answer.

"Fine. A pleasure to meet you," Mettakaruna said. He sat on the couch next to Tommy and looked up at Greve. "How can I help you?"

"I'm told that all the girls who were killed were Cambodian."

"Correct. Over the past seven years a total of eleven Cambodian girls were killed by six of General Chou Son Yee's men. As I'm sure Detective McKenna has told you, three more of those killings are documented on video and are available."

"Yes, he told me, but that's not what I'm getting at. Why just Cambodian girls?"

"Because they're readily available, impoverished people from an impoverished land. Thailand is full of them, mostly illegal immigrants, and they're considered something of a nuisance. Many of the women work as prostitutes, and our clubs employ a number of the more attractive ones. Illegally, because they aren't registered and don't have the proper documentation, but we do it."

"Do any of your other employees know that these girls have been killed?"

"Besides myself, only one other. You must have seen him in the film."

"The guy with the sword?"

"Yes, my brother-in-law and a trusted friend. Are you asking how we explain the disappearance of the girls who were killed?"

"Yes. After all, some of the other girls must've noticed when those eleven didn't show up for work again."

"My employers have worked out an efficient system that keeps those kinds of inquiries way down. First of all, the Cambodian girls are only hired on a short-term basis and our Thai girls don't normally associate with them. Three months is a long time for us to keep a Cambodian girl on. Second, we have two clubs. To keep our customers from getting bored, all the girls are frequently transferred from one club to the other, always on very short notice."

"So that girl wasn't missed at all?" Tommy asked.

"They never are. If our Thai girls even thought about her, they'd assume she was either fired or working at the other club."

"And the Cambodian girls?"

"We pay them well and they never ask questions. They just do what they're told."

"The killings only take place at the Leather Emporium?" Greve asked.

"Yes. That's the only club we've set up to accommodate the general's men. Our other club caters to the general public and the tourist trade."

McKenna thought that the questioning would go on for hours, but then the phone rang and he picked it up. "Brian, brace yourself for some bad news," Hurley said.

What could Hurley possibly tell me that I'd consider bad news? McKenna wondered. "Okay, I'm braced."

"Arthur McMahon is dead."

"Dead? I was talking to him around midnight last night and he sounded fine."

"Then I guess you weren't listening to him with a stethoscope on his heart. He's dead, died at two-ten this morning."

The news hit McKenna hard. The old man was tough to deal with at times, but McKenna liked him, respected him, and understood his feelings. He felt a surge of regret that he wasn't able to bring Dix and Hillman in before McMahon died, much less get them tried and executed. There simply hadn't been enough time left to McMahon. "Who told you about it?" he asked.

"I just got off the phone with Ginny. She was talking to him about Mettakaruna when he had the big one."

"So what now?"

"Not much has changed. I go on almost the same as before, and I guess you do as well."

"Almost?"

"Yeah, almost. I think we're dealing with a different kind of cat here, maybe one not quite as domesticated and ready to purr. She informed me that she's now a very wealthy woman, but she doesn't mind if she dies penniless in the poorhouse. There's only one thing she wants, and she'll spend everything to get it."

"I know. Dix and Hillman dead," McKenna said.

"Preferably writhing in agony and screaming in pain when the lights go out for them, but just dead will do in a pinch. She impressed upon me that she wants to get this over with as quickly as possible so she can get on with her life."

"Listen to me, Bob. If this goes on much longer, I have a feeling that she might be coming to you with some pretty crazy ideas. I don't want you to even consider doing anything rash."

"Rash? Me? Never," Hurley said. "However, I'm in business here and she's a wealthy woman. It's been my experience that the crazy ideas rich people have are usually expensive, doable ideas with just a little risk attached. I'm successful because I sometimes choose to take those risks."

"I see there's no talking to you. Do what you want, but could you keep me informed about what's going through her mind?"

"Brian! It's good old Bob you're talking to, remember? You're always in my thoughts lately."

Maybe true, McKenna thought, but he didn't feel good about it.

THIRTY-SIX

MONDAY, AUGUST 23, GRAMERCY PARK HOTEL, NEW YORK

Mettakaruna was a good chess player and he won every game during the first three days and most of them during the first week. Then things began to change. Mettakaruna had no new strategies and McKenna had already seen everything he had. By the third week, McKenna found him to be overcautious, unimaginative, and predictable in his moves. The games got longer, but McKenna won most of them. By the fourth week, the games were short again and Mettakaruna couldn't win. McKenna had broken him and destroyed his confidence.

The same thing had happened with the three videos. Getting them from Mettakaruna was another game that McKenna played by the rules, but ultimately won. That hadn't taken as long, just four days. McKenna had told him that the videos were peripheral to the case, so the NYPD wouldn't consider his price. Furthermore, since the videos weren't part of his immunity deal, the Thai government would be informed and presented with the facts on where the videos were made and by whom if they showed up anywhere else in the world. Naturally, Mettakaruna would be charged as an accessory to murder, and since he was living under a supervised suspended sentence in the U.S., his location would always be known. His arrest and deportation to Thailand would be a matter of course.

McKenna had left it to Mettakaruna to figure out that he had items for sale, but the only potential buyer he could safely sell them to was the NYPD. That realization did come to him and had considerably affected the asking price. On August 2 Greve authorized the purchase of the three videos for $18,000 which was, incidentally, the exact amount Mettakaruna needed to clear up his gambling debts in Atlantic City so the casinos would let him in again. On August 3 the videos were delivered by Mettakaruna's brother-in-law to the U.S. Embassy in Bangkok.

If all had gone according to plan, by August 16 General Chou should have had copies of the videos showing his men torturing and murdering helpless girls in the Bangkok Leather Emporium. Accompanying the tapes was a letter from Mettakaruna stating that the videos had been made on Dix and Hillman's orders. In his letter, Mettakaruna speculated that Dix and Hillman had planned to use the videos to blackmail the general into providing refuge for them in the event they needed it.

A moot point and very ungracious of them, Mettakaruna pointed out, since the honorable general was already giving them refuge without being blackmailed, but then an unfortunate situation had developed. Mettakaruna explained how he had been arrested while in possession of the videos and, worse, the unscrupulous American authorities were threatening to release the videos to the world press unless Dix and Hillman were turned over to the Thai police for deportation to answer charges in the U.S.

So sorry, Mettakaruna had written, but surely the esteemed general could imagine the consequences of continuing to provide his hospitality to Dix and Hillman if the Americans made good on their threat. He and his loyal men would be portrayed as barbarians by the world press, the American public would clamor for action against him, the DEA budget would increase and his profits would surely decrease, and the Thai government would be pressured to dislodge him from his sanctuary. Worse, with world opinion on their side, the unprincipled Americans might feel safe in taking direct military action against him to punish him for his hospitality and, incidentally, neutralize the largest source of heroin imported into the U.S. An unpleasant prospect, given their propensity to use cruise missiles and B-52s whenever they felt safe in doing so.

Mettakaruna ended by praising the general's wisdom and his demonstrated ability to always make the correct decision in difficult circumstances.

Enclosed with the letter was a color copy of the *In Charge* centerfold and a little note from Mettakaruna in which he had stated that the Americans in the Department of Defense were wondering if the unfortunate person in the photo was indeed the DEA informant Dronk Bai as alleged by those angry Americans in the Justice Department.

Getting the letter and the videos to the general had presented something of a problem. They couldn't go through the Thai authorities because the videos demonstrated Dix and Hillman's complicity in serious crimes in Thailand, prompting speculation that the Thai government would feel honor-bound to try the two in Thailand rather than turn them over to the Americans.

It was a CIA pal of Shields's who came up with the solution. Nine years before, there had been many villages in northern Laos where ethnic Vietnamese had lived for centuries. Unfortunately for them, they lived on land the general considered part of his expanding bailiwick, and the rising demand for heroin had necessitated the acquisition of more land to grow his poppies. He had dispatched a company of his troops led by one of his cousins to persuade the Vietnamese to return to Vietnam, a land they never knew. A short time later some of these Vietnamese villagers had straggled across the border into Vietnam with accounts of rape, torture, and wholesale murder.

Unfortunately for the general's cousin and his troops, these villagers found many sympathetic ears in the Vietnamese government. Vietnam had also long considered northern Laos to be an unofficial part of its bailiwick, so a battalion of troops had been sent across the border into northern Laos to reassert this claim and teach the general a lesson.

That they had done, hunting down and wiping out most of the general's troops there and bringing his cousin to Hanoi in chains, which was where he had remained, sentenced to nine lifetimes of making little rocks out of big rocks under intense prodding.

Fortunately for the general's cousin, according to this CIA friend of Shields's, the Vietnamese government so desired improved relations with the U.S. that they would be willing to grant any small favor asked in order to show their good intentions.

The small favor was asked and the general's cousin was released, given the videos and Mettakaruna's letter, transported across northern Laos under military escort, and dropped at the Thai border with instructions to give the package to the general for his consideration.

That had been on August 11. According to everyone's calculations and taking into account the difficulties of travel in northern Thailand, the letter should have been delivered a week ago and was apparently still being considered by the general.

Meanwhile, there had been a number of events on the home front. Ginny had a number of drastic ideas for a rapid resolution to the case and she was driving Hurley crazy, asking his advice on the feasibility of using mercenaries, international hit men, and other assorted crackpots to get Dix and Hillman one way or the other. Hurley had been able to put those ideas to rest, for the moment, but she did have one that he relished and implemented with the help of Paul Barrone and a few influential lawyer friends of Arthur McMahon. He located and contacted the families of the victims in New York, California, Arizona, Costa Rica, Chile, Argentina, Spain, and the Philippines and, on their behalf, instituted civil lawsuits around the world charging Dix and Hillman with the wrongful deaths of their relatives.

These lawsuits kept the case in the public eye in the countries involved, but they did something else that made Ginny smile. Since Dix and Hillman were fugitives and couldn't be served process and notice on these lawsuits, Hurley, through local attorneys, had requested that their assets in the Cayman Islands, Hong Kong, Thailand, Arizona, and California be frozen. These lawsuits also alleged that Hillman and Dix maintained identities and assets as Marvin Grossman, Richard Freeman, Reginald Johnson, and Justin Cox and the attorneys requested that assets held under those identities also be frozen.

Given the nature of the case and the attendant publicity, the courts all granted the request. The result was that, except for any cash they had with them in Thailand, Dix and Hillman were broke. All the blood-tainted money they had squirreled away during their criminal careers would be divided among the families of their victims.

One result of Hurley's action annoyed Big Ed, but delighted Ginny. Hillman's wife was rendered destitute. Everything they owned was in her husband's name and, with their joint bank account frozen, she was unable to cash a check or pay her bills. At Ginny's insistence, Hurley had also bad-mouthed her enough with the credit companies to ensure that her cards were cancelled.

Mrs. Hillman had been at the point of applying for food stamps when Big Ed gave her a suggestion to turn her financial situation around. "Get an agent," he told her, and she did. A good one, as it turned out, because he soon had the networks eating out of her hand. She found that the prices they were offering for an exclusive interview and "My Life with Him" were amazing.

During the celebration dinner, Mrs. Hillman happened to mention to her agent some videos and photos the police had, the ones of her and her husband enjoying marital bliss in their own special way. Upon hearing the news, her agent had such an attack of speculative greed that he had almost choked to death on his chateaubriand. He had only survived thanks to an alert waiter schooled in the Heimlich maneuver and a burning desire to live long enough to represent his new, wonderful client through her first twenty million, less, of course, his twenty percent.

"My dear Mrs. Hillman," he told her, "from now on, when the movie moguls are talking about the highest-grossing porn flicks, it will no longer be *Debbie Does Dallas* on their lips and greedy minds."

"But I only do those things with my husband," Mrs. Hillman had pro-tested demurely.

"Very admirable, but it's apparent that he's been doing those things and much more with anyone he can get his hands on—man or woman."

"I know that now. He's a horrible, perverted man, but that doesn't change me. Like I said, I only do those things with my husband."

"That's all right for now. The wonderful thing is that you already have a finished production starring a beautiful, sexy woman and one of the most evil sex-and-torture killers the world has ever seen. You'll be a star with guaranteed top billing and you won't have a money care in the world."

"Top billing?" Mrs. Hillman asked, confused.

"Of course top billing. Hollywood likes to plan ahead and I don't think your husband will be available for the sequel."

Something must have changed in Mrs. Hillman because she had been surprised to hear herself say, "Or to share in the profits."

———

The hotel phone rang as Mettakaruna was putting the final touches into his peanut and sesame sauce for their Thai roast chicken lunch, so McKenna answered it. "Hillman wants to talk to you," Big Ed said.

"He does? How do you know?"

"Got it from the tap on his wife's phone. He called her twenty minutes ago and left the message on her machine. Said he knew the police were probably listening in, but he wanted her to get the message to you in case we weren't."

"He say anything about how we're supposed to talk?"

"Just that he'd be calling her back at six o'clock tonight, California time. That's nine o'clock for you, so where are you gonna be?"

"Should be home, but I'll be at the office at eight."

"Fine. I'll have all her calls forwarded there starting at eight."

"Fine," McKenna said, and he gave Big Ed Greve's private number at the office. "Any indication where the call was coming from?"

"Northern Thailand or northern Burma was all the phone company could tell us. He's using a satellite phone, pretty sophisticated."

"You know this means they want to make a deal."

"Has to deal, I figure," Big Ed surmised. "Your letter must have worn their welcome thin with the general. He's gonna turn them in, but he's given them some time to get their best deal. The punks don't wanna go to jail in the Third World and they don't wanna die."

"So they've done some research?"

"Sure have. They'd much rather surrender to you and your I-won't-burn-anybody DA."

"What's your position if I can get them to surrender to me soon?"

"You know my personal position. I want them in the sheriff's jail here, but the final word rests with him."

"Have you talked to the sheriff yet?"

"Not yet. He's in L.A., trying to convince their sheriff that jail should be a bad place. They've got a new jail so nice there that Sheriff Joe says the only reason they've got guards is to keep people from sneaking in."

"Will you be able to get to him and have his official position ready by the time Hillman calls?"

"I'll get to him, and I'm sure he'll have something to say. Offhand, my guess is that he'll say that we've already got a deal between us, a deal that Dix and Hillman can't change with any promises or smooth talking."

"I agree, but I'm not the one who's going to be making the decision on this end."

"Whose decision will it be there?"

"Our police commissioner and, believe it or not, that very same Manhattan DA we were just talking about."

McKenna was relieved at the hotel an hour early, but not to go home. Brunette wanted to see him, so McKenna was at his office at four-thirty. "You're to go right in, Brian," Camilia told him. "The commissioner's expecting you."

Brunette was at his desk talking to the chief of patrol, but he just about shooed the chief out when McKenna entered. Once the door closed behind the chief, Brunette surprised McKenna with a pat on the back. "Looks like you're bringing this one home, buddy," he said. "Always knew you would."

"Yeah, but bringing it home where?" McKenna asked.

"Uncertain at the moment, but that's what we've got to talk about." Brunette sat on the edge of desk and McKenna took one of the chairs in front.

"I called Barrone and he stopped in," Brunette said. "We had an off-the-record heart to heart. He said that, personally, he'd much prefer to see them prosecuted in Arizona."

"Then nothing's changed there. How about his professional position on this?"

"Not much he can do or say as speaker of the city council. However, he did call the DA from here to try and get some indication on whether he'd seek the death penalty in this case. Got nothing from him, one way or the other."

"I'd be inclined to go on his past history," McKenna said. "He could have sought it before and got it just as many times, all big cases. He's not gonna change now."

"I agree, and so does Barrone."

"What about the sheriff? Have you heard from him?"

"An earful. He suggests we wait and hear what Hillman has to say before we go for each other's throats, but in his heart he wants them in Arizona. He was sure to point out a few times that we've got a deal about where they get prosecuted."

"Not much you could say to that," McKenna commented.

"But there is, and I did. I told him that it wasn't exactly a deal between us. It was more an accommodation that we reached under pressure from McMahon. He's gone now, and so's the pressure. The politics have changed."

Brunette's viewpoint surprised McKenna and he was uneasy with it. "I don't know. Sure there was pressure, but we still committed to McMahon."

"Does that mean that we're still committed to what's-her-name?"

"Ginny, and I think we are. I consider it a commitment we made to McMahon and family, and she's his family. She wants them bad and she prefers them dead."

"Have you spoken to her recently?"

"I called her to offer my condolences the day after McMahon died. She sounded pretty shaken up to me, but she still told me that getting Dix and Hillman was the most important thing in her life."

"Do you think you could convince her to be happy if we make a deal with them and bring them here?"

"I don't know if I could convince that lady of anything she wasn't ready to believe," McKenna said. "To talk to her, you'd swear she was a down-home-on-the-farm sweetie pie, but McMahon warned me that she was smart, tough, and determined."

"All right, we'll consider her part of the equation, but I'll tell you how I feel. I'd be content to let the sheriff have them, but I'm prepared to accommodate them if they tell us they want to surrender to us and take their chances here."

"Okay, first let's hear what they have to say. Then we'll all talk it over and see if there's a chance you, me, the sheriff, Ginny, and Barrone can be content."

"Not all happy, I'm sure, but I'd settle for content."

"One more thing," McKenna said. "I've read somewhere that we've got spy satellites that—"

"Already done. Shields got to somebody in the National Security Agency and they've focused one of their satellites on the northern Thailand area. They'll be able to tell within a hundred feet where Hillman is standing when he calls you."

"They can really do that?"

"Yeah, they're just like us," Brunette said, flashing the grin that showed his dimples. "They can do anything."

THIRTY-SEVEN

Greve, McKenna, and Tommy were in Greve's office by eight o'clock. There was a recorder hooked up to Greve's phone and a large map of Southeast Asia on his desk. The three men where all looking at the clock on the wall when the phone rang at five to nine.

McKenna almost picked it up, but didn't. Nine o'clock Hillman had said, so McKenna wanted to keep him off balance but on schedule. As the phone kept ringing, McKenna realized that Hillman had made a mistake by calling early. He was giving the NSA satellite more time to track his location. The ringing stopped.

"Was that wise?" Greve asked.

"I think so," McKenna said. "He'll call back."

"What makes you so sure?"

"His wife's machine didn't pick up, so he knows the call's being forwarded. Probably knows we're all sitting here waiting for him," McKenna said confidently.

That confidence had almost vanished by nine-ten. "We kept him waiting, so now he's keeping us waiting," McKenna said, but noted that Greve and Tommy were looking dubious. Then McKenna's cell phone rang. "I guess he hasn't called back yet," Shields said.

"Not yet, but he will. Were they able to find out where he's calling from?"

"Burma, but only about half a mile from a town called Mae Sai in Thailand."

As soon as Shields said it, Greve's phone rang. "Gotta go," McKenna said to Shields. He pushed the Record button on the tape recorder, then picked up the phone. "Detective McKenna."

"I'm delighted my message got through to you, Detective McKenna. This is James Hillman."

McKenna thought that Hillman sounded confident, and that annoyed him. He decided he would do everything he could to shake that confidence. "What is it you want to talk to me about, Hillman?"

"A number of things. First of all, do you know where I am?"

"Exactly, within a couple of feet, I'm told. Burma, just outside Mae Sai."

"It's called Myanmar nowadays, but I see that the general was right about our satellites. Very good."

"Yeah, we're wonderful. Get down to business."

"Not very polite, McKenna, but I can understand your attitude," Hillman said, still sounding confident. "Let me take this opportunity to congratulate you on tracking us down and making our lives fairly miserable."

"It wasn't just me. I had plenty of help."

"Regardless. We couldn't help but notice that we were doing pretty good in life until you came on the scene."

"Having lots of fun and making lots of money while torturing and murdering innocent people all over the world? Is that your idea of doing pretty good in life?"

"I didn't say that, and I'm not prepared to tell you anything about myself, yet."

"How about Dix? Is he there with you?"

"Standing right beside me. Wanna say hello to him?"

"Not yet. How about the general? Is he there with you as well?"

"No. At the moment we're avoiding the general's hospitality. You must know that we had nothing to do with those videos you sent him."

McKenna figured that Hillman was recording the call, just like he was, and that it was possible the general was also there, standing next to Dix and listening in. He saw no reason to remove any pressure from Dix and Hillman, so he decided it was time to lie. "That's not what I hear. According to Mettakaruna, everything was done on your orders. He said you even set up the cameras, placed them and hid them so well that the general's men never suspected you were having them filmed while they had their fun."

"That Mettakaruna's a greedy, lying little swine who's just looking to save his own ass!" Hillman shouted.

There goes his confidence, McKenna noted. "It doesn't matter much, but I'm inclined to believe him. Everything else he's told us has turned out to be true," he said in the calmest tone he could muster.

"What else has he told you?" Hillman asked nervously.

"Everything he knows, I suspect."

"Then you shouldn't be so trusting. For the record, we had no idea those videos existed until the package you sent the general arrived."

McKenna greatly appreciated Hillman's insistence on explaining the videos. He knew the denials were for Chou's benefit and, not indirectly, their own—all of which led McKenna to strongly suspect that Hillman had lied about two major points in their conversation. They were still under the general's protection, McKenna was sure, and there was a good chance that the general was standing right next to Hillman, listening to the conversation.

No reason to relieve the pressure, McKenna thought. "Whatever you say. Why don't you get to the point and tell me what you want."

"It's what *you* want that I'm prepared to offer. Maybe not everything you want, but enough to make you happy."

"Get on with it."

"I'm prepared to surrender to you in Thailand. I will waive extradition and accompany you to New York to be tried for the charges you've been making against me there."

"Only New York? What about the murder charges pending against you two in Arizona, California, and quite a few other places in the world?"

"Only in New York, but that's just part of the deal I'm offering. In addition, I will plead guilty to murder there as long as it's understood in writing that your DA will not seek the death penalty. I will accept a sentence of life without possibility of parole and serve my time in New York."

"Is that it?"

"No, there's more. As part of the deal, I'd need it in writing that I won't be integrated into the general prison population."

"You're not thinking this through, Hillman. Suppose our DA only seeks ten years? Then you'd have to face your charges in Arizona or California when you're released from New York, and they'd be sure to execute you."

"Then let me rephrase my wording. Change I'll *accept* a life sentence to I'll *receive* a life sentence without possibility of parole, and put that in writing."

"You really are afraid of dying, aren't you?"

"Not afraid, really. I'd just prefer to avoid the inevitable for as long as possible."

"How about Dix? Is he part of your deal?"

"Yes, a separate part. He's more optimistic than me and believes that the death penalty will be abolished. Besides, he proclaims his innocence and feels that you don't have enough on him to convict him of murder. He's a victim of circumstance, a man who just happens to be a frequent traveling companion of mine. He had no knowledge of any crimes I may have committed."

"Your position on that, if you don't mind?" McKenna asked, knowing just what was coming.

"As part of my guilty plea, I will sign a statement that I alone was responsible for the deaths of Cindy Barrone and Arthur McMahon. I acted alone and, while it's possible Jerome was in New York with me, he was nowhere near the Cloisters when they were killed."

"And the other crimes you're charged with all over the world?"

"Same answer, but I'm not saying I did any of them. Despite any *alleged* evidence you might have against me, he may have been with me before and after the crimes, but he wasn't present when the crimes were committed and took no part in them."

"Just a victim of circumstance, huh?"

"To the best of my knowledge."

"Very noble of you, Hillman. You're quite a guy, a man who's just managed to greatly expand the definition of facetious conduct," McKenna said sarcastically.

"Thank you. I'll take that as a compliment, although I'm not certain that was your intention."

"I assume that Dix is also prepared to surrender?"

"Maybe, but under slightly different circumstances. You want me to put him on to explain them?"

"No. We're getting along so well together, so why don't you do it?"

"Fine. Jerome will surrender to you with me, and he will also waive extradition and be taken to New York to answer your charges. Since you don't have anything to connect him to the crimes there except some questionable circumstantial evidence, he's prepared to be agreeable and plead to Manslaughter First Degree with the understanding, in writing, that he'll receive a sentence of ten years that must be served before he can be extradited anyplace else."

"Still very noble, but I'm going to tip my hand a bit. Then you can tell me if you and your pal should be rethinking his position. Interested?"

"I'm listening."

"Came across a glitzy little underground publication called *Serious*. Centerfold features a black guy and a white guy, good shape, just like yourselves. Anyway, the black guy and the white guy are whipping a girl named Cecilia Santiago near Herradura, Costa Rica. The girl turns up dead after being whipped to death and her brother was also found with her. He was also tortured to death, the only variation from your MO in New York."

"It was called *Serious*?"

"Jog your memory a bit. It's one of the rags you used to advertise your snuff films."

"So you say, but I'm not certain that alleged evidence of a crime in Costa Rica would be admissible in any proceeding against Jerome in New York."

"Maybe, maybe not, but a good DA might be able to set it in as evidence tending to connect your pal with the type of crime we've got in New York, a crime to which you've already pleaded guilty. Keep in mind that while you might like something about his position on capital punishment, he still is, after all, one of the best DAs in the business."

"That's it? A questionable piece of evidence that may or may not be admissible in New York?"

"No, I've got a bit more. I can place Dix on the subway leaving the Cloisters after the crime and I can also put him nine blocks away right after."

"Doing what?"

"Picking up the car registered to your pal-in-common Jason Robles, the same car he later picked you up with somewhere near the Cloisters at about eight-thirty that morning. You remember that, don't you?"

"Do you mind if I call you back in a few minutes?" Hillman asked.

"Good idea. See if you can talk some sense into Jerome. I'll be here waiting, interested to hear what his revised deal offer will be."

McKenna hung up the phone and looked to Tommy and Greve. "What do you think?" he asked.

"I think you've just boggled their minds," Tommy said.

Two minutes went by as the three men sat in silence. Then the phone rang again.

"Jerome's offer is now identical to mine," Hillman said without pre-amble.

"I thought so," McKenna said. "Now why don't you give me the threats?"

"The threats?"

"Yeah, you know. I think we're at the point where you tell me what you're going to do if we don't take you up on your offer."

"All right, if you insist. If you don't take our offer, we're going to head south."

"South, but still in Burma?" McKenna asked.

"Yes, a country where the U.S. government has almost no influence. We've got some cash and a dollar goes a long way here. I think we could stay as long as we like, and there's nothing you, the FBI, or the U.S. government could do to get us."

"Great plan, except for one thing. I'm looking at the map right now, got my finger on Mae Sai. And here you are. In Burma, sure enough, but I notice something else when I look at this map. Mae Sai and every place around you in Thailand, Laos, and Burma on the map I've got is colored yellow. Give me a minute to look at the legend and find out what that means."

"Don't bother, McKenna," Hillman said testily. "It means that we're in the Golden Triangle."

"That's right, the Golden Triangle. Now I'm told that Chou Son Yee is the supreme mucky-muck in that part of the triangle. Is that right?"

"That's correct."

"He's not just a namby-pamby titular ruler who can't run things in his own backyard, is he?" McKenna said for the general's benefit.

Hillman hesitated. "He's certainly not. He's a strong ruler in full com-mand of the area."

"Yet you're telling me that somehow you've escaped his hospitality so we could have this little chat."

"I said we escaped temporarily."

"But a strong ruler like the general could get you back anytime he liked?"

"If he wanted to, I suppose he could."

"I thought so. Do me a favor, would ya? If you're not looking at the general right now, could you give him a message from me the next time you see him?"

Hillman said nothing for a moment as McKenna waited, smiling to himself as he imagined Dix, Hillman, and probably Chou in a huddle. "Is the message just from you?" Hillman asked at last.

"Just me and the New York City Police Department."

There was another delay before Hillman said, "Okay, what's the message?"

"Tell the general that unless the Thais have you in custody for deportation to the U.S. within three days, I'm going to have a press conference, I'm going to release those videos showing the general's men torturing and killing those poor girls in your club, and I'm going to tell the press how the general is protecting you. Would you do that for me?"

"Yes, we'll do it."

"You might also remind the general that we've got an election year coming up, and you know how things get here around that time. The president might get an itch to show voters just how tough the Democrats are, so he might be hoping your pal will stupidly place himself in the Osamar bin Laden and Saddam Hussein circle to liven things up before the election."

"Is that your final word on our offer?" Hillman asked.

"It's my final word, but I'm not the one who makes the final decision. The details of our conversation have to be reviewed by a lot of people before I can tell you for sure. Call me back tomorrow, same time. See ya soon."

"Wait!" Hillman shouted.

"What? Another threat you forgot to mention?"

"Of a sort. If you and your superiors don't agree to our very reasonable terms, Jerome and I are going to kill ourselves and end this."

McKenna didn't try to suppress his laughter. Then he yelled to Greve and Tommy, "He says they're gonna kill themselves if we don't cave in."

Hillman was treated to the sound of three men laughing uncontrollably. Just when it was almost over Tommy yelled, "Ask him if they're gonna whip each other to death. I'd like to get a ticket for that show."

That kept the chuckles going until Hillman yelled into his phone, "McKenna! Are you there?"

"Yeah, Hillman, I'm still here."

"It wasn't a lie of any kind. We've talked it over and we've reached a sober decision. We'll do it if you force our hand."

"Let me get this straight. Two guys who are bargaining desperately to avoid the possibility of their execution are now threatening to kill themselves?"

"Basically, yes. Before you fall apart on me again, let me point out that your superiors are almost certainly looking forward to the fine publicity they'll get when we're captured and brought to justice in New York. Lots of press, lots of well-received speeches, lots of photo opportunities, lots of favorable editorials in the papers, and even more favorable coverage on national TV."

McKenna didn't want to admit it to Hillman, but it was a valid point. He didn't know what to say for a moment, but that delay was enough for Hillman to drive home his point. "Like you said, McKenna, there's an election year coming up and we're certain that whoever's running things in New York would like us there to share it with them. Talk to you tomorrow."

The line went dead, so McKenna hung up and turned off the recorder. Then he noticed that Tommy was still smiling, but Greve was serious and lost in thought.

"You don't believe they'd do it, do you?" McKenna asked Greve.

"It's not what we believe, probably not even what Ray believes that's important," Greve said. "This decision has to go way upstairs to the politicians who'd be affected if they did do it."

"It doesn't matter that we know their threat is bullshit?"

"I can't say for sure that it is," Greve countered.

"I can," McKenna said. "Death rows everywhere are full of murdering dirtbags like those two, dirtbags who value nobody's life but their own. They're not thinking suicide because they're all too busy working on their appeals to get their death sentence commuted to life without parole."

"I agree with Brian," Tommy said. "Those two would use any threat to bargain for what they can get, but they'd never kill themselves. If they can't get their deal, they'll still come in, take their chances with the system, and live a little longer while the process goes on."

"Even if you're both right, it's not our decision," Greve repeated. "Brunette will have to work it out with Arizona and the Manhattan DA."

THIRTY-EIGHT

McKenna called Ginny from home as soon as he got up. The phone kept ringing and he was about to hang up when Ginny answered.

"Brian, so good to hear from you. How are you?"

She sounded chipper, but McKenna knew that wasn't going to last. "Fine. I was afraid I was calling a little too early for you."

"Too early for me? Nonsense, I've been up for hours. I was just on the other line with Mr. Hurley."

McKenna checked his watch, amazed. Hurley up at eight-thirty in the morning? Ginny must indeed be a wonderful client, he thought. "Got some news for you that I hope you can live with," he said. "They're willing to surrender to me in Thailand with the understanding that they'll both do life without parole in New York."

"Excuse me, Brian. Could you repeat that?" Ginny asked. "I'm hoping I heard you wrong."

"Unfortunately, you didn't. They'll do life without parole in New York."

"That's news, but it's not great news. There's no chance that they can be brought to Arizona?"

"Sorry, no. The deal is New York."

"Because they don't want to be executed?"

"That's it."

"Then that's all the more reason they should be. What about the deal that was made with Mr. McMahon? Doesn't prosecuting them in New York break that deal?"

McKenna wanted to scream, "I think it does." He wanted to, but he didn't. Instead he remained loyal to the party line. "That understanding with Mr. McMahon was made under different circumstances than we find ourselves in now. They've threatened to commit suicide unless they're brought to New York to serve their sentence, and there's a fear they might do it."

"Commit suicide to avoid the death penalty? Brian, you don't buy that, do you?"

"Personally, no."

"So let me get this straight. In order to keep a deal with two murderers of the worst sort, somebody up there thinks it's okay to break a deal with an honorable man."

McKenna searched his mind for an argument to refute Ginny's simple statement, or at least soften it. He came up with a few that sounded vaguely plausible to him, but knew he would be wasting his time with her. "That's one way to look at it, but there are other ways."

"Do you think your deal with those two would float if Mr. McMahon was still alive?"

Ginny was asking all the questions that McKenna had hoped she wouldn't, questions he still had to answer. "Maybe with some difficulty."

"I see. But since Mr. McMahon's gone, the feeling in New York must be that I'm powerless to prevent it."

"You could make things difficult afterward, but you can't prevent it," McKenna said. "Neither can I."

"So I'm expected to accept this and keep my mouth shut because you've managed to make a deal to feed, house, and clothe them for the rest of their natural lives?"

"Like I said, it's not necessary, but it would make everybody involved much happier if you could accept it."

"You included?"

"Yeah, me too."

"Do I have to give you my answer now?"

"No. The tape of my conversation with them should be arriving via FedEx sometime after two. Listen to it, think about it, and give me a call."

"How long do I have?"

"I should be finalizing the deal at nine tonight."

"I'll do as you say, so expect my call."

"Thank you." McKenna gave her his cell phone number and hung up.

McKenna was at his desk typing the transcript of his conversation with Hillman when Brunette called. "Got the sheriff and the DA on board," he reported.

"Already?"

"Nothing to it. If it's viewed in the right light, there's something nice for everyone in this deal. Sheriff Joe won't be in the headlines for long, but he comes out looking tough and invincible without expending any further effort. 'Here's two filthy, low-life murderers who accepted life without parole in New York rather than stay in my jail and take their chances with one of our fine Arizona juries' is the way he's gonna play it."

"How's he going to deal with his public promise to have them prosecuted in Arizona?"

"He knows how to play that one, too, but he was nice enough to ask my permission. Big Ed will be standing next to you every step of the way, available for photographs and comment from Thailand to Central Booking here. He'll say every time he's asked that he wanted to bring them back home for justice as the sheriff had promised, but he was thwarted by that powerful, criminal-coddling Eastern Establishment."

"They'll understand that in Arizona, but it doesn't make us look too tough," McKenna said.

"Can't be what we're not. In Arizona we'll look good enough, but more than a shade shy of tough enough. We'll have to live with that, but it won't be hard because we made the DA happy."

"Not just content?"

"He didn't show it, but I'd say he's deliriously happy. Here we have the case that would entail the greatest public pressure for the death penalty he's ever experienced, and now he's out from under. All he had to do was approve the deal we presented him."

"At least somebody is happy," McKenna said.

"Then I take it that you weren't able to leave Ginny smiling."

"I'm a long way from that. Long way from content, for that matter. Unless she has a change of heart, the best we can hope for is 'resigned, but quiet' from her."

"Think she'll make waves?"

"She's going to call me after she listens to the tape. I'll know then."

Ginny didn't call and that made McKenna nervous. He was in Greve's office planning strategy with Greve and Tommy when his cell phone finally rang at eight-fifty. "I listened to the tape as many times as I could stand to hear his voice," Ginny said.

"And?"

"And I think you did very well with him. Showed him nothing but contempt and gave him no breathing room. It was great almost until the end."

"Thanks. I had hoped it would have been good right to the end, but you know how that turned out."

"There's just one thing more that's really bothering me that you didn't mention."

"The part about them being segregated from the other prisoners?" McKenna guessed.

"That's it. You're not going to let them live in prison the way they want to, are you?"

"Out of the question," McKenna said, thinking that he had found at least one thing to make her smile. "They're going to spend the rest of their lives elbow to elbow with all the other dirt."

"Thank God for that small favor, at least."

"Glad to be of service. Except for the big one, is there anything else I can do?"

"One little thing, but I don't know if it's possible. Randy stopped by today and he said—"

"One minute! Randy's in Virginia?"

"Sure. I see Randy all the time. He's a fascinating man, so smart and so interested in getting those two. Mr. McMahon really liked him and he's been a big comfort to me."

"He met McMahon?"

"Of course he did. Mr. McMahon had Mr. Hurley fly him in one weekend, right after he started working at that horrible bookstore. Mr. McMahon wanted to hear Randy's views on how things were going, and I think he valued Randy's opinion."

"What did Randy tell him, if you don't mind my asking?"

"Basically, just what's happened. Randy said that you, Tommy, and Big Ed are good and smart, but that you're luckier than the others. He told

Mr. McMahon that first he'd get the man who was selling the films and magazines for the killers, and then you'd get the killers and bring them in."

"Randy said this when? A couple of months ago?"

"At least six weeks ago. He also said that it was going to get complicated at the end."

How did I let this Randy out of my sight for so long? McKenna asked himself. Putting Randy and Hurley together? I must have been out of my mind! "When you say complicated, does that mean that he thought they'd wind up in jail in New York?"

"He said it was a possibility, no matter what deals were made. Randy said that you'd try to stay true to your promises, but he told us something I'll never forget. He said, 'This case has become a big, golden, political football and the end zone is always in New York.'"

"Did Randy happen to mention what he was doing in Virginia today?"

"He was here to see me, same as usual."

"Same as usual?" McKenna asked, finding it hard to believe where the conversation was going.

"Sure. He was off weekends from that horrible bookstore, so he'd fly in and spend Saturday night every once in a while. That was hard on him, so I flew out to meet him in San Diego once."

"Really?" McKenna said, amazed.

"It was wonderful. He took me down to Tijuana to his favorite Mexican restaurant. I had no idea that Mexican food could be that good."

Randy, Randy, Randy, what the hell have you been up to right under my nose? McKenna wondered.

"Am I shocking you?" Ginny asked.

"Not at all," McKenna lied. "Like you said, he's a fascinating man."

"But maybe a little old for me if you're thinking like my mother," Ginny said with the first giggle McKenna had heard from her since the night they had met. "She said she'd chase him herself, but she's ten years too old to catch him."

Good God! Enough of this Randy and his adventures! McKenna thought. "What was it good old Randy was saying when he stopped by today?"

"He was saying how he always wanted to be there when those two were caught."

"He wants to go to Thailand?"

"He realizes that he's not a cop anymore and that he has no place there if he'd be in the way, but he *has* worked on getting those two so hard for so long. You have to admit that he's contributed so much, so I was thinking that . . ."

"I agree. Randy has every right to be there if that would make him happy."

"It would. He'll never be able to thank you enough for this."

"Would it make you happy, too?"

"Certainly. I'll feel as if Randy was there representing Mr. McMahon and me when you put the handcuffs on them and drag them away. Of course, I'll pay all his transportation costs and any incidentals along the way."

"I'm afraid you'll have to do that. Have Randy give me a call tomorrow morning and I'll tell him what the travel arrangements are."

"I will, and thanks again, Brian. You don't know how much this means to me."

So now she's happy, McKenna thought after he hung up. Good going. That makes me happy and it'll be nice to put Ray's mind at ease.

Hillman called two minutes later at exactly nine o'clock. "Do we have a deal?" he asked.

"Not yet," McKenna answered. "That bullshit suicide story really worked wonders around here, but you didn't really expect your segregation proposal to fly, did you?"

"As a matter of fact we did. It's very important to us and we couldn't consider surrendering without it."

"More bullshit, and you just talked yourself out of a deal. Tell the general that he's got one more day to turn you over to the Thais or he'll be reading all about himself in every newspaper on the planet. See ya."

"Wait a minute, McKenna!" Hillman shouted. "How about a counter-proposal from you?"

"All right, how's this? Each of you will get an extra slice of salami on your sandwich every day for your first week in jail. I'm not authorized to go two slices, so hurry up and make your decision."

"Can I call you back with our answer?" Hillman pleaded.

"You can, but I won't pick up the phone. It's now or never."

"McKenna, we're educated, middle-class people. They'll kill us in jail, and how would that look for you?"

"I could live with it and still hold my head high, but it won't come to that. You're both big, strong lads and it won't be long before you find your natural spot in the jailhouse pecking order. Someplace near the dirty bottom, I suspect, but you'll learn what to do to survive and then you'll do it. Decision?"

"Do you still have your map?"

"I'm looking at it."

"Do you see a city called Chiang Rai?"

"I've got it. It's in the north, but it's colored yellow."

"The Thai authorities will confirm to you that it's quite safe there and not under the general's control. There is air service there from Bangkok via Chiang Mai, but I recommend that you charter a plane in Bangkok. We'll meet you in the lobby of the Little Duck Hotel at noon three days from now. That's Saturday here, Friday in New York. Is that acceptable?"

"That's good."

"There's an attorney in New York named Murray Plenhiem who says he knows you."

"Murray Don't Worry? I know him. Expensive, competent, defends all sorts of evildoers with money. You got any left?"

"Enough to pay him. He's ready to put our agreement into writing, so please have him confer with the DA to draw it up. Leave a copy of the agreement with Murray and bring one with you."

"I'll have it. Anything else?"

"No, that covers it."

"Good," McKenna said. "See ya soon."

"Unfortunately, this time you're right."

THIRTY-NINE

Shields offered to provide a military transport to bring the McKennas, Big Ed, Randy, Dix, and Hillman back from Thailand, but Brunette declined the offer after he found out how much such a flight would cost the U.S. taxpayers. Besides, both Brunette and McKenna preferred that the two be brought back like common criminals, not as criminal celebrities arriving on a plane especially arranged for them. That meant flying coach in the rear of the plane—uncomfortable, packed-in tight, handcuffed, and under guard for the long flight back, objects of curiosity and scorn from all the other passengers.

McKenna had been expecting a call from Bynum on Wednesday morning, but instead it was Hurley who called the office at noon. "Have you made your travel arrangements yet?" Hurley asked.

"Not yet. I was waiting to hear from Randy before I put the logistics into place."

"What's the deal? You and Tommy pick up Big Ed at a stop on the West Coast, then on to Bangkok?"

"That's it. I guess Randy will be leaving with us from New York?"

"Via Richmond, as you know by now. You traveling in coach?"

"You've picked up prisoners before, so you should know. When the city's paying, it's always coach."

"That's too bad. Hell of a long flight, and one I'd never expect one of my valued employees to suffer through packed in with the commoners. Randy will be up in first class, but lucky for you that I've got a deal you'll appreciate."

Uh-oh! A deal from good old Bob. Get ready, McKenna thought. "What's the deal?"

"Something that costs me nothing, but makes it easier on Ginny's finances and certainly more comfortable for you. Interested?"

"Barely, but go on."

"I've got more than three hundred thousand frequent flyer miles built up with United Airlines that expire in December. I'll never use them and Ginny's been so good to me that I asked myself, Why not use them to send Randy to Bangkok and save her a bundle?"

"United goes to Bangkok?"

"From New York via Los Angeles and Singapore. Perfect for you. Big Ed gets on in L.A., short half hour stopover in Singapore, and you're in Bangkok an hour later. If you'll go for it and do Ginny that favor, I'd be willing to—"

"Stop right there, Bob. I don't need anything from you. United will be fine."

"You don't want to hear the rest?"

"No, I don't."

"You'd like it. Costs me nothing and it'll make your trip much more enjoyable," Hurley said.

McKenna really thought at first that he didn't want to hear it, but then his curiosity got the better of him. "Okay, what's this wonderful thing you want to do for us?"

"Since you've agreed to be so nice to Ginny, I'm going to use some more of those miles to bump you, Tommy, and Big Ed up to first class so you can keep Randy company for the twenty-four-hour flight."

McKenna knew from infrequent experience that riding in first class, pampered and well fed with lots of room, did make the longest flight seem much shorter, but he didn't want to owe Hurley more than he already did.

Then Hurley put the icing on the cake with a sensible question. "It's a long flight back, and you've all got to be awake to guard those douchebags. Doesn't it make more sense to arrive in Bangkok well rested, refreshed, and feeling good?"

"Are you sure this isn't going to cost you anything?"

"Not a cent. Like I told you, the miles are going to expire with nobody using them. I accumulate so many miles flying my former civil servants to nice places that it happens to me all the time. Those frequent flyer miles keep expiring on me, unused and wasted."

"Okay, we'll take you up on that offer. Thanks, Bob."

"If you're interested, I've got just enough miles left over to bump you all up to first class on the way back. Three civil servants, one respected employee, and the two douchebags, all first class, all courtesy of good old Bob."

"Thanks anyway, Bob. Not interested. You've already done more than enough."

"What else are friends for?"

The conference with the DA and Murray Don't Worry was perfunctory. Hillman and Dix had called Murray with all the details of the deal and the deal memo Murray had prepared jibed perfectly with the DA's. McKenna had no changes to make on behalf of the department. It was signed by the DA, by Murray on behalf of Dix and Hillman, and by McKenna on behalf of the NYPD.

McKenna faxed a copy of the agreement to Big Ed and Ginny, then took the rest of the day off.

FORTY

WEDNESDAY, AUGUST 25, JFK INTERNATIONAL AIRPORT

It was just after 7:00 P.M. Tommy parked their unmarked car in the parking lot behind the Port Authority Police's headquarters building at the airport. They were traveling light, one piece of carry-on luggage apiece, and had just removed their bags from the trunk when McKenna's cell phone rang. It was Ginny and she sounded upset. "Brian, I meant to call you earlier, but things are so hectic here that it slipped my mind," she said. Thank God I caught you before you got on the plane."

"Ginny, calm down. Our flight doesn't leave until nine-fifteen. What's the matter?"

"My mother had a stroke this morning and we're on our way down to see her."

"I'm very sorry to hear that, Ginny. Is it serious?"

"We thought so this afternoon, but her doctor said she's stabilized now and out of danger. He says he won't know for a couple of days if there's any permanent damage, but we want to be there when she wakes up."

"We? You mean Randy and you?"

"Yes, of course Randy. He had his heart set on going to Thailand with you, but you know how he is. So kind and considerate, he insisted on going down to Florida with me."

"Yeah, he's quite a guy," McKenna said. "Where is he now?"

"We're at the airport, but we're having a tough time getting a flight down on such short notice. He went to see somebody about emergency reservations. Do you want me to have him call you when he gets back?"

"No, that's all right. Just tell him that we'll miss him."

"Maybe not. If everything works out with my mom, he's planning on meeting you in Bangkok or maybe Singapore for the flight back."

"Good. Then tell him we look forward to seeing him there and good luck with your mom."

"Thank you, Brian."

Big Ed got on in L.A. and was pleased to take his seat in first class. "Pardners, they sure do give a man enough room to stretch out up here," he commented.

McKenna couldn't help but notice that Big Ed didn't need much room to stretch out. Although the happy lawman certainly filled his wide seat width-wise, he had more than enough room length-wise because his legs weren't long enough for Big Ed to put his feet under the seat in front of him.

By the time they landed in Singapore sixteen hours later, McKenna felt that the long flight had been too short. They had been waited on hand and foot through all their delicious meals—breakfast, lunch, dinner, and breakfast again for the McKennas and breakfast, lunch, lunch, dinner, dinner, and breakfast for Big Ed. According to Tommy and Big Ed, the wine was as superb as the service, and they toasted good old Bob after every meal.

The service hadn't stopped with the meals. They had all been offered and had politely accepted so many hot towels that their fingertips were wrinkled, and between fitful naps, their pillows had been fluffed up and their blankets had been adjusted so many times by their very own delightful flight attendant that Big Ed said he would have been honor-bound under local custom to propose to her if they had been flying over Arizona.

Tommy and Big Ed both slept through their short Singapore stopover, but all were awake and fully rested when they landed in Bangkok an hour later at 9:00 A.M. local time on Saturday, twenty-four hours but two days after they had left New York.

"Are you sure we don't want to fly back first class?" Big Ed asked McKenna as their flight attendant brushed his jacket up and down with her lint brush.

"Let's talk about that later," McKenna said.

As arranged, Inspector Phaulkon of Thailand's National Police and Deputy Ambassador James Lawler of the U.S. Embassy were waiting for them at the gate. Lawler was polite and correct, but he looked like he didn't want to be there. Phaulkon was a smiling, friendly, middle-aged personality who received nothing but polite nods and deferential salutes as they whisked through Customs and Immigration without slowing down.

Once outside the International Arrivals Building, they all walked down the sidewalk bordering the terminal and soon boarded a waiting National Police van, but not soon enough for the McKennas. They thought the heat was oppressive for that time of morning and they felt their shirts sticking to their backs under their jackets, but Big Ed found the weather "refreshing."

"Don't worry," Phaulkon advised McKenna in his British-accented English. "Chiang Rai is in the mountains. The temperature is almost ideal there."

The NYPD had offered to charter a plane for the flight to Chiang Rai, but that hadn't been necessary. They would be flying there in one of the National Police's Gulfstream turboprops. The van drove through the airport along service roads to the edge of the runway where the plane was parked. Inside, the plane didn't have conventional seats. Instead, collapsible military net seats lined the bulkheads and occupying those seats were two squads of national police in full combat dress, complete with M-16s, grenades, and M-60 machine guns.

The new arrivals took seats near the front of the plane and McKenna noticed at once that the presence of the battle-dressed national police seemed to make Lawler uneasy, especially when they greeted Phaulkon with enthusiastic shouts and grunts. What put him closer to the edge was when the plane took off and the men began singing with gusto a military tune while slapping the butts of their weapons to keep up the rhythm.

"Inspector, is there the slightest chance that we're going into combat?" Lawler asked Phaulkon.

"Combat? Of course not, Mr. Lawler. Chiang Rai is completely under government control and has been for years. I don't think Chou Son Yee would dare to show his miserable face there."

"Then what is all this about?" Lawler asked, nodding toward the singing troops.

"Sometimes there are bandits."

"Bandits? We need all this for bandits?"

"Not really."

"Then why?"

Phaulkon shrugged. "The men like to dress up, the men like to sing, and the people in Chiang Rai like to see them all dressed up, singing, and looking mean like soldiers. It doesn't hurt to make everybody feel good."

Chiang Rai reminded McKenna of many Third World cities he had visited during his travels—partly modern, mostly lower-lower middle class by American standards, with touches of nineteenth-century architecture and rustic dress evident everywhere. Gleaming, new, modern buildings stood mere blocks away from, and sometimes right next to, much older, dilapidated structures lacking air-conditioning, heat, and indoor plumbing, but all these buildings served a purpose and were very much in use.

The Americans and the Thai police arrived downtown at eleven forty-five in a caravan of Toyota Land Cruisers and pickup trucks. The vehicles pulled to the curb in line one block short of a monumental old structure constructed entirely of large blocks of stone.

McKenna thought the building looked like the summer residence of the Dalai Lama—a medieval Tibetan castle ripped from its perch high in the Himalayas and transported somehow to the center of Chiang Rai.

"The Little Duck Hotel," Phaulkon said.

Maybe the last name I would have given to a building looking like that one, McKenna thought.

"Wait here a few minutes, please," Phaulkon said. He left the Americans sitting in the lead Land Cruiser and walked toward the hotel down the middle of the street, whistling and unconcerned with his hands in his pockets.

The police took their cue, left the vehicles in rapid order, and paralleled Phaulkon on the crowded sidewalks on either side of him. Each squad advanced in combat formation by sections. One section of four men would run forward twenty yards, fall to the ground, and point their weapons menacingly to the front, apparently ready to obliterate any opposition they might encounter there. The next section advanced through them and fell to the ground, and so the process was repeated with each combat squad keeping pace with Phaulkon.

Phaulkon seemed to be unaware of his impressive escort, but the citizens of Chiang Rai certainly took notice. At first they appeared to be shocked and fearful at this display of military proficiency taking place in front of them and disrupting their morning strolls. Women grabbed their children and cowered in doorways while men either fell to the ground or sought cover between parked cars.

Then the truth hit them, seemingly all at once; there was no danger present on the streets of Chiang Rai—it was just their police having some military fun on a very nice day. Those who had been fooled stood up, women let go of their children, and people appeared at the windows to watch. The children were the first to clap, but it was infectious. Every military move performed by the advancing squads brought squeals of delight and approval and more clapping.

The hotel doorman tipped his hat and opened the door for Phaulkon, a process he nonchalantly repeated ten times as police followed him in. The rest of the cops took up a defensive position in a semicircle around the hotel entrance, delighting the citizens with their fearsome and menacing display. A crowd of hundreds gathered on the sidewalk across the street from the hotel, clapping every time one of the cops so fearlessly guarding the hotel entrance doffed his helmet to acknowledge his fans.

One cop approached the Americans, trotting down the sidewalk followed by squealing children running to keep pace with him. He drew himself to attention at the side of the Land Cruiser, paused a moment to catch his breath, and announced, "The hotel had been secured. It's safe to come in."

"Thank God and thank you," McKenna said. "We all feel much better now." The cop turned and marched back to the hotel with the Americans following.

The lobby was decorated as McKenna had expected the interior of a castle would be, complete with tapestries hanging from the stone walls, lighting provided by chandeliers, and woven rugs covering the floors. The furniture was Chippendale, with leather sofas and overstuffed leather armchairs scattered around the large room.

Phaulkon sat on a sofa facing the bank of brass-doored elevators, reading, appropriately enough, a copy of the *London Times*. His men were placed throughout the lobby, looking military with their weapons held at the ready. The reception clerk and the bellboys had taken seats in front of the reception desk to better enjoy the show.

The McKennas, Big Ed, and Lawler approached Phaulkon.

"They're here," Phaulkon said without looking up from his paper. "They'll be down in five minutes."

"How do you know that?" McKenna asked.

"They told the clerk when they checked in last night that they were expecting company at noon. At eleven-thirty they called to have their luggage brought down and it was," Phaulkon said, pointing to six suitcases stacked on a trolley next to the reception desk. "Their company's here and it's five to twelve, so I'm assuming they'll be down in five minutes."

"What names did they use?"

"James Hillman and Jerome Dix."

"Were they alone?"

"No. There's four of Chou's men with them. Guarding them to ensure that they keep their appointment with you, I assume. Chinese, unsettling types. The clerk said that they didn't appear to be gentlemen and he'll be happy when they leave."

"Were they armed?"

"They didn't show the clerk any weapons, but I would think so. In any event, they're not as well armed as my men, so I'm not anticipating any problems."

He's right about that, McKenna thought. We certainly do have the better show, and the name of the game here is showmanship.

At two minutes to twelve Phaulkon neatly folded his newspaper, placed it on the sofa, and stood up. "Kindly take seats and relax for a while, if you would," he said to the Americans. He shouted a command and four of his men rushed to the elevators and stood with their weapons pointed at the doors. Phaulkon then walked to the reception desk and stood leaning against it as he also watched the elevator doors.

Phaulkon's polite message to the Americans had been clear: It's my show for now, so kindly refrain from interfering. They complied and took seats that afforded them a good view.

At one minute after twelve the doors of one of the elevators opened and there stood Dix, Hillman, and their four guards. They walked out and a shouting match in Thai ensued between the guards and the cops facing the elevator with their M-16s leveled.

McKenna felt it was a tense situation. He thought the cops wanted the guards to surrender and place their hands in the air, something the guards were not prepared to do.

The confrontation was ended by Phaulkon with a few shouted commands. The cops slung their weapons on their shoulders, placed their hands together with their fingertips near their lips, and bowed. The guards reciprocated with the same action, bowing and smiling. The unfortunate misunderstanding over, a few pleasantries were exchanged, and the guards marched out the front door without looking back, leaving Dix and Hillman standing in front of the elevator doors.

McKenna would have known them anywhere, although the effects of the tropical sun had made them closer in appearance. Hillman was still coffee-colored, but Dix was deeply bronzed. Both were muscular, with their physiques accentuated by the close-fitting open-neck polo shirts and tailored slacks they were wearing. Both wore loafers and Hillman was holding a leather briefcase.

Their faces didn't belie their ages. Although McKenna knew that both were over fifty, they could have just as easily passed for forty. Their appearance was that of two successful businessmen relaxing here in Thailand while waiting to close a deal with the locals.

Phaulkon approached Dix and Hillman and bowed slightly. "Jerome Dix and James Hillman, I am Inspector Phaulkon. It is my unpleasant duty to inform you that you are under arrest and will remain in my custody until you are transferred to the custody of the American authorities tomorrow morning. Kindly hand me the briefcase and submit to a search by my men."

Dix and Hillman responded with a formal nod but didn't say a word. Hillman gave Phaulkon the briefcase and then both Dix and Hillman raised their arms while they were searched by two of the Thai cops. Their wallets and passports were removed from their pockets by the cops and handed to Phaulkon. When the search was complete, the cops looked to Phaulkon and he said something to them in Thai. The cops took handcuffs from pouches on their belts and rear-cuffed the two.

After Dix's and Hillman's luggage was searched in their presence, Phaulkon opened the briefcase. He quickly closed it and motioned for the Americans to come over.

"What's in it?" McKenna asked Phaulkon.

"Their clean socks, a change of underwear, toilet items, and lots of money."

McKenna turned to Dix and Hillman. "How much money you got in there?"

"A hundred eighty-one thousand, four hundred dollars," Dix replied.

Then it was Phaulkon's turn. "How much U.S. currency did you declare when you entered Thailand?"

"Together, about eighteen thousand dollars," Dix said.

"Are you aware that all cash business transactions in foreign currency in excess of roughly ten thousand dollars American must be reported to the Ministry of Banking and Currency within seventy-two hours?"

"Yes, we're aware of that and we'd intended to report it as soon as we returned to Bangkok."

That wasn't sitting well with Phaulkon. "When did you make the transaction?"

"Yesterday."

"And what was it you sold in return for this money?"

"Material of an artistic nature."

"What was the total purchase price?"

"One million dollars."

"Then where is the rest of the money?"

"We owed it to the purchaser for food and lodging. He deducted his fee before he paid us," Hillman said, smiling innocently.

"I see. Rather expensive accommodations, I'd say, but it's not up to me to say where you chose to stay or what you chose to pay. However, our courts have ordered that your assets be seized and held pending the resolution of personal lawsuits that have been entered against you in other countries."

"I understand that you're just doing your duty, Inspector, but we need some of that money to pay necessary legal fees," Dix said. "We're told that under American law, money needed to pay past legal fees for a criminal defense cannot be attached."

Phaulkon turned to McKenna. "I don't know if that makes much difference in Thailand, but is it true?"

"I can't say for sure, but since the lawyers write the laws with themselves in mind, I'd say it probably is," McKenna answered, then turned to Dix. "Who told you that? Murray Plenheim?"

"Yes. He sounded very sure of himself and said that the Thais wouldn't keep his money."

"How much is he charging you?"

"One hundred thousand as a retainer."

"A hundred grand to draw up a simple plea agreement? Even for Murray, that's rather steep, isn't it?"

"We have an understanding that the retainer will also cover his fee for any lawsuits we may bring if any of the provisions of our agreement with you are violated."

"In any event, what happens to this money will be decided by our courts," Phaulkon said. "I don't know if your lawyer should have much reason to be optimistic about getting paid if this is all you've got."

"Don't we get to keep any of it?" Hillman asked.

"Just enough to pay your hotel bill."

The flight back to Bangkok was uneventful. The Americans stayed in the front of the plane with Phaulkon and the prisoners were in the rear, guarded by the police. Not another word passed between the prisoners and the Americans. The McKennas and Big Ed were dropped at the Airport Holiday Inn, then Phaulkon, Lawler, and four of the cops took Dix and Hillman to court in Bangkok. Lawler would represent the U.S. government before the court and he was armed with the agreement between Dix, Hillman, and the Manhattan DA.

If all went according to the agreement, Dix and Hillman would waive extradition and they would be brought to the United Terminal at seven-thirty the next morning where custody of the prisoners would be transferred to McKenna for their eight o'clock flight to the U.S.

Just in case, Lawler and the embassy's legal staff were ready if Dix and Hillman repudiated the agreement in court. According to Lawler, it could then take as long as a week before they were placed in McKenna's hands, but in any event they would be going back to the U.S in handcuffs.

McKenna knew he should, but he couldn't get to sleep. He still felt rested after his first class experience, so he called Tommy's room and found that Tommy was suffering from the same problem. Another call revealed that Big Ed was also up and about, so the three decided to see the town and have dinner out. They changed some money at the desk, left the hotel, jumped into a waiting taxi, and an hour later were stuck in traffic in downtown Bangkok. The driver recommended a restaurant that turned out to be quite good, very close, and relatively inexpensive. They hadn't had lunch, so Big Ed had an opportunity to amaze the McKennas once again with his capacity.

After their two-hour dinner, they hailed another taxi. "The Leather Emporium, please," McKenna told the driver.

"Sorry. Club very good for some people, very expensive, but very closed," the driver said.

"When does it open?"

"I think never. Police close," the driver said, not understanding why his statement was making his passengers smile.

"Take us there anyway," McKenna said.

The driver complied with the unusual request and, fifteen minutes later, found himself wondering what made foreigners so crazy. As he waited across the street, his passengers had stood solemnly outside the closed and boarded club for ten minutes without a word passing between them. Suddenly the short, fat one began dancing in a circle and whooping while the other two stomped their feet and laughed hard and loud as they clapped a song for him.

What could be the fun in that? the driver wondered.

FORTY-ONE

At 6:00 A.M. the McKennas and Big Ed were at the United ticket counter to reserve their seats. They had six coach tickets and requested seats at the rear of the plane, but found they had been upgraded to first class at the direction of the United front office in New York. The ticket agent couldn't explain it, but McKenna felt Hurley's hand in it somewhere. He cursed Hurley softly while Tommy and Big Ed applauded him loudly.

As required by all airlines, McKenna filled out the forms stating that he was a police officer transporting prisoners and requesting permission from the captain to be armed during the flight. That permission was granted, so the McKennas and Big Ed removed their guns from their suit-cases and put them on under their jackets in the men's room. They were waiting outside the terminal when the police van pulled up right on time at seven-thirty.

Phaulkon and two cops got out and McKenna signed some forms for him. Then Dix and Hillman were let out of the van, handcuffed with their arms behind them.

"To make it easier traveling on you two, we're gonna take off those handcuffs and cuff you in the front," McKenna announced. "At the slightest hint of any trouble from either of you, Lieutenant Taggart here tells me he's got enough restraining equipment in his suitcase to tie you up so tight that you won't even be able to smile. Understood?"

"You won't get trouble from us, McKenna," Dix said. "We're resigned to our fate and ready to do our time."

"How about you, Hillman?" McKenna asked, but Hillman was focused on Big Ed. "Are you Lieutenant Taggart from Arizona?" he asked, obvi-ously concerned.

"Been keeping up on your news, have you?" Big Ed asked. "Lieutenant Ed Taggart of the Maricopa County Sheriff's Department, that's me."

McKenna noticed that Big Ed's statement also had Dix disturbed.

"Don't worry, you big sissies. Your deal with Detective McKenna stands," Big Ed added. "Much as it pains me to say it, you're not gonna die in Arizona. I'm just along for the ride."

Hillman and Dix looked at each other and smiled, obviously relieved.

The McKennas and Big Ed were taking no chances. Dix and Hillman had been placed in the window seats in row 2 and both were still front-cuffed. Big Ed sat next to Hillman and Tommy sat next to Dix, boxing the prisoners into their seats. Both prisoners had their seat belts fastened, but Tommy and Big Ed had theirs open. To reduce the danger in case a struggle ensued, McKenna carried Tommy's and Big Ed's guns. He sat behind Tommy in row 3.

Both Hillman and Dix had been delighted to learn that they were riding first class to their life without parole, and as Dix had said, they seemed resigned to their fate. Hillman asked McKenna for his copy of the deal memo and McKenna gave it to him. Hillman read it word for word while enjoying his coffee and croissant stuffed with fresh strawberries and whipped cream. When he finished reading, he folded the agreement and stuffed it into his pocket.

Dix napped during the circuitous landing approach to Singapore, but Hillman looked out the window and pointed out the landmarks on the ground to a totally uninterested Big Ed. To each one of Hillman's sightings, Big Ed said, "Take a good look 'cause you're seeing that one for the last time."

The plane had landed and was taxiing to the gate when the flight attendant approached McKenna. "Captain Cook would like to have a word with you in the cockpit," she whispered in his ear.

"Be right back. Holler if you need me for anything," McKenna said to Big Ed and Tommy. He noticed that Dix had awakened and both the prisoners were looking at him with undisguised interest. He followed the flight attendant to the closed cockpit door. She tapped on the door lightly four times and the copilot let McKenna in and closed the door behind him.

Captain Cook was at the controls and McKenna saw through the windshield that he was guiding the plane to the United terminal a hundred yards away. "I just heard from our people in the terminal that we've got something highly unusual happening at our gate," Cook said. "Don't mention that I told you so, but I thought you should know."

"I understand. What is it?"

"The Singapore police are there in force and they've asked for our passenger list."

"Has that ever happened before?"

"I've never seen it."

"Was the list given to them?"

"Of course. If you're in Singapore, you'll learn quickly to give the police here anything they ask for."

"Very strict?"

"I'll say. You'll get a five-hundred-dollar fine here every time you throw a butt on the sidewalk and they hang a tourist every couple of years for possession of marijuana."

This has got to have something to do with Dix and Hillman, but what? McKenna wondered. Could it be that they're here to arrest them for using those forged passports back in June? Highly unlikely since our prisoners are already in custody and headed for prison for the rest of their lives, but if that is it, how did the Singapore cops know to look for Dix and Hillman on this particular flight?

A number of gnawing suspicions began forming in McKenna's mind. He thanked Cook for the information and went back into the cabin.

Tommy, Big Ed, Hillman, and Dix were all staring at him with curiosity etched in their faces.

McKenna looked from Dix to Hillman and thought he saw more than curiosity there. He thought he saw fear.

"What's happening?" Dix asked.

"That's something I was hoping you could tell me. If you two have ever killed anybody in Singapore, I think we've all got a big problem brewing here."

McKenna got a piece of his answer from both sources. The look on Dix's face changed from curiosity tinged with fear directly into sheer terror, but Hillman had another response. Two, really. He quickly unbuckled his seat belt with his cuffed hands and was starting to stand up when Big Ed hit him so hard in the solar plexus that he projectile vomited his croissant, strawberries, and cream onto the back of the seat in front of him. Hillman then collapsed in his seat, panting heavily while Big Ed refastened his seat belt for him without the slightest opposition.

"I'd say that's a big 'yes' from Mr. Hillman," Tommy observed. "Are the cops gonna board the plane?"

The answer came from Cook over the intercom. "Your attention please, ladies and gentlemen. We will be at the gate in a minute, but there's a small problem. At the direction of the Singapore police, all passengers are to remain in their seats with their seat belts fastened. They advise me that any passenger who fails to obey these instructions will be arrested and held in Singapore."

A murmur rose from the passengers throughout the plane, but nobody got up and even the flight attendants took seats and buckled up.

"Anybody got a plan?" Big Ed asked.

"Yeah, I do," McKenna said as he took his seat. "From what I hear about this place, I'd say it's time we fasten our seat belts."

They did, and that was when Dix voiced his opinion. "McKenna, we've got a deal? Remember, we've got a deal," he shouted. "Don't let them take us."

"I know we've got a deal. I'll do what I can," McKenna replied, but he couldn't help noticing that Big Ed was having a fit of the chuckles.

"McKenna, don't let them take us," Dix shouted again, and Big Ed couldn't help himself. He put his hand over his mouth to try and stifle his laughter, but it was no use.

"McKenna, pleeeease don't let them take us," Dix shouted, and Big Ed was over the edge. He laughed so hard and so loud that his shoulders shook and his face turned bright red. He turned in his seat to look at McKenna and tried to say something, but the words wouldn't come out through his laughter.

"Pardner, are you trying to tell me that you apologize for this unprofessional display of yours?" McKenna asked.

Big Ed just nodded his head and kept laughing.

"Fine. I accept your apology and I forgive you," McKenna said evenly, anger rising in him. The he noticed that Tommy's seat was shaking, but Tommy at least was still maintaining some quiet control.

"Don't you two jokesters realize yet that we've been had?" McKenna said as the flight attendant got up to open the door.

"Had? Had by who?" Tommy yelled back.

"Figure it out, but I'll give you a hint," McKenna said. " 'Gee, fellas, I've got all these frequent flyer miles that are gonna expire and I just hate to waste them.' "

"Hurley!" Tommy shouted. "That conniving bastard engineered us to Singapore! I can't wait to get my hands around his fat, lying vocal cords."

Before McKenna had a chance to really fan Tommy's rage, a well-dressed Chinese man entered the plane and stopped in front of McKenna. He was followed by six cops dressed as the much bigger, much tougher, much meaner brothers of the Thai police.

"Detective McKenna, I am Assistant Superintendent Kwan of the Singapore Police. It's my duty to inform you that I have warrants ordering the arrests of James Hillman and Jerome Dix."

"For murder?" McKenna asked.

"Yes, for the murder of Nancy Lee."

"Nancy Lee? Chinese?"

"Half Chinese. She was what we call a Peranakan, half-Chinese and half-Malay.

"When was the murder?"

"September ninth, 1982, as close as we can figure out."

"Were Hillman and Dix indicted here?"

"Yes, the warrants are based on indictments."

"When were they indicted? No, let me guess," McKenna said. "Was it yesterday?"

"As a matter of fact, it was yesterday."

"And were these indictments based on information supplied by one Mr. Bob Hurley?"

Kwan smiled for the first time. "You had me going there for a moment, Detective McKenna. No, it wasn't a Mr. Hurley. I don't even know a Mr. Hurley."

"Not Hurley? Then you must know a Mr. Randy Bynum. He'd be a rather recent acquaintance of yours."

Kwan's smile vanished. "Yes, I do know Mr. Bynum."

"Then I'll make you a little bet. I'll bet that you and good old Randy watched quite a bizarre film yesterday."

Kwan said nothing. He just he shook his head and smiled, so McKenna upped the ante. "I'm even willing to go better than that. Your hundred to my thousand, I'll bet there was a film and that film was supplied by him."

"I wouldn't bet against you on anything, Detective McKenna, and I'm a betting man. The film is quite bizarre and features, we believe, James Hillman and Jerome Dix torturing Nancy Lee to death."

Has to be the film Nolan told Chipmunk about, McKenna thought, and Nancy Lee being half-Chinese and half-Malay might account for Nolan thinking she was Hispanic. Let's see. "I'm not willing to bet too much on this one, but did they behead Nancy Lee at the end of it?"

"Detective McKenna, have you seen this film?"

"No, but I've heard about it."

"From a very reliable source, obviously."

"A source that wasn't made available to me, but that's another story for another time. Tell me, are you aware that we were bringing Dix and Hillman to the U.S. to serve a life sentence without the possibility of parole?"

"Yes, I'm aware of that."

"Then I guess you don't feel that punishment is adequate and just?"

"Under the circumstances, my government feels that no, it's not. We feel your punishment falls far short of the punishment such killers would deserve."

"What circumstances?"

"It's very complex and would take a while to explain."

"So I guess you're going to hang them?"

Kwan's smile returned. "Only if they're found guilty of the crime."

"Then let me rephrase my question, Superintendent, and let's be candid with each other. They're guilty, so *when* are you going to hang them?"

"Fair enough. Then let me rephrase my answer," Kwan said, still smiling. "Soon."

Upon hearing that, Dix began to moan, softly at first, then louder and louder.

Kwan looked at Dix, amused, but Kwan's men looked mystified by Dix's display.

Finally, Tommy had enough. "Shut up, you sissy, and take your medicine like a man," he ordered. "Don't you realize that you're now representing all the red-blooded, murdering American degenerates and here you are bawling in front of these foreigners. Think how ashamed of you the other American degenerates would be if they were here now."

McKenna thought that Tommy's reasoning was sound, but it hardened Dix too much for his own good. He shouted, "You pricks ain't hanging me," and he fumbled with his seat belt with his cuffed hands.

Kwan said something in Chinese to his men and one of them pushed past the others and fired two taser darts into Dix's chest just as he got the belt open.

The effect on Dix was instantaneous as the fifty-thousand volts short-circuited every nerve synapse in his body. He stiffened for a moment, then slumped in his seat. The only movement evident in him was a twitch in his right thumb and his rapidly fluttering eyelids.

"These two desperadoes we were saddled with sure turned out to be morons, didn't they?" Big Ed asked no one in particular. "If these hombres said they were gonna hang me, I'd have enough sense to just ask for a blindfold and a cigarette."

"And you would be Lieutenant Taggart?" Kwan said.

"Would be? Hell, I *am* Lieutenant Taggart."

"And you are the other Detective McKenna?" Kwan asked Tommy.

"Wrong, Superintendent. "I'm *the* Detective McKenna. The other Detective McKenna is sitting behind me."

Kwan appeared to be confused, but only for a moment. "In any case, I have another unpleasant duty to perform," he said. He reached into his pocket, took out three subpoenas, and gave one to each. "These subpoenas are for the prisoners' preliminary hearing tomorrow and compel you to give testimony and provide evidence on any matter that would assist the court in determining their guilt or innocence. However, my government has decided not to legally bind you to testify."

"That means we can stay on this plane if we want to?" Big Ed asked.

"If you feel you must. However, if you stay and testify, my government will pay all reasonable expenses including meals, hotels, and airfare back to the U.S."

"Tommy and I will need a few minutes before we can give you an answer," McKenna said. "We'll have to call our boss and ask if he'd like us to testify for the folks who just stole our prisoners."

"I guess I should do the same thing, but let me ask you one thing first," Big Ed said. "Do you have enough to hang them without our testimony?"

"I imagine so," Kwan said.

"Then why would you need us?"

"More is always better, isn't it?"

"True, but I've got a better answer," McKenna said. "The State Department would be less likely to pitch a big bitch to Singapore over this if three American cops testify voluntarily against Dix and Hillman before they hang them."

"I'm sure my government also considered that," Kwan admitted. "Now, could you please stand up so my men can remove the prisoners?"

Tommy and Big Ed unbuckled, got up, and stood behind McKenna's seat. One of Kwan's men cops attempted to revive Dix by smacking his face a few times and he partially succeeded. The cop lifted him up by the belt buckle and Dix, though semiconscious, slapped at the cop's hand. Dix received another fifty thousand volts for his impertinence before he was carried off the plane.

"I can walk as slow or as fast as you like, I'm not sassy, and I'm not slapping anybody. I'm ready to go," Hillman declared to Kwan once Dix was out. And he did, escorted by two of Kwan's men.

"They have our handcuffs on," Tommy protested.

"They'll be returned to you outside," Kwan assured him. "There are also phones near the gate. You can call your superiors from there."

"Is Randy out there?" Tommy asked.

"Mr. Bynum? Yes, he's here."

"Did he come to town by himself?" McKenna asked.

"No, he has a woman with him. I believe she's connected somehow to Arthur McMahon."

"You knew Arthur McMahon?"

"No. I was never in a position to know him, but our prime minister thinks quite highly of him."

"Why would that be, I wonder?"

"Didn't you know? Arthur McMahon was the lobbyist hired to represent our interests in your congress. He did a splendid job, managed to have the Big Seven economic summit held here a couple of years ago."

"No. Didn't know that, but I guess I should've."

Tommy and Big Ed followed Kwan and his men to the gate outside. Cook was standing at the cockpit door when McKenna passed. "You staying or going?" Cook asked.

"Don't know yet and it might take a while to decide. How long before you have to take off?"

"Almost as soon as I can. Your police business has put us behind schedule and lots of our passengers have connecting flights to catch in L.A. If I take my time here and lollygag a bit, maybe half an hour."

"Are there any more United flights going back today?"

"Two-fifteen this afternoon. We've got one leaving here for New York via Hong Kong and San Francisco."

"Wonderful. If we're not back in half an hour, then don't worry about us."

"Hope to see you. Good luck."

McKenna rejoined Tommy and Big Ed at the gate check-in counter in the terminal. Bynum and Ginny were watching the Singapore cops remove the McKennas' handcuffs from Dix and Hillman in the waiting area of the next gate. Bynum had his arm around Ginny and she looked ecstatic.

McKenna noticed at once that Bynum had once again transformed himself, this time into Randy the Fortune 500 CEO of the Year, dressed to impress in his Savile Row suit, gold-rimmed glasses, Rolex watch, and those Bally loafers with the little tassels. He projected a regal air, as if he had just paused to take in a show his subjects had provided for his amusement.

"Wanna go talk to them now?" Tommy asked McKenna.

"In a minute. I've still got some things to work out in my mind. Don't want to say something now that I'll regret later."

"Feeling double-crossed, are we?" Big Ed asked.

"Aren't you?"

"Not at all. I've already been double-crossed, remember? They weren't going to Arizona, so right now I'm feeling kinda good."

"How about you?" McKenna asked Tommy.

"You want the real truth?"

"I think so."

"Okay, if you insist. I've been double-crossed on this case right from the start. Worked this case hard for eighteen years, and then the other McKenna gets tossed the ball for the touchdown. True, I didn't know there were two of them, but over the years I've worked up more than enough hate for my killer to cover them both. I wouldn't have chosen this way, but I'd like to see them hang."

"So Randy's not a bad guy?" McKenna asked.

"That depends," Big Ed said.

"On what?"

"On who played the first joke on who. As I recall, you two started it when you left him standing in a parking lot in San Diego with some bullshit story."

"Okay, we started it," McKenna admitted. "But we had no choice. We had to."

"Because your boss told you to?"

"Yeah, that's right."

"And he took it pretty good, didn't he?"

"Exceptionally well," McKenna admitted. He knew where Big Ed's line of reasoning was taking them, but he still wanted to hear it put into words.

"And who's Randy's boss?"

"Hurley or Ginny, don't know which by now. Could even be that Randy's the real boss, working them both to get us where we are now."

"In any event, back home we'd say it was a pretty good joke he just pulled on you. The famous Double-Triple Payback, and we don't get to see that every day."

"Yeah, it's turning out to be a real knee-slapper," McKenna said. He knew he had just received a lecture, and it gave him quite a bit to think about. He needed more time before he could decide if Bynum had really crossed the line and made himself an enemy.

While thinking it over, McKenna watched Hillman and Dix. The two prisoners had been searched again and Dix had come to his senses. He was able to get up with some help, but he still appeared confused as he and Hillman were shuffled down the long corridor toward the terminal entrance. Kwan had the handcuffs, so he looked around and spotted the owners.

That was when Bynum saw them. He gave his old pals a small, friendly wave, then pointed them out to Ginny. She also had a wave and a smile for them and looked as if she wanted to come right over, but Randy gave her a tug and they stood there, waiting.

Kwan handed McKenna the handcuffs. "Well, are you staying or going?"

"We need a few minutes more."

"I understand, but I have urgent things to do and must leave with my men," Kwan explained. He took a card from his pocket and gave it to McKenna. "If you decide to stay, give me a call and I'll make the hotel arrangements." Kwan turned and walked down the corridor. Since he was the boss, there was no reason for him to hurry.

Time to get to the bottom of all this, McKenna thought as Bynum and Ginny walked over arm in arm, appearing happy, innocent, and very friendly.

"How do you wanna play this?" Tommy asked.

McKenna was relieved to hear the question. Even though his traveling companions were delighted with this turn of events, Tommy had told him that he was still in charge and making the decisions. "By ear," McKenna said.

There was an uncomfortable silence as Ginny, Bynum, Tommy, and Big Ed stood looking at each other, so McKenna felt it fell to him to break the ice. "How's your mom doing? Sure hope she came out of that stroke all right."

"Miraculous recovery, thank you," Ginny said, smiling sweetly at McKenna. "I hope you're not too angry with us."

"I was, but I've managed to work the edges off it. There have been broken promises and dirty tricks all along the way. I thought we were doing pretty good at it until you two showed us today how the game is really played."

"Thanks for the compliment. I was hoping you'd take it that way," Ginny said. "So you're staying to testify?"

"Don't know yet. I have to call my boss and Big Ed has to call the sheriff for the answer to that one."

"You have to convince them to let you stay."

"Why? Singapore's gonna hang them whether we testify or not."

Ginny looked to Bynum for the answer.

"True, but it's a question of when," Bynum said. "The government here is very cost conscious, so if you stay they'd likely have the trial in a couple of days. They're paying the expenses, so they'd figure to save a bundle on airfares flying you guys and cops from all over the world back and forth."

"What cops?"

"Morro, for one. He's on his way here, but I'm sure there'll be cops testifying from every place those two acted up."

"When did Morro find out that they'd be snatched by Singapore?"

"Talked to him yesterday. He didn't ask for any details and I didn't volunteer any, but he sure sounded delighted. Said he wouldn't miss it for the world. Kwan got to the cops in the Philippines and got the same reaction from them. They'll be here tomorrow."

"So whenever it happens, this is gonna be a Moscow-type show trial?"

"I expect so. They're gonna hang them anyway for what they did to Nancy Lee, but they'd rather have world opinion on their side."

"Cops showing up from everywhere with their grisly crime scene photos should do that," McKenna surmised.

"But you guys are still the three most important players," Bynum insisted. "You're the ones with the most evidence and you're the ones who tracked them down and put the whole thing together."

"If you say so," McKenna said, but he knew Bynum was right. "But I'll tell you one thing. It doesn't bother me if Singapore has to spend a bundle after the stunt they pulled on us today."

"Please don't be vindictive about that, Brian," Ginny pleaded. "Talk to whoever you have to, but please stay and let's get this over with."

"Like I told you, it's not my decision. It rests with my boss and he's been known to have a vindictive streak all his own when he gets stepped on."

"I know you can sway him if you want to."

"Maybe, but I'm not going to try. I'm thinking that I'm too close to this thing and you two to judge what's the right thing to do right now. It's entirely his call."

"You can't mean that," Ginny said as she tugged on Randy's arm. "We'll see you later and you can tell us how you convinced him to let you stay."

"Wait! You're not leaving, are you?" McKenna asked.

"Have to," Bynum said. "Got a lot of phone calls to make and we've got a little celebration planned."

"Aren't you going to tell me how you and Hurley came up with that video?"

"Sure, when I see you later."

"We might not be there."

"I'm not worried. You'll be there," Randy said as he and Ginny turned and headed down the corridor.

"Hold on! Where's this celebration of yours gonna be?" Big Ed yelled.

"If you're any good, you'll find us," Bynum yelled back over his shoulder.

It was a challenge Big Ed and Tommy were anxious to answer, McKenna knew, but he had more pressing matters on his mind. The Singapore passengers had boarded their plane and it would be leaving soon. He and Big Ed went to the phones for their decision while Tommy went back onto the plane to get their luggage, just in case.

McKenna knew that a decision this big would ultimately rest with Brunette, but he didn't want to break the chain of command. He called Greve at the office, but it was nine o'clock in New York and he wasn't in. McKenna had him beeped to his pay phone in Singapore.

Greve called ten minutes later. It took McKenna another ten minutes to explain what had happened and he got the reaction he had expected. Greve was livid over the Randy stunt and he wanted McKenna and Tommy on the next plane back, but he told McKenna to stand by for a call from Brunette.

While McKenna was waiting for Brunette's call, he watched their plane leave the gate. Meanwhile, Big Ed had reached the sheriff at his office. It had taken a long conversation to explain what they were doing in Singapore, but Big Ed looked happy when he hung up.

"Well?" McKenna asked.

"Sheriff Joe ain't much put out by all this. Said since he can't have his way with them, no skin off his nose if somebody else gets to hang them."

"Did he tell you to stay and testify?"

"Said he doesn't care. Since he doesn't have to pick up the hotels and airfare, he put it up to me to decide."

Brunette called back ten minutes later. "Heard you're having some problems, buddy," he said. "What do you wanna do, stay or come home?"

"I could go either way on this, so I'm leaving it up to you," McKenna said.

"Passing the buck, huh? I could go either way, too."

"Ray, you're the one who's going to have to live with all the implications on this. I'm under some pressure here and maybe I'm too close to see what's best."

"Tommy?"

"Yeah. He wants to stay and so does Big Ed. He's got carte blanche from the sheriff to do what he wants."

"I see. Well, here it is. Tell Tommy I'm sorry, but I'm gonna back Greve up. You might also mention to him if he squawks about it that he should be mad at his good pal, not me and not you."

"I don't know if he'll see it that way."

"Then tell him he'll probably be back there to testify at the trial, whenever that will be."

"You're gonna send us back and make them happy at their show trial?"

"Why not? I'd say that there's nothing we can do that'll get Dix and Hillman back here, so why not get some good publicity in the world press when we show off all the good work you two have done?"

"Okay, I'll tell him."

"Well?" Tommy asked as soon as McKenna hung up.

"Greve wants us home and Ray's backing him up. However, Ray says we'll probably be back for the trial."

"That's too bad, but I can live with that," Tommy said. "Did Ray mention anything about sending us here for the hanging?"

"No, it didn't come up."

"No matter. I'll come here on my own for that if I have to."

The McKennas turned to Big Ed to see what he would do and got the answer they expected from him. "I'm with you guys. Let's get our tickets changed and get out of here."

They carried their luggage to the United ticket counter at the front of the terminal. McKenna gave the pleasant young Chinese ticket agent their tickets and explained that they wanted to catch the two o'clock flight out. No problem, there was room in first class, she told him, but unfortunately there was a $75 surcharge to change each ticket.

McKenna gave her his American Express, she swiped it through her credit card machine, and McKenna received his first premonition of disaster as he read her face. "I'm very sorry, but this card isn't valid," she explained. "Do you have another?"

"Not valid?" McKenna heard himself stupidly ask, but he gave her his Visa and she swiped that one, too. The look on her face turned from nervously apologetic to fearful as she read the message coming up on her machine. "I'm very sorry. This card isn't valid, either, but I'm sure it's just a mistake," she said. "Please give me a minute while I call the credit card company."

"Go right ahead, I can't imagine what the problem is," McKenna said, but he could. The ticket agent picked up the phone and a rapid conversation ensued in Chinese while she continued smiling at him.

"What's going on?" Big Ed asked.

"Quite a bit. Get your passports and your ID ready."

"Why?"

"Because Hurley reported our credit cards stolen and this nice young lady is very busy talking to the police right now."

"That can't be," Big Ed exclaimed. "How the hell would he be able to do that?"

"Easy for him. All he needs is our social security numbers and our mothers' maiden names. That's what they ask you for when you report your cards stolen. Child's play for Hurley."

"I understand he's a lowlife, but even he wouldn't do that," was Big Ed's initial opinion on the matter.

"Oh yeah? Turn around," Tommy said, and Big Ed did. He couldn't miss the two cops running toward them from the far end of the terminal with their guns drawn or the police car pulling up outside with roof lights flashing.

"What now?" Big Ed asked.

"Well, obviously we're not leaving today," McKenna said.

"Obviously."

"So while you're thinking about what's one better than that good old Double-Triple Payback, I suggest we assume the position."

And they did, leaning face forward against the ticket counter, hands on the counter in plain view next to their passports and police ID, and their legs spread far apart. They had achieved the perfect position by the time the fastest of the Singapore cops arrived and correctly placed the business end of his pistol in McKenna's left ear.

FORTY-TWO

A very unfortunate and inexplicable misunderstanding, the ticket agent, the credit card companies, and the cops had all agreed after the necessary intercession downtown by Assistant Superintendent Kwan. What really had them all perplexed was that the Singapore police's investigation had revealed that Tommy's and Big Ed's credit cards had been reported stolen as well.

Certainly unfortunate, but not entirely inexplicable, the McKennas and Big Ed knew. However, they had felt it would be unwise to educate their hosts and the card companies on how such a thing could happen after they remembered that Hurley had previously engaged in numerous, probably criminal credit card shenanigans on their behalf.

After a hurried conference, the McKennas and Big Ed decided that testifying at the hearing was a great idea, and they told Kwan so. He in turn was more than happy to arrange their deluxe rooms at Raffles, one of the best and most famous old hotels in the world, and to advance them $500 to cover other necessary expenses they would be sure to encounter while guests of the city.

After checking into their fine rooms and enjoying a fine meal from room service, they shaved and showered while the concierge had their suits pressed. Refreshed and suitably dressed, they were ready to answer the Randy Challenge and have some questions answered in turn. They called six of the best hotels in town without locating either Bynum or Ginny, so some footwork was needed. They went outside and hailed a taxi.

"Is there a Mexican restaurant in town?" McKenna asked the driver.

"Yes, two Mexican restaurants."

"Are they far from here?"

"Very close. Everything good very close in Singapore. Big city, small country."

"Are they close to each other?"

"Holland Village, both side-by-side next door.

McKenna didn't know what that meant, exactly, but it didn't sound as if getting to either of them would present a problem. "Is the food very good at either of them?"

"I think so, both very good. Very many rich people go there. Come out very-very happy, say food very-very hot."

"Then take us to the closer one, please."

The taxi driver glanced back at McKenna, slightly perplexed, but he shrugged his shoulders and took off.

As their taxi driver had said in his own way, El Felipes Cantina and Cha Cha Cha were next door to each other. "Sorry, don't know which one closest," he said.

"Obviously, El Felipes Cantina is twenty feet closer to Raffles than Cha Cha Cha," McKenna said. He paid the driver and added on the customary stupid-tourist tip, so everybody was happy.

From the outside Cha Cha Cha looked like it would be slightly more expensive than El Felipes, so the McKennas and Big Ed reasoned it was slightly more likely that the celebrating Bynum and his very rich, very happy girlfriend were in Cha Cha Cha.

They were, the center of attention as they mariachied their way around the dance floor of the crowded restaurant while the Chinese band dressed as Mexican cowboys played and sang a good rendition of "El Rey" in Spanish, a very hard thing to do without pronouncing a single *r*. As soon as Bynum saw them at the door, he stopped dancing, held up his arms to stop the music, and announced to all that, as he had been promising them for hours, his good friends had arrived. From the dance floor, he then introduced the three famous American detectives and told how they had brought those two murderous, despicable, cowardly villains to Singapore for well deserved and certain justice.

Randy and Ginny must have been there developing lifelong friendships for hours while waiting for them, McKenna supposed, because he, Tommy, and Big Ed received a thunderous round of applause. A crowd formed around them to congratulate them and ask details of the hunt for the men who had so horribly murdered their poor Nancy Lee.

None of the Americans thought it wise to mention that they had never even heard of Nancy Lee until that morning, so they just shook hands, nodded a lot, and smiled their way through the crowd until they reached Randy and Ginny's table fifteen minutes later. In the interim, patrons had been moved and tables had been rearranged to prepare suitable places for them between Bynum and Ginny, their two wonderful old pals.

Half an hour after entering the restaurant, the McKennas and Big Ed were finally left alone with Randy and Ginny to sit together and work their problems out. Drinks were served and merely sipped at by everyone. McKenna was sitting next to Ginny, so he began the healing process. "Sorry we're late, but we were unavoidably delayed."

"No apologies necessary. We understand," Ginny said. "Are you very mad at us again?"

"Annoyed is more like it. We're saving our real anger for Hurley for that credit card stunt."

"You shouldn't be upset with him. The credit cards were my idea," Ginny admitted. "He didn't want to do it."

"He didn't?" McKenna asked, amazed.

"No. Absolutely refused until I told him that he should reconsider opening his new offices in Washington and Richmond to handle all that corporate work we thought was on the way. Only then did he see things my way."

"I see. To Hurley's way of thinking, he had no choice. Okay, you win. I won't be too mad at him."

"But now you're mad at me again?"

"You have to admit, it was a case of classic overkill. But don't worry, I'll get over it."

Big Ed picked up the ball. "Who was this Nancy Lee and why's she so important around here?"

"She was a girl with a future when she was alive, a significant footnote when she disappeared seventeen years ago, and a national heroine since the people here found out that she'd been tortured and murdered by Dix and Hillman," Bynum explained.

"They never found her body?" Tommy asked.

"Nope. She was fifteen at the time, lived in the Clementi section of town, near the docks. She had a report due for school, last seen leaving the library when it closed at nine o'clock on the night of September ninth, 1982. Dix and Hillman kidnapped her and they must've had a boat rented. They tell us here that the film was shot on Pulau Sebarok. Uninhabited island off the coast, great views of the skyline. McMahon knew right away it was Singapore."

"Then they dumped her body in the ocean after they were through with her, I guess," Big Ed said.

"Her body and her head, but she was sure missed. Young girls don't disappear in this town, especially girls like Nancy Lee. Pretty, honor student, class president, and a very close family. Her father was an editor for the *Straits Times*, one of the big local newspapers, so her disappearance caused quite a fuss. They rounded up all the usual suspects and questioned everybody who ever knew her. Came up with nothing, but she was headline news for a while, and the *Straits Times* still runs a tearjerking article about her every September ninth."

"So everybody knows who she is?" McKenna surmised.

"Everybody, and those that didn't yesterday do now. Kwan released the news this morning and it's been all over the radio and TV. You can imagine what the *Straits Times* is gonna have to say about this whole case tomorrow."

"I can imagine, and I hope that Dix and Hillman get to read it," Tommy said. "Killing that poor girl in Singapore was the stupidest thing they ever did and I want them kicking themselves over it, and hopefully each other."

That caused everyone to smile except McKenna. "Why don't we talk now about how the police here got their hands on that film?" he suggested.

"Wouldn't you rather eat first?" Randy asked. "I'm getting hungry again and the food here is great."

"No. First let's get this out of the way."

"Okay. Mr. Hurley was trying—"

"Stop right there," McKenna said. "Randy, if I hear you call that back-stabbing snake 'Mr. Hurley' one more time, I'm gonna puke. Please call him 'Bob,' 'Hurley,' or anything else you like, but please, not 'Mr. Hurley.' "

"Brian, getting that film wasn't Mr. Hurley's idea," Ginny said. "He was just following Mr. McMahon's orders, and Mr. McMahon specifically instructed him not to tell you anything about it."

So what do I say to that? McKenna wondered. It's certainly not appropriate to mention that the dead guy who loved her enough to leave her millions turns out to be the back-stabbing snake in question. "Sorry for the interruption, Randy. Please go on."

"Bob was trying desperately to find Nolan with no luck for a while. Then he found out that Nolan had co-signed for some student loans for his daughter, and he checked it out. Found out she was graduating from UCLA Berkeley last June and he figured Nolan would be there for that. We went there to check it out and found him."

"Is that when Hurley loaned you all that fancy jewelry?" McKenna asked.

"Yeah, putting the squeeze on Nolan put him in a very generous mood. Loaned me everything I needed for my smut king role."

"How did Hurley squeeze Nolan to get the film from his prince?"

"Pretty straightforward. Nolan was to tell the prince that Hurley found out about the film from the Russian dealer who sold it to him. Nolan was to also tell him that Hurley would publicize the kinds of films the prince liked to watch in his spare time if he didn't give it up."

"I see," McKenna said. "And if Nolan didn't play ball, Hurley was going to get to the prince and tell him that Nolan was the blabbermouth?"

"Exactly, which would mean Nolan would be out a very nice job. For good measure, Hurley also gave Nolan the list of every cat house where the prince had used his cards in the past ten years, and you know that sort of fun is frowned upon back home in Saudi Arabia."

"Of course. They would have chopped the prince's head off in a public execution as soon as all that stuff was made public. How long before Hurley got the film?"

"Two days, Federal Express. Cost him nothing."

Ginny's not complaining, but I bet it cost McMahon a bundle, McKenna thought. Dix and Hillman are certainly the losers, but good old Bob might be the biggest winner in this case.

FORTY-THREE

The hearing was a one-sided, all-day affair before a single judge in a small courtroom crowded, almost exclusively, with reporters from the local press and the international wire services. Everything the prosecutor and his witnesses said was entered into the record with very few objections from the public defender assigned to represent Dix and Hillman. The entire morning and much of the afternoon was spent establishing and certifying the credentials, experience, reputation, and expertise of the government's witnesses; their testimony on the matter at hand came in the late afternoon and very little time was spent examining what they had to say about the defendants and the crimes they may have committed.

Dix and Hillman sat impassive and shackled in the dock as one witness after another said little more than yes, there was a heinous murder or murders at such and such a time and place; yes, I was assigned to investigate the murder or murders as either the primary investigator or the investigative supervisor; and yes, through my own efforts coupled with information supplied to me by the other competent and experienced investigators present, I have developed evidence that leads me to strongly believe that those two sitting over there committed the murder or murders I had been assigned to investigate.

Kwan was the last to testify and he spent less time on the stand than any of the cops from all over. He stated simply that he was in possession of strong evidence that, considered in conjunction with relevant and conclusive information supplied to him by the other esteemed witnesses already heard by the court, led him to strongly believe that the defendants had tortured and murdered Nancy Lee in the State of Singapore on or about September 9, 1982.

Not a single piece of evidence was presented to buttress the witnesses' beliefs nor, apparently, was any deemed necessary by the court for the purposes of the hearing. Since the credentials, experience, reputation, and expertise of the witnesses had already been certified to the court's satisfaction, their beliefs on the matter were never challenged by the public defender. The indictments of Dix and Hillman for the murder of Nancy Lee were upheld, and at the request of the government, trial was scheduled for Wednesday, two days hence.

The scheduling of the quick trial date was the only time the public defender rose to voice an objection. He argued that one day wasn't sufficient time for him to prepare an adequate defense for his clients. How much time are you requesting? the judge asked.

Two weeks, Your Honor.

Ridiculous and overruled. Citing the expense being borne by the state in order to have the esteemed witnesses present to testify and the terrible inconvenience being borne by the esteemed witnesses who were voluntarily in Singapore and so far from their homes and busy schedules, the judge sternly informed the public defender that two weeks was out of the question.

However, the judge was prepared to be gracious and he changed the trial date to Thursday, giving the public defender an extra day to talk to his clients, interview the government's witnesses, investigate the evidence, and prepare his defense. To make things easier on the public defender and his staff, the judge informed him that all cases scheduled to come before any court in which the defendant was represented by his office would be adjourned until the following week. Anything else? the judge asked.

There was, and those requests were also granted. All witnesses were instructed by the judge to make themselves readily available to the public defender for interview; they were also instructed to permit the public defender and his staff to examine all evidence in their possession and to answer completely and truthfully all questions he may pose to them.

On Monday night the McKennas' files arrived from New York, Big Ed's files arrived from Phoenix, and Bynum's old files arrived from San Jose. All were delivered to them at the Raffles.

The cops from Spain arrived on Tuesday morning with their files on the murders in Barcelona. After a short meeting with the state prosecutor, they were also installed in the Raffles on the same floor as Morro and the Philippine cops.

On Wednesday morning at nine o'clock the McKennas, Bynum, and Big Ed met in the hotel's conference room with the chief public defender, his crime scene expert, his document expert, his ballistics expert, and two of his legal assistants. The public defender and his assistants questioned the Americans closely about their work on the case while his experts pored over the files and made copies of any reports that interested them. The session was nonconfrontational and the Americans found the public defender, and especially his assistants, to be polite, respectful, and, at times, even deferential.

The three things the public defender found most interesting were the

Serious photos, McKenna's reports on his questioning of Mettakaruna, and the item Big Ed had saved for last, the Hillman home movies. After viewing one of the Hillman fun sessions, he decided that the formal work session was over.

It was then time for the informal tea session. "You know, I was going to ask you all if you were absolutely certain if Hillman and Dix were the same men who appear in the government's film," the public defender confided. "However, I realize after seeing those movies that a question like that would make me appear stupid."

"Have you seen the government's film?" Bynum asked.

"Yes, last night. Horrible, and the almost-naked black man wearing the mask while whipping Nancy Lee is definitely the almost-naked black man cavorting with Mrs. Hillman and the almost-naked black man whipping that girl in the magazine you just showed me."

"So you know that Hillman, at least, is guilty?" McKenna asked reflexively, a question no U.S. defense attorney would ever answer.

But the public defender did. "Without a shadow of a doubt, and so is Dix. Any doubts I had were cleared from my mind this morning after going through your files. They tortured and murdered Nancy Lee, but they still must be properly defended before they hang."

"Haven't they already told you they did it?" Big Ed asked.

"No, they deny ever having killed anyone. Very foolish, considering the strength of the government's case."

"They're lying to their lawyer?" Big Ed exclaimed incredulously. "Can you imagine that there was a time when we considered those two morons to be master criminals?"

"It's possible they foolishly believe that I'm in league with the government," the public defender explained. "In any event, they tell me that their own lawyer will be here tomorrow, a Mr. Plenheim."

Murray Don't Worry is coming here? "Could that be true?" McKenna asked.

"Could be. As is usual in capital cases, they've been granted unlimited telephone privileges and the guards tell me they're always on the phone."

"Would you mind answering a few questions for us?" Tommy asked.

"If I can and if it's proper for me to answer them."

"Is all the information in our files going to be admissible?"

"Why wouldn't it? Whatever you and your scientific experts wrote is true, isn't it?"

"Of course."

"Then why not?" the public defender asked, but then he got it. "I see. You're talking about your American rules of evidence."

"Yes. Back home, even if the evidence the police present is reliable and valid beyond the shadow of a doubt, there's many other things to be considered before a jury ever gets to see or hear it."

"You're talking about how the evidence was obtained?"

"That, and what the cop knew and even what he was thinking when he obtained it. If everything isn't right according to our latest court decision, the evidence is ruled illegally obtained and inadmissible."

"I've heard that. I hope I'm not being insulting and I don't consider you naive, but we consider the American rules on evidence to be very strange. Here we sometimes have improperly obtained evidence, but it's still considered by the courts if it's reliable evidence."

"So you don't let murderers walk on a technicality?"

"Preposterous! There are very few murders here and all are publicized. If such a thing were ever to happen, the government would be seriously criticized."

"Are there *any* repercussions when improperly seized evidence is presented to the courts?" McKenna asked.

"Yes. The officer who seized it is disciplined, but we would never release an obviously guilty murderer because a policeman made a mistake or violated a procedure. Think of what would happen if he killed again."

"Think about it?" Tommy said. "Back home we see it."

"Really?"

"Not frequently, but often enough."

"Really?"

Now who's being naive? McKenna thought. This poor guy, a sharp lawyer living in his orderly, common-sense world, can't believe that rules that make no sense at all can be common legal procedure where we come from.

Wednesday afternoon and early evening were spent with the state prosecutor, a very nice session since he elected to discuss his case and plan strategy, courtesy of the city, in a private dining room at The Golden Phoenix, one of the city's pricier Chinese restaurants. The cops from all over were all there, comparing notes, exchanging information, and offering up for discussion any weaknesses they thought present in the case. All their worries were examined by the state prosecutor and subsequently dismissed, including McKenna's.

McKenna had reasoned correctly, according to the state prosecutor, that the information that had been obtained from Mettakaruna was important to the state's case. Therefore, McKenna had thought it best to have Mettakaruna flown to Singapore to testify under oath about all the things he had told McKenna.

Incorrect, McKenna was told by the state prosecutor, an unnecessary expense for the state and something that could prolong the trial another day. His line of reasoning was that McKenna, an experienced and sophisticated interrogator, had believed Mettakaruna, had acted on his information, and had never found any of it to be false. McKenna would be permitted to testify on what Mettakaruna had told him, the state prosecutor was sure. If the court believed the testimony because McKenna believed it, as would probably happen, all well and good. If not, the state prosecutor was sure he still had enough to send Dix and Hillman to the gallows without costing the state airfares, hotels, and meals for a man who, after all, should probably be charged in Singapore as an accessory to murder.

Right after their dinner the state prosecutor announced that the preparation of the state's case was complete except for the work he would do at home that evening. "See you all tomorrow morning" were his parting words after he paid the check.

Tommy and Big Ed decided to stay and further discuss the case, but McKenna declined their invitation and returned to the hotel.

By nine o'clock McKenna had worked out in the hotel's gym and taken a half-hour nap, when he answered a knock at his door.

It was Murray Don't Worry, correctly dressed but appearing tired and down. "You got anything to drink in there, McKenna?" he asked.

Professionally, McKenna detested Murray since he was an extremely competent defense attorney with a bagful of legal tricks and maneuvers designed to cloud evidence, ridicule prosecutors, prolong trials, confuse juries, malign cops, and inconvenience willing witnesses to the point where they no longer showed up. On the other hand, McKenna liked Murray personally because Murray was always a funny and candid, upbeat kind of guy, an urbane realist who made no apologies nor bones about his trade.

"Murray, I've been dreading your visit ever since I found out you were coming. What took you so long?"

"I'm lucky to be here at all. Took me most of the day to wrest my money from those bumpkins in Bangkok."

"But you did?" McKenna asked, surprised.

"Only half of it, unfortunately. I'm ashamed to tell you that I have to send them legal bills to cover the other fifty thousand of mine those greedy pricks are holding."

"Murray, that money's slated to go to your clients' many victims. It won't be staying in Bangkok for long and I'm surprised you were able to get what you did."

"They'll make on it, believe me. Charged me almost two grand in court costs to get my own money. C'mon, invite me in and pour me something stiff and tall."

"Murray, so nice of you to drop by. Why don't you come in and have a drink?"

While McKenna was at the minibar mixing Murray his usual scotch and scotch on the rocks, Murray sat on the bed and began reading the *Straits Times*, the Singapore newspaper which had full coverage of the case and was locally considered to be the voice of truth.

"Don't just read it, study it because that's your case," McKenna advised. "It's the first piece of evidence you'll be battling tomorrow."

"A newspaper story is evidence?"

"They call it an opening point. They like to save time and money here, so they figure that since everybody knows the facts in this case, they won't waste time establishing each and every one of them."

"A newspaper story?" Murray repeated.

"You'll get a chance to contest anything in the story that you disagree with, but there's a problem for you there."

"It's all true?" Murray guessed.

"Almost. It's not just a newspaper, it's a very good newspaper."

"Good God!"

"Afraid so, and I've got some more bad news for you. All that the judges in this case are interested in is the truth, and they want it the quickest, easiest, and cheapest way they can get it."

"Good God, how uncivilized. How's a bright Jewish boy from Queens supposed to make a living around here?"

"Maybe be a doctor?"

"Out of the question. I'd wind up lying awake nights worrying about other guys like me cooking up those good-paying malpractice lawsuits. Did I hear you right when you said judges?"

"You did. Three judges, no jury. Meaning that the state here isn't going to supply you with your audience of gullible rubes to watch and enjoy that wonderful you-smart-people-certainly-can't-believe-my-client-did-that routine of yours."

"Good God!"

Murray had finished his second scotch and scotch by the time he was satisfied that he knew everything there was to know in the article. Then he closed the paper and eyed McKenna shrewdly. "How long do we know each other, Brian?"

"Maybe fifteen years."

"And in all those fifteen years, have I ever lied to you or done you dirty?"

"Yes, many times."

"But not countless times?"

"No, just many."

"See, I like you and I know you like me. Now, I don't really expect you to tell me, but I really wish you would. What weaknesses do you see in the state's case?"

"Ordinarily, I wouldn't. But just this one time. Considering the way they operate here and according to the state's prosecutor, there aren't any."

"Okay, be that way. Don't tell me."

"Murray, I'm telling you the truth. In the States you'd make them miserable and have them stuttering, same as always. But here there really aren't any. It's airtight."

"Good God! They always told me that something like this could happen to me, but I never believed them," Murray said, covering his face with his hands. "I'm gonna be the first lawyer I know to ever lose a client to the gallows."

"Murray, no lawyer in New York has ever lost a client to the gallows. We don't execute them, remember?"

"I know, but that makes it even worse."

"At least you're paid," McKenna offered.

"The only bright spot," Murray said, but even that didn't put a smile on his face. Then he stood up, rubbed his eyes, and pulled himself erect. "Those two are certainly murdering, heartless scumbags, but they're my murdering scumbags. Do me a favor and mix me up another toddy while I conjure up a way to get them out of this."

"Murray, you're a credit to your miserable species and for some reason I admire you for that. Please get out."

FORTY-FOUR

At eight o'clock the next morning Murray was present in the large courtroom where the trial would be held and he received another series of shocks. Eight in the morning was considered to be before dawn by most judges in New York, yet the three judges trying the case were behind the bench in the almost-empty courtroom, fully awake and keeping current on the case by reading that morning's *Straits Times*.

Then Murray noticed something that gave him more to think about. There was another judicial bench set up at the side of the courtroom; no one was sitting there yet, but Murray immediately feared the worst. Since his usual drug-dealing, always-guilty clients knew that prison involved unprofitable down time in their careers, they were always ready to finance an appeal if Murray couldn't get them off with his ordinary bag of tricks. Consequently, Murray had become known among judges as that one bothersome attorney who really was ready to appeal every adverse ruling if he lost his case.

All judges hate having their decisions reversed upon appeal, so they became cautious to a fault when dealing with Murray's complex, inane motions and his countless, frivolous objections. Sometimes Murray still lost, but along the way he filled another bag of tricks that frequently enabled him to fool the scholarly appeals court judges who hadn't been present to observe firsthand his shenanigans in court.

Then the situation Murray feared came to pass. A scholarly looking judge with the *Straits Times* under his arm took his seat behind the small bench. An appeals court judge, Murray knew, one who would not take part in judging the case, but would observe the proceedings in order to later issue a speedy ruling on anything that occurred during the trial that might be construed by either the defense or the prosecution as the basis of an appeal.

An appeal had been Murray's one hope, a way of delaying sentence while he searched through cases in other countries that ran their courts on the British model. He felt there was a good chance he could come up with some obscure point to delay sentence, and Murray knew that delay was a defense attorney's best strategy.

The presence of that appeals court judge in the courtroom forced Murray to realize what everyone else already knew: Singapore was going to hang his clients, and it was going to be soon. He turned and walked out of the courtroom, trying to put the best face on things. He succeeded by the time he reached the door. A hundred grand would have been nice pay for two days of work, he reasoned, but fifty grand wasn't bad for doing nothing.

By nine-thirty the courtroom was packed with reporters, but their complexion had changed. Most were big names from the world press, along with many prominent TV reporters. Cameras were not permitted, but the first row was reserved for the press's artists. The second row was reserved for the international cops, but the crowd of reporters outside was so thick that McKenna and the other cops had to be escorted to their seats by court officers. After Dix and Hillman were led into the dock, the row of artists came to life and began sketching them.

The trial began with a reading of the *Straits Times* article into the record without objection by either side. Next a map and photos of the spot on Pulau Sebarok Island where Nancy Lee had been murdered was entered into evidence. Then came the film, and everything after the lights were turned back on in the courtroom was anticlimactic. Even the hardened reporters used to covering wars, ethnic cleansings, and famines were revolted, and McKenna could see that the artists seated in from of him were drawing Dix and Hillman as evil, vile devils with whips splattered with the blood of their helpless victim.

McKenna couldn't agree more. He had dreaded seeing the film, and after five minutes of viewing he couldn't stand to see any more. He sat through the rest of it, seeing but not watching as he concentrated on transporting his mind elsewhere. He was aware of the cruel, perverted action on the screen, but he didn't focus on it and only brought himself back to the courtroom when it was finally over.

After the lunch break one of the Hillman home videos was played for purposes of identification, and then Dix was stripped to the ankles in the courtroom. McKenna could tell from the looks on the judges' faces that they had no doubt they were looking at the two men they had just seen torturing Nancy Lee to death.

The rest of the afternoon and all the next morning was taken up by the testimony of the police as they described their cases. It was superfluous. Dix and Hillman had already been convicted by the film, and all the cops knew that their testimony on the horrible murders in their own countries was being elicited by Singapore to justify the final sentence to the rest of the world.

At the conclusion of each cop's testimony, there was always the same question from the state prosecutor: If this trial were being held in your country with the evidence now available, do you believe that the defendants would be convicted of murder in the case you have just described in your testimony?

McKenna was the last to testify and he gave the same answer every other cop did, thus validating the proceedings as well as the sentence in the eyes of the world press.

The verdict was pronounced after the lunch break on Tuesday. To absolutely no one's surprise by that time, they were found guilty of the murder of Nancy Lee. Dix and Hillman had sat impassively when the verdict was announced, and they didn't answer when the presiding judge had asked if they would like to make a statement before sentence was pronounced.

They were to be hanged, of course, but the sentence contained two surprises. The hanging was set for the following Friday, seven days hence, but on Thursday Dix and Hillman were to receive twenty strokes each from the rotan. Like their victims, they would be beaten before they died.

The Spanish cops, the Philippine cops, and Morro all returned home after the trial, and McKenna was inclined to do the same, but Big Ed's, Tommy's, Bynum's, and especially Ginny's hatred was long-term and would follow Dix and Hillman to the gallows, and probably beyond. It wasn't enough for them to hear the sentence pronounced and know that Dix and Hillman would be beaten and hanged. They wanted to be there as the sentence was carried out. They wanted to see them beaten and they wanted to see them die.

McKenna figured that he would spend plenty of time in self-analysis over his decision later, but he let himself be talked into taking a week's vacation in order to watch a beating and execution.

Although no appeal had been filed by either side, on Monday the appeals court judge issued a ruling that surprised no one. He had found no defect in the evidence, testimony, or verdict. The execution would proceed as scheduled.

Barrone arrived on Wednesday. He had intended his visit to be low-key, but the Singapore government wouldn't permit that. He was surprised to receive a reception at the airport fit for a head of state, and then he was cajoled into a press conference where he thanked the government of Singapore for helping him to close the most painful experience of his life. He was asked if he was satisfied with the verdict, and he informed the press that he was generally against capital punishment. However, he admitted that in this case and with those defendants, yes, he was very satisfied.

It didn't stop with Barrone. Many other relatives of Dix's and Hillman's victims also came to see them die. Their arrivals in town were all reported in the local press, and all were asked their opinion on the sentence. All said they were pleased, and despite the cost of the trip, all were happy that Singapore was the place Dix and Hillman had been tried.

Ginny surprised everyone on Thursday when she announced that she didn't want to attend the beating. Although McKenna was interested in how men who had so viciously beat so many would handle being on the receiving end, he didn't want to witness it to find out. The others were content to respect their decision, so McKenna and Ginny had lunch in the Raffles cafe while Tommy, Big Ed, and Bynum went to the prison.

Big Ed, Tommy, and Bynum had been in a jovial mood when they left, but they returned somber. "They handled it well," Bynum reported, but he sounded disappointed when he said it. "Certainly better than I would've. Those two took a real professional thrashing with hardly a whimper."

Breakfast on Friday was another somber affair. What had started out to be something most of them had been looking forward to had turned into something they dreaded. But they all went, maybe to put an end in their minds to the whole horrible affair.

The building where beatings and executions took place was actually outside the prison, but the rear of the barnlike structure abutted the walls. It was larger than McKenna had expected, but certainly not large enough to accommodate the throngs of reporters outside. Surprisingly, there were very few local citizens in the crowd, leading McKenna to conclude that the people of Singapore had become blasé about executions.

Kwan was waiting for them at the door. He waved them through the cordon of police guarding the entrance and escorted them in past the families of the victims and the reporters privileged enough to have gained access. About two hundred people were inside seated in chairs arranged around the gallows dominating the center of the large room. McKenna noticed that, like himself, most of them appeared to be wishing they were somewhere else. Barrone was already seated and waiting for them, three rows from the gallows.

McKenna sat between Tommy and Big Ed. Like them, he had nothing to say as he waited and tried to read the thoughts of the other witnesses to the execution, people who had come so far seeking closure to the most bitter chapter of their lives. All were silently focused on the stage at the center of the room.

The gallows could have come from a Hollywood Western set, except it wasn't a temporary wooden structure. Constructed of steel, it was intended to be used again and again. The railed stage was ten wide steps above the ground, and two nooses hung from a steel beam ten feet above the stage.

The execution was set for noon, and at five to twelve Dix and Hillman were led through a steel door in the prison wall. They were dressed in orange prison jumpsuits, rear-cuffed, wearing leg irons, and obviously suffering the effects of the beating they had received the day before. They reminded McKenna of Scrooge's dead partner Marley; Dix's and Hillman's leg irons clanked with each painful, stiff step they took toward the gallows. Their eyes never left the gallows as they lurched forward, escorted by the four uniformed guards holding them by their arms. Another two guards followed the slow procession, and bringing up the rear was the hangman, dressed in a black suit.

As the procession proceeded up the gallows steps, Dix and Hillman grimaced in pain each time they raised a leg on the way up. They were obviously determined to make a good show of it and didn't let loose a whimper as they kept their eyes focused on the nooses above them.

Once up, the hangman placed a noose around Dix's and Hillman's necks without ceremony of any kind. There were none of the preliminaries that McKenna had expected; no prison chaplain consoling the condemned men, no formal reading of the death sentence, and Dix and Hillman weren't asked if they had any last words for posterity or the crowd watching below. It was to be another example of Singapore efficiency, a necessary, unpleasant chore best finished quickly.

Dix kept his face forward, staring impassively at the crowd until the hangman placed a black hood over his head and his world went dark. His guards took two steps back, leaving him standing alone with the noose around his neck.

Then it was Hillman's turn. He also had been staring forward at the crowd, and it seemed to McKenna that Hillman's eyes were fixed on him. That changed when the hangman attempted to slip the hood over his head. Hillman was held firmly by his two guards and had no place to go, but he turned his head to the side, away from the hood. "I hope you're all happy now! I hope you're really happy," he screamed, and then he straightened himself up and the hood slipped on without further fuss. The hangman went to a shelf built into the rail of the gallows as Hillman's guards also stepped back.

The guards looked to the hangman, waiting. Except for Dix and Hillman, every eye in the room was on the hangman who stood looking at his watch with a finger poised on the button built into the shelf.

Reflexively, McKenna looked at his own watch and saw that the second hand had just ticked past the eight. Twenty seconds to go, so he gritted his teeth and noticed that every witness in the room was staring at their watches.

Correct to the second, the hangman pushed his button, and the trap door under Dix and Hillman fell open. They silently dropped four feet and into Eternity after one jarring speed bump along the way.

McKenna kept his eyes on the gallows only long enough to see that the bodies were motionless. Then he took in the room and concluded that Hillman didn't get his last wish. Not a living soul there seemed happy.